GAGE

BY
DELORES FOSSEN

First published in Great Britain 2013
by Mills & Boon, an imprint of Harlequin (UK) Limited,
Eton House, 18-24 Paradise Road, Richmond, Surrey TW9 1SR

© Delores Fossen 2012

ISBN: 978 0 263 90348 5
ebook ISBN: 978 1 472 00699 8

46-0313

Harlequin (UK) policy is to use papers that are natural, renewable and recyclable products and made from wood grown in sustainable forests. The logging and manufacturing processes conform to the legal environmental regulations of the country of origin.

Printed and bound in Spain
by Blackprint CPI, Barcelona

Imagine a family tree that includes Texas cowboys, Choctaw and Cherokee Indians, a Louisiana pirate and a Scottish rebel who battled side by side with William Wallace. With ancestors like that, it's easy to understand why *USA TODAY* bestselling author and former air force captain **Delores Fossen** feels as if she were genetically predisposed to writing romances. Along the way to fulfilling her DNA destiny, Delores married an air force top gun who just happens to be of Viking descent. With all those romantic bases covered, she doesn't have to look too far for inspiration.

Chapter One

Gage.

Lynette Herrington's eyes flew open, and she jack-knifed to a sitting position in her bed.

Something had caused her to wake up.

But what?

With her breath gusting, her heart racing, Lynette glanced round her bedroom and then at the clock on the nightstand. Just past four in the morning.

Outside, a bad storm was playing havoc with the massive oaks on the side of her country house. The wind slapped at the branches, fanning them over the security lights mounted on the eaves. Rain slithered down the windows and made snaky shadows in the room.

"It's just the storm," she mumbled. That's what had pulled her from a deep sleep.

But something about that explanation didn't feel right.

She reached for the lamp switch, but the sound stopped her cold. It was hardly a sound at all, and the storm practically drowned it out, but Lynette was positive she heard something she didn't want to hear.

A single footstep.

"Don't scream," someone warned her. It was a man. And he was right next to her bed concealed in all those rainy shadows. "I won't hurt you."

Lynette's heart jumped to her throat, and she did exactly what he'd warned her not to do. She screamed. Or rather that's what she tried to do, but he muffled it by clamping his hand over her mouth.

"I said I won't hurt you," he repeated.

Lynette didn't believe him. She clawed at his hand and reached for the drawer of her nightstand where she kept a loaded .38. And by God, she knew how to use it. She wouldn't just let this man attack her or do heaven knows what else without her fighting back.

But the man fought back, too. He didn't let go of her, and whichever way Lynette turned and twisted to break free of him, he seemed to anticipate her every move. She couldn't reach the gun, and he was a lot stronger than she was.

Oh, God.

Was this how her life would end? With an intruder killing her in her own bed?

The fear of that caused her to freeze. But only for a moment. That's because she remembered she had a very big reason why she had to keep fighting. And why she had to win. She drew back her fist so she could punch him in the face.

"Gage sent me," the man growled.

It took her a moment to hear what he'd just told her. It was another moment before those words sank in. That was the only thing on earth he could have said to make her stop. Lynette quit struggling, and her gaze rifled to the man.

Gage.

Just the sound of his name put Lynette's heart in her throat again. It warmed her. And cut her to shreds all at the same time.

"Gage is dead," she whispered when he eased back his hand. "How could he have sent you?"

Unless…

Oh, mercy. She wanted to believe Gage was alive—especially since she'd never seen his dead body. Was that what this man was here to tell her? That Gage wasn't dead after all?

She was too afraid to hope, but she did anyway.

"No," he mumbled as if he knew exactly what she was thinking, and he stepped several inches away from her. "Before Gage died, he asked me to keep an eye on you. He made me promise."

His voice was like gravel, husky and raw, and Lynette studied what she could see of him. Tall. Lanky. He wore dark jeans, a black shirt and a black leather jacket.

There was a cowboy hat, also black, slung low on his forehead so that it was hard to see his face. He'd probably done that on purpose, since he was obviously trying to prevent her from getting a good look at him.

"Who are you?" she demanded.

He stepped deeper into the shadows. "It's best if you don't know my name."

"I disagree with that," Lynette snapped. "You're in my bedroom at four in the morning. How did you get in? All the doors and windows were locked, and I have a security system."

"I disarmed the system," he readily admitted. "And I'm pretty good at dealing with locks. Especially your locks. They're really kind of wussy, and you should look into upgrading."

He sounded cocky about that, and it made her trust him even less than she already did. Lynette wanted to scream again. Or at least get her gun so she could try to defend herself from this name-dropping intruder. Heck, he might not even know Gage. Maybe he'd just learned enough about her to realize that he could use Gage's name to get her to listen.

She didn't intend to listen for long.

"Go ahead," the man offered. He tipped his head to the drawer. "If holding a weapon on me will make you feel better, then do it."

Well, he was chock-full of surprises, but if this was some kind of reverse psychology, she wasn't biting. Lynette jerked open the drawer and grabbed the .38 as fast as she could. She didn't aim it at him, exactly, but she pointed it in his general direction. And she would take aim if he didn't give her some answers and give them fast.

"Start talking," she demanded.

He lifted his shoulder. "Gage said you'd probably want proof that he sent me," he casually tossed out there.

"I do." And then she would also want to know who this man was and why he was here.

The timing was certainly suspicious.

Dangerous, even.

"Gage told me a lot about you." That's all he drawled for several moments, and it was a drawl. Easy and cocky like the rest of him. "He said you owned the town newspaper, that you bought it a couple of years ago."

"So?" She tried to sound cocky, too, but failed. Her voice was shaking almost as much as her hand. Clearly, she wasn't as accustomed to break-ins as this guy was. "That's public record. Tell me something that isn't."

Another shoulder lift. "When Gage was twenty-one, he got Hodgkin's. Something very few people know."

True. At Gage's insistence that information had been limited to his family and the doctors in San Antonio who'd treated him. Still, that info alone wouldn't convince her to trust this man.

"Gage and you eloped when he was twenty-two and you were nineteen," he continued nearly right away. "But you had the marriage annulled a few weeks later because your father disapproved of the relationship."

Lynette's eyes narrowed. "You could have learned that from just about anyone who lives in Silver Creek. People here still gossip about it."

"Your father is Ford Herrington, a businessman and now a state senator, and he hated Gage," the man stated as if he hadn't heard her. "Your father thought you could do a lot better than a Ryland cowboy cop, and you caved in under the pressure and did as he wanted."

Now, she aimed the gun at him because these weren't very reassuring answers to prove that Gage had indeed sent him. "Again, not convincing. Any town gossip could have told you that."

But this intruder had managed to hit a nerve that was still raw after all these years. Because what he said was true.

Lynette had caved in.

"If this is all the proof you have, you can get out because this conversation is over," she informed him.

"It's not all I have."

He let that hang in the air for a few seconds before he stepped from the shadows, and she saw his face when he angled his head. He wasn't as young as she'd originally thought. There were some wrinkles around his eyes and on his forehead, and his neatly trimmed beard was flecked with gray.

"I need to get something from my pocket," he said, "and I'd rather you not shoot when I do that, okay?"

He waited until Lynette gave a crisp nod before he reached inside his leather jacket and took out the *something*. Whatever it was, it was small, but it made a plinking sound when he dropped it on the nightstand. Even though the room itself was dark, the outside security lights flickered off the white-gold circle.

It was Gage's wedding band.

Or one exactly like it.

Lynette picked it up with her left hand, keeping her gun in place in her right, and she reached out again to turn on the lamp.

"No." The man snagged her wrist. "Not a good idea."

That sent a chill through her, and she was about to ask why, but he released the grip he had on her, took a penlight from his pocket and handed it to her. It was small, as well, but it did the job. Lynette could see the etched swirls on the outside of the wedding band and the inscription inside: Gage's and her initials. And there was something else.

TLF.

"'True love forever,'" the man provided. He made a show of clearing his throat. "Cute. But not very accurate, huh? Two weeks isn't anywhere close to *forever.*"

Lynette shot him a glare. Then, she swallowed hard. This man could have found the ring wherever Gage had last left it, looked into her past and then guessed what the initials meant. He could have done that for a variety of reasons—especially money. Maybe he thought he could get her to cough up cash for this part of her past.

But whatever was going on here, the ring itself was real. That was the ring she'd bought for Gage the day they got married.

"How did you get this?" she asked.

The man shrugged again. "Gage gave it to me. In case you needed to be convinced about him asking me to keep an eye on you."

"I still need convincing," Lynette assured him. "You knew Gage well?"

He nodded.

Lynette waited, then huffed. "I'd like a few details so I can tell if you're lying. How did you know him?" She had to take a breath to finish. "How did Gage die?"

"I worked with him in the CIA." He paused as if weighing each word carefully. "And you know how he died. The agency told you."

"No. The agency told his family. His five brothers. I got a phone call two days after the fact from his brother Grayson, who's the sheriff. All he said was that Gage had been killed while on a classified assignment at an undisclosed location. He didn't know anything else. Or maybe he just hadn't wanted to share it with me."

Even now, eleven months later, that was another slice to her heart. Of course, Lynette couldn't blame Grayson, since she hadn't exactly stayed on a friendly basis with the Rylands, and she couldn't very well tell them that the estrangement was for their own benefit.

And for their safety.

That would have only created questions that she couldn't answer. Still couldn't.

"Gage's last assignment was in South America," the man went on. "Things didn't go as planned, and we were ambushed. He was shot, and right before he died he gave me that ring and made me swear to keep an eye on you."

Oh, God.

Now, those were the details that felt real. And convincing. Painful, too. It felt as if someone had clamped a fist around her heart and was squeezing the life out of her. She couldn't breathe. And everything inside her started to spin.

"Gage is really dead?" All she could manage was a broken whisper to ask that question.

The man made a sound, something akin to a *duh*. "You knew that."

"Yes." But until this moment, Lynette had hoped and prayed that it wasn't true. She blinked back tears. "I know it now."

She fought the pain and the panic rising inside her. Later, she would grieve and try to come to terms with losing him. *Really* losing him. But first, she had to deal with her intruder. Despite the horrible news that he'd just delivered, she doubted he'd come here in person to confirm Gage's death. He could have done that with a phone call.

"Why would Gage ask you to keep an eye on me?" Lynette asked.

"Who knows? He was dying, and men don't always use their last breath to make a wise request."

She didn't miss the venom in his voice. Probably because he believed she'd done Gage wrong. And she had. But Lynette had had her reasons way back then, and she didn't intend to explain them to this man. Or anyone else.

Some secrets were best left secret.

"I did as Gage asked," the man continued as his glare drilled into her. "I kept an eye on you. I ran some cybersearches. I even followed you a few times."

A chill rifled through her. Mercy. She hadn't noticed anyone following her in the eleven months since Gage's death. That shook her to the core. Because if this man could do that without her knowing, then others could have done it, as well.

"How much do you know?" she risked asking.

He stepped closer. "Enough to realize you're in way over your head." He paused. "Your father's a dangerous man, and he has dangerous allies. You've been digging into their files and business records, and I can promise you, that's not a good idea."

Lynette forced herself to remain calm. Well, on the outside anyway. Inside, there was a firestorm. There weren't many people who would have labeled her father as dangerous.

Powerful, yes.

Ruthless, even.

But Lynette and apparently this intruder were part of the small handful of people who suspected that her father was much, much more than the political facade that he'd created.

"I did look into his business dealings," she admitted. "But I stopped."

He stared at her, studying her. "Why?" His roughly barked question hung in the air.

"I decided other things were more important," she settled for saying.

"What things?" he snapped.

Confused at his intense emotion over what was a personal matter to her, Lynette shook her head. She had no intentions of telling him. "*Things* that have nothing to do with my father or with you."

"Tell me why you stopped." He paused between each word and spoke with clenched teeth.

Okay. That helped cut through the fear and the pain. A year ago she probably would have nicely tried to talk her way out of this, but there was a proverbial line drawn in the sand, and this cowboy had just crossed it.

Lynette got to her feet. "Enough is enough. So what if Gage asked you to keep an eye on me? Well, I don't want your eye or anything else on me. Get out now!"

She pointed the gun right at his chest.

He huffed and propped his hands on his hips. "What if I'm wearing a Kevlar vest, huh?"

Lynette blinked. "What?" And she wanted to ask if he'd missed a dose of meds or something. Because he was either ice-cold under pressure or he was crazy.

Another huff, and he grabbed the barrel of her gun and aimed it higher. "If I'm wearing Kevlar, then a chest shot will just temporarily knock the breath out of me, crack a rib or two and then piss me off. If I'm the big bad threat that you think I am, then go for a head shot. No Kevlar there."

Lynette just stared at him. "Who the heck are you?"

He leaned in so close that she caught the scent of the rain on his clothes.

And maybe something else…

"I'm the man who's going to save your life, darlin'," he growled. "And you'll let me do it because of that promise I made to Gage. You're going to take a suitcase from your closet, pack a change of clothes, and you'll leave with me *now*. We're moving fast, light and without any more arguments or questions from you."

He started to step back. Back into the shadows, but Lynette caught on to his arm and yanked him closer. Well, she tried anyway. He looked lanky, but the muscles in his arm were rock-hard and, despite the rough pull she'd given him, he didn't budge even a little.

Lynette reached to turn on the lamp again. She wanted a better look at his eyes to see if she could recognize something. *Anything.* But he ripped the lamp's electrical plug from the wall socket.

"I thought I made it clear—no light," he insisted. He pointed to the rain-streaked windows. "Because there could be someone bad out there. If he's not already here, he will be soon. And trust me, Gage didn't send this guy to keep an eye on you."

Lynette's gaze darted to the window, and she would have moved closer if the man hadn't latched on to her shoulder and anchored her in place.

"Who is this *someone* out there?" she demanded.

He cursed, and his grip melted off her. "A hired gun. And he has orders to kill you."

Chapter Two

Well, so far this plan just plain sucked.

Despite the near darkness, Gage Ryland could see the color drain from Lynette's face, and with her chest pumping for air, she sank back on the edge of the bed. Even with the bad blood and old baggage between them, he hated to see her like this. Frightened.

And in the worst kind of danger.

Maybe she would be frightened enough to cooperate, because Gage really had to get her out of there fast.

"You're lying," she said.

Denial. That was a predictable reaction. Too bad he didn't have time for it. "I wish," he mumbled.

While he was wishing, Gage wished he had a better plan, because this one *sucked*. It was taking too long, and there was way too much touching and close contact going on.

Too much emotion.

And Lynette wasn't the only one of them responsible for that. He hadn't expected this to feel like a bandage being ripped from a raw, unstitched wound. But that's exactly how it felt. This trip down memory lane wasn't doing his heart or his gut any good.

He should have just waited outside her house in the storm and killed the would-be killer, quietly disposed of the body and then kept watch for the next assassin that would come her way.

And there would be others.

He was sure of that.

It was the *there would be others* logic that Gage had used to justify putting on this middle-age disguise and risking everything to warn Lynette of the danger. Not just of this danger but of those assassins that would come even after he managed to neutralize this one.

Well, he'd warned her all right, along with feeding her a boatload of lies about a promise he'd made to a dead man.

No promise.

And the dead man was standing smack-dab in front of her.

Of course, Lynette couldn't learn either of those things tonight. Or ever. In the only way that mattered, Gage was dead to her, and it had to stay that way even if a little part of him wanted to confront her about the way she'd sliced and diced his heart all those years ago. But while a confrontation might make him feel marginally better, it wouldn't do much to help the situation.

Her closet door behind him was already open. Gage knew that because he'd opened it not long after he'd broken into her house, and he pulled out her overnight bag that he'd located on the shelf. But Lynette only pushed it away when he tried to hand it to her.

"Who's the hired gun and who sent him?" she demanded.

All right. The denial was already over. Well, maybe. At least she was asking questions again, and the sooner Gage furnished her with answers, the sooner he could convince her to leave this place and go into hiding. Best not to spend much time in this room with her.

Especially with her wearing a paper-thin white gown that hugged her body. A body he remembered a little too well.

Yeah.

He had to hightail it out of there ASAP.

"The hit man's name is Freddie Denton," Gage explained.

Thanks to a throat spray that the CIA used to help with disguises and covers, his voice was like a Texas gravel road. He didn't sound anything like himself.

He hoped.

Gage also hoped he could finish this rescue plan before the effects of the spray wore off. He figured he only had about an hour, tops, and the minutes of that hour were ticking away fast. Not good, since she was staring at him as if he'd lost his mind. She sure wasn't moving or doing what he'd told her to do.

He huffed and doled out some more details. "An informant called to let me know that Denton was on the move and making arrangements to pay you a visit."

"A visit?" she questioned.

Gage gave her a flat look that probably didn't translate well beneath the layers of prosthetic makeup and dark brown contacts. "Denton doesn't make social calls. He kills people for a living, and he's very good at what he does."

She kept her chin high, but her breathing was still way too fast. "Then if he's a known killer, why haven't you arrested him? Especially since you're a CIA agent, like Gage was."

Oh, man.

Yeah, it'd been years since he'd seen Lynette, but he didn't remember her being this, well, courageous or mouthy. He'd counted on her screaming—which she'd done—and then begging him to get her out of there. She hadn't exactly begged for the latter, but Gage would still do it.

However, these questions were eating into their escape time.

"No one has arrested Denton because he doesn't leave evidence behind, that's why," Gage settled for saying. "He kills witnesses and anyone else who gets in his way."

But Lynette only shook her head and kept staring at him.

Gage didn't bother with another huff. It was making his throat sore so he got started on something he'd wanted her to do. He put her overnight bag on the bed next to her.

"Pack," he insisted.

She didn't stop staring. "Convince me why I should."

This stubborn streak was getting old fast.

He got right in her face and slowed his words so that she would grasp each life-threatening one. "About two and a half hours ago Denton left his house in Houston, and he was armed with an assault rifle, night-vision goggles and a map to your house. It's my guess that with the rain-slick roads, he'll be here in five minutes."

Actually, it would probably be about fifteen, but Gage wanted to up the urgency here.

Her breath rattled in her throat. Because of the darkness, he couldn't clearly see her eyes, but Gage knew they were a deep ocean blue. And right about now, she would no doubt be fighting back tears and the terror. Lynette wasn't accustomed to hit men and danger. Prior to this, her father had kept her just out of reach of that.

Gage had tried to do the same.

But he'd failed.

This would be brutal, but she needed to hear it. "I figure Denton will do one of two things. He'll try to gun you down through that bedroom window the moment he arrives, or he'll just wait until morning when you walk out your front door to go to your car. Either way, you'll be dead…unless you leave with me right now."

Her forehead bunched up. "And who hired Denton?"

"I'm not sure—yet." Gage checked his watch. The minutes were ticking off fast. If he didn't convince her soon, he'd have to use the tranquilizer packet he had in his coat pocket. "I suspect it was your father or one of his slime-ball business associates you were investigating."

Gage knew their names: Nicole Manning and Patrick Harkin. Names that Lynette already knew, as well, because *(a)* she'd known the pair most of her life, and *(b)* she'd been conducting a pseudo-investigation into some of their business deals that dated back as far as two decades.

Good intentions.

Bad idea.

Real bad.

"When you started playing Nancy Drew and digging into your father's records, I think it made Patrick and Nicole very nervous," Gage clarified. Since she wasn't packing yet, he did it for her. He grabbed the first outfit he could reach in her closet, jeans and a top, and stuffed them into the overnight bag. "One of them could have hired Denton. Or maybe your father decided to cut his losses and put a permanent end to your snooping."

"Not my father," she whispered. Lynette pulled in a long breath and repeated the denial. "He wouldn't send someone to kill me."

Gage could have argued that, but he'd learned the hard way he would just be wasting his breath. Lynette was never going to believe her father was the bottom-feeding monster that he truly was.

"Besides," she added. "I've already stopped looking into their records."

He studied her face to see if that was a lie. It wasn't. "When did you stop?"

She hesitated. "Nearly a month ago."

Gage didn't miss that little hesitation, but he let it pass for now. "Well, I don't think your daddy got the memo about that." He didn't bother to tone down the sarcasm. "And even if he did, he might have thought you were still too much of a liability."

He went to her dresser drawer, grabbed a handful of underwear. Yep, a lacy bra and panties similar to the ones that'd been tossed onto the chair in the corner, and he crammed the items into the bag.

"What exactly were you looking for in those records?" Gage asked her.

Her gaze snapped to him again, and she scowled. "It doesn't matter now. I'm no threat to my father or to Patrick or Nicole. I can call them and let them all know that."

Gage had to risk touching her again when Lynette reached for the phone. "And what will you say to them?" He got his hand off her as quickly as he could. *"Daddy, I know you hired a hit man to kill me, but I promise I'll be a good girl. Again,"* he added in a mumble.

Hell.

That was a fit-of-temper kind of response, and Lynette obviously latched right onto it. She stood, slowly, and stared at him. She also aimed her gun.

At his head.

She was a fast learner.

"I'm doing something I should have done the moment I found you in my bedroom," Lynette warned him. "I'm calling the sheriff."

Great. Just what he didn't need. His big brother Grayson in on this stupid-butted plan. That couldn't happen for a lot of reasons, so Gage grabbed her hand again when Lynette reached for the phone on the nightstand.

"You can't," he let her know.

"I can," she let him know right back. "If there's really a hit man on his way here, then the sheriff can stop him."

"Yeah. Or the sheriff can get killed by a pro who knows how to do just that." Grayson and he had never seen eye to eye, but Gage wasn't going to let Denton gun down his brother. Or for that matter gun down Lynette, despite this sudden stubborn streak.

Lynette tried to throw off his grip, and Gage had no choice but to grab on to her and put her against the wall.

The clicking sound surprised him.

It surprised the heck out of her, too.

Lynette's eyes widened, and she looked down at the trigger she'd just pulled. The gun was no longer aimed at his head. But rather the ceiling.

"Your bullets are in my pocket," he explained once he got his mouth working again. Sheesh. His heart was beating a mile a minute, and that didn't happen very often.

She made a sound of outrage and kept struggling to get away from him. "You unloaded my gun?"

"Yeah, before you woke up. And in hindsight, it was a smart move, don't you think?" Gage grabbed both her wrists in his left hand and shook the .38 loose in case she tried to bash him in the head with it.

"Hell," he grumbled. "I didn't think you'd actually pull the trigger."

And for some stupid reason, that nearly made him smile even though the aim at the ceiling meant she was just trying to fire a warning shot. Still, she'd fired. His ex had grown a spine. *Finally.* Under different circumstances and if her delays weren't a threat to their lives, he might have approved.

Gage's near smile went south though when she tried to knee him in the groin. She got darn close, too. Her kneecap rammed into his thigh and had him seeing stars.

"Time for the tranquilizer," he grumbled. He took out the plastic packet from his pocket.

"No!" Just like that, Lynette stopped struggling. "Please. No drugs. I'll do whatever you say."

Gage stopped, too, and he stared at her, trying to figure out what this was all about. "It's just a mild sedative. It won't hurt you. You'd be out ten minutes, tops."

"I don't want to be unconscious. It's a phobia I have." Lynette held his stare and put some steel in her voice. "Now, let go of me so we can leave. Denton will be here soon."

Yeah. And Gage was more than a little suspicious that Lynette had suddenly realized the need for them to get the heck out of there—especially since he hadn't made much headway with her until now with the tranquilizer threat.

Gage let go of her, stepped back, and with some major suspicion, he watched her grab the bra and panties from the chair and then go to the closet. He didn't think she had another gun in there, but she might try to use something to club him. Gage didn't believe for one minute that he'd actually convinced her that leaving was the only way for her to stay alive.

So, what was she up to?

Had she managed to find a weapon in that closet?

"Don't look," she insisted. "I want to put on some clothes."

Gage didn't look. Not exactly. But he didn't trust her enough to give her complete privacy.

Lynette somehow managed to get on the underwear

while her gown was still draped over her body. The gown finally hit the floor, and she immediately slipped into a loose blue dress. If there'd been time, he would have suggested jeans or something that covered more of her. But that would have required him seeing her half-naked again.

He was pretty sure that wasn't a good idea.

"I left my raincoat at my office, but I can use this," she explained, pulling a cherry-red trenchcoat from a hanger. She put it on over the dress and slipped on a pair of shoes.

Gage checked both, including the coat pockets. Too bad that required more touching. Those pockets were deep, and the search for a possible weapon sent his hand skimming against her thigh.

Oh, yeah. This plan sucked.

She huffed, maybe at the hand-to-thigh contact and mumbled something about him being a pervert. Lynette grabbed the overnight bag from the bed.

And Gage's wedding ring from the nightstand.

Something he'd been about to take for himself.

"If Denton comes in the house looking for me," Lynette mumbled, slipping the ring onto her index finger, "I don't want him to find it."

Neither did Gage, but he had to wonder why that was so important to Lynette. It couldn't be because she still had feelings for him.

No.

Couldn't be that.

She'd had their marriage annulled ten years ago, and the few times he'd seen her since, Lynette hadn't been just distant, she'd been downright ice-cold. Not just to him but to his family, as well. So, what was with her grabbing that ring?

Too bad Gage didn't have time to find out.

"What?" she asked, probably because he was staring holes in her. She moved closer.

Her gaze connected with his.

That kind of deep eye contact was something else that shouldn't happen. The *windows of the soul* theory might be all bunk, but he didn't want to risk Lynette seeing the real person behind those colored contacts and disguise.

"Let's go," Gage ordered. He picked up her gun and his penlight, stuffed them into his jacket pocket and led her out of the room and into the hall.

In his research he'd learned that Lynette had only owned the place two years, so this was Gage's first trip here. That's why he'd taken a couple of minutes to familiarize himself with the layout.

And even a few seconds to watch her sleep.

He wasn't proud of that. It had seemed more like a violation of her privacy than breaking in. After all, the breaking in had been necessary, but there was no logical explanation for why he'd nearly lost his breath when he'd seen her lying there in bed.

So many memories.

So many vivid images of her naked body.

She'd been right to call him a pervert.

Gage mumbled some profanity. Oh, good. Now, he was feeling hot in all the wrong places. Sadly, Lynette could do that to him even though his brain didn't want another dose of what she doled out. He'd barely survived their last showdown.

"How do we know Denton isn't already out there waiting for us?" Lynette asked.

It took Gage a moment to switch gears, which should have been a big fat clue for him to get his mind off her and back on the plan. "Because I left a sensor wire on the road

about an eighth of a mile from your house. If he'd driven
over it, the monitor in my jacket would have gone off."

"Assuming Denton stays on the road," she pointed out.

It was an assumption all right, but Gage was banking on the fact that Denton didn't know anyone was onto
him. Gage was also banking on the fact that he was just
as good of a shot as Denton. Maybe better. Still, he didn't
want to test that theory because it would mean Lynette
would be in the middle of a gunfight. The plan was for
her to stay alive, not to be shot in cross fire.

Gage pulled his weapon and expected the gasp he
heard Lynette make. "You said Denton wasn't here yet."

"It's just a precaution to have the gun ready," he explained.

But it might become a necessity. He wasn't walking
out that door without something to defend them.

They went through the dining room. Then the kitchen.
Gage kept his eye on Lynette in case she tried to grab a
knife or cast-iron skillet to club him over the head, and he
cracked open the back door. The rain and storm muffled
sounds he would have preferred to hear, but he didn't see
anything suspicious.

"Let's go," he ordered.

"On foot?" she asked. When she dug in her heels, Gage
took her by the arm and led her onto the porch.

"I left my vehicle on the Old Creek Road. About a five-
minute walk." Something she no doubt already knew.
"Eight minutes if you keep dragging your feet."

"I'm dragging my feet because I'm not sure I should
trust you."

"Yeah. I got that. You tried to shoot me, remember?"

"I tried to shoot the ceiling," Lynette snapped. "Not
you. But maybe I should have. After all, you broke in to
my house." She mumbled something he didn't catch. "Of

course, you made sure I couldn't shoot you. Just how long were you in my house before I woke up?"

Gage would take that secret to the grave, and if they didn't hurry, he might be in the grave, a real one, sooner than he'd imagined.

He tuned out her mumblings and protests and kept watch around them. When he was as sure as he could be that it was safe, Gage pulled her off the porch and onto the soggy ground.

The rain immediately assaulted them, and he hoped his disguise would last a little while longer. All he had to do was get her to his SUV and drive about ten miles to the small regional airport where he had a plane and pilot waiting to whisk her away to safety.

But *all he had to do* could be complicated in too many ways. Especially since she was still dragging her feet. Gage gave her a rough jerk to get her moving at more than a snail's pace.

"Gage wouldn't have asked a man like you to keep an eye on me," she snarled when he pulled her again.

He was about to assure Lynette that she was wrong, but the monitor inside his coat beeped.

Just one soft little sound.

But it was more than enough for him to know this plan was about to get a lot more dangerous. That's because Denton was ahead of schedule. He'd either driven like the wind or tagged someone else closer to come after Lynette, because Gage didn't think this was someone else paying a social call at this hour of the morning.

"Stay low and behind the trees," Gage warned her. Which shouldn't be hard since her backyard was littered with pecans and oaks.

He looked over his shoulder to make sure Lynette understood. But the only thing he saw was the wild fear in her eyes. Before he could even try to calm her down, she shocked the heck out of him.

She threw the overnight bag right at him.

Because Gage hadn't been expecting it, he rammed into a tree when the bag rammed into him.

And Lynette took off running.

Gage didn't take the time to curse or remind himself that he should have kept a closer watch on her. He just went after her, the mud and the rain sloshing all around his boots and probably doing a real number on his disguise.

Lynette was a lot faster than he'd figured she would be, maybe because she knew which mud holes and tree roots to dodge. Gage didn't. And he stumbled over a few before he finally managed to snag her by the shoulder. In the same motion, he dragged her behind the nearest tree.

"Let me go!" she said in an angry whisper. She punched at him again and tried to get away.

Oh, man. He didn't have time for this. Gage kept her tight in his grip and reached in his pocket for the tranquilizer. He couldn't risk Denton hearing her and coming straight into the backyard. It would prevent them from escaping, and he didn't want to hide out for what could be a half hour or more in the rain and behind a tree with a woman hell-bent on beating the tar out of him.

"This will keep you calm," he promised her, ripping open the packet of the liquid sedative. And it'd make her temporarily unconscious—a real bonus right now. "It'll be safer carrying you than chasing you down."

"No. Please." Lynette frantically shook her head and shoved away the packet that contained the drug-soaked cloth. "You can't. It might hurt the baby."

Now, it was Gage who froze.

"Baby?" he spit out. "What baby?"

Chapter Three

Lynette hadn't intended to blurt out her baby news.

She hadn't wanted a soul to know that she was pregnant. Not yet anyway. But she couldn't allow this man to use a tranquilizer or any other drug on her. At this early stage of her pregnancy, she had no idea what kind of damage it could do to her unborn child. It might even cause her to miscarry.

The man glared at her, and Lynette didn't know why her baby news would cause him to react this way. Nor did she care. She was tired of fighting. Tired of this man. And tired of the entire situation of hit men and danger. If he was so determined to get her to safety, then Lynette was going to cooperate.

Well, maybe.

If she got a chance to escape again, she would take it in a heartbeat, but she wouldn't do that if it meant further risk to her child.

"Denton?" she reminded him when he just stood there gawking at her. "He tripped the sensor, remember? And that means he'll be here any minute."

He shook his head as if to clear it and caught on to her arm again. "Yeah."

Yeah? That was his only explanation for his extreme reaction about her pregnancy? It certainly didn't mesh with the smart-mouthed cockiness that he'd shown her up to this point. Unless he was planning on doing something or taking her somewhere that wouldn't be safe for a pregnant woman. Of course, a hit man wouldn't be safe, either.

"Come on," he finally snarled.

The return of the surly tone was actually a relief. Sort of. But it was more of a relief when he caught on to her arm again. For a moment Lynette thought they might start running. After all, a hit man on their tails warranted running. But he kept the pace at a light jog as they slogged their way through the mud and grass.

Maybe he was being considerate now that he knew she was pregnant. Or maybe things weren't as urgent as she'd thought.

The slash of light changed her mind about the *lack of urgency* and robbed Lynette of what little breath she'd managed to keep.

Headlights.

No doubt belonging to Denton's vehicle.

Well, they were Denton's headlights all right *if* this mouthy intruder had told her the truth. Lynette couldn't be sure about him. Something definitely wasn't right, but she didn't know what. Still, if he'd wanted her dead, he could have managed that before she ever woke up.

Not exactly a comforting thought.

The headlights of the approaching vehicle suddenly went dark, causing her heart to pound even harder. Her intruder had no reaction. Not even slightly tensed muscles. And she could tell that because he practically had her in a bear hug as they jogged.

"Denton's out of his car," the man mumbled.

Lynette had no idea how he knew that, especially since they were a good twenty yards from the house and even farther from the road. Added to that, it was still pitch-dark. But then, there was another light. A tiny streak that had the man mumbling some profanity.

"He has a flashlight," he whispered. And he yanked her behind the nearest tree.

He positioned her so that the front of her body was against the towering pecan. He pressed himself against her back, and he was big enough that he created a shield of sorts.

They waited there, the seconds crawling by, with her heartbeat crashing in her ears and the rain swiping at them with each gust of wind. The man, her self-proclaimed protector, kept his gun ready and aimed, the barrel sticking out just slightly from the tree trunk.

"It's Denton all right," he whispered.

Lynette tried to blink the rain from her eyes so she could pick through the darkness and see what had made the muscles in her *protector*'s chest and arm turn to iron. Now that the headlights were off, she could no longer spot the car.

But thanks to her security lights that rimmed the eaves of her house, she saw the shadowy figure.

A man dressed in dark clothes. And he was indeed carrying a rifle.

Her stomach clamped into a hard knot. Lynette had held out hope that Denton wasn't real, or that he wasn't an actual hit man, but that rifle proved otherwise.

Sweet heaven.

What was she going to do?

She hadn't had time to finish her backup plan to move from Silver Creek, and now it might be too late. Denton could complicate things because once this was over, there'd be an investigation. She'd have to call the authorities. And that would mean bringing in Gage's family. There was no way she could keep the intruder's visit a secret.

"Keep quiet," the man warned her in a whisper. "And don't you dare think about running again." He kept his attention pinned to Denton.

Lynette had indeed considered running again, but she had to pick her poison here. An intruder or a likely hit man.

Some choice.

It was the intruder. *For now.*

She watched as Denton skulked toward the house. Straight toward her bedroom window. He lifted the rifle and fired, the bullets crashing through the glass panes.

Lynette clamped her hand over her mouth to muffle the gasp. The blasts slammed through her and robbed her of her breath and any hope that all of this had been some scare tactic. If she'd been inside, those bullets would have ripped through her. She'd be dead right now.

The man behind her made an *I told you so* sound. But that sound had no sooner left his mouth than he sucked in a quick breath. And Lynette knew why.

Denton looked inside the window, his face right against the now gaping hole that his bullets had left. He pulled back his shoulders, and then his gaze skirted all around the yard.

Oh, mercy.

He'd apparently realized that he'd just shot at her empty bed.

Lynette prayed that Denton would go inside, and then she and her Gage-appointed protector could get out of there. That rifle could fire just as deadly a shot into the yard as it had into the house.

"Get ready to move," the man whispered when Denton stepped onto her back porch.

Lynette did. Well, she got as ready as she could considering the ground was practically a mud bog and that her nerves were in shambles. The moment that Denton stepped inside her house, she and the man started to run. And this time, it wasn't a jog.

They *ran*.

The security lights didn't give them much illumination this far out, and it was next to impossible to see where they were running. Lynette hoped they didn't trip and fall.

The sound nearly caused her to do just that.

It was a thick blast, and it ripped through the darkness. Not from inside the house. No. It was much worse than that. This shot had been fired outside and in their direction.

The man latched on to her arm and pulled her behind another tree. Just in the nick of time. A shot slammed into the trunk of the oak and sent a spray of splinters everywhere.

Lynette couldn't think, couldn't breathe. She could only pray that the shots would miss and would end soon. Every bullet was a risk to her, her baby, and yes, even to this man she didn't completely trust.

Again, the man positioned himself so that he was shielding her, except this time he was pressed even harder against her until he had her flattened against the tree.

He reached out with his right hand and returned fire.

Since his gun was so close, just inches from her head, the blast was deafening. Lynette put her hands over her ears. Too late. Everything inside her was clanging, and that only revved up her fear and adrenaline.

Denton fired another shot into the tree.

Then another.

With each one Lynette knew this nightmare was real. But why? Why had someone sent Denton after her? Yes, she'd looked into those business deals in her father's files, but she hadn't found anything that incriminated Patrick, Nicole or even her father. She certainly hadn't found anything that would warrant her death.

Unless…

Oh, God. Was that it?

Did this have to do with her pregnancy? Had her father learned the secret that she'd paid dearly to have hidden? If so, then Denton was the least of her worries.

"Level your breathing," the man warned her. "Or you'll hyperventilate."

Lynette tried to do that. She tried to stop herself from spiraling into a panic, but it was hard to remain calm when this close to death. If she died, so did her precious baby.

"Stay ahead of me," he ordered.

Lynette had no idea what he meant by that until he shoved her away from the tree and in front of him. He pushed her to start running again. And that's exactly what Lynette did. She ran with him behind her, once again acting as her human shield. Gage must have somehow convinced this guy to risk taking a bullet for her.

But why?

Why had Gage thought of her safety during his last moments on earth?

Later, that was something she wanted to know. If this man would tell her, that is. So far, he'd been short on explanations and long on details that anyone could have learned. But Lynette had to know—had Gage somehow managed to forgive her during those last moments of his life?

Was this man the proof of that forgiveness?

If Gage had managed that, it wouldn't ease her immediate grief, but it might help with other things.

She slid her hand over her stomach.

Another shot.

Lynette braced herself for one of them to be hit, but this shot also slammed into the tree. Her rescuer had no doubt planned it that way because he kept them weaving in and out of the clump of trees, using them and his body to keep her out of the path of Denton's bullets.

"Watch out for the ditch," he reminded her.

Good thing, too, because Lynette had forgotten about it, though she'd walked near it dozens of times. Falling at this point could be a fatal mistake. They leaped over the foot-wide ditch and kept running.

Too bad the shots kept coming their way.

"Denton will have to reload soon," he let her know. "And then he'll run after us."

That didn't help keep her breathing level. Lynette didn't want to believe him, but unfortunately, he'd been right about everything so far. Maybe when this was done and they were safely out of here, he would tell her more *right* things. Like how she could stop this from happening again.

Just like that, the shots stopped. Apparently it was reloading time. And Lynette and the man automatically sped up, going from a jog to a sprint.

She was thankful that she was in good shape, and the irony was just the day before she'd asked her doctor if it was okay to continue jogging. He'd given her the green light. However, her obstetrician certainly wouldn't recommend her running for her life to dodge a hail of bullets.

The man shoved aside some low-hanging cedar branches and pulled her into the dense shrubs and underbrush at the edge of her property line. Though it was late September, everything was in full leaf, and the foliage scratched and slapped at her. Still, she felt safer here than out in the open.

Well, she felt safer until the shots started again.

And yes, Denton was indeed following them. These shots were closer than the others had been.

They broke through the wall of thick shrubs, and Lynette spotted the dark waters of the creek coiling around the rock and sand banks. She also spotted the dark-colored SUV. It was parked on the narrow dirt road—exactly where the man had said it would be. Another truth in his favor.

But they didn't head toward the SUV.

Much to her surprise, he latched on to her arm and practically dragged her into a clump of hackberries. Lynette was about to remind him that the idea was for them to get the heck out of there, but he put his mouth right against her ear.

"Denton's too close to us for us to escape," he whispered. He positioned them side by side so that he had a good angle to view the dirt road and the SUV. "If I start the engine, he'll hear it."

Lynette shook her head. "But you could drive out of here fast." In fact, she was going to insist on it. The farther and faster away from Denton, the better.

"The road's too straight for that. Denton could, and will, disable the SUV by shooting out the tires, and then we'd be forced to get out while he still has a rifle trained on us."

That sounded, well, logical. Something she didn't want to hear right now. Lynette didn't want logic. She wanted to get out there and away from the assassin trying to kill them.

"Just wait," he added in that same hoarse whisper. "If Denton comes this way, I'll see him." He paused so long that it drew Lynette's gaze up to his. "I'd prefer him alive so he can tell me the name of the scumbag who hired him."

Yes. Lynette hadn't considered that, but it was something she needed to know. That was the first step in stopping this and keeping her baby safe.

But would Denton tell them?

Maybe if this man pressed him, and Lynette didn't care how hard he pressed. She didn't care if he beat Denton to within an inch of his life. She had to know what had brought all of this down on her.

So, they sat and waited. With her breath racing. Her heart pounding. And the fear, overwhelming. She had to get out of this alive.

Because the hackberry trees were choked together, they actually created an umbrella of sorts, and they got a reprieve from the rain. His Stetson helped, too, because she was tucked partly beneath its brim. Still, despite the trees and her trenchcoat, she was soaked to the bone because she hadn't taken the time to button up. Maybe it was the chill and the adrenaline, but Lynette's teeth started to chatter.

"Shh," the man warned.

When the chattering only got worse, he hooked his left arm around her and pulled her inside his leather jacket and against his body.

Instant warmth. And comfort. Something she hadn't expected from this stranger.

Lynette drew her knees up to her chest and buried her face into the heat from his chest and shoulder. It didn't calm her exactly, but it helped. So did the fact that he had those diligent eyes trained on the area around them.

The rain made it hard to hear anything, but she listened for any sound that might alert them that Denton was near.

And she heard it.

The snap.

As if someone had stepped on a twig.

The man no doubt heard it, as well, because she felt the muscles in his arm tense just slightly. Barely a reaction and a drop in the bucket compared to hers. He eased away from her, probably to get ready to fire, and Lynette readied herself, as well. She pulled in her breath.

Taking in the man's scent.

Not the rain-slick leather jacket or even the T-shirt beneath.

She took in *his* scent.

Despite hearing that twig snap, Lynette looked up at the man. It was too dark to see his face, but she tried to recall every detail of it when she'd seen him in her bedroom. The wrinkles around his eyes, the gray in his beard and hair. None of those things was familiar.

But his scent was.

It stirred through her, warming her in a different kind of way than his body had. But then, Lynette shook her head.

No.

It couldn't be.

She stared at him, trying to see something in his face that would match the scent, but the sound had her attention snapping away from him. There was rustling movement in the underbrush to their right.

Just a split second of sound.

Before Denton came crashing through.

Denton pivoted, turning that rifle right on them. Her heart stopped. Her breath froze in her lungs. But the man with the familiar scent didn't freeze. He bracketed his right wrist with his left hand. Took aim.

And he fired.

He pulled the trigger twice, and even though Lynette

couldn't see exactly where the shots had gone, a few moments later, she had her answer. She saw Denton crumple into a heap on the ground.

"Hell," the man grumbled.

He kept his gun aimed at Denton, stood and cautiously went closer to the hit man. He bent down, touched his fingers to Denton's neck and added another *hell*. "He's dead."

Dead. Not exactly good news, because he wouldn't be able to tell them who'd hired him. As bad as that was, Lynette still didn't wish him alive.

But she did want something else.

She had to know.

Lynette stood and stepped from the cover of the hackberries. The rain immediately slapped at her, just as it was doing to the man in the black leather jacket and Stetson. She walked closer and drew in his scent again.

Oh, God.

She hadn't said that aloud, but he must have sensed some change in her body language.

"What?" he snapped, staring down at her.

Lynette shook her head and stared back. She was terrified to speak. But there was no chance she could stay silent and not ask the question.

"Gage?"

Chapter Four

Oh, hell.

This rescue had just gotten a lot more complicated.

Gage shook his head and tried to cut off the complication at its proverbial knees. But Lynette only shook her head, too, and she reached up and touched his face. Or rather she touched the thin sheet of prosthetic makeup that had created the wrinkles around his eyes and the fake beard.

"Gage," she repeated on a rise of breath.

And it definitely wasn't a question.

Since she looked ready to rip the rest of the makeup off his face, Gage took Lynette's arm and practically dragged her to the SUV. He had a lot to do now, more than he'd originally planned, and he doubted he could dodge her question for long. Especially since she seemed so darn sure of who he was.

But how the devil had she known?

This disguise had fooled enemy agents. Heck, it could have probably fooled his brothers. So, how did Lynette figure it out while running for her life from a hit man?

"Gage," she repeated when he stuffed her into the passenger's seat.

Gage groaned and hurried, getting behind the steering wheel as fast as he could. He had to put some distance between them and the hit man in case the guy had brought backup with him.

"You're alive." Lynette's breath broke, and a hoarse sob tore from her throat. She clawed at the prosthetics, ripping them off.

"Hold that thought," Gage told her. He wasn't completely immune to the emotion, or the fallout that would happen from this, but he had to make a call. Then, he'd figure out a way to deal with Lynette.

It wasn't going to be pretty.

He pressed the button on the secure phone on the dash, and his handler, Sherman Hendricks, answered on the first ring.

"Lock on to my coordinates," Gage instructed. "I just left a dead body in the woods, and I need the area to be sanitized. There's also an overnight bag near the residence, and it'll have to be moved."

In other words, a full cleanup of the dead assassin and the overnight bag in case his prints were on it. No one could know Gage had been there.

Well, no one except Lynette.

Gage didn't see a way around this big discussion that Lynette and he were about to have, so he ended the call to start some damage control.

"How did you know?" Gage was unable to stop himself from asking. He was good at his job. Damn good. And it was a little insulting that a civilian had figured it out in under a half hour.

"Your scent," she said in a breathy whisper.

Gage gave his armpit a quick smell but clearly didn't detect what Lynette had.

"No one else has that scent," she clarified, which of course, didn't clarify it much. She bolted across the seat and threw her arms around him. "It's you. It's really you."

Well, that wasn't the reaction Gage had expected.

Nor was the hungry kiss she planted on his mouth.

Her lips tasted of the rain and the salt from her tears. And of Lynette. Yeah, after all this time, he remembered exactly how she tasted. So, maybe it wasn't too much of a stretch for her to remember his scent.

Considering though that they hated each other, it was still a puzzling memory to latch onto.

The kiss continued, punctuated with her sobs and mumbles, and Gage finally had no choice but to pull over. Not a good time for it, with the body of a hit man only a mile away, but he didn't want to wreck.

Without thinking it through, Gage kissed her right back, that taste coiling through him. Oh, man. He'd missed her almost as much as he hated her.

Almost.

However, he was having a hard time remembering the hatred part while playing lip-lock with his ex. He kissed her far harder and deeper than he should have, but then considering he shouldn't be kissing her at all, he was getting his money's worth from this particular mistake.

Thankfully, the kiss didn't last much longer. Just seconds. Before Lynette stopped and pushed away from him.

"You let me think you were dead!" she shouted. And she planted both her hands against his chest and gave him a hard shove. "How could you do something like that to me? How?"

It took Gage a moment to recover from the scalding kiss, the shove and the quick change in Lynette's mood. "I had no choice."

"No choice?" she howled. The tears streamed down her cheeks. And she gave him another shove. "Everyone has a choice, Gage, and you let me and your family believe you were dead."

She stopped cold, stared at him. "Or does your family know the truth?"

He shook his head. "They don't. There are only two people who know—you and the man I just called." And for some very dangerous reasons, it had to stay that way.

Lynette cursed. Shoved him again. "You jerk!" And then she called him something worse. *Much* worse. "How could you do that to us?"

"How? I did it to save all of your lives!" And he immediately hated the outburst. Hated that he felt bad for the lies that had been necessary. "You think it was easy for me to give up my life? My family?"

He didn't add Lynette's name to that little tirade, felt a little guilty about it, and then Gage reminded himself that she was pregnant with another man's child.

Hell.

He'd only been fake dead for eleven months. Of course, Lynette and he hadn't been anything close to a couple for years. Ten years to be exact. But Gage was still riled even if he didn't have a right to be.

For that matter, Lynette didn't have a right to be riled, either. He reminded himself of that, too, and put some steel back in his attitude. Except he didn't have time to put that attitude into a mind-your-own-business snarl because she spoke before he could.

"Why did you do this?" she demanded. Now, she was the one with attitude.

Gage debated mentioning that part about her not having riling rights for anything related to him, but he didn't want this to launch into a long argument. He had to give her a quick, sterile explanation, so he could get her to the airport for the trip to safety. Then, he'd be out of her life.

Again.

And he didn't want to know why that suddenly didn't

feel like the perfect solution that it had been just thirty minutes ago.

Oh, wait. He did know.

It was because of that blasted kiss.

Sheesh. When the heck would he learn to quit thinking with any other organ that wasn't his brain? Because the rest of his body, especially parts of him that were still affected by Lynette, wasn't prone to making good decisions.

"Well?" she pressed. "I deserve an answer."

No, she didn't deserve anything from him, but he'd give her one anyway.

Mostly, it would be the truth.

"When I was on assignment last year, I killed a notorious international drug dealer, Rodney Dalvetti."

While he thought about how to continue, how to word this, Gage put the SUV in gear and started driving. He also picked off the rest of his now worthless disguise.

"Since Rodney had murdered a hundred people or more," he explained, "I didn't take his death too hard. But his brother, Sampson, did. Turns out Sampson's plenty upset about losing his rabid sibling, and he blames me for the shoot-out that his brother started."

Lynette used the heels of her hands to swipe away the tears. "This Sampson Dalvetti is after you?"

"*Was.* And when he couldn't find me, he swore that he'd come after my family. You, too, since he had his minions dig around and find out that we'd once been married." He shot her a glance. "I guess he figured he'd use anyone and everyone to draw me out so he could kill me."

"Oh, God," Lynette mumbled.

"Yeah, that was pretty much my reaction, but I added a lot more words when I heard what was going down."

Gage could protect himself, but he had five brothers, four sisters-in-law and a handful of nieces and nephews.

Plus, Lynette. That was a lot of people to try to protect, and he knew that sooner or later, Sampson would get to one or more of them. Gage also figured that Lynette would be at the top or near the top of Sampson's kill list.

Well, maybe.

Sampson had made it clear with his threats that he would take out Lynette. Gage wasn't sure why Sampson had locked in on her, especially since Gage had had little communication with her since the annulment. But that was a question for another day. A day when he had Lynette tucked away so that Sampson couldn't reach her.

"The only way I could keep you all safe was for Sampson to believe I was dead," Gage spelled out for her.

Still staring at him, she stayed quiet a moment. "You could have told me the truth," she whispered. "I would have kept your secret."

He shook his head. "Couldn't risk it." Though he had considered it. Well, he'd considered telling his brother Grayson, so he could make sure Sampson stayed away from Silver Creek. But in the end Gage had decided he was best suited to do that. And he had. That's how he'd learned about Denton targeting Lynette.

Lynette swiped away more tears, and she looked so sad, so distraught, that it had Gage shaking his head.

"I figured it wouldn't matter to you if I was dead or not," Gage reminded her. "Especially since I've been out of your life a long time now."

And he glanced at her stomach in case she missed the snarky reference.

Her eyes widened, and she got that deer-in-the-headlights look before she dodged his gaze completely. "But yet you came back to save me from a hit man." Another pause. Another headshake. "Why?"

And she didn't sound appreciative. But cautious. Afraid, even.

What the heck was going on in her mind?

The immediate danger was behind them. He'd gotten her out of there, and he would take the final step to ensure her safety. So, why the feeling that there was something else going on here?

"Why save me?" she repeated.

Again, Gage chose his words carefully. "My handler, the person I just called," he clarified, "got word from an informant that Freddie Denton had been hired to take you out. I needed to make sure he wasn't connected to Sampson so I came."

"And was Denton connected?" she pressed.

Gage shook his head. "I don't think so."

Of course, that didn't explain why Gage had come himself to take on this particular assignment. His handler could have sent another agent. But Gage had wanted to do this. One last thing for Lynette. Not because he felt he owed her. No way. However, he'd thought this would finally close those old wounds.

So far, he was batting a big fat zero in that wound-closing department.

"You're sure Denton's not connected to Sampson Dalvetti?" Lynette asked.

He got his thoughts back on track and hoped they stayed there. "I can't be positive, but the money trail for Denton's payment doesn't have international origins. Dalvetti usually deals with banks in the Cayman Islands."

"He could have made an exception to throw you off his scent," she pointed out.

Gage lifted his shoulder. "Yeah. But I verified that Dalvetti still believes I'm dead. There'd be no reason to come after you unless he's pretending to believe that I faked my death."

Now, it was Gage's turn to pause. "Of course, that leaves your father and his business associates. One of them could have hired Denton."

She made a sound of agreement, nothing else, and Gage took the turn to the small country airport. Lynette obviously noticed the route, knew where it led, but she didn't say anything. Maybe that meant she wouldn't give him any lip about getting on the plane that was waiting for her.

"Denton knew where your bedroom was in the house," he tossed out there. "He didn't look around. He got out of his vehicle, walked straight to the window and fired." And he gave her some time to think about that. "Dalvetti's never been to your house."

She shook her head, sucked in her breath. "Maybe he broke in, studied the layout and told Denton?"

Gage copied her headshake. "If Dalvetti had broken in, he would have kidnapped you. As a minimum." More likely, he would have killed her on the spot. "I doubt Denton got your floor plan from Dalvetti, and I know Denton didn't arrive any earlier to case the place."

Lynette stayed quiet a moment. "So, someone told Denton where my bedroom is."

Oh, yeah. "Someone who knew the floor plan."

"Someone who knew *me*," she corrected. "Someone who's been to my house."

Bingo.

"I've narrowed it down," Gage continued when Lynette didn't say anything about the accusation he'd just tossed out there about her father. "Of course, your dad, Ford, is tops on the list of suspects who could have hired Denton. But I haven't been able to rule out Patrick or Nicole."

Another sound of agreement, but like before, that was the only thing Lynette volunteered. Of course, she already knew what these people were capable of. Both Patrick and Nicole were ruthless in business and their personal lives. Ford was a couple of steps past the ruthless part. Except Lynette might disagree with that. She'd certainly jumped to defend her father when he'd torn them apart.

"All three have been to your house?" he asked.

"Yes," she verified after a huff.

"None of them would approve of you snooping in their dirty dealings. So, why did you?" Gage came right out and asked. Maybe this time, he'd get a real answer and not more of those noncommittal sounds. The woman was nearly as good at dodging the truth as he was.

In addition to that sound, which put his teeth on edge, Lynette shivered, prompting Gage to turn up the heat. And he waited. Waited some more. Then, more. Until time was just ticking away.

He cleared his throat and repeated his question. "Why?"

Still, she took more long moments before she opened her mouth. Moments they didn't have. "After you died… after I *thought* you died," she corrected, "I decided it was time to try to figure out exactly what my father and his associates were doing."

The explanation stopped there. Cold and way incomplete. "Why didn't you just find a rattlesnake or two to play with? It would have been safer."

That earned him a glare. "Because I wanted to know the truth about my father."

Wow. Not something he'd expected her to say. "Can you deal with the truth?" he fired back.

Her glare got worse but then softened almost immediately. "I was looking for proof that he had something to do with my mother's death."

Yeah, Gage knew something about that. Her mother had died from a so-called accidental drowning when Lynette was just a kid, nine years old. A lot of people had wondered if Ford had killed his wife, Sandra, after rumors of an affair.

Rumors of an affair between Sandra and Gage's own grandfather, Chet McLaurin, who was then the sheriff of Silver Creek.

Even now, after all these years, it hurt to think about losing his Granddaddy Chet. The rumors hurt, too. Though his grandfather had been a widower during the alleged affair, it had put a stain on his good name when folks whispered about a possible involvement with a married woman. And not just any married woman but the wife of the rich and powerful Ford Herrington.

"Did you find anything about your mother?" Gage pressed.

"No." She looked at him. "And I didn't find any link to my father killing your grandfather, either."

That didn't mean it hadn't happened.

The timing was suspicious since his grandfather had been gunned down by an unknown assailant just weeks after her mother's drowning. It was bad enough that during that same month Lynette and he had both lost people close to them, but then shortly after, Gage's own father had abandoned the family. Boone Ryland had just walked out without warning. Gage and his brothers had been devastated. Their mother, too, since she committed suicide not long after he left.

A lot of bad things had gone on around that time.

And Gage figured Ford Herrington could have started

the whole ugly ball rolling by killing his wife and her supposed lover.

"That was the worst summer of my life," Lynette mumbled. "Well, one of the worst. Another was when you got Hodgkin's." And she sounded all torn up about it.

He had to be wrong about that. These old memories couldn't mean anything to her now. If they had, then she would have tried to contact him during the past decade. She hadn't. And after a couple of years of waiting for that, Gage had shut out all thoughts of her.

Until now.

Hard to shut her out when she was just inches away and after that kiss.

"Even though you were sick, there were still some parts about that summer that were good," she said, her voice practically soundless. But somehow Gage managed to hear her anyway.

"Oh, you considered the good part our marriage?" he growled. "Except it didn't last long enough for the ink to dry on the license. Not much good about that."

No glare from her this time. Something he figured that she'd toss at him. In fact, it was the opposite reaction. Her forehead bunched up, and she started to nibble on her bottom lip.

"You hate my father because he forced me to get that annulment," Lynette mumbled.

Gage couldn't argue with that. It was true. But it was also true that he hated Lynette for not standing up to the man. Ford got away with what he did only because Lynette had allowed him to have his way. She'd backed down when Gage had needed her to stand up to her father.

Gage decided to take this conversation in a slightly different direction—or rather a backtracked one. His SUV was quickly eating up the miles to the airport, and while the conversation made him feel marginally better, it wasn't giving him the answers that he might be able to use to get to the bottom of this.

"I take it you didn't find any dirt on your mucked-up dad?" he concluded. "But we both know there's plenty of dirt to find. How hard and how long did you look?" Better yet, what had she found?

"There is dirt. I'm sure of it. But I didn't find it in any of the files in his office." She paused. More lip nibbling. Another pause. "I even tried taping him in the hopes that he might let something slip, but he must have known something was up, because he grabbed my purse and found the recorder that I'd tried to hide."

Of course, he would have. Ford was very good at reading people, and he was suspicious by nature. At least that's how Gage remembered him and all the dirty looks and snide comments he'd made when Lynette and he were dating.

But Ford had another side, that fake face he put on for the world to see. Gage had also gotten a glimpse of that when they'd first told Ford about their elopement. Maybe because they'd told him in front of witnesses, including the justice of the peace, Ford had been all calm on the outside. But there must have been some fire beneath all that calmness or else he wouldn't have talked Lynette into the annulment.

"Why'd you quit looking for the dirt on your father?" Gage asked. "And don't get me wrong— I'm glad you quit. Less snooping will keep you alive. But why'd you try to close up Pandora's box after you opened it?"

"I had my reasons," she snapped.

And apparently those were reasons that she wasn't planning to share with him. He'd probably find out anyway, because he was going to do some deep digging of his own when he had Lynette on safe ground.

Gage pulled into the tiny airport parking area, stopped and spotted the plane on the runway. Good. No hitch in that department. The pilot was there, as well, tucked underneath the awning of the maintenance hangar. In other words, this last leg of the plan was a go—despite the rocky start with the hit man and the kiss. What Gage should do was get Lynette's butt on the plane *now* and never look back.

But the need for those answers gnawed away at him, and he just couldn't let go of it yet. Especially one answer in particular.

"And what would those reasons be for stopping the investigation?" he pressed, and he braced himself for another snapped response.

Which he didn't get.

With her mouth tight, she just stared out at the wipers slashing the rain off the windshield.

"Okay. You won't tell me," he fired back. "Then, let me guess. You fell in love with someone. Or maybe it wasn't love. Maybe just lust. You landed in the sack with him, and when you found out you were pregnant, you figured you'd better not do anything to get yourself and that baby killed."

More silence.

That didn't help the anger roaring inside him. "At least tell me that this SOB is willing to marry you now that you're pregnant."

"We haven't discussed it," she mumbled.

Gage cursed. "Was this like a one-night stand?" He didn't wait for an answer. Which he should have. He also should have dropped a subject that was none of his business. But he didn't. He just had to get in one more jab to go along with the knot that this news had put in his gut.

"There is such thing as safe sex, you know?"

Even though Gage wasn't too happy about any kind of sex with Lynette that didn't involve him. Yeah. That was petty since they weren't together. Heck, they didn't even like each other anymore.

Still, it stung.

This pregnancy was a couple of steps past stinging. Maybe because part of him—the immature part still hanging on to the past—remembered that once, years ago, Lynette and he had planned to have kids of their own.

A whole brood of them, she'd insisted. To make up for her being an only child.

Gage had siblings, five of them, so he didn't have the same need as Lynette did, but yeah, he'd wanted kids back then. Now... Well, *now* didn't matter. His future was sealed as long as Sampson Dalvetti was alive, and since Gage hadn't been able to get to him in the past eleven months, he wasn't counting on eliminating the drug lord anytime soon.

Lynette pointed to the plane. "I'm supposed to get on that?" she asked.

It took a moment to get his jaw unclenched, and it didn't happen until after he cursed himself for going off on another thought tangent. "You are. You're supposed to stay gone until I can figure out who's trying to kill you."

She pulled back her shoulders. "You mean you're continuing the investigation into my father and the others?"

"Damn straight." It was the only way to end this.

Lynette shook her head. "It's too dangerous. If my father learns you're alive—" Again, she stopped cold.

And Gage intended to find out why this was a forbidden subject with her. She knew how he felt about Ford.

Gage hated the man, and the feeling was mutual. There was no reason for her to keep skirting around the obvious.

"You think your father will try to kill me?" Gage concluded. "Well, that's a chance I'll have to take, because if I don't stop him, or the person responsible, then you'll never be safe. You'll never be able to have a normal life. Guys like Freddie Denton will just keep coming after you."

She frantically shook her head. "I won't be safe if my father finds out you're alive. He'll put things together. He'll start digging."

Lynette sucked in her breath as if she'd said too much.

But she hadn't said nearly enough.

Fed up with the lack of answers, Gage caught her by the shoulders and turned her toward him. "I know Ford hates my guts, but why would my being alive make your father come after *you*?"

She tried to dodge his gaze, tried to turn away from him, but Gage held on, and he got right in her face. "Why?" he demanded.

She started shaking her head and didn't stop. "I can't."

"Yes, you can." And Gage didn't say it nicely. "If you don't tell me, I'll get the answer from your father."

Lynette gasped. "Please. You can't," she repeated. "It'd only make things worse."

Probably, but it was just a bluff. Still, that didn't mean he was going to let her get on that plane until he had what he wanted. An answer.

"Why would your father come after you if he finds out I'm alive?" he pushed. Gage glared at her, to let her know he wasn't just going to let this go.

Her gaze came to his, finally, and it seemed as if Lynette changed her mind a dozen times before she opened her mouth. "Because my father will figure things out about the baby."

Well, that was a reason he darn sure hadn't expected to hear.

Gage tried to work it out. Did Ford disapprove of the baby's daddy? But he shook his head. Then, what the heck would that have to do with Lynette's and his safety?

Especially Gage's.

He moved closer, and met her eye to eye. "I'm missing something, and you're going to tell me what this pregnancy has to do with me."

Lynette swallowed hard, and her breath rushed out in a thin stream. "Gage, the baby is *yours*."

Chapter Five

Lynette knew that telling Gage the truth could be a massive mistake. Everything at this point could be a wrong move for her, and she'd already made too many of those.

Maybe it was the shock of seeing him and learning he was alive. Maybe that spontaneous kiss of relief had melted her brain. And maybe it was this blasted attraction that just wouldn't die. Whatever the reason, she hadn't been able to stop herself from blurting out what would no doubt be a bombshell for him.

The baby she was carrying was his.

Gage stared at her as if she'd lost her mind, but it wasn't exactly shock she saw in his expression. More like total disbelief. "Lynette, I haven't had sex with you in ten years," he reminded her.

Yes, ten years, one month and four days.

Yet she still remembered every inch of his body. His touch. The things he said to her in those intimate moments. That made her one sick puppy.

Or something worse.

Lynette was afraid to put a label on that *something worse* but a one-man woman came to mind. Despite smothering all the good things she had once felt for him, the memories still haunted her.

"You want to explain to me how I could have gotten

you pregnant?" But he didn't give her time to answer. "Did someone come to you, someone pretending to be me?"

"No," she quickly assured him. "I'm pretty good at detecting the real Gage versus a fake one." And there was no way he could argue with that. She'd certainly found him out soon enough despite the disguise and the altered voice.

He huffed and made a circular motion with his hand to prompt her to continue with her explanation about the pregnancy. Lynette debated where she should start and decided to go with the beginning.

"When you were twenty-one and got Hodgkin's, we were already making plans to get married." She tried to keep her voice level. And failed. "The doctors in San Antonio told you the treatment could make you sterile. We'd talked about having kids down the road, so you stockpiled some semen."

She paused to give him time to absorb that.

He didn't absorb it well.

Gage cursed, a long string of profanity. "The hospital kept it after all this time?"

Lynette nodded. "Until about six weeks ago. When the hospital couldn't reach you, they called me because you'd listed me as your emergency contact. They wanted my permission to dispose of it since it'd been there so long. I, uh, took it instead."

There were few times that she could remember when Gage had been gobsmacked, and this was one of them.

He cursed again and scrubbed his hands over his face. "Why the heck would you do this?"

"Because I wanted a baby." *Your* baby—something else she kept to herself. In fact, there were other things she had to keep secret, as well.

Things that could make this situation even more dangerous than it already was.

"Plus, I thought you were dead," Lynette reminded him.

"Yeah, but my being dead wouldn't prevent the fallout from Ford if he found out the kid is mine."

"My father didn't know about the frozen sperm, and I had no plans to tell him. In fact, I don't intend to tell him about the baby, period. I'd planned to be out of Silver Creek before I started showing."

"And you thought he'd just let you leave?" Gage asked.

"No. But I've been making arrangements for a new identity in a place far away from here so I can raise this baby and have the life I always wanted."

"A life with my baby." He punched the steering wheel. "Lynette, I'm not exactly in any position to be a father."

"I know." She couldn't say that fast enough. "And I don't expect you to be."

Did she?

Well, she hadn't expected him to be because she'd thought he was dead. But now…

No.

She couldn't go there, either.

Gage wasn't really back in her life. He was just here to save her.

"All right," he said, and repeated it. "I need you to get on that plane and leave. I'll try to figure out who's after you and how to stop it."

That seemed like the goodbye she'd been expecting, and Lynette wanted to hang on to this moment just a little longer. "I could stay and help you."

"No deal." Another of Gage's sayings. In this case, he delivered it with a stubbornness that she had no trouble hearing.

Lynette opened her mouth to argue. She didn't want Gage shouldering all the danger. But then she thought of her unborn child. Their baby. If she stayed, the baby would also be in danger.

"You'll go," he insisted. He glanced at her stomach again to let her know they were on the same wavelength. "Who else knows the baby you're carrying is mine?"

"Just you and me."

"What about the doctor in San Antonio who contacted you?" he pressed.

She shook her head. "I didn't tell him I'd planned to be inseminated."

"No, but it isn't much of a stretch for him to figure it out. Someone could have followed you to the hospital and then paid off the doctor."

Another headshake. "I was careful, and I didn't have the insemination done there. I went to Houston, used a fake ID, and had it done at a private clinic where I paid to make sure my records would stay confidential."

He stared at her. "And all these precautions were because of your father?"

"Yes," she admitted, though she knew that would only lead to more questions.

It did.

Gage turned toward her. "Do you finally realize how dangerous a man he is?"

"Yes." Again, it would mean more questions. So, Lynette continued before Gage could ask them. "Ten years ago when my father found out we'd eloped, he said I had two choices. I could have the marriage annulled, or he'd kill you."

No profanity. No glare. But thanks to the lights on the runway, she could see his eyes, and the aha moment of truth. A truth she'd kept from him for a decade.

"And you believed him?" Gage pressed.

"Oh, yes." Lynette had to take a deep breath. "He convinced me after he confessed that he'd murdered my mother and gotten away with it."

There. She'd finally said it aloud. The words, the fear. The horrible secret she'd been carrying in her heart for so long that it was now part of her. Not just part of her past but her future.

Now, Gage cursed again. "You should have gone to Grayson. He could have arrested Ford."

"There was no evidence, just his confession that only I heard. He told me that before I could make it to the sheriff's office, you'd be dead and at least half your brothers, too." That required another deep breath. "I couldn't take the risk of losing you."

Ironic, since she'd lost him anyway.

Gage had hated her after the annulment. Still did. Well, maybe. He'd certainly responded to that kiss of relief. But Lynette couldn't pin her hopes on one kiss. Especially a kiss that could have been left over from the old heat between them. He could still lust after her without wanting anything to do with her.

"Ford wouldn't have killed me," Gage insisted.

"He convinced me otherwise." And that's all she could say for several seconds. "Remember, I disappeared for a week after we got married?"

"Oh, yeah. I remember. And that's when you told me you'd had the marriage annulled."

It was hard to deal with those old memories that were still so raw and painful, but Gage had to know. It might make him understand the danger. Not from men like Freddie Denton or Sampson Dalvetti. No, this danger was much closer.

"My father had me committed to an insane asylum in

Mexico," she explained, trying to sound clinical. "Let's just say it wasn't a fun place, and he did that to me to prove that he had complete control of me and my life."

Gage's mouth dropped open. "He put you in a crazy house?"

"He did. And he called me every day to remind me that he could keep me there while he murdered you." She stared at him. "Gage, he did that and didn't leave a paper trail or any trace of what he'd done."

He turned her to face him. "You should have told someone."

"I did! I told the authorities in Mexico, but my father had fake doctors' reports saying I was paranoid and needed to be institutionalized. He has a lot of power. A lot of friends in the right places to do whatever wrong he wants to do."

Gage didn't answer, but she could see his jaw muscles stirring. He let go of her and stared out at the rain and the runway.

"After I thought you were dead, I dug into those files because I was looking for some proof that he'd killed my mother," she continued. "I figured I could send him to jail for the rest of his life."

Gage shot her another glare. "If he sent you to the crazy house and killed your mother, then he'd kill you. It was too dangerous for you to go looking for proof that could put you in the grave."

"I know. And that's why I stopped after the doctor called from San Antonio."

Another aha flash went through his eyes.

"I quit looking for proof of my father's guilt because I wanted a baby. And I wanted to keep my baby safe."

"Clearly, you failed at that," he mumbled. "Why'd you use my sperm and not some anonymous donor from a sperm bank? That would have been a heck of a lot safer for you if your father found out."

She hesitated, carefully considering her answer. Gage probably wouldn't want to hear that the only baby she wanted was his. No. Not with everything that'd happened between them. Besides, it might make him feel as if she were trying to pressure him to coming back into her life.

"Going through a sperm bank would have added another step to the process," she settled for saying. "To keep my father from finding out, I would have had to create another identity to get a donor. It just seemed simpler to use what the doctor in San Antonio was offering me rather than go to another source."

Gage looked at her, and Lynette braced herself for the next set of questions. The ones where he would press for the truth about what she'd just told him. Or maybe he'd want to know how she felt about that decade-old annulment. She couldn't tell him that it'd crushed her. That it had left a wound inside her that would never heal.

No. Gage couldn't know that.

Because it would make him go after her father. Not with the cool head of a CIA operative, either. Gage would confront him in a hot moment of temper, and there would be one of two outcomes.

Gage would kill her father.

Or her father would kill him.

Without proof that her father had done the unspeakable crime of killing her mother, Gage would look guilty of killing an innocent man. One with lots of power and money. A man that Gage had let plenty of people know that he hated and would like to see dead.

The wave of nausea hit her so quickly that she hadn't felt it coming. Lynette took a deep breath. Several of them. It didn't help. She hadn't had a twinge of morning sickness, but maybe that's what this was. Or maybe she was just sick at the thought of never seeing Gage again.

But it was worth the price to keep him alive—especially now that he hadn't been killed eleven months ago.

Lynette buttoned her coat and reached for the door handle to open it. "Where are you sending me?" she asked.

He didn't answer right away. He continued to stare at her. "To a friend who's a federal marshal over in Maverick County. He'll keep you safe."

She hoped that was true. Hoped that safety was even possible at this point. "Will my father or another hit man be able to trace where the plane is going?"

"I'll take care of that," Gage promised. "I'll contact you when everything's been resolved."

She believed him. Well, she believed he would try anyway. "And you'll be careful?"

"Deal. Hey, I'm a careful guy," he added, splashing each word with his trademark drawl and cockiness.

Mercy, this was torture, knowing that Gage would have to face down a killer while she was tucked away in another county with a marshal.

Since there was nothing else to say that wouldn't get her in more trouble, Lynette just nodded and opened the door of the SUV. Gage did, too, on the driver's side. But before her foot even touched the ground, Gage caught on to her and yanked her back inside.

"What's wrong?" she asked.

He didn't get a chance to answer. In front of them, on the runway, the small plane burst into a ball of flames.

GAGE DIDN'T THINK about what had just happened. He went on autopilot, relying on his training and experience. The second he had Lynette on the seat, he threw the SUV into gear, slammed his foot on the accelerator and got them out of there.

Fast.

"The plane blew up," Lynette said. She wasn't just shaky. That was pure panic Gage heard in her voice. "The plane blew up." She just kept repeating it while she stared back at the ball of flames.

Yeah, it'd blown up all right. That meant they had an even bigger problem than he'd anticipated, and he had anticipated some pretty bad things.

"Why did it blow up?" she asked, the panic going up a notch.

"I'm not sure." But he had to find out. Somehow.

Gage glanced at the secure phone attached to the dash. It was supposed to be untraceable, but Gage couldn't take the risk that someone had managed to tap in to it. He also couldn't risk calling his handler, Sherman Hendricks. Sherman wasn't dirty. He was positive of that, but it didn't mean someone around Sherman hadn't discovered that Gage was still alive and betrayed him.

"Who did this?" Lynette asked. She still had her attention fastened to the rear window. Her eyes were wide, and she was shaking all over.

"I don't know that, either. Not yet. But put on your seat belt," Gage ordered.

With the slick, wet roads and the speed he was going, conditions were ripe for an accident. That was the last thing they needed if someone was already on their tails.

Lynette did put on her seat belt, though he didn't know how she managed with her hands shaking like crazy. "I was supposed to be on that plane."

Stating the obvious, but it was unnecessary to remind Gage of that, and he couldn't let *what could have been* distract him now. He got off the airport road and took the first side road he could.

"Did the pilot blow up the plane?" Lynette asked.

Possibly.

And that was another reason Gage couldn't call his handler. Sherman had also arranged for the pilot, who was a former operative. Hell. If they had a leak in communication or a mole, it was a really bad time for it. Gage needed backup and resources, and at the moment he was short on both of those.

"I'll get answers soon," Gage promised her. "But first, I have to get you someplace safe."

She shook her head. "Is that possible?" Her shaky voice hadn't calmed even a little. Probably because she'd had a double whammy of danger this morning.

"Eventually, I'll find somewhere for you to go." It would take some doing since he couldn't contact anyone in the CIA for help, not until he'd cleared up the possible leak issue.

"Oh, God." She dropped her head against the back of the seat and slid her hand over her stomach.

That shot a new round of alarm through him. "Are you okay? Are you having pains or something?"

It hit him then. She could lose the baby. She was only weeks into this pregnancy, and the trauma of all of this could cause her to miscarry.

That hit him even harder than the explosion.

Until minutes ago, Gage hadn't known about this baby. He darn sure hadn't planned it, either, but he would do everything within his power to keep Lynette and the child safe.

"No pains," she assured him. "I'm just scared for the baby and us."

So was he, but Gage kept that to himself. Lynette was

barely holding it together as it was, and she didn't need to know that he was shaking in his boots.

Oh, man.

He'd faced enemy fire and cold-blooded assassins, but that felt like Little League compared to this.

She glanced behind them again, but Gage already knew there wasn't anything to see now that the airport and flaming plane were out of sight. No one was following them, and to make sure it stayed that way, he rolled down his window and tossed out the secure phone.

"Just in case," he told Lynette.

"In case of *what?*" she asked.

He didn't intend to answer that, either. It wouldn't do her or the baby any good for him to go through all the nightmarish scenarios that could play out.

"Just in case," he repeated.

That obviously didn't ease any of her concerns, but it was a necessity. Now, the question was—what was the next step? Gage went through his options and discarded them as quickly as they came.

Until he got to the last one.

Hell.

It was the only one that made sense. But it wouldn't be easy. Still, he had to put his personal feelings and issues aside and consider what was best for Lynette.

Though it wouldn't be easy for her, either.

"Are we going back to my house?" she asked, taking him by his arm.

"No." Not a chance. That's exactly where he'd directed a CIA cleanup team to go. A team that might have dirty agents who could leak their location. He didn't want Lynette near the place.

Gage turned onto the main road, and almost immediately he saw the lights from the town. Silver Creek.

Home.

Where he wouldn't be welcome.

But hopefully Lynette would be. Well, maybe she would be after Gage explained some things.

"Where are you taking me?" she asked. The concern was rising again.

Not just in her but in Gage, too.

Because in a few minutes he would walk into the sheriff's office and face the brothers who thought he was dead.

Chapter Six

Ahead of them on the road, Lynette spotted lights from a squad car.

The blue flashes of light whipped through the darkness and the rain-streaked windshield. Someone, probably one of Gage's brothers, was no doubt responding to the explosion at the airport. Maybe they'd find something that would ultimately lead to an arrest.

Her father, Nicole or Patrick.

Any one of them could be behind this.

Any one of them could want her dead.

That was suddenly crystal clear to her. The hit man was proof of that. Ditto for the exploding plane. But while Patrick or Nicole could be the culprit, this felt like her father's doing. Not getting his pristine hands dirty but rather hiring someone to blow her to smithereens.

And he or the person responsible had nearly succeeded.

She was about to remind Gage that they should get as far away from this place as possible. But Gage slowed down and turned into a parking lot.

A familiar one.

She looked at Gage as if he'd lost his mind. "This is the sheriff's office," she pointed out.

"Yeah." And that's all he said.

She huffed. "But your family doesn't know you're

alive. Plus, there's the danger with the drug lord guy coming after them if he finds out you're not dead."

Another *yeah*. He parked, turned off the engine. "I'm aware of all of that. I also know that anything I do at this point is a risk." He paused. "But doing nothing could be an even bigger risk."

Maybe. But when she thought about that, she shook her head. "We could go to a city like Dallas or Houston and get lost in the crowd."

He looked at her, his head cocked to a familiar angle. "My brothers will protect you with their lives."

They probably wouldn't protect him though. There was bad blood because he'd left after the annulment and had had only minimal contact with them since. He'd turned his back on his family, and that wouldn't earn him a warm, fuzzy welcome.

Especially since he was riding in on the heels of danger.

"This is just so we can regroup," Gage explained. "We'll tell as few people as possible and then leave as quickly as we can."

Because they sure as heck didn't want the news to get back to Sampson Dalvetti. The problem was it was very difficult to keep secrets in a small town. Lynette had managed it so far with the pregnancy....

But she froze.

And remembered that her father was a devious man with all those resources to help him with his deviousness.

Oh, mercy.

If her father knew about the baby, then he could have been so enraged that he would have sent that hit man.

"Let's do this fast," Gage told her. "I don't want you out in the open any longer than necessary."

She didn't budge. "Let me go alone. And you can disappear again. It'll be safer for you."

"Yeah. But not safer for you. I'm not leaving you in a parking lot in the rain. Heck, I'm not leaving, period, until I know you're protected."

She tried to object, tried to make him understand this was a bad idea, but Gage didn't listen. He hurried from the SUV, took Lynette by the arm and he got her moving toward the back entrance of the sheriff's office. The second he had the door open, he shoved her inside and then stepped protectively in front of her.

The sound of the movement and door must have alerted someone because Lynette heard footsteps. A moment later, Gage's older brother Mason appeared in the hall.

She silently groaned. Mason wasn't the friendliest of the Ryland clan. In fact, he looked far more dangerous than the criminals he arrested as a Silver Creek deputy. Thankfully, they didn't cross paths a lot because Mason did the bulk of the work to run the family ranch.

Mason made a slight sound. Barely a reaction at all. "So, you're alive," he snarled.

Gage gave his usual "yeah."

Not much of a welcome-home outpouring. Unlike hers. She'd kissed Gage, for heaven's sake. Something that shouldn't have happened. The brothers stood there, staring at each other, and it seemed to her as if they had an entire discussion without saying a word.

Mason finally lifted his shoulder. "Anyone else know you're back from the grave?"

Gage shook his head. "Just Lynette and my handler." He stepped to the side so that Mason could see her. "It has to stay that way. Who else is here?"

"Just me. Grayson and Dade are on their way to the

airport to check out the explosion." Mason paused. "Did you have anything to do with that?"

"Indirectly," Gage admitted. "The pilot and plane were supposed to get Lynette away from here."

"Someone tried to kill me," she volunteered. "A hit man."

Mason's eyebrow swung up. "Who'd you piss off?"

She shook her head. "I'm not sure."

"There's a slim possibility it's connected to me," Gage admitted. "There's a good reason I let everyone believe I was dead."

"Who'd you piss off?" Mason repeated, directing it this time to Gage.

"The wrong person." Gage paused then mumbled something she didn't catch.

"What's wrong with your voice?" Mason asked.

"A failed attempt at a disguise. It'll wear off soon." Gage huffed. "I need to use your phone. A landline."

Mason hitched his thumb to the office behind him. "Anything else?"

"Watch Lynette for me. Don't let her out of your sight."

As if he knew his order would be obeyed and obeyed well, Gage walked past his brother and disappeared into the office. Mason looked at her, at her wet dress, coat and hair.

"You knew he was alive?" Mason's question had an edge to it. But then, Mason always seemed to have an edge.

"No. Not until about an hour ago when he broke in to my house." It seemed like an eternity since that'd happened. Her entire world had been turned upside down in that hour, and she suspected Mason was feeling some of that, too.

Mason studied her, as if checking for some clues in her body language. "So, what's going on?"

She wearily shook her head. "We're not sure. A drug lord threatened to kill all of you. And me. That's why Gage faked his death. He figured if the drug lord thought he was dead, there'd be no reason to come after us."

"That's Gage. Always too stubborn to ask for help. Well, until now. But I suspect his help-asking has more to do with you than him." Mason studied her some more. "Are you two back together or what?"

"No." And she couldn't answer fast enough. Lynette even hiked up her chin and tried not to show any doubts. "Gage got word of the hit man, and he came to save me. That's all. I was supposed to get on that plane, leave and go to safety so that he could get out of here, too. But someone blew it up and messed up those plans."

Mason stayed quiet a moment. "So, what now? Gage just leaves again and pretends to be dead?"

Lynette hated the thought of it. Seeing him even for this short time had reopened all the old wounds that had never fully closed. Never would.

But yes, that's what had to happen.

Mason pulled in a long breath and motioned for her to follow him. She did and didn't bother to ask where he was taking her. He led her down the hall to the bathroom and pulled out a handful of paper towels.

"Thanks." She wiped her face and clamped onto her bottom lip when another wave of nausea hit her. Lynette slapped her hand on the wall to keep from staggering.

"You okay?" And there was so much concern in Mason's voice that Lynette forced herself to give him a quick nod.

"Fine," she lied.

He just kept staring her, and when his gaze dropped

to her stomach, Lynette thought she might panic. Mercy, was he suspicious that she might be pregnant? He couldn't be, because this was a man who could definitely put one and one together and come up with the correct answer.

Fortunately, Gage saved the moment, again. He came out of Mason's office and into the hall with them.

"The pilot's alive," Gage told them. "But other than that, we don't know anything else about the explosion."

"We?" Mason challenged.

"We," Gage repeated but he didn't clarify. He looked at her. "Are you okay?"

"Yes," she snapped.

At the same moment, Mason said, "She looks like she's about to throw up."

"It's been a rough morning," she added in a mumble and shot them both a *back off* stare. She didn't need any more questions about her or her sudden queasiness.

Gage flexed his eyebrows and thankfully moved on. Maybe because he understood it wouldn't help matters if Mason figured out she was pregnant. "I'm making arrangements for you to leave for a safe house."

"Hope it's safer than the plane was," Mason growled.

"It will be," Gage promised. "In the meantime, can she stay here?"

"Of course," Mason said without hesitation. "You'll stay, too?"

Gage shook his head. "Best if I work behind the scenes."

That earned him one of the Mason's infamous scowls. "In other words, you want me to lie and not tell the others you're alive."

"For now." Gage's attention went from his brother and back to her. But he didn't get a chance to tell her what-

ever he was about to say because the bell over the front
door jingled.

The bell meant they had a visitor.

Gage didn't wait in the hall to see who'd just come in.
He ducked back inside Mason's office and slapped off the
lights before he peered around the doorjamb to get a look
at who had just entered the sheriff's building.

Mason cursed, and for a moment Lynette thought the
profanity was for Gage's response or maybe even this
whole mess of a situation. But then she followed Mason's
gaze toward the front of the sheriff's office.

And to the two people who'd just stepped inside.

No. Not this. Not now. Their timing couldn't have possibly been any worse.

Lynette saw Nicole Manning, her father's longtime
girlfriend, campaign manager and business associate.

However, Nicole wasn't alone.

Senator Ford Herrington nailed his gaze to Lynette and
made a beeline down the hall toward her. Toward Mason.
And toward Gage.

Oh, God.

Lynette tried to brace herself for the worst.

GAGE HADN'T THOUGHT this morning could possibly get
any more complicated, but he'd obviously been wrong.

Two of their suspects had just walked into the sheriff's
station, and there was no time to get Lynette or himself
out of there.

Lynette shot him a *stay put* glare. Mason, too. And
then his brother thankfully stepped in front of Lynette.
Mason also drew his gun, and while Gage couldn't see
Nicole's and Ford's reactions, he'd bet his favorite snake-
skin boots that they weren't good ones.

"The firearm isn't called for, Deputy," Ford grumbled

in that high-class ice-cold voice of his. And Gage hadn't missed the demeaning way he'd referred to Mason as a *deputy.* In Ford's mind that was one step below hoof grit. His opinion of Gage was even lower than that.

Maybe his opinion of Lynette, too.

Gage wished the man would give Mason and him an excuse to shoot first and ask questions later. But then he rethought that. It was the last thing he wanted to happen because Lynette would be in the line of fire again.

Two attempts on her life were enough.

Besides, Ford was too smooth to pick a fight with witnesses around. No. For him, it was all about appearances. A perfect public image reserved for everyone but his enemies. He was probably planning to send Lynette back to the crazy house in Mexico.

"Lynette, you're here," Nicole said. No ice for her. The woman sounded concerned, but Gage knew that could be faked. After all, Nicole slept with Ford on a regular basis, and she'd no doubt learned some of his tricks.

"She is here," Mason verified. "But the real question is—why are *you* here?"

Gage smiled. No one had ever accused Mason of being a nice guy, and he gave them back as much snark as Ford had doled out to him.

"I called my daughter's house," Ford calmly explained, "and when she didn't answer, Nicole and I drove over to check on her."

"We were worried," Nicole added. "Especially when we saw that someone had broken your bedroom window."

Broken, not shot. Of course, maybe Ford knew the difference, especially if he'd been the one to send the hit man who'd shot through that glass.

"Someone tried to kill me," Lynette said.

Oh, man. She sounded shaky, and he hated she had to

go through this. If Gage had thought for one second that revealing himself would make this better, he'd be out in that hall with them.

But it wouldn't make things better.

It might spur on her father or someone else to try to kill her again. Right here, right now. After all, he was betting that Nicole was carrying a weapon in that purse that he'd managed to get just a glimpse of before he'd had to duck into the office and out of sight.

"Any idea who'd try to kill Lynette?" Mason asked. He still didn't ease up on the snide tone, and he asked it in such a way to let them know that he not only knew the answer, they *were* the answer.

"No," Ford and Nicole said in unison.

"Why would we?" Ford continued.

Mason shrugged. "I figured you must have suspected Lynette was in some kind of danger. I mean, why else would you call her at such an early hour and then have driven over there in this storm?"

Gage heard Ford step closer, and he ducked deeper into the dark office. "Is that an accusation?" Ford challenged.

"It's a question," Mason clarified. "A simple one. I was kind of hoping for a simple response."

The seconds crawled by.

"I was worried about her," Ford spoke up. The facade was back in place now, and he sounded like a concerned daddy. "I'd tried to talk to Lynette yesterday, and she seemed frazzled, or something."

"It was the *or something*," Lynette answered. "I was busy at work and didn't have time for your call. Besides, I didn't want to talk to you."

Gage smiled again. Lynette really had developed some sass when it came to her father. Too bad it had come ten years too late.

"Why did you try to call me this morning?" Lynette pressed. "And why bring Nicole in on this? I don't trust her, and I don't want her or you doing welfare checks on me."

"So, now you're accusing me?" Nicole snarled. "You'd better think before you speak."

"I have," Lynette assured her. "I think about you a lot. My father and Patrick, too. And what I'd like is for you both to leave. If you aren't going to tell us why you're really here, then you're of no help."

But Gage didn't hear anybody jumping to leave.

"Who tried to kill you?" Ford asked. He took down his tone a notch.

Now, there was movement. Lynette stepped closer to her father, and Gage silently cursed. He didn't want her closer. He wanted her tucked safely behind Mason and his gun.

"He didn't tell me his name," Lynette simply stated. "He just shot and ran."

That was partly true. The hit man had indeed run— after Lynette and him.

"So, it could have been a botched burglary attempt," Nicole suggested after blowing out what sounded to be a breath of relief.

"Could be," Lynette agreed, but there was no agreement in her voice. Lynette stared at the woman so long that Gage had to wonder what had snagged her attention.

"There," Nicole concluded. "The mystery's solved, and the sheriff can start looking for a burglar. Maybe it was a kid who got scared when he realized you were home."

"Maybe." But there was still no hint of agreement. "Now, if you don't mind, Mason here has to take my statement, and I have to fill out an insurance claim for the broken window. Then I'd like to get some sleep. Nearly getting killed has made me a little cranky."

Gage saw Ford's hand snake out, and for one horrifying moment Gage thought this was all about to come to a head with Mason pulling his gun. And both men firing. But Ford only aimed his finger at her.

"You need to be careful," Ford warned. It didn't exactly sound fatherly, but the words were right. He added, "Call me after you've had time to rest."

"Of course," Lynette replied. Again, there was no hint of cooperation in her voice. Just the opposite.

Gage finally heard the sounds he wanted to hear. Footsteps. Followed by the bell jangling over the door. He was ready to step out when Mason motioned for him to stay put.

"Anything else, Nicole?" Lynette asked.

So, the woman hadn't left with Ford after all. Why? But Gage figured he'd soon hear the answer.

"Your father's under a lot of stress," Nicole finally said. "You need to cut him some slack."

"Why would I do that?" Lynette snapped, and she folded her arms over her chest.

Even though Gage couldn't see Nicole's face or expression, neither Mason nor Lynette seemed pleased with her presence or this waffling conversation.

"Ford makes it hard on everyone when he's under stress," Nicole added. "Especially on me."

Lynette made a sound of weary amusement. "I doubt he's been any harder on you than he has on me. You know what he's capable of, and yet you still go to his bed. If you're looking for sympathy, you won't get it from me."

"It's not sympathy," Nicole said, her voice quivering on the last word. "It's self-preservation. For all our sakes, Lynette, back off."

Gage heard more footsteps, and the bell jangled again.

"She's gone," Mason told him. "Now, would both of you mind explaining to me what the heck is going on?"

Gage walked to the doorway and tried to assemble an explanation that would be short, sweet and effective. "Someone hired a hit man to come after Lynette. I suspect it's because she was trying to learn some things about her father and his business associates. Nicole, included. That's why Nicole's running scared and gave that cryptic warning."

Mason swung his attention to her. "Does this have to do with your mother's death?"

"Maybe," she admitted, and she seemed surprised that Mason zoomed right in on that. "My father told me he killed her, and I was looking for proof."

Mason cursed. "You should have come to Grayson or me with this."

"Too dangerous." Lynette said, then paused. "My father's a dangerous man."

"Never doubted it for a minute," Mason said. He looked back at Gage. "So, Ford sent this hit man because Lynette figured out the truth?"

Gage had to shake his head. "It could have been Nicole."

"Yes," Lynette verified.

Gage remembered the look Lynette had given the woman. "Did you see something that made you more suspicious?"

Lynette stayed quiet a moment. "Something wasn't right, but I'm not sure what. It was almost as if Nicole was scared. Not just of me but my father."

"She's not usually scared of him?" Mason pressed.

"No," Lynette answered. "Nicole has a warped sense of right and wrong when it comes to my father, and she could have done this to protect him. Plus, she's no doubt had some dirty dealings of her own, and maybe I got too close to learning the truth about her."

"What about Ford's business partner, Patrick Harkin?" Mason asked.

"Also a suspect," Gage answered. Mason clearly understood the dynamics of what was going on here. No surprise though. He'd been a deputy sheriff for fifteen years, and there wasn't much that went on that Mason didn't know about.

"I stopped my investigation," Lynette told his brother. "But I might have stopped too late."

Mason gave a weary sigh. "Or this could have come from that drug lord you mentioned." He looked at Gage for verification.

And Gage couldn't deny it. There was only a slim chance that Sampson Dalvetti had done this, but he couldn't rule it out completely.

This time Mason huffed. "So, what's the plan? I don't want to face a drug lord or Ford and his crew unless we have something worked out."

Gage had already been going over this in his head, but the devil was in the details. The possible danger, too. "I need Lynette in protective custody until I can get this safe house nailed down. And I also have to disappear while I do that. Deal?"

Judging from the look on Mason's face, he was about to disagree with some part of the plan. But he didn't have time to voice that argument.

The back door flew open.

So fast that Gage barely had time to react. He took hold of Lynette, dragged her behind him and drew his gun.

Chapter Seven

Lynette had tried to prepare herself for the worst—another hit man—but it was Gage's brother Grayson who came through the door. Grayson's attention went straight to Gage, and he stopped cold.

"Yeah, he's alive," Mason announced. No emotion in his voice. Unlike Grayson's face.

There were a lot of emotions there, including shock and anger. Those came first, but then Lynette saw something else. Something stronger. Relief.

Maybe.

Grayson hurried up the hall, grabbed on to Gage and hugged him. Okay. She could breathe a little easier. It had been relief, and Lynette knew exactly how Grayson felt. Gage's eldest brother had been more of a father than a sibling.

"I could beat you to pulp for letting us believe you were dead," Grayson told him.

"I didn't have a choice," Gage whispered. He pulled back and met Grayson's gaze. "Still don't. I'll explain it all later, once Lynette is safe."

Grayson looked at Lynette. Then, at Gage again. "Are you two back together?"

"No," Lynette assured him, but since Mason had asked her the same darn question just minutes earlier she wondered just how obvious the heat was that was still zinging between Gage and her.

Heat that had to end.

She hoped reminding herself of that would work.

Gage wearily scrubbed his hand over his face. "Look, I know I don't have a right to ask, but I need you and Mason to keep Lynette safe while I do some things."

She grabbed Gage's arm. "Things that don't involve my father, right?"

"Things that involve your safety," he answered. Which wasn't at all an answer to her question. He looked at his brothers. "The plane that blew up was supposed to get Lynette out of here."

Grayson shook his head. "The fire chief thinks the explosion wasn't an accident."

She didn't believe it had been, and Lynette was having a hard time getting past the fact that she'd been within just seconds from death.

Grayson turned his attention to Mason. "Why don't you go ahead and take Lynette to the ranch?"

"The ranch?" Gage challenged. "It's not safe enough."

"Oh, these days the ranch is plenty safe," Mason assured him. "We've had some trouble over the past couple of months so we increased security. Plus, all my ranch hands know how to shoot."

Lynette knew all about the trouble. There'd been several attempts to break in to the place and even some shootings. But the talk of the town was that the ranch had become more like a fortress. That was partly because all five of Gage's brothers lived there, and they were all in law enforcement. So was one spouse, and another spouse was the assistant district attorney.

"A lot has changed since you've been gone," Grayson

continued. He held up his left hand to show Gage the wedding band that was there.

"I heard." Gage shrugged. "I had my handler keep tabs on all of you. You and Eve are married with a baby on the way. I'm happy for you both. You and Eve belong together."

"Funny," Grayson commented. "We always said that about Lynette and you."

"Yeah, funny," Gage grumbled.

The silence was long and awkward. Lynette didn't volunteer anything. She'd already blabbed enough for one night. If she'd kept her mouth shut about the baby, she might have been able to talk Gage into leaving. Into going someplace safe.

But she doubted she could do that now.

She hadn't been sure of what Gage's reaction would be to her pregnancy, though she had thought about it. Actually, she'd thought about every possible aspect considering Gage. That he was alive. That he would return. But none of the fantasies involved him risking his life to save her.

"Can you take Lynette to the ranch now?" Gage asked Mason.

Mason nodded, but Lynette didn't budge. "I need a moment alone with Gage," she insisted.

Grayson exchanged glances with Mason, and they started up the hall toward the front dispatch desk to give Gage and her some privacy.

"What are you going to do?" Lynette came right out and asked.

He lifted his shoulder as if the answer were obvious. It wasn't, and she let him know that with a scowl.

"Safe house preparations," he clarified. "I need to get a report on the explosion and the hit man cleanup."

She waited for more, much more, but that's all he

said. "Will I see you again?" Lynette hated that her voice cracked and tears burned in her eyes.

Great. Nothing like a sobbing hormonal woman for Gage's send-off into what would no doubt be a life-and-death situation. She didn't think for a minute that Gage was only going to do those two things he'd named.

Lynette waved Gage off when he started to pull her into his arms. "I can stand on my own two feet," she reminded him.

And herself.

In fact, she'd spent years trying to overcome the fear that her father had put inside her.

Lynette cursed the tears that came anyway.

"Right now, you look like you're about to fall off your own two feet," Gage whispered, and put his arms around her despite her protest. "No shame in that. You're tired, cold, and you've been through two sets of trouble already, and the sun hasn't even come up."

"Three sets," Lynette corrected. "You didn't include yourself."

"Yeah," he mumbled. He pushed her still wet hair away from her face and used the pad of his thumb to swipe off the tear that streaked down her cheek. "I always was trouble for you."

Trouble in a body that still heated her up in one second and infuriated in the next.

That was Gage.

Their relationship had never been easy.

"You should come with a warning label attached," she whispered. "Especially one attached to the zipper of your jeans." That part of him was just as much trouble for her as the rest of him. Maybe more.

"Oh, yeah? What should that warning label say?"

Amusement danced through his eyes while the Texas drawl danced off his words.

She could think of a few. *Caution: Hot.* Or maybe *Danger Ahead.*

"Do not remove," she settled for saying and hoped that the joke would lighten the mood.

It didn't.

"Will I see you again?" she repeated, fearing a no and a yes equally. Either one would be yet another complication.

"Afraid so." He brushed a kiss on her cheek. It was a peck but not chaste.

Gage's mouth was never chaste.

Their gazes met, and he was so close that Lynette could give him a real kiss. Like the one in the SUV. And she thought about it, she really did, especially since his *afraid so* could be a lie. This might be the last time she saw him again.

Lynette stared at him, trying to remember every detail in case this was indeed the last time. His dark brown hair was a little too long as usual. Gage always managed to look like a rock star who'd just climbed out of bed. Rumpled. Kissable. Hot.

But one of the details was wrong.

"Your eyes," she mumbled.

"Colored contacts." He touched his index finger to first his left eye and then his right. No more brown.

Lynette smiled at the gunmetal-gray eyes that stared back at her. "Killer eyes, I used to call them."

"How romantic. Guys like to hear that kind of talk from a woman." But he smiled, too.

Her smile faded just as quickly. Killer as in they always did her in. Those eyes still worked magic on her. And that couldn't happen. Even though it would rip her heart apart again, it was best to let Gage go.

But maybe she could risk a goodbye kiss.

"We've got company," Grayson called back to them.

It broke the kissing urge in a snap, and Gage stepped into the first office he reached, and as he'd done before, he turned off the lights.

Good thing, because Patrick Harkin entered the building.

"Lucky us," Lynette mumbled. "Patrick is here."

Gage groaned, and Lynette agreed. She was too tired for another round with another suspect. But she doubted she could avoid it completely. Her best bet was just to make it as short as possible.

"I heard about the explosion at the airport," Patrick greeted. "I wanted to find out what happened."

Maybe it was an honest question, but when Patrick looked at her, something inside her snapped. No more need to make this short. She was riled enough to ask questions and force the answers out of him.

"Did you hire someone to try to kill me?" Lynette demanded.

Gage groaned again, and she went up the hall so that he wouldn't have a chance to grab her and pull her into the room with him. She was tired of playing the whiny victim here. She wasn't helpless, and Patrick was about to learn that the hard way.

"I have no idea what you're talking about." Patrick's tone suddenly didn't seem so casual. "Nicole called me and said a burglar tried to break in to your house."

"Not a burglar. And he didn't try to break in. He fired shots into my bedroom window and tried to murder me."

Patrick looked appropriately shocked. "I had nothing to do with that."

"Didn't you?" she pressed. She went closer, hoping to violate his personal space and then some. "Because I don't trust you, and I think you have plenty to hide." Lynette went even closer. "But here's the bottom line, Patrick. This stops now. Hear me? *Now!*"

He shook his head, as if ready to deny that, but Lynette waved him off. "I'm thinking anything you say right now will be a lie so just save your breath."

Mason stepped to her side. "So, did you hire a nut job to kill Lynette?"

Lynette knew Mason was far more intimidating than she was. It felt good to have someone on her side again, and it didn't feel as if she were leaning on him. Just the opposite. She'd missed this camaraderie with Gage's family.

"No, absolutely not," Patrick insisted. His expression morphed from surprised to indignant concern. "I'm a businessman, for Pete's sake. Besides, I don't have a reason to kill her or anyone else."

"Yes, you do," Lynette corrected. "At least you think you have one, but when I was doing all that snooping around, I didn't find anything that implicates you in a crime."

"I'm still looking," Mason added. "In fact, this little visit just makes me want to dig harder to see what's put that fear in your beady little eyes."

Patrick's face turned bright red, and it seemed to take him several seconds to put his temper in check. He turned his narrowed gaze to Grayson. "You need to call off your brother, or you could find the sheriff's office slapped with a lawsuit for slander."

Grayson shrugged. "It's not slander if it's true." He casually checked his watch. "Tell you what—it's barely 6:00 a.m. Too early for an interrogation since I haven't even had my coffee yet. But come back at 8:00. We'll talk then. Or rather, you'll talk, and I'll listen."

"Is that an order?" Patrick demanded.

"Yes, it is," Grayson answered, and Lynette nearly cheered.

"Fine," Patrick spit out. "I'll be here, but I'm bringing my lawyers." He stormed out, slamming the door behind so hard that the bell clattered to the floor.

"I'll send you a bill for that," Mason called.

They stood there long enough to make sure Patrick wasn't going to come rushing back in.

"I'll get Ford and Nicole in here at the same time so Dade and I can interrogate them all at once," Grayson explained. "With their tempers, one of them might blow up and say something incriminating."

"Don't count on it," Lynette mumbled. "Especially from my father. His sheep's clothing hides the wolf very well in public. Besides, his lawyers aren't going to let him speak."

Another shrug from Grayson. "Maybe one of the other two will rattle, then." He looked at Mason. "Go ahead and take Lynette to the ranch."

It was time. Gage and she had technically already said their goodbyes, and now she somehow had to make it out of there without crying.

Mason and she started down the hall, and Gage stepped out. He gave her a look. That's all. No words. But he followed them into the parking lot.

The sun hadn't come up yet, so they only had the overhead security lights. Mason paused in the doorway and glanced around, his attention swinging from one side of the parking lot to the other. He also put his hand over the gun in his shoulder holster before he led her straight toward a cruiser that was parked next to Gage's SUV.

She looked over her shoulder to get one last look at Gage, but the sound stopped her cold. It was barely a sound at all, more like some movement that she caught from the corner of her eye.

"Get down!" Mason shouted.

He didn't wait for her to respond. He grabbed her and pulled her to the side of the cruiser.

Just like that, Lynette's heart was in her throat again, and the fear returned. The questions, too.

What was going on now?

Other than the possible movement, Lynette hadn't seen anyone in the parking lot, but Mason and Gage apparently had.

Both had their weapons drawn.

She followed Mason's gaze to the front part of the parking lot. Toward the street. More specifically, toward the hardware store directly across from the sheriff's office. There was a thin alley there, pitch-black, and she didn't have to be a lawman to realize it would be the perfect place for a hit man to hide.

But was it another hit man?

They waited for what seemed an eternity with her fears rising and with their attention locked on that alley. Mason didn't move a muscle, and from what she could see of Gage, neither did he.

Lynette was on the verge of deciding this was all a false alarm when there was another sound. Not movement this time. It happened fast, a zinging sound ripping through the air, and something slammed into the SUV.

"A shot," Mason mumbled along with some profanity.

Oh, God. Her heart dropped again. It hadn't been a regular blast— She'd already heard her share of those this morning. This one sounded as if it'd come from a gun rigged with a silencer. And she knew that couldn't be good. Someone was trying to kill them and trying not to be heard. Probably so that the sheriff and any deputies inside wouldn't come running.

The gunman ran though. He came out of the alley, sending a stream of shots their way. Nonstop. The bullets pelted into the SUV and the concrete surface of the parking lot. Mason shoved her lower to the ground and crawled over her back. Protecting her. Just as Gage had done in the woods when Denton was firing at them.

Lynette caught just a glimpse of the gunman as he darted out of the alley and disappeared from her line of sight. But apparently not from Mason's.

"He's at your six o'clock," Mason yelled to Gage.

"I got him," Gage answered.

Lynette tried to pick through the darkness and the rain to see the threat, but Gage apparently had already located whatever or whoever was out there.

Gage took aim.

Fired.

Since his gun didn't have a silencer, the two shots blasted through the parking lot.

And then nothing.

Everything seemed to freeze. Except her heartbeat. It was pounding so hard that Lynette thought her ribs might crack.

Even though Mason was practically all over her, Lynette could see Gage from beneath Mason's cover. With his weapon ready and aimed, Gage took slow, cautious steps toward the street. Lynette saw it then.

The man on the ground.

She pulled in her breath. Held it. And prayed that the guy didn't get up and start firing again. But he didn't move. Gage made his way to him, stooped down and touched his fingers to his neck.

"Dead," he relayed to Mason.

Mason stood, and somehow so did she. It was the second time today she'd seen a dead man, and it didn't get easier. She was thankful for that. Thankful, too, that Gage had managed to save her once again.

But this couldn't continue. Sooner or later, a gunman might get lucky, and it could cost them everything—including their lives. It was bad enough that she was in danger, but now she'd brought that danger to his family. Maybe to the entire town, because anyone nearby could have been shot with a stray bullet.

"You know who he is?" Mason asked.

Gage nodded and quickly made his way back to Lynette. "His name is Walter Jonavich. He's a hit man who often pairs up with Freddie Denton, the guy who tried to kill Lynette earlier."

Oh, mercy. She used the cruiser to steady herself. "You don't think Denton brought along someone else, do you?" she managed to ask.

But Gage didn't answer her, which was an answer in itself. And that answer was *yes*. Then Gage got her moving.

"I'll call for a cleanup," Gage told his brother. He headed straight for one of the cruisers. "But I'm getting Lynette out of here *now*."

Chapter Eight

Gage pulled the cruiser to a stop directly in front of the guesthouse on the Ryland ranch. The main house was much larger and just a quarter of a mile away, but he'd decided against taking Lynette there. According to his conversation with Grayson, the guesthouse and the grounds around it were equally safe.

And this way, Lynette and he wouldn't have to deal with the rest of his family.

Well, not yet anyway.

Eventually he would have to decide how to handle all of this—the danger and his so-called homecoming—but for now he just wanted to get Lynette inside, so she could get her mind off the fact that she'd nearly been killed. Again.

Gage should have anticipated that Denton wouldn't come alone. But he'd screwed it up. In hindsight while Denton was at Lynette's house, his sidekick, Walter Jonavich, probably had been at the airport putting an explosive device on the plane. Of course, one of their other suspects could have done that, too, but the bottom line was that someone had known that Lynette was supposed to be at the airport and on that plane.

And it was that someone who clearly wanted her dead.

"How long will we stay here at the guesthouse?" Lynette asked, pulling his attention back to her.

"A day at the most. We'll leave as soon as the safe house is ready."

She nodded. "Thanks," Lynette added when he opened the passenger's side door to help her out. She stood, looked up at him and met his gaze. "But you can get that worried look off your face. I'm fine. The baby's fine."

"Yeah, because we got lucky." And Gage would never forget that something as fragile as luck had played into this.

"No. Because you're a good shot."

She gave his arm a friendly pat and walked ahead of him and into the single-story cottage-style guesthouse. Everything about it looked homey, from its fresh white exterior to its porch complete with a swing and rocking chairs. Heck, it even had a picket fence and flower beds.

It was a place with fond memories.

It'd once been his grandfather's house, and after he had been killed twenty years ago, the family had used it for guests and for the occasional ranch hand or two before Mason had built a massive bunkhouse to accommodate the workers.

But years ago, this house had served a different purpose. When Lynette was seventeen, Gage had sneaked her in so they could have sex for the first time. Over the next two years, they'd come back. For more sex and some heavy-duty make out sessions.

It'd happened so often Gage used to get aroused just driving past the place.

Lynette looked back at him, the corner of her mouth lifting as if she knew what he was thinking. "It's been a while," she mumbled.

A while that seemed like yesterday. It was way too

fresh in his mind, and especially his body, and Gage started to wonder if this might be as big a mistake as his plan that'd already backfired.

Still, he didn't stuff her back in the cruiser and drive away. Like a moth to a flame he followed Lynette past the gate and into the yard.

"Bittersweet," she added, and paused on the bottom step so she could take the place in.

Oh, yeah. It was exactly that.

"You cried after the first time," he reminded her. That, too, was a darn fresh memory for something that'd happened fourteen years ago.

She made a sound of agreement, went up the steps and opened the front door. "Because I thought you wouldn't respect me."

Surprised, Gage shook his head. It was the first time he'd heard an explanation for those tears.

He followed her into the living room and shut the door. Gage also armed the newly installed security system that Mason had told him about. "I never did understand that logic. Did you lose respect for me?"

"Never," she mumbled.

At least that's what he thought she said.

Never meant a lot to him, considering all the crap that had happened after their so-called marriage. Of course, he'd probably misunderstood her.

She took off her shoes, which were caked with mud from their run through the woods. "I need to grab a shower."

Good idea. Anything to help her relax. And it might help if he had her out of his sight for a moment or two so he could get his bearings. He felt off-kilter, and it wasn't a good time for that. Best to keep his mind on the assignment of protecting Lynette rather than taking arousing trips down memory lane.

"After your shower, you should eat something," Gage added. "Mason said he had one of the ranch hands stock the fridge for us."

Lynette nodded.

Gage nodded.

But she didn't move.

Neither did Gage, though he knew he darn well should be hoofing it out of there, away from her and away from the stupid mistake he was thinking about making.

Lynette glanced into the open door of the bedroom. And at the bed where she'd lost her virginity to him. It was covered with the same patchwork quilt.

Then, she glanced at him, as if waiting for something. "I can *feel* the memories here," she whispered.

So could he. He could feel them in every part of his body. Especially the parts involved in creating those memories that they still felt.

She turned, just a little, and he saw her breasts rise and fall with her suddenly shallow breath. Lynette probably didn't know it, but she was sending out a signal that his body had no trouble interpreting.

She ran her tongue over her bottom lip.

Okay, so maybe she did know about the signal-sending. Maybe she wanted exactly what he wanted. Being on the same page could be a good thing. Or bad.

Really bad.

That still didn't stop him.

Forcing any of those *really bad* doubts aside, Gage went to her, and in the same motion he hauled her into his arms.

"What are you doing?" she asked. Her voice was all

breath and filled with more of those signals that yelled for him to take her now.

So, that's what Gage did.

"I'm dealing with what you started earlier in the SUV," he let her know.

Yeah, it was stupid to finish something that would only lead to more stupidity, but Gage was about a mile beyond being able to put on the brakes.

He put his mouth to hers and kissed her.

There was a lot of emotion built up inside him. He hadn't realized just how much. But he had realized, too many times to count, what Lynette did to him. Not just to his mouth. But to his entire body and mind.

She didn't stop him. She kissed him as if this was the first and last kiss she'd ever have. It was always like that with them. Life and death. Now or never.

Especially the *now* part.

The kiss fired up an urgency that Gage hadn't felt, well, since the last time they'd had one of these fiery kissing sessions. And he decided—what the heck. He might as well do this right.

He put her back against the wall so he could run his hands down her body. First her sides, then her breasts. Touching her made him crazy, but Lynette upped the ante by grinding her body against his. Sex to sex.

The woman knew how to make him crazy, too.

"We shouldn't be doing this," Lynette mumbled and then coiled her arms around him and dived back in for kissing, round three.

Gage couldn't agree more. They shouldn't be doing this. They had way too much to do than to be French-kissing against the wall.

That still didn't stop him.

But another thought at least caused him to slow down. "Are you okay? I mean, will this hurt the baby?"

She shook her head. "It won't hurt the baby," she assured him.

The words had barely left her mouth when Lynette pulled him back to her for another kiss. And Gage knew things were going to get way out of hand, especially after he shoved up her dress and located the flimsy lace panel on the front of her panties.

She went limp, the opposite of his reaction, and she made a sound mixed with both immense pleasure and hesitation. Yep, even through the fiery haze in his head and body, he heard the hesitation.

Gage pulled back a little, but he kept his hand in place. He touched her with his fingers through the lace.

"We have to think this through," she said. It would have been a good suggestion if she hadn't sounded on the verge of a climax and if she hadn't moved against his fingers, seeking his touch. "My head's not on straight right now."

Nothing was straight, he wanted to tell her.

Gage kept touching her, and he watched her eyelids flutter down. She made that sound again. The sound that heated every inch of his body that wasn't already scalding hot.

"You're a really good kisser, and I haven't had sex in a long time." She punctuated that with a breathy moan and ground her body against his fingers.

He touched her again. Kissed her, too.

Then stopped.

"How long of a time?" he risked asking.

She looked at him, but Gage caused her eyes to haze over again by sliding his hand into her panties and touching her the way he wanted. Naked skin to naked skin.

Judging from her reaction, she wanted it, too. So Gage slid his fingers into that wet, slick heat.

"Ten years," she whispered.

He was so caught up in sending her straight to a slippery climax that it took a few seconds for that to register. It didn't register well.

"Ten years?" he repeated. Gage stopped touching her.

But Lynette put his hand right back where it'd been.

"Don't read anything into it," she grumbled.

"Ten years as in when we were together?" he pressed. "That was the last time you had sex?"

She didn't answer verbally, but everything about her face and body language said *yes*.

"Oh, man." He paused. "Oh, man!" And that was all Gage could get out for several moments. "How the hell could I not read anything into that?" he asked. "Am I the only man you've ever been with?"

Lynette tried to move away from him, but Gage held her in place. Probably not the brightest idea he'd ever had with his erection between them.

"Don't read anything into it," she repeated. "It just took me a long time to get over you, that's all."

He looked at her face, flushed with arousal, her nipples that were drawn tight and puckered against her flimsy white lace bra. And her swollen lips from their kissing assault. She looked like sex. Smelled like it, too. And it was crystal clear what she wanted him to do.

"But you got over me?" he challenged.

She looked him straight in the eyes. "I did."

A different set of emotions roared through him. Bad ones that sent his blood boiling in a different way. "Tell me that lie again, Lynette, and I'll strip off those panties and take you where you stand. I'll be gentle with you because of the baby, but I *will* take you."

Her chin came up. "It's true. I got over you."

He might have believed her. If she hadn't made that hot shivery sound when his breath hit against her mouth.

Gage stared at her, sizing her up as he'd done with the enemy. But she wasn't the enemy. She was his ex-wife, and no matter what she said, Lynette hadn't gotten over him.

Hell.

There was no way he could ignore that. No way to stop without doing something to finish this.

He'd already broken all the rules anyway.

So, Gage slid his hand down her belly and back into her panties. He didn't kiss her, because he wanted to see her eyes. And he wanted her to see him.

For starters. He touched her. He'd given Lynette her first orgasm. Maybe her only orgasms. And he was in a crazy mind to do it again.

"Gage," she whispered.

If it'd been a warning, he would have backed out of this. It wasn't one. Far from it. She lifted herself, wrapping her legs around his waist. No more talk that they shouldn't do this. No more anything except her moving into the strokes of his fingers.

Gage wanted to be inside her. And he considered it. But there was going to be enough hell to pay without this becoming full-blown sex against the wall.

Lynette said his name again. And shattered into a thousand little pieces. Gage gathered her in his arms, gave her a moment to catch her breath and then took her to the bed.

Not for sex.

Though his body reminded him of how uncomfortable he was right now.

Still, he had to get some things straight.

"You've gotten over me," he repeated, but it wasn't a

question. The next one wouldn't be, either. "You haven't had sex with another man in ten years. Now, what the devil am I supposed to do with that information?"

She sat up, fixed her clothes and glared at him. Yeah, it was a glare all right. "You're to do nothing with it."

It didn't take long for Gage to figure out why they were having this conversation and not putting this bed to better use.

"This is about your father threatening to kill me," Gage tossed out there.

"It's not a threat. He *will* kill you."

"Not if I kill him first."

She grabbed on to both his arms and got right in his face. But this time, there was no hazy passion glazing her eyes. "And then what? You're arrested and put on death row for killing a state senator?"

Gage didn't even consider that a possibility. "It doesn't have to go down that way. I could force his hand. I doubt it would take much since he already wants me dead."

"And then you've stooped to his level. I won't let you do that for me."

"Then how about I do it for the baby?" he fired back.

"No!" And Lynette didn't whisper it, either. "We do this the right way. We find the evidence to stop him, and we use the justice system to put him in jail for the rest of his life."

"And what if we can't do that?" Gage didn't have to add more because they were both thinking that, with her father around, their baby wouldn't be safe.

"If it comes down to that, then I'll goad him into a fight," Lynette countered. "I'll be the one to kill him."

Gage said a curse word that was so bad that she blinked. "No way will I let you do that. And for the record, it *is* my fight."

He would have said more, cursed more, but the house phone rang, the sound shooting through the room.

"This discussion isn't over," he warned her. Gage snatched up the phone. "What?"

"Having fun?" It was Mason, and he could no doubt tell from Gage's tone that he'd interrupted something.

"Not yet."

"Well, I don't think the fun stuff will start anytime soon."

Gage groaned. "What's wrong?"

"I'm on my way to the guesthouse with the computer so you can watch Grayson's interviews with Nicole, Patrick and Ford." Mason paused. "If the interviews actually happen, that is. You aren't going to believe what they're trying to do to Lynette."

Chapter Nine

Lynette hurried from the shower. Getting the mud and muck off her had felt more like a necessity than a guilty pleasure while Gage and Mason were setting up the equipment so they could watch the interviews. Each second she'd stayed in the steamy hot water, she'd thought of nothing else other than what Mason had told Gage.

You aren't going to believe what they're trying to do to Lynette.

Lynette would believe it because she'd been dealing with them her entire life. She figured all three—Nicole, Patrick and her father—were capable of pretty much anything, and the only thing she could do was shower, ditch the dirty dress she'd been wearing all morning and try to brace herself for the worst.

She found a pair of sweatpants and a denim shirt in the closet and made a mental note to have someone pick her up some clothes and underwear from her house. Her hair was a mess, but clean now, so she combed it with her fingers and made her way back into the living room where she discovered the interview was already in progress.

On the laptop screen, Nicole, Patrick and her father were in an interrogation room at the sheriff's office, all seated at a metal gray table. Grayson was across from them. And behind the three suspects were six lawyers.

"Why are they all in the same room?" she asked Mason. "Shouldn't Grayson be interviewing them separately?"

"He took their initial statements separately, but the three insisted on doing this interview together. Since they haven't been charged with anything, Grayson agreed to accommodate them. Especially since he's trying to defuse something."

"Defuse what?" And Lynette was almost afraid to hear the answer.

Gage got up from the sofa the moment she came in and stepped in front of the screen. He caught on to her arm. "It's not good," he started. "Nicole and your father are trying to have you committed to an asylum."

She was just tired and angry enough to laugh. "Again?" But she couldn't quite choke back those horrible memories of being there. Gage must have seen that in her eyes.

"I'm not going to let that happen," he assured her.

"Neither am I," she let him know with confidence she didn't totally feel. She tipped her head to the laptop screen. "Can they hear us?"

Gage shook his head. "But Mason can text Grayson any question you want him to ask them."

"Good. Then text and ask how they're planning to have me sent back to that place when I'm not insane."

Lynette figured that would prompt a *back to that place?* question from Mason, but he didn't react. Which meant Gage had either filled him in or Nicole and her father had. It was an embarrassing secret, like being a battered spouse, but she figured she'd kept it hidden long enough.

"Your father and Patrick have yet to say a word," Gage explained. "They've let their lawyers do the talking. Nicole, however, has been a regular chatterbox. She says she has documentation to prove you're mentally unstable."

Her stomach tightened. "It's a lie."

"I know," Gage said.

Mason made a sound of agreement. "Our brother's wife Darcy is a hotshot lawyer. We've already got her on this."

Yes, but it could take days, weeks even, and it would embroil Gage's family even deeper in this. "I'll call my father and tell him to back off."

Gage gave her a flat look. "You think that'll help?"

"No. But it'll infuriate him that I'm not begging Nicole and him to play nice."

The corner of Gage's mouth lifted. But then it faded. "Don't call him. I don't want to give him any reason to send another hit man after you."

She shook her head. "We're not even sure he's behind this." Lynette pointed to the screen again where Nicole was babbling on and on about how unstable Lynette was, that Grayson was a fool to believe anything she said.

"Nicole must think I found something on her when I was digging in those old files," Lynette commented.

"Did you?" Mason asked.

"No," she said with plenty of regret. She wished she'd found a mountain of evidence. "So, how do I stop her?"

Gage ran his hand down her arm. "We let Darcy take care of the commitment papers. She said as a minimum she could request an independent medical evaluation for you. That could take days."

"Do we have days?" Lynette asked.

Gage didn't lie—something she appreciated. He just shrugged.

So, that took care of her, temporarily, but it didn't take care of the others. "In the meantime, your family is in danger."

"Don't worry about the family," Mason assured. "We've got all the spouses and the kids covered."

"You're sure?" she pressed. "Because my father and those other two vipers next to him are dangerous. And clever. My father made my mother's murder look like an accident, and I'm sure he can do it again."

Again, Mason didn't look even slightly surprised. "Can we prove it yet?"

"No," Lynette answered. "And trust me, if I could I would trade myself for that confession. That way, at least he'd see the inside of a jail for what he did."

"And you'd be dead," Gage reminded her. "Not going to happen." His hand slid from her arm to her stomach.

That's when Lynette realized that Mason was watching them. His left eyebrow slid up.

"Lynette's pregnant with my baby," Gage admitted. "But no one can know."

Mason made a *hmm* sound. "I knew you two were back together."

"We're not." Again, said in unison.

"It's a long story about the pregnancy," Gage added.

"I know how babies are made," Mason joked, and turned back to the screen.

"Not this baby," Lynette mumbled.

The joking mood vanished. Her father, Patrick and their respective lawyers all stood and exited the interrogation room. So much for Grayson getting them to say anything incriminating.

But Nicole didn't budge. She stayed put, and maybe that meant she was going to give them something. Anything. At this point, Lynette would take a crumb of information if it put them on the right track.

"Lynette's on a vendetta to prove I'm a criminal," Nicole continued.

She huffed, paced, folded her arms over her ample chest. Everything about Nicole screamed that she was a kept woman—the surgical enhancements, the perfect hairstyle, manicure and expensive wardrobe. But Lynette knew Nicole was no dummy. And she wasn't always loyal to Ford. Over the years, the two had fallen out too many times to count. If that happened now, if Nicole and her father ended up on opposite sides, then it could work in their favor.

"I'm going to stop Lynette before she ruins my reputation beyond repair," Nicole continued. She aimed a determined look at Grayson. "If you don't abide by that court order, I'll have your badge."

Then she exited, her lawyers trailing along behind her.

"What court order?" Lynette asked.

Neither Gage nor Mason jumped to answer. Which meant this was bad.

Gage stepped closer to her again. "Grayson has twenty-four hours to escort you to the mental health facility for evaluation."

Oh, God. "And admittance," Lynette supplied.

"Darcy's working on it," Mason reminded her.

Gage continued, "Nicole pulled strings to get that court order. And Darcy's checking into that, too." He lifted her chin, forced eye contact. "There's no way you're going back," he repeated.

Mason turned off the laptop and stuffed it and the equipment into a bag. "I've got to get back to the office and help out Grayson with the investigation. You can handle things here?"

Gage nodded. "When the safe house is ready, I'm moving Lynette."

"Sounds good to me," Mason drawled. He slung the

equipment bag over his shoulder and headed to the door. "They can't serve that court order if they can't find her."

The court order was the least of her worries, but it was a worry.

"Any news on that second hit man?" she asked Gage.

"Not much. I suspect he came with Freddie Denton. Maybe in a backup car. I have someone checking into that."

Yes, no telling how many wheels were turning to try to figure who was behind this and what he or she would do next. After the stunt Nicole had just pulled, the woman was now at the top of her suspect list. Of course, it didn't mean that her father hadn't put Nicole up to doing this.

It made Lynette angry and light-headed just thinking about it, and she headed back to the bedroom in search of some socks. She located a pair in the top dresser drawer.

Gage stayed in the doorway, his shoulder propped against the jamb. Lynette sank down on the foot of the bed. The memory bed. And here she was again in the same room, same bed.

Same man.

And her body was begging her to forget all her worries and seduce Gage. Not that it would require much to get him on the bed with her. They were both operating on a short sexual fuse.

But sex was not going to satisfy them for long.

They had too many things to work out first.

Heck, she wasn't even sure Gage would be around an hour from now much less long enough for them to resolve a decade of hurt and separation.

"I remember the first time I saw you naked," he said. "It was on that very bed, and I thought I'd died and gone to heaven."

Lynette put on the socks. "Gage, that's not helping."

He pushed himself away from the jamb, strolled to her. "It wasn't meant to help." He pulled in a long, weary breath and eased down on his knees in front of her, his body in between her legs.

"Gage," she warned.

"Lynette," he warned right back.

He reached up and pushed her hair from her face. Just that simple touch went through her. Always did.

Gage groaned softly, slid his hands up the outside of her thighs and to her backside. "We have some things to work out before sex," he told her. And he leaned in and buried his face against her breasts.

Just like that her argument started to dissolve.

"But at least all the secrets are out of the way," Gage added. "You know I'm alive. And I know about your father's threat and the baby."

The argument returned in her head. Because all the secrets weren't out of the way.

Well, not one secret anyway.

And it was a huge one.

"What?" Gage asked. He was doing the mind-reading thing again. And would have no doubt pressed her for the truth.

But the phone rang.

Gage gave her a suspicious look, got to his feet and snatched the phone from the nightstand. He didn't say anything, probably because there was no caller ID screen on the old-style phone.

Lynette waited, breath held, and prayed this wasn't bad news. She'd already had enough.

"Hendricks, you have news?" Gage finally said.

Sherman Hendricks, Gage's handler at the CIA.

She watched Gage's expression and body language.

There wasn't much in either to help her figure out what the handler was telling him.

"No," Gage finally said. "Just get that safe house ready." And with that, he hung up.

Lynette got to her feet and faced him.

"It's not good." That's all Gage said for several moments. "The informant who gave us info about the hit man didn't just give the information to us. He gave it and more to the drug lord, Sampson Dalvetti."

Her breath vanished, and she had no choice but to sink back onto the bed. "Dalvetti knows you're alive?"

"It's possible. In fact, Dalvetti might have hired both hit men so he could test the waters. He could have sent them after you. And then leaked it, knowing that if I was alive, it would get back to me."

Oh, mercy. If so, then it'd worked. Dalvetti had maybe figured that Gage would come back from the proverbial grave to save her.

And he had.

But at what cost?

"I'm sorry. So sorry," Gage whispered. He pulled her into his arms.

"You saved my life," she reminded him.

"Yeah. But I'm the one who could have put you in danger in the first place."

She was about to disagree with that, but the phone rang again. He leaned over and punched the button on the base of the phone to put the call on Speaker. However, as a precaution he didn't identify himself.

Good thing, too.

Because it wasn't his handler's voice that greeted them this time.

"Lynette?" the caller said. It was her father.

Gage put his finger to his mouth in a keep-quiet gesture so she wouldn't answer.

"Lynette," Ford continued, "I've called every number at the Ryland ranch, so I figure if you're not listening, you'll get the message." He paused. "I know that Gage is alive."

Her heart went to her knees.

Gage mouthed some profanity. Was this a fishing expedition, or did her father truly know?

"I want to talk to both of you," Ford insisted. "We have things to settle."

Lynette wanted to tell him that talking wasn't going to settle anything between them, but she didn't want her father coming after Gage.

But Gage stood and moved closer to the phone. "Ford, what do you want?" he asked aloud.

Lynette nearly screamed and gave him a look that read, *Have you lost your mind?* Gage ignored her.

"I want to speak to you both, face-to-face," her father informed them. "*Now.* I'm not far away, but your armed ranch hands won't let me onto the property."

"Good," Lynette spoke up. "Because I don't want you here."

"Yes, you do," her father disagreed. "I can call off Nicole, but that'll only happen if you both agree to speak to me."

"Is that so you'll have a better chance at gunning us down?" Gage asked.

"Despite what you think of me, I don't gun down people in broad daylight." He huffed. "I just want to talk to you and my daughter."

"No," Lynette stated as clearly as she could through clenched teeth. "And how exactly did you find out Gage was alive?"

Her father took his time answering, as if he was giving thought to his answer. "If you want to know that, then
meet with me. I'll tell you."

Lynette huffed. She didn't want to know it at the risk
of her father trying to kill Gage or her.

But Gage turned toward her. Studied her. He mumbled,
"I'm sorry." Before she could ask what the devil he meant
by that, Gage turned back to the phone. "All right, let's
meet," Gage said to her father.

"No!" Lynette insisted.

Gage touched her arm, rubbed gently. Probably a gesture meant to soothe her, but it didn't work. She was far
from soothed. She was angry, shocked and frustrated that
her father had found out about Gage now. The timing
was not good.

"It might help," Gage whispered.

"It might not," she whispered back. "This could be
some kind of trick to draw you into a fight."

"That's why you won't be doing this meeting." Gage
brushed a kiss on her cheek and turned back to the phone.
"Meet me outside the guesthouse. Just me."

"Lynette, too," Ford fired back.

"No deal. Whatever you have to say, you can say it
to me."

Chapter Ten

Gage wasn't sure it was the brightest decision to confront Ford, but he was damn tired of the man trying to run roughshod over Lynette. Ford had gotten away with it for, well, all of her life, and maybe the man just needed a good dose of his own bullying tactics.

"I don't want you to do this," Lynette repeated. "It's not safe."

He figured she'd repeat it again before he walked onto the porch to face Ford. "I'll make it safe," Gage promised.

Thankfully, the guesthouse phone had a direct line to the main house and to Mason's ranch office. That's the button that Gage pushed.

"Ford Herrington's at the end of the road," Mason informed him the second he answered.

"Yeah. I'm meeting him to settle some things."

Mason paused. "Lynette couldn't talk you out of it?" He didn't wait for an answer. "You always were the hard-headed one."

Gage couldn't argue with that. "How many ranch hands are with Ford right now?"

"Two. I had them stand guard at the top of the road so we wouldn't get any unexpected visitors. Both are armed, and I trust them."

Good. If Mason trusted them, then so did Gage. "Call

them for me and have them escort Ford to the guesthouse. I'll meet them out front."

Mason paused again, and Gage waited for his brother to try to talk him out of this confrontation, but then Mason just cursed and hung up. One down, another to go. He looked at Lynette, who was fuming, and knew this was another argument he had to win.

"Why don't you get something to eat while I talk to your father?" Gage knew the lame suggestion would fall on her deaf ears so he played dirty. He glanced down at her stomach. "Think of the baby. It's not good for you to go this long without eating."

Her eyes narrowed, and she called him a bad name that questioned his intelligence and his paternity. But she turned and headed for the kitchen.

"I'm watching from the window," she informed him.

Good grief. He wasn't the only hardheaded person in the room. "Stay back. Away from the glass."

That got her whirling around to face him again. No more narrowed eyes, but there was worry in them now. Gage went to her, slid his arm around her. Kissed her.

Then, kissed her again.

"That won't work," she snarled against his mouth.

"Yeah. It will. Because you're going to think of the baby again and play it safe."

"That's not fair."

"I know. But I can't carry this baby," he reminded her. "Only you can do that. And that means I do the caveman stuff and you grow us a healthy child."

Gage didn't miss how easily the *us* had flowed off his tongue. There was a lot for them to work out before there was an *us,* and it started with this meeting with Ford.

He drew his Glock from his holster, took a deep breath and stepped onto the porch. Gage also checked to make sure Lynette wasn't right by the window. And that she was eating.

A winner on both counts.

She was munching on an apple as if she were in a race to finish it, and while she was close to the front door and window, she was staying back.

It didn't take long—less than a minute—for the truck to come to a stop in front of the guesthouse. An armed ranch hand was on either side of Ford, and they all got out. The ranch hands stopped at the white picket fence gate. Not Ford. He walked toward Gage.

"That's close enough," Gage told the man when he made it to the bottom step. It was still drizzling and Ford didn't have an umbrella, but Gage hoped the discomfort of the weather would speed things up. He didn't want Ford on the grounds any longer than necessary.

"How did you find out I was alive?" Gage tossed out there for starters.

Ford lifted his shoulder. "I have my sources."

"And those would be?" Gage pressed.

"Confidential."

Gage wished he could wipe that smugness off Ford's weaselly face, but that would only make this ordeal last longer. Best to hear what he had to say and then get him far away from the ranch.

"I haven't told anyone you're alive," Ford insisted.

Gage didn't believe him, but he had more important things to discuss. "Call off Nicole."

He lifted his shoulder again. "I'll try."

"On the phone you said you could do it. That's the only reason I'm out here."

"I said I would if you both agreed to talk to me." Ford made a show of looking at Gage. "You're not *both*."

Gage heard the movement behind him and cursed a

blue streak. That's because Lynette opened the blasted door and came out onto the porch with him. He shot her a warning glance, which did no good whatsoever.

"Now, you have both," Lynette snarled. "Call off your lover."

Her father seemed more than pleased that he'd gotten his way.

"I'll put pressure on Nicole," Ford told them. "I know some of her secrets." He paused a heartbeat. "Yours, too." And he was looking at Lynette when he said it.

Hell. Did Ford know about the baby?

It wasn't something Lynette could keep secret for long because she would soon start showing, but Gage hadn't wanted Ford to put two and two together and come up with the conclusion of the baby being Gage's. That would only start another war between Ford and him. Gage needed some security measures in place so that Lynette wouldn't be anywhere near her father when he learned she was pregnant.

"Yes, secrets," Lynette repeated. She tried to step around him, but Gage blocked her. He couldn't hog-tie her and put her back inside the house, but by God, as a minimum he could shield her body with his. "You mean like the secret you told me about my mother?"

A muscle flickered in Ford's jaw, but that was his only response. "That was a long time ago."

"Yes, there's no statute of limitations on murder," she fired back.

Gage didn't want to take his eyes off Ford, but he turned around and gave Lynette another warning glance. This was turning ugly fast.

"There's also a law against bribing a public official," Ford said, pulling Gage's attention back to him.

Gage braced himself for Lynette to ask what the heck that meant, but she didn't say anything.

Oh, man.

"You didn't think I'd find out?" Ford snapped, his attention still nailed to Lynette. "I *always* find out everything you do."

"What are you talking about?" Gage just came out and asked.

Ford got that smug look again. "She didn't tell you?" He clucked his tongue. "Lynette's one for secrets. All that digging into my personal files prompted me to do some more digging, too. She bought a condo in Dallas, and she used an assumed name. Did she tell you that?"

No. But Gage guessed that's where she'd planned to go when she could no longer hide the pregnancy. It was a smart move, but it hurt for Gage to think she'd had to do these smart moves on her own. And because they'd been necessary.

"What does that have to do with bribing an official?" Gage pressed.

"I need to talk to you," Lynette whispered to him.

That put a big knot in his belly.

"See, it's different when it's your secrets being blabbed, isn't it?" Ford questioned. "I figured you'd done the right thing about the annulment, especially after I'd made it so clear what the consequences would be if you didn't. Imagine my surprise when last month I discovered you'd bribed an official. A judge, no less."

Gage shook his head. "What the hell is this about?"

Ford smiled. "What my daughter needs to tell you is that you two are still married."

LYNETTE FELT THE BLOOD drain from her head, and she was sorry she'd wolfed down that apple, because she was suddenly queasy, too. She'd intended to tell Gage about the annulment. Or rather the lack of one.

But she darn sure hadn't wanted to tell him like this.

She looked at Gage, lowered her voice, so she could tell him something meant only for his ears. "I bribed a judge in Kerrville to fake the annulment."

Gage blinked. Looked at Ford then her. "We're still married?"

Lynette nodded. "Don't read too much into it," she added.

He stared at her. The same stare he'd given her when she'd told him he was the only lover she'd ever had. There was a reason for that.

She'd always considered herself a married woman.

That, and she hadn't wanted another man. Just Gage. And her father was going to do everything in his power to make sure she didn't get him.

Not then, not now.

"Any reason you didn't tell me this?" Gage asked her.

She tipped her head to her father. "The reason is standing out there in the rain."

"I told her I'd kill you if she didn't get the annulment," Ford volunteered. "Never wanted her to drop in bed with the likes of you. Her tramp of a mother already did that with your kin."

Some venom went through Gage's eyes, and he turned that venom on her father. "It takes a special kind of man to use a threat like that on a nineteen-year-old girl. But guess what? Lynette and I aren't kids anymore, and I've been trained to take out scum like you."

"Is that a threat?" Ford snapped.

"You bet it is." Gage took one step forward, and in the same motion, he pushed her behind him. "If you come near Lynette, if you utter another threat to her—veiled or otherwise—you're going down."

Ford chuckled. "You'd kill me in cold blood, *Agent* Ryland?"

"No." Gage's voice got eerily calm. "I'd wait until you pulled your gun first. But trust me, I'm faster. I can get a bullet in your brain so quick that before you blink, you'll already be in hell."

Oh, mercy.

Lynette had to do something to defuse this. It was already past taking a dangerous turn.

"I'm about to faint," Lynette whispered to him. And she prayed she sounded convincing enough. "Please. I don't want to fall. It might hurt the baby."

That got Gage moving. "Get *him* out of here," Gage told the ranch hands.

Gage kept his eyes on her father and his right hand on his gun, but he looped his left arm around her and got her inside. He kicked the door shut, lifted her into arms and took her to the sofa.

"Should I call the doctor?" Gage asked, looking down at her. No more venom in his voice. Just worry.

Well, for a couple of seconds.

"You're not about to faint," he accused. Gage cursed. "That's playing dirty, Lynette."

She came off the sofa. "I didn't want you in a gunfight with my father. This is what I've been trying to prevent for over a decade."

His anger and frustration returned with a vengeance. Gage kicked a wood magazine holder next to the sofa and hurried to the door. He looked out. Cursed some more. And locked it as if he'd declared war on it. He reholstered his gun and started to pace like a caged tiger.

"I'm not sorry for what I did," she let him know.

Still pacing, he aimed his index finger at her. He also tried to speak, but the anger didn't let the words come. Not that she wanted to hear what he had to say right now. Lynette had warned him that talking to her father would be bad, and Gage hadn't listened.

"I'm not sorry about the nonannulment, either," she added. Best to clear the air about that, as well, since Gage was going to stew for a while.

The burst of temper drained her, and Lynette dropped back down onto the sofa. Gage studied her a moment, and his pacing took him back to the door where he armed the security system. He then paced to the kitchen and came back with a Lone Star beer and a pint-size carton of milk.

"Drink," he ordered.

"Well, since you asked so nicely..." Lynette took the milk.

"Don't," he warned her. "If you'd told me we were still married—"

"My father would have picked a fight with you sooner," she interrupted. "Just remember, there's a reason I tried to make him think I'd gone through with the annulment."

His thumb whacked against his chest. "Yeah. To save me. Lynette, I didn't need saving. Not at that price!"

"The price was worth it to me."

He gulped down a good portion of the beer, and it was obvious he was still wrestling with the bombshell that her father had just delivered. "How much did it cost you to bribe the official?"

She took a moment, drank some milk, dodged his gaze. "Ten thousand," she mumbled.

His mouth dropped open. And she knew why. Her father was rich, but he'd never shared that wealth with her. She'd worked for every penny that she had in the bank.

Which wasn't much, considering she had a mortgage for the condo in Dallas and her house in Silver Creek.

"Where'd you get that kind of money?" Gage demanded.

She decided it was a good time to avoid his gaze some more. "I sold my mother's jewelry."

The profanity was there, in his eyes, but he didn't voice it. Instead, he sank down onto the coffee table across from her. "Not her gold heart necklace?"

Lynette nodded. "All of it."

"What about your wedding ring?" he asked.

"I kept that." She didn't manage to say that above a whisper, but Gage no doubt heard it loud and clear.

Lynette undid the top button on her shirt so she could reach her bra. She pulled the ring from the tiny pocket she'd sewn into the right cups of all her bras and held it up for him to see.

"My father has a bad habit of searching my place when I'm not there," she explained. "I figured it was best if I kept it on me as much as possible. Less chance of him finding it." She slipped the ring back into her bra. Rebuttoned her shirt.

Now he cursed, but there was no anger in it. "If you tell me you're over me, I'll…"

"Take me where I stand?" she finished, hoping the levity would help.

He shot her a scowl. "I'll make you take a nap." Gage groaned. "If you'd just told me…" He didn't finish that, either. Didn't need to.

"It probably seems selfish and a little crazy on my part, but I wanted to hang on to the marriage as long as I could because it was my way of hanging on to you. I knew that you'd get on with your life. That you'd find someone else and when you did, I'd planned to get a quick annulment so you wouldn't be committing bigamy." She paused. "But you didn't find anyone else. Not that I know of anyway."

Another scowl. "No." He drained more of the beer. "And I didn't have to sell something I loved or keep a secret that burned into my soul."

"Yes, you did," she reminded him. "You left your family. Faked your death to save me and your brothers. If we're comparing our martyr badges, I think they're about the same size."

He looked at her. "So, where does that leave us?"

Lynette drank her milk. "Our martyrdom failed. Even after all these years, we're right back where we started. Married and in danger."

"Yeah." And that's all he said for a long time.

Except this time around, the danger was even worse. Because it wasn't just Gage and her. Their baby was now involved in this.

Gage set his beer aside, stood, and without warning, he scooped her up. "You're taking that nap," he growled. *"Alone,"* he added, heading for the bedroom. "I have some things to work out."

"You're not leaving?" she asked.

"No." A moment later, he repeated it along with a heavy sigh and deposited her onto the bed. "I don't want you here by yourself."

His gaze dropped from her face, to her body.

All of her body.

Lynette could have seduced him to make him stay in the room with her. She could keep an eye on him that way and make sure that he didn't go after her father.

Of course, seducing Gage had other benefits, too.

Her body was always burning for him. Plus, she was already on the bed with him just inches away, and she

knew his weak spots. Some neck kisses would get this
seduction started the right way.

But she had some things to work out, as well.

Like how she was going to neutralize her father. She'd
been trying to work it out for ten years now, and it was
past time she came up with a permanent solution.

But what?

Her investigation had failed to turn up anything, but
maybe that just meant she had to dig deeper or in a different place. Maybe she could get someone at the asylum in
Mexico to spill what her father had done to her. It wasn't
a good angle, but it might be the only one they had.

"I'll keep digging," she promised him.

He shook his head. "After you rest."

Gage leaned down, and for a moment she thought he
had changed his mind about joining her. But his mouth
didn't go in the direction of hers. Instead, he dropped a
kiss on her stomach.

On the baby.

The moment was so perfect, so sweet, that it brought
tears to her eyes.

"Get some sleep." He threw the covers over her and
walked out.

Lynette watched him stride away in those jeans that
hugged his best asset. Well, one of them anyway. His
heart was at the top of that asset list.

A tear spilled down her cheek.

Loving Gage seemed to be something she couldn't
stop. Even though loving him was the fastest way to get
him killed.

Lynette pulled the covers to her chin and knew that
the only way to save him was to say goodbye.

Again.

Chapter Eleven

Gage's eyes flew open. He groaned and got up from the sofa where he'd fallen asleep. His thirty-minute catnap had turned into four hours. His body had needed rest, but he should have been thinking and planning instead of dozing off.

Planning how to bring Ford Herrington down.

He stumbled toward the bedroom, and nearly had a heart attack when he didn't see Lynette where he'd left her.

"I'm in the kitchen," she called out to him.

He turned to hurry to her, bashed his knee against the doorjamb and had to go into the kitchen limping. But the hurrying up wasn't necessary. Lynette was seated at the country-style kitchen table eating—Gage looked at her plate—pancakes smeared with crunchy peanut butter.

"You okay?" she asked, glancing at the knee that he was rubbing.

Gage nodded. "You?"

She nodded, too. Lynette slid some of the pancakes onto another plate and passed them his way.

His stomach growled, and Gage realized the only thing he'd had to eat or drink in the past twenty-four hours was a beer. Hardly food for thoughts and planning. He grabbed a fork from the drawer and dug in. It wasn't steak and eggs, his favorite, but it was good.

"Thanks," he mumbled.

Lynette poured him a glass of milk, set it next to his plate and then sank down in the chair across from him. Uh-oh. That look in her baby blues told him this wasn't going to be a conversationless meal.

And they *should* talk, he reminded himself.

But for a moment he let himself take all of this in. Lynette and he doing something as ordinary as sharing a meal. Of course, ordinary and Lynette didn't fit. An oxymoron. She was anything but.

"What are you looking at?" she asked. And made him smile when she ran her hand over her shoulder-length blond hair to smooth it down.

"You," he admitted. "You're prettier now than when you were seventeen. Wouldn't have thought that was possible, because you caught a lot of eyes even then."

She blushed. Made him smile again. "Look at yourself in the mirror, Gage Ryland. You're the hot guy every girl in high school wanted in their dreams. And in their beds. I was just lucky enough to get you in mine."

The last part had her looking uncomfortable and glancing away. "Sorry," she mumbled.

He shrugged. "You don't have to say the words aloud to make me think of being in bed with you." And he waited to see where that would take him.

Apparently, not far.

When her gaze returned to his, she looked serious again. "When I was at the asylum in Mexico, there was a nurse, Rosa Mendez, who was nice to me. She seemed to believe me when I told her that I'd been sent there against my will and that I wasn't crazy. I want to see if I can find her. Maybe she'll have some proof that my father had me committed there illegally."

Gage gave that some thought, but he didn't have to think long or hard to see where this could go.

"I doubt Ford left that kind of loose end behind." And if he did, he would just neutralize her before she could give them anything they could use. However, he didn't say that to Lynette. "But I'll check into it."

And he would make sure this Rosa Mendez had some protection. Of course, protection hadn't worked so far.

"It could be a good lead," Gage assured her with confidence he didn't feel.

She nodded, stared at him. "If you don't swear to me that you'll stay away from my father, then I'm leaving when I finish these pancakes. I'll call Mason to come and get me, and I'm out that door."

Oh, man. That was an ultimatum he hadn't seen coming. "It's not safe for you to go."

"And it's not safe for you if I stay."

Gage had another bite of the pancake that he no longer wanted. "No deal. Your father won't quit just because I back off."

"Maybe not. But he might if I tell him I'm going to the press, that I'll do an interview with every tabloid in Texas, and I'll tell them how he confessed to killing my mother."

Gage started shaking his head. She ignored him.

"I'll tell my father that I'll convince the new assistant district attorney, who happens to be your sister-in-law, to take the case to a grand jury. I've never had anyone in the D.A.'s office on my side, but I do now with Darcy." She paused. "I'll also tell him that the way to stop me is to leave you the hell alone."

Gage groaned, stood and went to her. He pulled her

to her feet and then into his arms. "What the devil am I going to do with you?"

One thing he did know. Lynette was not going to fight his battles for him.

She didn't exactly melt against him. "You're going to agree to leave for a while until things settle down."

He blinked, pulled back so he could see her stubborn face. "I'm not going anywhere."

"It's not a choice. If you want to drop kisses on my baby belly and make me cry." Her voice quivered a little, and she cleared her throat. "If you want a chance for us to try to work things out, then you have to leave."

He stared at her. "Let me get this straight. Both scenarios involve leaving. You in the first one. Me, in the second. That's going to be hard to do because I don't intend to let you out of my sight until the danger has passed. Remember the hit men who tried to kill you?"

"I remember." She swallowed hard.

Gage hated that he shoved those nightmares right back at her, but he wasn't backing down. "No one will do more to protect you and this baby than I will," he promised her.

She opened her mouth to argue, but thankfully the phone mounted to the wall rang. Without taking his attention from her, he reached over and pushed the speaker button to answer the call.

"Gage," the caller said.

Not Ford or one of his brothers. But his handler, Sherman Hendricks.

Gage didn't miss the tone in Sherman's greeting, and he reached to take the call off Speaker. But Lynette stopped him. She gave him a look, reminding him that she had the right to know. And she did.

"This is about Dalvetti?" Gage asked his handler.

"Yes." Sherman's pause was long enough to make Gage

more than uncomfortable. "We've confirmed that Dalvetti knows you're alive."

Gage automatically went to the window, lifted the blinds and looked out. "How'd you confirm it?"

"Dalvetti left a message with the informant who told us about the hit man who was after Ms. Herrington. The now-dead informant. Dalvetti carved the message on the guy's chest and stomach. It said, *This time Gage Ryland dies for real.*"

Gage checked to make sure Lynette was okay. She wasn't. She sank back onto the chair. He cursed himself for not doing it sooner, but he grabbed the phone from the receiver and took the call off Speaker. Of course, the damage had already been done.

"The safe house is nearly ready," Sherman continued. "We had to take even more precautions than we normally take."

And those extra precautions might not be nearly enough. "Finish the preparations for it and send two agent decoys there. Because Dalvetti might have an informant in the CIA."

Sherman didn't jump to say that wasn't possible. It was. And both of them knew it. Dalvetti could already know the location of the safe house. Heck, he could know that Lynette was with him.

"What are you going to do?" Sherman asked.

Gage looked out the window again. "I'd rather not say. I trust you, Sherman, but the less you know, the better." Gage didn't wait for him to agree. "How long do I have before Dalvetti comes here?"

"A day, maybe less."

Well, it wasn't good news, but it was better than the drug lord being on the front porch.

"I'll be in touch," Gage promised Sherman.

By the time he hung up, Lynette was on her feet again and coming toward him. "Gage" was all she managed to say.

The fear on her face was enough to make him sick, and so that he wouldn't make that fear worse, Gage clamped down his own feelings.

"The safe house wouldn't be a good idea," he explained. "But I can do things to make you safe."

Gage sat and pulled her onto his lap. It was wrong to leach comfort from her this way, but by God, he needed to have her in his arms right now. That didn't stop him from taking the phone again and calling Mason.

"I'll make this quick," Gage said the second Mason answered. "The drug lord is coming to Silver Creek, and it won't take him long to find the ranch. You need to get everyone out of here."

If Mason had a reaction to that, he didn't voice it. "How much time do we have?"

"Do it as fast as possible. You have a place to go?"

"Dade's wife has a place in San Antonio. We had to use it a couple of months ago when there was trouble at the ranch." Mason paused. "But we have a little problem this time around. Eve just went into labor."

Eve, Grayson's wife. Gage loved her like the sister he'd never had, but it was not a good time for her to be giving birth.

"Grayson's on the way to the hospital with her," Mason added.

Of course he was, but Grayson would be tied up with the delivery and he wouldn't be thinking about security.

"Kade's heading to the hospital to be with them, too," Mason went on.

Good. His little brother Kade was an FBI agent and

could protect them. That would leave Dade and Nate to get the wives and children to San Antonio.

"I'm staying with you?" Mason asked as if he'd already grasped the plan that Gage hadn't even come up with yet.

"I'd like family backup," Gage admitted.

"Then you got it." And Mason didn't hesitate.

Until that moment Gage hadn't realized how much he'd missed his family. And how lucky he was to be a Ryland.

"What about Lynette?" Mason asked.

"I'm handling that now."

Gage glanced at Lynette to see how much he had to handle with her. But she wasn't panicking. If anything, now that the initial shock had worn off, she looked resolved to the danger.

That riled him even more.

Danger should have never entered her life, and now she had so much that heaven knows what the stress was doing to her and the baby.

Gage had to do something.

But what he couldn't do was go off half-cocked. His instincts were to cram Lynette into the nearest vehicle and drive out of there fast. But there had to be some things in place first. And he didn't want to take Lynette to the house in San Antonio with the others because the danger might follow them there.

"Call me when you've worked things out with Lynette," Mason insisted, and he ended the call.

"Good news," he started. "Eve's having her baby."

Lynette managed a smile of sorts. Brief and barely. But there. She slid her hand over her stomach and was hopefully thinking one day she'd be there, safe in the hospital. Giving birth.

That seemed like an eternity from now.

"There could be a bright side in all of this," he said to

her. "Maybe your father, Nicole or Patrick didn't try to have you killed after all."

"Maybe," she repeated, clearly in deep thought. Lynette wasn't a coward, but right now she had to be worried about the safety of the baby she was carrying.

Gage was worried, too.

Because even if Ford wasn't guilty of attempted murder, he'd still murdered. Sooner or later, Gage was going to have settle that score.

He pulled her closer, careful not to touch any part of her that would distract them. Lynette and he had a problem with touching. It always turning to kissing and kissing led to sex. She didn't need that right now. And he vetoed his body's suggestion that it would help her get her mind off things.

Nothing was going to do that.

"How will Dalvetti come after us?" she asked, slicing right to the point.

"Not us. *Me.* You'll be at the main house with Mason and as many armed ranch hands as he has guarding you."

She stared at him. "You're going after Dalvetti?"

Gage figured a lie would just put more fire in her eyes. "I have to. If I don't, he'll try to use you and my family to get revenge against me."

A thin breath left her mouth. "You could stay at the house with Mason and me."

He shook his head. "I have to end this, Lynette."

"But it's dangerous."

"It's my job. It's what I do, and believe it or not, I'm really good at it." He shrugged. "Well, most days. I screwed up with the informant."

"No. You didn't. Because Denton would have killed me and the baby if you hadn't stopped him."

Gage had a hard time even imagining that, and he

didn't care how many people he had to take down to keep her safe.

"I know I wasn't in on the planning stage of this baby," he said, "but so you know, I want it."

He expected that to soothe her because the words sure as heck soothed him and put things crystal clear in his mind. But she grabbed on to his arm—hard.

"That sounds like a goodbye, and it'd better not be."

He shook his head. "No goodbye. I'm coming back, and we'll work out the rest. Got that?"

Gage wanted to hear her answer, but the blasted phone rang again. Because it could be his handler with more information, he answered it right away.

"It's me," Mason greeted. "The others just drove out of here using the back way to get to the highway. Don't worry. We have that trail closed off for any other traffic. But they had to use it this time because there's a visitor at the end of the road where the two guards are. It's Patrick Harkin."

Not now. "What the heck does he want?" Gage barked.

"To talk to Lynette and you. I gotta say, you two are popular with the scumbag crowd. Patrick says he wants to explain how Ford found out you were alive."

Definitely not now. "Tell him to call me tomorrow." Gage doubted he would be there then.

"I tried that. Tried telling him I'd arrest him for trespassing, but he claims it's important. Says it has to do with the drug lord."

"Dalvetti?"

"The very one," Mason verified. "I'm on my way to the guesthouse now so I can bring the computer to monitor the security cameras. If you want, I can have one of the ranch hands escort Patrick to the front yard."

No, it wasn't what Gage wanted. He didn't want Patrick within a mile of Lynette. But Gage also needed some answers. *Any* answers that would stop an attack, and Patrick might be able to provide those.

"I'll meet you in the yard in a couple of minutes," Gage told him. He hung up and immediately turned to Lynette. "And this time, you *will* stay inside. You won't argue about it, either," he added when she opened her mouth.

"I wasn't going to argue. I was going to tell you to be careful. And to give me a gun for backup. I've been doing target practice in the woods behind my house, and I'm a good shot."

Gage didn't doubt it, but he knew he didn't want Lynette having to shoot a gun at anyone. Still, he opened the cabinet above the fridge and saw that it was still there. His grandfather's old Colt .45. He checked to see if it was loaded. It was. And he put it in her waiting hand.

"Stay inside," Gage repeated. "Away from the windows." He pressed a kiss on her cheek. And decided that was a sucky way for him to go out that door.

So he kissed her the right way.

He snapped her to him and put his mouth to hers. Yeah. The right way. His lips, moving over hers. He waited for the slight moan that he knew she'd make.

She made it.

And he kept the kiss long, slow and deep. Gage pulled away from her and was pleased they were both breathing hard. If he was going to muddy the waters with Lynette, he might as well do a thorough job of it.

Or so he kept telling himself.

He was doing that so he could justify the way he was complicating the heck out of things. He wasn't free to think about a relationship with her. Not yet. And even after this situation with Dalvetti was over, they still had obstacles to face.

Gage drew his gun and stepped outside. The rain had stopped, finally, and it was late afternoon, still plenty of light. For now. But it wouldn't be long before the sun set. It also would be a god-awful long night without some kind of information that Gage was hoping he'd get from the weasel of a visitor.

He glanced toward the ranch house and saw Mason driving up in the rust-scarred pickup truck that had seen better days. It was his usual mode of transportation, and he wouldn't budge on getting anything new. In the other direction, Gage spotted one of the ranch hands escorting Patrick. Not in a vehicle.

But walking.

The other ranch hand was still at the end of the road next to the sleek black luxury car. Patrick's, no doubt.

"His car died," the ranch hand called out. "He couldn't get it to start."

"Then he'll be walking back into town," Mason said, stepping from his truck. He had a stuffed-full equipment bag. "Because I'm not tying up any of my men for the likes of him."

Gage couldn't agree more. Now, he just needed to hurry this along so he could make sure the guesthouse was as safe as it could be.

"I need to put this inside," Mason let him know, and he carried in the equipment bag. A few seconds later, he came back out. "I told Lynette to boot up the laptop so we can keep an eye on all the security cameras."

Good idea. As long as she stayed put.

"Start talking," Gage said while Patrick was still walking toward the guesthouse.

"You have a big problem," Patrick answered.

"If you're here to state the obvious, then you can turn around and leave," Gage answered back.

When Patrick reached the fence, he started to open the gate, but Mason stopped him. "You can state more than the obvious from right where you are."

Patrick's mouth tightened, and he eyed them both as if they were scum. Which made Gage wonder—if he hated them so much, then why was he here? Gage doubted the man had good intentions, but sometimes bad intentions worked just as well. Especially if Patrick could give them anything that would put an end to Dalvetti and his threats. It was telling that Patrick even knew about the drug lord. It meant he had at least something.

"Ford isn't going to let this go," Patrick went on.

Again, it was the obvious, and Gage's eye roll let him know that. "The subject you wanted to discuss was Dalvetti." But Gage paused. "Unless Ford has some connection there. If so, spill it and don't waste any more of my time.

Patrick swallowed hard. "I want a deal. Immunity from prosecution."

A deal? It wasn't totally unexpected, but it didn't have anything to do with Dalvetti. Or it damn well shouldn't.

"What have you done that would warrant prosecution?" Gage asked when Patrick didn't add more.

Patrick glanced around. The look of a man on edge. "Ford has some things on me. Things he said he'd leak if I don't cooperate and do as he says." He paused again. "He wants me to kidnap Lynette so he can get her the psychiatric help she needs."

Gage tried very hard not to curse. But he failed. "Lynette's not crazy. Ford is. And what kind of dirt does he have on you?"

More glancing around. "Business deals. Buried away a long time ago. You'd never find them, but Ford apparently kept copies of things."

"I'll bet he did." Gage glanced around, too. The weasel was making him nervous, and he still hadn't spilled anything about Dalvetti. "So, why come to me? Why not just go on being Ford's lackey?"

He dipped down his head a little. "Because I don't want to be part of what Ford's trying to do to Lynette."

"You're just a regular do-gooder, aren't you?" Mason snarled.

Patrick's next round of glances included his car. It was just a glance, but Gage had dealt with scum long enough to know something was wrong.

Gage lifted his gun. "You've got five seconds to tell me why you're really here, and your explanation better include the name Dalvetti."

Patrick shook his head.

Gage took aim at him.

Patrick threw his hands up in the air. "Ford made a deal with Dalvetti." He said the words so quickly that it took Gage a moment to understand what he'd blurted out.

"I'm sorry," Patrick said. "I didn't have a choice."

Hell.

"What did you do?" Gage demanded.

Patrick only shook his head again.

Gage looked at him. At the stalled vehicle. And at the ranch hand near the car.

"Get down!" Gage shouted to the hand.

The ranch hand immediately dived to the side, but it was already too late.

The car exploded in a fireball.

Patrick dropped to the ground, his hands sheltering his head.

"What did you do?" Gage yelled to Patrick.

Patrick kept his head down, but Gage heard him loud and clear. "Dalvetti is *here*."

Chapter Twelve

The sound of the explosion sent Lynette racing to the window.

Oh, God.

Patrick's car had blown to smithereens. Just like the plane at the airport.

She watched Patrick drop to the ground, saw him say something that had Gage throwing open the door and running inside toward her.

"Get down," he told her.

Mason was right behind him, his phone sandwiched between his shoulder and his ear, and he was barking out instructions to someone on the other end of the line.

"What's going on?" she asked Gage.

He caught on to her arm and headed for the bathroom. Without a word, he pulled back the plastic curtain of the tub-shower combo, and he put her inside.

Gage looked her straight in the eyes. "According to Patrick, Dalvetti and your father are in on this together. And Dalvetti is here on the grounds."

Everything inside her went still. The calm before the storm, no doubt. But it was going to take a few seconds for it to sink in that a cold-blooded killer was at the ranch and that her father was perhaps responsible for his being here.

Not perhaps, she amended.

Almost certainly.

This is exactly the kind of destructive stunt he would pull, and he would have no trouble sending Patrick to do his dirty work.

"Where is Dalvetti?" she managed to ask.

Gage shook his head. "I don't know, but I'll find out."

And that meant he would go out there looking for this monster.

Lynette caught on to his arm, to beg him to stay inside, but Mason called out to them. "The ranch hand near the explosion is okay. He hasn't seen anyone other than Patrick."

But then, Mason cursed.

Her breath froze. And she waited to hear the bad news that had caused the profanity. There was no mistaking from Mason's tone that it would be *bad.*

Gage hurried out of the room, and Lynette moved in the tub so she could see them in the doorway of the bedroom. Mason was carrying the laptop and showed the screen to Gage.

"Someone's blocked all the feed from the security cameras," she heard Gage say. "We can't see a thing."

No. That couldn't happen. They needed those cameras to pinpoint Dalvetti's location. Especially with the sun setting. There were plenty of places for him to hide and then sneak up on the guesthouse.

"I'll keep an eye on Patrick and the front of the guesthouse," Mason let him know, and he handed Gage the laptop and headed back out.

"How bad is this?" she asked.

Gage came back into the bathroom and put the laptop on the side of the tub. "If the feed comes back on, let me know. If Dalvetti or someone else is using a jammer, he might not be able to keep an interference signal for long."

Lynette looked at the screen. No images. Just white static.

Gage disappeared into the living room where she could hear him rummaging around, and he came back with his grandfather's Colt, extra ammunition and a walkie-talkie.

"Mason brought the walkie-talkie in the equipment bag," he explained. His gaze finally came to hers and held. "If Dalvetti gets past Mason and me, shoot him."

She wanted to ask what were the odds of him making it into the house, but Lynette really didn't want to know. Because there was only one way Dalvetti would manage to make it inside, and that's if Gage and Mason were dead.

That couldn't happen.

Somehow they all had to make it out of this.

"I'll be careful," Gage promised her before she even demanded that he say it.

He popped a kiss on her mouth and left again. This time, she heard him leave by the front door.

Lynette hugged her knees to her chest, but she kept the Colt in her hand. Ready. Well, hopefully. She'd done lots of target practice, but she doubted a man like Dalvetti would just stand there while she took aim and shot him.

And he might not be alone.

He'd probably brought some hired guns and a lot of weapons with him. Worse, he might even have had help from her father planning this attack.

She listened, trying to pick through the sounds outside. She heard voices, and there was movement around the exterior of the guesthouse, but it was impossible to tell what was going on.

There was a slight clicking sound, and Lynette's attention flew to the laptop screen. It was no longer white static. The images came on, one by one, until there were six of them on the screen. Each shot showed a different camera angle of the ranch.

Still holding on to the gun, she pulled the laptop closer, her gaze rifling over each one.

Finally, she saw Gage.

Thank God.

It wasn't the best camera view, but he was in the yard in front of the guesthouse. A rifle was in one hand and his Glock was in his shoulder holster. He was hunched down as if prepared for an attack. However, the white picket fence wouldn't give him much protection if bullets started flying. Patrick was in the shallow ditch just in front of that fence, looking ready to run off in a panic.

Lynette didn't care a flip about his fear, because Patrick had had a part in setting all of this up. In fact, he'd no doubt used this meeting to distract them in some way so that Dalvetti could jam those cameras and come onto the ranch.

Her attention darted to all the monitors. She saw Mason on one of the other cameras. He was somewhere behind the guesthouse and was directing ranch hands. The men, at least a half dozen of them, were all armed and scattering out. She prayed it would be enough.

The other cameras were positioned in the back pasture, the road and the front and rear of the main house. Things looked normal. Definitely no sign of Dalvetti, her father or any other gunmen. But then, her father wouldn't do this in person. No. He wouldn't put himself in danger, only others. Including Gage and her baby.

That sent a shot of raw anger through her.

When this was over, she had to figure out how to stop this from happening again and again.

Lynette kept her attention pinned to the laptop. And because she was watching so closely, she saw the movement. Not near the guesthouse but near the entrance to the ranch where Patrick's car was still blazing.

Two men came bolting from across the road.

They were dressed in dark green camouflage clothes and were armed with assault rifles. Behind them trailed another man, also armed with a rifle and other guns holstered in an equipment belt.

The last man was no doubt Dalvetti.

Lynette had never seen a picture of him, nor had she even heard a description, but she was certain that's who it was. He moved like a man in charge. Like a man on a mission of murder. And he and those men were using the smoke from Patrick's vehicle for cover.

Lynette jabbed the button on the walkie-talkie, and she both saw and heard Gage answer.

"The cameras are working. Three men just crossed the road near Patrick's car," she relayed with her voice shaking.

"Keep watching and stay put," Gage warned her again.

She saw him use the walkie-talkie to speak to someone else. Mason, she realized. Because Mason said something into his own walkie-talkie and started toward the road.

When she started to get dizzy, Lynette realized she was holding her breath. She wouldn't be any good to Gage and the others if she fainted, so she reminded herself to breathe.

The three guys in camo made it to the burning car but then climbed over the white fence that lined each side of the road. The opposite side of the guesthouse, but still with those rifles, they were possibly already in firing range.

Lynette pressed the button on the walkie-talkie. "The three men are in the east pasture now. They're using the fence and the smoke from the explosion to hide."

Gage didn't respond right away, but she saw him turn in that direction. "I see them." He clicked off the walkie-talkie.

Just as the shot blasted through the air.

Gage dived for cover on the side of the porch steps. Some of the ranch hands hit the ground. Mason ducked behind a tree. Patrick crawled closer to the fence but stayed in the meager cover of the ditch.

Another shot.

She couldn't see which of the three men were shooting, but she did see Gage lift the rifle. He also levered himself up and out of the meager cover of the steps.

Gage fired.

So did Mason.

Lynette watched their bullets tear into the wooden fence. The shots, however, didn't stop the trio.

More bullets came, and one slammed into the guest-house. But not just into the guesthouse—in the bedroom just yards from where she was. She pulled the computer onto her lap and sank down lower into the tub. She couldn't risk one of those shots hitting her because it would endanger the baby.

She hated these men, Dalvetti and her father for every shot, for every drop of fear she felt with Gage putting his life on the line. But it only made her more determined to finish this once and for all.

The next shots shattered one of the windows in the bedroom. There was a window in the bathroom, as well, but it was on the back side of the place. Mason seemed to be positioned to stop anyone from making it back there.

She hoped.

But she also hoped that he wouldn't be hurt putting himself in harm's way for her.

The bullets started again and continued. Nonstop.

All of them aimed at Gage and the guesthouse. Several slammed into the trucks parked outside. One pinged against the rooster weather vane on the roof.

Mason leaned out from the tree and returned fire, a hail of bullets blasting through the air and into the fence.

Lynette had switched back to the screen with Gage when she saw the movement. Not the gunmen. But Patrick. He drew a gun from the back waist of his pants.

Oh, mercy. Was he going to try to shoot Gage? Lynette reached to press the button on the walkie-talkie to warn him, but Gage shouted something. Lynette couldn't hear what over the noise from the blasts, but Patrick froze.

The gunmen didn't.

One of them came up from the fence and took aim at Gage. Lynette wanted to scream for him to watch out, but he wouldn't hear her. Plus, the sound of her voice could be a distraction that could get him killed. Gage ducked down just in the nick of time, and the bullet went into the stone steps.

She watched, her breath in her throat, as one of the gunmen started running toward the guesthouse. He stayed low and dived back down when Mason sent a couple of shots his way.

Gage got up, positioned himself and took aim again with the rifle. He waited. And the moment the gunman reared his head again, Gage fired.

The gunman flew back, and Lynette saw the shock on his face before he hit the ground. If he wasn't dead, he soon would be, and Lynette felt nothing but relief.

One down. Two to go.

She didn't have to wait long for a second gunman to start firing. The shots bashed into the porch again and Gage thankfully dropped back down into cover.

How many times had he faced danger like this?

It sickened Lynette to think about it, especially since this sort of thing was probably part of his job description. It sickened her even more that she'd had a part in this. If she'd just managed to neutralize her father, he couldn't have done whatever he'd done to bring this killer literally to their doorsteps.

She touched the wedding ring that she'd put on her index finger. A poor substitute for Gage, but it calmed her a little. So did the prayers she said.

Suddenly, everything went quiet.

No shots. No sounds. Gage and the others seemed frozen, waiting.

Lynette waited, too, and kept praying that it was over. Her gaze flew over the screen, but she saw nothing. And for a few seconds, she thought maybe her prayers had been answered. Maybe the gunmen were dead.

But no.

The man reared up from the fence. No rifle this time. It was a big tube-looking device, and even though she'd never seen one, Lynette's first thought was that it was rocket launcher.

He aimed it at the guesthouse.

Now, she yelled for Gage to get down, and she turned, flattening her stomach against the tub. She braced herself for the blast that would likely rip the place, and maybe her, apart. But all she heard was another gunshot.

Her attention flew back to the screen.

And to Gage.

He had taken aim at the gunman, but the man and his rocket launcher were already tumbling to the ground.

Patrick, however, was standing, and it was his gun pointed in the direction of dead gunman number two.

Of all the ways Lynette had thought this would play

out, she hadn't expected Patrick to try to save them. If that was indeed what he'd done.

More movement.

She saw the third man, the one she believed to be Dalvetti, running away. The man was in a full sprint.

Gage started to run, as well, and, with the rifle gripped in his hand, he vaulted over the fence and raced after the man.

Lynette wanted to hurry after Gage, to back him up, but she knew that wouldn't help. Gage had told her to stay put, and she would. Even if it was killing her to do that.

Some of the ranch hands followed Gage, but Mason hurried to the front porch, positioning himself between Patrick and the guesthouse. Probably because Mason didn't trust Patrick. Or maybe he was worried Dalvetti would circle back and come after her.

The seconds crawled by, and she had no idea how much time passed. It seemed hours as she watched Gage run after the man who'd just tried to kill them.

Soon, too soon, Gage disappeared from camera range.

It had been torture watching the gunfight, but it was even worse now that she couldn't see Gage at all. Maybe it was all the recent danger in her life, but her thoughts ran wild, and she hoped that Gage would make it back safely to her.

The front door opened, but Lynette could see that it was Mason. "You okay?" he called out.

"Yes," she lied. She hadn't been hurt, but it would take a lifetime or two to forget seeing those bullets come at Gage like that.

"I killed him," Patrick called out to Mason. "Did you see? I killed him."

"I saw," Mason answered. "I'll give you a gold star

later." Mason kept his attention fastened to the end of road where she'd last seen Gage.

Lynette watched both the road and Patrick. But thankfully Patrick still seemed to be on their side. Like Mason, he was caught up in watching the rest of this nightmare unfold.

She heard Mason curse, and there was nothing that could have prevented her from leaving the tub. Lynette raced to the door, praying that she wouldn't look out and see Gage wounded. Or worse.

It was Gage all right. And he was running back toward the house. Alone.

Gage cursed, too. "He got away."

Because her legs turned to rubber, she grabbed the door. Mason caught on to her.

"We'll get him," Mason promised her.

But she wasn't sure that was a promise Mason or anyone else could keep.

Gage jumped the fence and made it to her, barreling up the steps two at a time. He took over the duty of holding on to her, but he pulled her into his arms.

"We're leaving," he whispered. *"Now."*

He didn't say anything else. Gage took the Colt from her, stuffed it in the back waist of his jeans, and they hurried toward the bullet-riddled truck.

Chapter Thirteen

Gage parked the truck directly in front of the back entrance to the sheriff's office. After what had happened the last time they were here, he didn't want to take any chances, and he darn sure didn't want them to be out in the open any longer than necessary.

He hurried Lynette to the door that he knew would be unlocked, temporarily, because Gage had called ahead to arrange it. He didn't want anything slowing them down.

And he didn't want any more unnecessary risks.

There were no guarantees that Dalvetti wouldn't come after them here, but it was the safest place Gage could come up with on such short notice. It was a start, but he needed to make it as safe as possible for Lynette.

So he could go after Dalvetti and her father.

Gage was going to end this.

Now that he had the hall light to see her face, Gage gave Lynette a quick check. No signs of injury. Well, not physical ones anyway. But he didn't want to know what all this stress and danger were doing to her and the baby. He certainly wasn't dealing with it well. He wanted someone to pay and pay hard for this.

"Gage," he heard someone say at the exact moment he heard footsteps.

He looked up the hall and spotted his baby brother

Kade and a petite brunette with a rifle making their way
toward them. Gage wasn't sure of the reaction he'd get.
He had turned his back on his family ten years ago when
he left town.

And on Lynette.

Now, he had some fences to mend if he wanted to get
back into the fold.

He did want that, he realized.

Not just because he wanted family around for his child,
but because he needed them.

Gage locked the door and walked closer, bracing himself for Kade's reaction. He'd spoken to Kade about un-
locking the door, but it'd been a ten-second conversation
at most. Too short to determine his brother's feelings
about his return from the dead.

But Kade only smiled and pulled him into a long, hard
hug.

"Glad you're back," Kade whispered. "Wish it were
under better circumstances."

"Me, too," Gage agreed.

Kade pulled back, stepped to the side and eased his
arm around the brunette's shoulder. "My wife, Bree. Bree,
this is your other brother-in-law, Gage."

Bree smiled. "I have a lot of them." She shook Gage's
hand with a grip a lot firmer than he'd expected from
someone who barely came up to his shoulder, and then
she looked at Lynette. "Are you doing okay?"

Lynette gave a hollow laugh. "Been better."

"Yes, I heard. Mason called, told us all about it. A
shoot-out with a drug kingpin isn't my idea of a restful
evening, either."

Gage could attest firsthand that was true.

"How are the twins—Leah and Mia?" Lynette asked

Bree, making Gage realize that she had kept in touch with his family. Or at least kept up with the gossip.

Bree nodded. "They're good. Growing like weeds and probably giving the nanny some gray hairs because they're still not sleeping through the night." Bree combed her gaze over Gage. "You can tell you're a Ryland. You look like the rest of them. I'm betting you're as hard-headed, too."

"Oh, he is. The worst of the lot." Kade flexed his eyebrows and managed a thin smile. A smile that quickly faded. "Nate's on the way here. You haven't seen Dade or him yet."

Gage shook his head. "But I don't want them here if it means putting the rest of the family in danger. They have wives and kids to protect."

"We're working on that," Kade assured him. "Grayson's at the hospital with Eve. She's still in labor."

"Might be a long one," Bree added in a mumble.

Gage silently cursed Dalvetti and Ford again. Lynette and he should be at the hospital, happily awaiting the birth of Grayson's firstborn, but instead they were on the run for their lives. And maybe putting others in danger by being in danger themselves.

"Dade's in San Antonio with the others," Kade continued. "But SAPD, Nate's men, will take over security detail when Dade comes here."

So, the plan was for him to have four brothers and a very capable-looking sister-in-law for backup.

Gage wasn't going to refuse any of their help.

Lynette came first, and that meant swallowing his fears about their safety. Plus, there was the fact that he didn't trust anyone as much as he trusted his siblings.

"Darcy dropped by earlier," Bree explained, looking at Lynette now. "She brought you some clothes and toiletries that she got from your house. Your cell phone, too. Darcy wasn't sure which clothes to pack so she just got some things from your closet and drawers."

"Whatever she brought will be fine, I'm sure. I'll thank her the next time I see her."

Bree hitched her thumb to the stairs. "There's an apartment you can use to get some rest and a shower if you want. It's not much more than a flop room, but no one is going to get in this place to come after you."

"Bree's former FBI," Kade supplied. "And both of us have sniper training."

That might come in handy, and it was a reminder that Bree obviously fit well into the family. Kade had done good.

"If it comes down to needing long-range shooters," Kade continued, "we can use me and Bree." But then he huffed. "Even though I'd prefer Bree not be in the line of fire."

Bree came up on her toes and kissed him. "I can take care of myself."

"I'd rather not risk it."

Gage understood that, too. And he wouldn't take the chance, either. It was obvious his kid brother was crazy in love, and it would make Kade just plain crazy if he knew his wife's life was at more risk than necessary. He'd work it so Bree was on protection detail for Lynette. Neither woman would probably like that much, but he didn't want them on the front lines.

"Too bad Patrick's not a suspect," Lynette mumbled.

Yeah, too bad. "Patrick took out one of Dalvetti's men," Gage explained.

That seemed to surprise Kade as much as it had surprised Gage. "You think that means Patrick's not behind any of this?" Kade asked.

Gage shook his head. "I'm not sure. Heck, Patrick could have set up that entire attack and then killed the gunman just to take blame off himself."

Kade and Bree made sounds of agreement. Lynette, too. So, Patrick was still on their short list of suspects despite having done them a favor. That list wasn't getting any shorter, and it might be a while before they could eliminate a name or two.

"I just want this to end," Lynette said. Gage heard the fatigue and knew the adrenaline crash was coming. He was sure feeling it.

"It will," Kade promised her. He gave Lynette's arm a gentle squeeze. "This is our fight now, too."

So, four brothers and a sister. But even that didn't mean good odds. "Sampson Dalvetti is rich and ruthless. He won't come alone. He's probably regrouping right now and assembling a new team of assassins."

"I read his file," Kade said. "He's not stupid, either, and that means he probably won't come here gunning for trouble. Not in the middle of town."

Gage hoped that was true, but he wasn't going to base Lynette's safety on hope. No. He had to get Lynette settled into the apartment, make a few more security arrangements, and then he needed to call her father.

Something Gage didn't intend to tell Lynette.

There was a knock at the front door, and all of them turned in that direction. All of them groaned. Gage and Kade cursed, as well.

"I'll get rid of her," Kade mumbled, and he headed toward the glass door where Gage could see Nicole waiting and knocking again.

"You think she got that court order to put me back in the loony bin?" Lynette asked.

Gage shrugged and tried to give Lynette a reassuring

glance. When that didn't work, he kissed her, and then followed Bree and his brother.

Apparently, this long-assed day wasn't over yet.

"Why don't you wait upstairs in the apartment?" Gage suggested to Lynette. But as expected, she went with him to the front door.

And he couldn't blame her. Nicole was trying to railroad her, and Gage could understand Lynette's need to face down the woman.

Kade unlocked the door but used his body to block Nicole from coming in. "What do you want?" he snarled.

"Your help." Nicole's voice didn't sound any steadier than Lynette's.

Nicole looked past Kade, and her attention landed on Lynette. "I need your help, too."

"Really?" Lynette challenged. She folded her arms over her chest. "With what? You want me to have myself committed to the asylum so it'll cut down on the time you're spending on this witch hunt?"

"No. That *witch hunt* is over. On my part anyway. I can't say the same for your father or Patrick."

"Patrick?" Lynette challenged. "So, now he'll try to have me committed?"

Nicole groaned softly and shoved her perfectly styled hair from her perfectly made-up face. "I don't know what Patrick will try to do. Kill you, maybe. Because he believes you're trying to send him to jail."

"We are," Gage volunteered. "If he's done anything that warrants jail. Did he?"

For a moment Gage thought she might answer, but Nicole only shook her head. "I have enough enemies without making one of Patrick." She looked at Lynette again. "I'm here because of your father." She paused a heartbeat. "Ford knows."

Nicole dropped her gaze to Lynette's stomach.

And to the baby.

"Ford knows," Nicole repeated.

KADE AND BREE LOOKED at Lynette, and they obviously wanted an explanation about what the heck was going on.

Lynette wanted the same thing.

Gage kept his right hand over his gun, but he moved closer to her, until they were shoulder to shoulder. And he waited just as Lynette did, because she wasn't about to volunteer anything to Nicole. This could be a fishing expedition.

"Ford knows you're pregnant," Nicole clarified.

So, no fishing expedition. Lynette pulled in her breath and wondered just how bad things would get now. Pretty bad. Because this would only enrage her father even more, and it might even explain why Dalvetti had attacked them.

"You're pregnant?" Kade asked.

Lynette nodded.

"It's Gage's baby," Nicole supplied. "Ford knows that, too."

Gage stared at Nicole. "Am I supposed to care a rat's butt that my spit wad of a father-in-law knows my wife is pregnant?" Gage glanced at his brother. "Yeah, Lynette and I are still married. Long story."

"I didn't get the annulment," Lynette volunteered.

Gage shrugged. "So, maybe not so long after all." He turned back to Nicole. "Did you think I'd be shaking in my boots? Well, I'm not. And if Ford sent you here—"

"He didn't," Nicole interrupted.

"Then why the heck are you here?" Gage demanded.

Nicole looked away, mumbled something that Lynette didn't catch. "Ford blackmailed me into starting the paperwork to have Lynette committed. I, uh, did some things. Things that Ford said Lynette found when she was investigating me."

Lynette shook her head. "I found nothing, and you're only implicating yourself by coming here like this."

"I had to warn you," Nicole countered.

Gage gave the woman a skeptical look that Lynette was certain matched hers. She was even more skeptical because Patrick had come to the guesthouse to make a similar whine, and it had been the start of Dalvetti's attack.

"It's true. I'm trying to help you," Nicole insisted. "All I ask in return is immunity if any charges are filed against me."

Sheesh. Another immunity deal. Both Patrick and Nicole must think she'd dug up some pretty smelly dirt for them to react this way.

"No deal," Gage assured Nicole.

Lynette mumbled an agreement. She'd had enough from all the vipers involved, or potentially involved, in this. "If you don't mind, Gage and I will decline your *help.*"

"Fine," Nicole snapped. But she didn't budge. Her red-lacquered mouth tightened into a fine line.

"If there's nothing else…" Gage prompted. He nudged Lynette to get moving.

"Wait!" Nicole called out.

Lynette and Gage did, but it took several seconds for Nicole to continue. "About a year ago, Ford had a tracking device put on your car. When you went to San Antonio to see that doctor, it only took Ford about an hour to bribe him into telling him what you were up to."

Lynette cursed the fear that coiled through her, and then she cursed that her father had violated every moment of her privacy. She didn't want him having even a thought of her precious baby in his monstrous mind.

"Ford didn't think you'd go through with the insemination," Nicole added. "He thought you'd realize how much he hates Gage and do the right thing."

Lynette met her eye to eye. "I did the right thing." And since she was as tired of the fear as she was this conversation, she turned again to go to the apartment.

"Ford brought that drug dealer here," Nicole called out.

That stopped Lynette, only because it stopped Gage. Lynette wondered if Nicole was aware that Patrick had made the same accusation.

"What do you know about Dalvetti?" Gage pressed.

Nicole drew in a weary breath. "I know Ford would do anything to get you out of Lynette's life."

Gage lifted his shoulder. "Hard to do that now that she's carrying my baby."

Now, Nicole swallowed hard. Maybe faked. Maybe real. She also glanced away from them. "Ford has no intentions of letting this baby arrive into the world."

The rage that went through her was instant. Gage tried to catch on to her, but Lynette scrambled over the reception counter. She latched on to Nicole and slammed her against the glass door.

Lynette tried to speak, to yell, scream, anything, but the words couldn't make it through her clamped throat. How dare her father threaten her child.

Gage eased her away from Nicole, but then he got in the woman's face. "Tell Ford I'll deal with him soon."

The fury in Gage's voice was nothing compared to the look he shot Nicole. The woman gave a shaky nod and hurried out the door.

Lynette stood there, watching Nicole scurry away.

Oh, God.

She could feel the showdown coming. And Lynette prayed that Gage wouldn't die trying to protect their child.

Chapter Fourteen

Gage glanced around the apartment above the sheriff's office to see if he'd done everything to make it as safe as possible.

He'd pulled down the blinds. No lights were on. The door was locked. He had two guns, a rifle, and the windows were rigged with security sensors that would alert them if anyone tried to break in. He had a cell phone, walkie-talkie and a landline phone.

Of course, the best security measures were downstairs. Mason, Dade, Nate, Kade and Bree.

The Rylands were on duty. Or as Mason always liked to say "justice isn't just coming—it's already here." Gage was counting heavily on that to get them through this night.

Gage glanced around the apartment again. Double-checking. He couldn't see anything that needed correction. Now, all that was left was to make Lynette get some rest. That might not be easy since she was watching him like a hawk. No doubt worried that he'd go off half-cocked to confront her father about the threat he'd made to the baby.

And he *would* confront Ford.

Gage just wouldn't do it half-cocked though.

No, it was best to do these things with a cool head.

Hopefully, he could choke down his anger and do that. But Gage was actually looking forward to beating some sense into Ford even if there would be consequences to pay for that.

"You didn't eat much," Lynette told him.

She was seated on the sofa finishing off one of the sandwiches Nate had brought. Gage had had to play dirty again when she'd at first said she wasn't hungry. He'd asked her to eat for the baby's sake.

And she had.

Not just the sandwich but some milk and an apple. He made a mental note to use that trick again if necessary.

"I'll eat more later," he promised. But right now, he felt like a wet gym bag, and this might be the only lull he got to wash off some of the grime from the earlier attack. He took his grandfather's Colt from the back waist of his jeans and put it on the countertop of the makeshift kitchen. "I need to grab a shower."

Gage hadn't tossed that out there without thinking it through. He knew it couldn't be just a shower. Because there was no way he would leave Lynette in the room alone. Of course, he could get one of his brothers to sit with her, but he preferred them doing guard duty downstairs so that all the windows and doors were covered.

"You'll have to come in the bathroom with me while I shower," he said.

She stood, slowly, and even in the dim light he saw her turn toward him. Also slowly. She was staring at him. He could feel it.

And he could also feel the air drain right out of the room.

"Are you keeping on your clothes for that?" she asked.

He gave her a scowl that she couldn't see, but she no

doubt knew it was there. "No," he mumbled. "And that should make things interesting, huh?"

"Not if I can't see you," she mumbled back.

Oh, yeah. This was going to be torture. But necessary. When he told her the part about his going after her father, Gage would want to pull her into his arms. To steady her, and to steady himself. He didn't want her keeling over from the smell of gunshot residue, sweat and mud.

Even if a shower could lead to things best left alone.

He walked ahead of her into the tiny bathroom. Since there was only one small window, it was even darker than the main room, and Gage intended for it to stay that way. He didn't want to risk that someone could use the lights to target them with a long-range rifle. And he had firsthand knowledge that Dalvetti liked to arm his goons with rifles.

The rocket launcher had been a surprise though.

Gage hadn't heard of the man using one before. Maybe that had been Ford's little contribution to the assault. But Ford, Dalvetti or his men hopefully wouldn't get close enough to the sheriff's office to use a weapon like that. That's because Mason had set up barricades that blocked off streets on all sides. Plus, one of Kade's coworkers and Kade were on the roof with sniper rifles. If Dalvetti tried to get near the place, he'd be stopped. For good.

"Stay put," he warned Lynette when she was in the doorway of the bathroom. "I'll hurry."

He stripped down, fully aware that she didn't take her attention off him. Heck, he would have done the same if she'd been the one going bare. In fact, maybe he could reverse it when he was done. Seeing Lynette naked would make him feel a whole lot better.

For a few seconds anyway.

And then that good feeling would lead to sex. As much as Gage wanted that—and he wanted it bad—he wasn't sure she needed him inside her while she was going through all this emotional turmoil.

"You got a tattoo," Lynette commented. She sank down onto the floor, her back against the closed door.

Obviously, the room wasn't as dark as he thought.

"Yeah." A heart with a dagger through it on his right shoulder. "I was pretty mad about that annulment I thought you got."

She laughed, and the sound rippled through him.

Gage mentally cursed, threw back the shower curtain and turned the water on as hot as it would go. He probably should have chosen cold, but he was already sure he was fighting a losing battle here.

He took his time, lathered up twice, rinsed and re-rinsed, hoping that exhaustion would cause Lynette to fall asleep—something both the baby and she needed. He needed it for them, too, so it would give him one less thing to worry about. But when Gage turned off the water and opened the curtain back up, Lynette wasn't asleep.

She was staring at him.

Correction: she was *waiting* for him.

Gage knew her well enough to know the difference.

He waited, too, hoping that sanity and common sense would kick in.

Nope, they didn't.

He had the willpower of a termite on wood when it came to Lynette.

"You're sure you're up for this?" he clarified.

"I'm not the one who needs to be up." And she chuckled again.

Gage groaned.

Yes, this would be a special kind of sweet torture.

He grabbed a towel, dried his face and stepped from

the tub. The two-second debate he intended to have with himself didn't even last that long. A split second, tops.

"Let's just go for it," she whispered, "and we'll work out the rest later."

There was no way he could refuse that, especially since he'd already reached the same conclusion. "Deal," he agreed.

Dripping wet and already burning for her, he hooked the towel around the back of her neck, dropped down and pulled her to him. Everything happened fast. Like a train wreck.

Like a fantasy.

His mouth took hers, and the thoughts in his head, and the doubts, turned to ash.

"Gage," she whispered.

That got through the ash, and he realized that his name coming from her lips was what he wanted most.

Well, one of the things he wanted anyway.

He amped up the kiss, letting himself savor the taste of her. Man, he'd missed her. His body had been with other women—something he'd keep to himself—but in his mind, he'd only ever made love to Lynette. Even when he hated her, or believed he did, he couldn't stop himself from thinking of her.

And now, he didn't have to think.

He was with her again.

Good thing, too, because she dropped some kisses on his neck that created more ash in his brain. She didn't stop there. Lynette coiled her warm arms around him and pulled him closer until she was pressed against him and it was impossible to tell where her body ended and his began.

The kiss got hotter and hungrier in a hurry.

Lynette and he could never just keep things simple.

They kissed until they finally had to break for air or
suffocate. They gasped for breath and then went right
back at each other. A kissing battle, raging. But as he
could have predicted, kisses only made his body want
more.

He did *more*.

Gage slid his hand up her top and touched her breasts.
She was perfect. Small and soft. He got the reaction he
wanted— She made a breathy moan and climbed into his
lap with her sex aligned right against his. It was good.
Old memories slammed with new ones that they were
about to make.

But it wasn't enough.

He needed her naked, and he needed to be inside her.
Gage stripped off her top. Her bra. And kissed her the
way he wanted to kiss her.

She made another breathy moan.

And she did some touching of her own. Her hand dal-
lied on his chest, pecking at the coils of hair there, but
then she moved downward. To his stomach.

Oh, man.

He'd forgotten that she knew all his hot spots. Those
all-knowing fingers went down his stomach and to pay-
dirt territory. She wrapped her fingers around his erection.

That sped things up. After he got his eyes uncrossed,
that is.

Gage considered taking her into the other room and to
the bed, but he doubted they'd make it there. Since they
were already on the floor, that'd have to do.

Lynette had the same idea because without breaking
the kiss, she started to lower herself onto the floor.

"No deal. The floor's hard and cold," he reminded her.
"It'll leave tile marks on your butt."

She chuckled, but there was a nervous edge to it. "Then figure out something fast."

He did.

Gage turned her, putting her back against the door again, and he yanked off those loose sweatpants and panties so her butt was on the rug, not the tile.

Naked, finally.

There were no more obstacles. He fastened her legs around his waist and lifted her back onto his lap.

Gage kept kissing her and wanted to apologize for the short foreplay, but it was clear she didn't want foreplay any more than he did. She drew back her hand, and Gage pushed into her.

His head exploded.

Thank goodness other parts of him didn't do the same.

But it was a challenge. She was made for him. Made to send jolts of pleasure through every inch of him. Maybe Lynette felt the same about him, because she stilled for a moment.

He heard a sound he didn't want to hear.

And he froze. "You're crying?"

"Good crying," she assured him. "I've missed you more… Well, just more."

Gage held his breath, waiting.

"I'll respect you in the morning," she added.

He might have smiled at her joke if she didn't start moving, her hips pushing forward to take him deeper inside her. Gage tried to keep things gentle. He caught on to her hips, to set the pace and slow things down.

That didn't work, either.

Her mouth came to his, and she smothered him with one of those scalding-hot French kisses. *Slow down* went out the window. Taking her was all that mattered now. Finishing this.

Finishing *her*.

Gage slid his hand between their bodies, to add some touches to the now frantic strokes. It wouldn't take much. He knew as much about her hot buttons as she knew about his. That's why she took that kiss to his neck.

Yeah.

More pay dirt.

Gage felt his vision blur but kept touching her. Even when she shattered around him, he touched her.

He kissed her.

Lynette's mouth was on his when he gathered her into his arms. And Gage let himself fall fast and hard.

Chapter Fifteen

Other than the bad timing, Lynette had no regrets about having sex with Gage. She'd waited a long time to be back in his arms, and she would deal with the regrets later.

Especially one.

She didn't want Gage to feel trapped in the life she had created for herself. A life with a baby. There probably weren't any CIA assignments nearby in Silver Creek, which meant, well, he could feel trapped.

Of course, she didn't want him trapped in her backup plan, either. That's what the condo in Dallas was all about. She'd already created a fake identity and arranged for a job there so she could keep her pregnancy and baby from her father. With that cat now out of the proverbial bag, she wasn't sure where she should go. Or what she should do. But she didn't want Gage caught up in this unless it was what he wanted with all his heart and soul.

She'd seen no signs of that.

Yes, he wanted her. Her body. Even the baby. But she wasn't sure he'd gotten past what had happened all those years ago. She certainly wasn't sure he loved her.

Later, once she'd caught her breath and he'd caught his, she'd give him an out. And she had to brace herself in case he jumped at the chance to take it. Ten years was a long time, and she might not know this Gage as well as she'd known the kid who had proposed to her all those years ago.

Gage scooped her up off the floor, and with them both stark naked, he walked into the main room and deposited her on the bed. But not before giving her one of those mind-numbing kisses to make her head fuzzy again and her body hot.

"Don't get dressed yet," she whispered when he started back toward the bathroom where he'd left his clothes. Hers, too.

"My brothers will be here soon," he reminded her. "I need to go over the security plans with them and make sure every inch of the place is protected."

All that was necessary, but it would also be a reunion, the first time they'd been together in years. Lynette figured they had some catching up to do.

"Give me a minute." And she pulled him onto the bed with her.

Yes. That was her body's first reaction. She'd just had Gage, literally, but holding him naked like this was almost as good as the sex.

Almost.

She ran her hands over his chest and to his back, where those corded muscles responded to her touch. And then her hands went lower.

"Playing?" he teased.

"Remembering," she countered.

She put her face against the curve of his neck and took in his musky male scent. Oh, mercy. It was the best kind of memory. That scent had her numb, and just like that she was ready for him all over again.

Gage did some playing of his own. He pushed her hair aside, his fingers lingering on her face.

"You should come with a warning label," he said, repeating what she'd told him earlier. "Dangerous curves ahead."

She laughed, and it felt so good to be in this moment with Gage. But the moment couldn't last. Both knew it. And that's why he kissed her again.

"When this is over, we'll talk," he assured her. He didn't elaborate or even mention the subject. Didn't have to. He wanted to have an *us* talk, and she needed to have an *out* talk. She feared both.

"Maybe we'll even do more of this," Gage added.

More of this sounded perfect and made Lynette want to delay the talk for months and months because it might lead to Gage leaving again.

"My brothers," he reminded her, and he left her to get his clothes. "You stay put, though. I want you and the baby to get some rest."

She needed rest. There was no denying that, but she had no intentions of being naked in bed when his brothers stopped by to see him.

"Bring me back my bra," she reminded him. She didn't want her ring to fall out and get lost.

"Bra detail," he joked. "My favorite."

Lynette gave a weary sigh, got up, as well, and in the murky light she located the overnight bag that Darcy had packed for her. Even though she couldn't actually see the jeans, top and underwear, she put them on and welcomed the clean clothes.

Her cell phone, too.

Lynette turned it on and saw the eleven missed calls from her father. He'd left voice mails, too, but she didn't even bother with them.

"Rest," Gage repeated when he came out of the bathroom. He put her bra in the overnight bag. And to make sure that *rest* would happen, he picked her up again, put her back in bed and draped the comforter over her.

"I'd rest better with you."

"You wouldn't rest at all with me." He kissed her again. "I'm staying close, on the stairs, and I'll leave the door open so I can see you. Sleep," he insisted. "Tomorrow, we'll work out what we're going to do about Dalvetti."

Maybe by then this fuzzy haze wouldn't be clouding her head. Heck, while she was hoping, maybe Dalvetti and her father would wipe each other off the face of the earth.

Lynette watched through the murkiness as Gage walked away from her and to the door. When he opened it, she could just make out the others who were already there. Four of his brothers—Nate, Dade, Kade and Mason. Nate and Dade hugged him. Spoke in whispers. And Gage eased the door partially shut, so that she could see only him.

And he could see her.

She tried to listen to what they were saying. There was a lot of catching up to do, and she wondered if Gage would tell his brothers that he was still married to her and that they had a baby on the way. Lynette also wondered if he would tell them how he felt about her.

Because he sure as heck hadn't told her.

With that thought she drew in an exhausted breath, and even though she fought it, Lynette couldn't keep her eyelids from drifting down.

She fell asleep with the taste of Gage's kisses still on her lips.

GAGE WAITED until he was sure Lynette was asleep. His brothers were waiting for that, too, even though he hadn't actually said that there were things he preferred that Lynette didn't hear.

Things she wasn't going to like.

"Lynette's pregnant," Gage said in case one of them hadn't gotten the word. Apparently, they had. Later, he'd explain how the pregnancy had come about, but that could wait. "If this danger continues, I'm worried she could lose the baby." He was more worried that he could lose her.

"So, what's the plan?" Dade asked without hesitation.

That put a lump in Gage's throat. It'd been a while since someone had had his back like this. "I'm starting with Ford Herrington. He's a killer, plain and simple, and he's not going to stop until someone dies. I'm sure that I'm on top of his to-murder list, but he's brought Lynette into this, and it has to stop."

"A showdown," Nate concurred. "How? When? What do you need from us?"

"I need Lynette protected first." Gage looked at Mason, who had his back against the stairwell wall, his feet crossed at the ankles. Then Nate. Then Dade. "I need you to stay here and make sure no one gets to her."

"Bree can give Mason some backup," Kade suggested. "Both deputies, too."

Gage nodded. No doubt Kade wanted that so he could keep his wife out of direct harm's way. Gage understood that completely. But even with six lawmen guarding Lynette, he worried it might not be enough.

"Call in anyone you trust from the ranch," Gage continued. "I can't use my people because there might be some kind of leak in communication. But I want to make this building a fortress, and that includes more people on the roof who can stop a sniper or rocket launcher attack."

All of them nodded.

Kade turned to him. "And what will I be doing?"

"You'll be here, too, and keeping a safe distance from

me," Gage assured him. "I have no plans to make Bree a widow."

"Sounds like you're planning to make Lynette one," Mason growled. "If Kade keeps a safe distance from you, that means you're pretty much going in somewhere alone."

Gage couldn't disagree with that. "I'll call Ford and arrange a meeting at the city hall building. Before I make the call, Mason and I will already be in place there, and Mason will be on the roof watching in case Ford tries to pull something."

"Ford *will* try to pull something," Nate spoke up.

Still no argument from Gage. "I don't want to take any more of you away from this building. Lynette comes first, understand?"

"So, you're just going to meet with Ford and have a nice friendly chat?" Mason asked, and he didn't bother to take out the snark.

Now, Gage could disagree. "It won't be friendly. But one way or another the danger from him stops tonight. Then, in the morning I can deal with Dalvetti—*alone,*" Gage added before any of them could ask.

"Last I heard there was no *I* in team or brothers," Mason mumbled.

"I can't risk your lives."

"To hell you can't," Mason fired back. He stooped down so they were all eye level. "You want to stop Ford Herrington tonight, then put us all to good use. Together, we can stop him."

Gage stood, shook his head. "Protect Lynette," he repeated.

He didn't wait for their assurances. Didn't need them. They might not agree with his plan, but they would do it. And right now, keeping Lynette and his baby alive was the only thing that mattered.

Chapter Sixteen

The beeping sound woke Lynette. She sat up in the bed and automatically reached for Gage, only to remember that he wasn't there. He was with his brothers.

Lynette tried to settle her breathing. Her stomach, too, since the sudden movement had caused a wave of nausea to come over her. She prayed this wasn't the start of a bout of morning sickness, because the timing sucked. There were already too many things on Gage's and her minds.

She heard the beep again, and this time she realized it was her cell phone, letting her know that she had another voice mail. Lynette glanced at the clock. It was nearly midnight. And there was only one person who'd call her at this hour.

Her father.

And she didn't want to speak to him.

She threw back the covers and looked around. Listened, too. She could no longer hear the whispered conversations on the stairwell. That caused her to jump from the bed, and despite the sick feeling in her stomach, she hurried to the ajar door.

No one was on the stairs.

And the place was way too quiet.

Except for her phone. It beeped again.

Lynette grabbed the cell from the bag and jammed

the button to retrieve her calls, and she quickly learned that she'd been right. It was her father. She pressed another button to listen to the message that he'd left just seconds earlier.

"I'm meeting with Gage at the courthouse in ten minutes," her father's recorded voice said. "Call me now."

Oh, God.

Lynette's hands started to shake, but somehow she managed to return the call. "What have you done?" she asked the second he answered.

"Nothing. Not yet anyway. Gage called me earlier and set up a meeting at the courthouse. I got the distinct impression he was going to try to kill me."

No. Gage couldn't arrange a meeting like this behind her back. It wasn't just dangerous. It could be suicide.

"I'm assuming no one else is listening in on this call, but just in case, I'll mince words."

A veiled threat was no doubt coming, and Lynette tried to brace herself for it. What she wanted to do was reach through the phone and tear her father to shreds. But for now her best bet was to listen to what Gage and he had done and then try to figure out how to keep Gage alive.

"Gage and I are going to *talk*," her father said. There it was, the veiled threat. "If you don't come, too, then you'll be very sorry. You could lose the things that matter most to you. And Gage, well, Gage could lose a lot more than that."

His words fired through her and nearly brought Lynette to her knees.

"If you call Gage to warn him," her father continued, "then it'll only make things worse. I'll see you in a few minutes. Oh, and, Lynette, this would be a good time to obey your father."

Lynette slapped the phone shut, hurriedly put on her

shoes and grabbed the gun that Gage had left for her on the dresser. She ran down the steps, praying that her father had been lying and that she'd find all the Rylands there.

She didn't.

No one was in any of the offices that she raced past, and the lights had all been turned out. Something was wrong.

"Gage?" she called out.

"Stay there," someone answered. Not Gage. But Kade. He came out from the pitch-black reception area by the front door, and he made his way down the hall toward her.

"Where's Gage?" she asked, and she felt the terror crawling up her spine.

That feeling only got worse when Kade didn't answer right away. "He's meeting with your father."

Oh, mercy. The call wasn't a hoax. Her father had managed to set up what she'd thought would be impossible. "It's a trap. My father just called and said if I didn't show up at the courthouse that I could lose Gage. I have to go to that meeting."

Kade shook his head. "Gage's orders are for you to stay put. Don't worry," Kade added. "We've covered the entire place. Nate, Bree and some other FBI agents are on the roof. Dade is guarding the back of the building. Dalvetti and his men can't get within a quarter of a mile of this place without us knowing."

"But I could tell by the way he was talking that my father intends to kill Gage at the courthouse."

Kade caught on to her arm to keep her from bolting. "Gage has everything set up. Some of the ranch hands are watching the courthouse to make sure Ford doesn't pull anything. And Mason is there, too. He's on the roof of the adjacent building."

It wasn't enough. Not nearly enough. "Gage went in alone to that meeting?"

Kade didn't answer. He didn't have to. Because she knew that's exactly what Gage had done.

"I have to help him," Lynette insisted.

"You can't. Gage wants you to stay here."

Lynette threw off his grip and got right in Kade's face. "I'm not asking for your permission. I'm helping Gage, period."

She started down the hall toward the back exit, but Kade raced after her. He took her arm again and whirled her around.

"Gage said I was to tell you to think of the baby," Kade warned. "You can't put the baby in danger."

It took a moment for Lynette to steady her voice so she could speak. "I won't endanger the baby. I'll do everything to stay safe, but I have to help. I can't lose Gage. Not again." She stared at him, even though she could barely see his face. "Please."

"I can't let you go," he argued.

Lynette couldn't outmuscle him, and even though she hated to pull her gun on him, she would if it came down to it. Of course, Kade probably knew that she had no intention of shooting him. Her only intention now was to get to Gage in time to save him from her father.

"Please," Lynette repeated. "What if it were Bree out there instead of Gage?"

Another pause. Then Kade cursed. "But Gage will throttle me if I let you go."

"You're not letting me go. I'm doing this on my own."

She remembered seeing a jacket in Grayson's office so she hurried there to get it. Not for the warmth but so she could slip the gun in the pocket. She didn't want to go running up Main Street brandishing a Colt .45. Lynette located a raincoat, some extra ammunition, and then she spotted the tiny tape recorder on Grayson's desk.

It was a long shot, and it certainly hadn't worked in the past, but it might come in handy.

"Reconsider this," Kade warned her.

"No." And she didn't even have to think about her answer. She ran to the back exit and prayed she would get to Gage in time.

FORD HERRINGTON WAS LATE.

Gage checked his watch again and cursed. When he'd called Ford nearly two hours ago, the man had assured Gage that he was *eager* for them to talk.

Right.

More like Ford was eager to try to finish Gage off.

But that was all right. Gage didn't care why Lynette's father had agreed to meet with him, he was just glad all of this was about to come to a head.

"See anything?" Gage asked Mason through the walkie-talkie. Mason and two of his ranch hands were on the roof. Waiting. Just like Gage.

"Nothing other than Herman Smith staggering home drunk. All okay down there?"

"Peachy," Gage mumbled, and he clicked the button to end the conversation so he could keep watch around him.

The lobby of the courthouse wasn't exactly sprawling, but it had a curved staircase feeding off one side and a wide hall off the other. Plus, there were the doors and windows. It did have one big bonus though— It was surrounded on all four sides by parking lots and the street, and there wasn't a vehicle out there now that he had sent the night watchman home.

Neither Dalvetti nor Ford would make it across those open spaces without Mason or the ranch hands spotting them—especially since Gage was betting neither would come alone.

Another bonus to the courthouse was there were no convenient nearby buildings where gunmen could hide. Lynette's one-story newspaper office was on the left side. It was locked up, and he'd seen the red light blinking on the activated security alarm when he'd looked in the window.

On the front and back side of the courthouse were streets that Mason had blocked off. Someone could perhaps get through the barricade by ramming into it, but it would take a big vehicle and a determined driver.

That left the right side where there was a hotel under construction. Unfortunately, there were places to hide inside, which was why one of the ranch hands had specific orders to keep his eyes on it at all times.

Gage checked the time again. Cursed some more. And he thought of Lynette. Of how just hours earlier he'd taken her hard and fast on the bathroom floor. Hardly romantic. He owed her something better.

Hell, he owed her something better than him.

He truly had been trouble for her, and he wasn't sure he could give her the normal, quiet life that she craved.

"Incoming," Mason said over the walkie-talkie. "It's Ford, and he has two goons with him."

Gage immediately pushed aside the thoughts of Lynette, took a deep breath and readied himself. "I'll let them in."

"All of them?" Mason questioned.

"Yeah, I'll be careful." Gage cut off whatever Mason was about to argue, and clipped the walkie-talkie to his belt so his hands would be free.

He went to the front door, unlocked it and then stepped back into the shadows at the edge of the hall. There was a gun in his right hand, another in the back waist of his jeans, and his jacket pocket was crammed with extra ammunition. He wasn't much for wearing Kevlar, but for this meeting Gage had made an exception and borrowed one from Grayson's office.

Ford had killed at least once, and Gage was betting that his goons and he wouldn't hesitate to kill again.

One of the goons came in first with his gun already drawn. Then Ford, followed by the third man holding a weapon. All wore dark clothes and stayed by the door. The guards looked around, probably trying to figure out the best place to take cover if shots were fired.

But there wasn't any cover.

It was another reason Gage had picked this place. If it came down to it, he could dive into the hall. Not exactly out of the line of fire, but it was better than trying to get back out that door.

Of course, he was outnumbered three to one.

"Check for bugs," Ford ordered the men. One stayed by him, but the other pulled a handheld device from his pocket. A transmitter detector. And he began to prowl around the room.

"What about Ryland's walkie-talkie?" one of the men asked.

Gage glanced down at it. "You want it? Come and get it."

"Hold off on that," Ford told his men. "He has some hand-to-hand combat skills, and I don't want to give him the opportunity to use them on you. Besides, no one on the other end of the walkie-talkie can hear what we're saying unless Gage pushes the button. He won't do that if he wants this meeting to continue."

Yeah, Gage wanted it to continue. And end. With Ford out of the picture one way or another.

"Gage," Ford repeated like profanity. "You've come to make a deal with me."

"I have." Best to keep this simple. "I want you to back off and leave Lynette alone."

"I can't," Ford quickly answered. "She has to pay for her disobedience. Imagine, my own daughter doing that. My only blood kin. I'm sure you know how painful something like would be."

Gage figured that could be a reference to the baby. Maybe even a cleverly worded threat. But he didn't bite. Not yet anyway.

"Look, we both know you're dirty," Gage continued, "but Lynette isn't going to look for proof of that. She stopped her investigation."

His bug-searching goon gave Ford a thumbs-up. "No one's listening but us."

Ford smiled then shook his head. "Lynette stopped her investigation too late."

"It's never too late," Gage countered.

Another headshake. "You seem to believe I have complete control over all of this. I don't. Patrick and Nicole are shaken up, too, and if one of them believes Lynette found anything incriminating, they'd be willing to do something about it. So, you see, I'm not the only person who might want to stop my daughter."

"She didn't find anything," Gage supplied.

"They think she's lying." Ford paused. "Lynette stopped digging for one reason— She decided that she wanted to test-drive motherhood. But I'm betting she found plenty before she got pregnant with your bastard child."

Okay, that chipped away at the temper that Gage was trying to keep in check. "Not a bastard," Gage calmly corrected. "Lynette and I are still married."

"An abomination of a marriage. That makes your baby an abomination, too."

"No, it makes this baby a Ryland." Gage huffed. "Are you trying to make me want to kill you? Because that's not necessary. I already want you dead."

There was just enough light that Gage saw Ford smile again. He motioned for his men to stay put, and he started toward Gage. Gage didn't aim his weapon at the man, not exactly, but he kept it ready just in case.

"Then go ahead." Ford came closer. Closer. And stopped just a few feet away. He outstretched his arms. "Shoot me. Right here, right now."

It wasn't even tempting. Okay, it was. But just briefly. "Pull first and I will."

"Chicken?" Ford taunted.

"Sane," Gage taunted back. "Can you say the same? And before you answer that, remember you killed your wife, had your daughter committed to the loony bin, spied on her, had her stalked. And now you want her dead."

All traces of Ford's smile vanished. "I never wanted Lynette dead. I just wanted a daughter who would love and respect me."

Gage wondered if Ford really wanted that or if he was just blowing smoke. "Committing multiple felonies is not the way to get love and respect."

"I'll never admit to those things," Ford snapped. "I don't care if anyone else is listening or not."

Gage shrugged. "That's not a way to get love and respect, either."

Definitely no smile this time. Ford's eyes narrowed. "You're just like your grandfather. He was cocky, too."

Gage hadn't intended to go there tonight, but he would now that Ford had opened the door. "Did you even have any proof he was sleeping with your wife?"

"Oh, yes. I followed her to his place. The place you later used to bed Lynette. The shame of the mother passed down to the daughter."

It turned Gage's stomach to hear this man's venom, especially when the venom was directed at Lynette. And at his grandfather.

"Did you kill him, too?" Gage came right out and asked.

Now, Ford smiled. "Wouldn't you love to know? Oh, and just so we're on the same page. If you're still alive when this conversation is over, you won't be leaving until my men have searched *you* for a wire. I like to keep my secrets safe within my own family."

Gage didn't intend to let Ford or one of his goon-guards lay a hand on him.

"So, I think what we have here is a stalemate," Ford continued. "You're not leaving with Lynette, and I'm not stopping until I find out what she learned from snooping in my private files."

"Yeah, you're right, we do have a stalemate." And that's all Gage said for several seconds. Ford's guards were already looking antsy, and a good, long pause would only add to it. "Well, maybe not. After all, I'm a better shot than either of those Neanderthals."

"I thought you didn't want to kill me."

"No. I do." Another pause. "It's just when your men get nervous enough—and they will—they'll fire. You'll pull your weapon, too. It's a reflex. Anyone armed would, and I know you're armed with a slide holster. Ankle, too." Gage took a step closer, lowered his voice to a whisper. "And when you pull is when you'll die."

And the staring match began.

Gage wasn't bluffing, so that helped. But he wasn't

sure how much longer it would take to make those two start firing.

The walkie-talkie made a soft buzzing sound, and without taking his eyes off Ford, Gage used his left hand to click it on.

"We got trouble," Mason said. Before Gage could even manage a word, his brother added, "It's Lynette. She just pulled up in a cruiser and parked in front of the courthouse steps."

Gage cursed.

Ford smiled.

"Lynette's not alone," Mason added. "Nate, Dade and Kade are with her."

That was good. Except there was something in Mason's voice that said otherwise. And there was definitely something up with Ford.

Why the devil had Lynette risked everything to come here?

Gage was sure he wouldn't like the answer.

"Lynette and the others aren't our only visitors," Mason explained. "Dalvetti and his men rammed through the road barriers I put up, and they just arrived, too."

There wasn't enough profanity in Gage's vocabulary to cover what he felt. Lynette was here. Why, he didn't know, but he did know she was in grave danger.

"Cover Lynette," Gage insisted, already heading for the door while he kept watch on the three vipers inside.

Gage pointed his gun at the two guards. "On the floor, hands behind your head."

They looked at Ford, and Gage held his breath. He didn't have time for this, and if they didn't do as he ordered, he'd have to neutralize them. Maybe a shot or two to the kneecaps. Yeah, he'd have to answer for it later, but it would give him a fighting chance at saving Lynette.

Ford gave his men a nod. Just that simple gesture. And the two lowered themselves to the floor. It was probably some kind of trap, a move they'd planned, but Gage had to deal with Lynette first.

Gage had barely taken a step when he heard something else that he hadn't wanted to hear.

A blast. Outside.

Right where the cruiser was parked.

Chapter Seventeen

The second that Kade brought the cruiser to a stop in front of the courthouse, Lynette tried to bolt. She had her gun drawn and ready, and she had to get to Gage *now*.

But Nate clamped his hand on her arm to stop her.

Good thing, too.

Because Lynette hadn't even gotten the door open when there was an explosion.

Her heart jumped to her throat.

Chunks of concrete and asphalt slammed into the cruiser, shaking it like an earthquake. One of those chunks flew into the front end and gashed the metal hood directly into the engine.

"I think someone just used a rocket launcher on us," Kade spit out. "Thank God they missed."

Yes, thank God. But it'd still done a lot of damage.

She couldn't see who'd fired it and didn't have time to look around. Dade dragged her into the backseat with him. He shoved her onto the floor and covered her body with his.

She heard Nate and Kade scrambling around in the front seat, and it was only a few seconds before Mason's voice poured through Kade's walkie-talkie.

"It's Dalvetti and his men. Three of them, all hiding behind the new hotel," Mason added. Each word was punctuated with a burst of his heavy breath. "I just took out the guy with the launcher, and none of the others has one."

Oh, mercy. Lynette was thankful Mason had managed to do that much. But it meant killers were still out there, and while they might not have another rocket launcher, they almost certainly had guns.

"Any of you hurt?" Mason asked.

Lynette did a quick inventory. The cruiser was damaged beyond repair, and they'd been darn lucky that the blast hadn't landed on them. She was certain all of Gage's brothers were thinking *I told you so,* but Lynette didn't regret her decision.

Not yet anyway.

"Where's Gage?" she shouted to Mason.

"Inside." Mason paused a heartbeat. "With your father and his two bodyguards."

Not bodyguards. Goons. Goons who would try to kill him if her father didn't do the job first.

"I've lost contact with Gage," Mason added a moment later.

He couldn't have said anything else that would have put that much terror in her. Sweet heaven. Were they holding Gage at gunpoint? Or had they already hurt him? She refused to even consider that it might be worse than that.

"Gage can handle himself," Mason reminded her.

Maybe, but he was outnumbered and therefore outgunned. Now, here they were pinned down, and they had to get to him so they could help.

"Where are Dalvetti and these gunmen?" Kade asked Mason. But the question had no sooner left his mouth when someone fired again.

This one slammed right into the driver's side of the cruiser. Whoever was shooting, the Rylands and she were clearly the target. And worse, the cruiser was disabled. There was no way Kade could drive them out of there.

The next bullet had a different sound and angle, and it took her a moment to realize it'd come from the roof of the courthouse.

"I got another one of them," Mason let them know. "Not Dalvetti himself though. He's staying back."

More shots, and this time they didn't come at the cruiser. There was a gunfight going down on Main Street, just yards from sleepy little shops.

"Is Lynette okay?" she heard someone ask.

Gage.

It was his voice now on the walkie-talkie.

"I'm fine. Are you all right?" Lynette couldn't ask Gage fast enough.

"Mad as the devil for you coming here." But his voice softened. "Yeah, I'm okay. Just trying to take out Dalvetti's men while playing stalemate with your father."

Lynette didn't like the sound of that. Or the next round of bullets. The shooters were hitting the cruiser again. One of the bullets gouged into the already damaged windshield.

"To heck with this," Kade snarled. "We have to get Lynette out of here."

More bullets came at them, nonstop now, but she could also hear Mason and the others on the rooftop returning fire. As Dade pinned her down on the floorboard, she was able to catch a glimpse of Gage.

Alive and unharmed.

He stepped out from the courthouse doorway and fired in Dalvetti's direction.

"Is it safe to get Lynette and the rest of us in there?" Kade asked.

"No. But from the looks of things out there, we don't have a choice. Get her in as fast as you can."

Kade did move fast. So did Dade. He pushed her to the side of the cruiser that was facing the courthouse doors. She was already wearing a Kevlar vest that Dade had given her before they left the sheriff's office, but as Gage had pointed out, that wouldn't help with a head shot.

"We're moving now," Dade told his brothers.

Lynette didn't know what Nate and Kade would do with that information, but they knew. While Dade got her out of the cruiser, both Nate and Kade started firing at Dalvetti and what was left of his hit squad.

Dade and she barreled up the three steps, and she got a closer look at Gage. She felt both the overwhelming relief in one breath, and in the next, she felt the overwhelming fear. With the bullets flying, they might not be *alive and unharmed* for long.

Gage didn't look directly at her. He kept his attention fastened to the shooters by her office. He took aim. And fired.

Three thick blasts.

She heard someone groan in pain, and from the corner of her eye, Lynette saw one of Dalvetti's gunmen fall to the ground.

When she made it to him, Gage latched on to her and pulled her inside. Dade was right behind them, but he stayed in the doorway and started delivering some shots of his own at Dalvetti.

"Why did you come?" Gage demanded. *"Why?"*

She shook her head and hated the worry and fear in his voice. "I didn't have a choice. My father called and made a veiled threat that if I didn't come, he'd kill you."

Gage took aim at the men on the floor. But then he glanced around the lobby and cursed. "He got away."

Because the thoughts and fear were flying through her head, it took her a moment to realize what Gage meant. She looked around, as well, and didn't see the one person responsible for all of his.

Her father was gone.

HELL. THIS WAS NOT the way Gage wanted all of this to play out.

All he'd wanted was to negotiate some kind of truce with Ford and then leave so he could take Lynette far away from Silver Creek. That way, all of them would have walked out alive.

But now, things had gotten complicated in a dangerous way.

Because Lynette was here.

And her father wasn't.

"Get down," Gage told Lynette, and he pointed to the staircase banister.

Gage was betting Ford hadn't used the stairs to escape since the stairs were right by the door where Gage had been standing. And shooting.

If *escape* was what Ford had actually done.

It was possible the man was lurking in that dark hall and was ready to strike. After all, there had to be a reason Ford had told Lynette to come here. Later, Gage would figure out what that reason was, and he was pretty sure he wasn't going to like it.

"Disarm these two," Gage told Dade. "And cuff them if you can."

The walkie-talkie buzzed again, and Gage hit the button while he inched his way toward the hall.

"The only one left outside is Dalvetti," Mason relayed. "I took out his other man. That's the good news. The bad news is that he's in a Hummer, and he's driving straight toward the courthouse. I think he's planning to drive up the steps and bash it through the front door."

Well, Gage hadn't thought this could get worse, but he'd obviously been wrong.

Gage looked out the front glass door where Nate and Kade were shooting at a massive black Hummer that was flying across the parking lot. The windows in the vehicle must have been bulletproof, because no shots seemed to be getting through.

They had seconds at most to get out of the path of that vehicle.

"Move!" Gage told Dade, who was still in the process of disarming Ford's henchmen.

Gage grabbed Lynette and started running. Yeah, it was a risk to use either the stairs or head to the hall, but at the moment the biggest risk of all was staying put. He started up the stairs with her.

Dade left the men and hurried to the back of the foyer by the hall. Neither of Ford's men stayed put, and Gage couldn't blame them. They scrambled out of the way.

"Watch out for Ford," Gage called down to warn his brother.

But he wasn't sure Dade heard him because at the exact moment Gage shouted that warning, Dalvetti's Hummer tore up the steps and came crashing through the doors.

Glass and wood flew everywhere, like missiles shooting in every direction. Even though Lynette and he were only halfway up the stairs, Gage stopped, shoved her behind him so that she wouldn't get hit with the flying debris, and he got ready to fire. So did Dade.

But not for long.

One of Ford's gunmen must have figured out this was a good time to make a bad situation worse because he drew a gun from the waist of his pants and took aim at

Dade. His brother dived into the hall just in the nick of time, and he came up ready to return fire.

The gunman's shot slammed into the wall, and he scrambled for cover, as well, on the side of a table stacked with pamphlets.

Behind him, Gage felt Lynette move and realized she, too, was taking aim at the second henchman who'd drawn his weapon. She fired, the blast roaring through Gage's head.

She missed.

And Gage volleyed his attention between Ford's men and Dalvetti's car. The windows were heavily tinted so he couldn't see the drug lord inside, but Gage had no doubt he was there. Ditto for his brothers outside. Nate, Kade and Mason would soon be coming in to help. The trick would be to make sure that none of them got killed in the process.

Especially Lynette.

When she took another shot at her father's men, Gage pushed her back down. He appreciated the help, but he didn't want her to be an easy target, not when shots could come from so many different directions.

"Stay down and watch behind us," he told her. Just in case he'd been wrong about Ford not using the stairs. He didn't want her father or anybody else sneaking up on them for an easy ambush.

There was another shot in Dade's direction, but Gage couldn't look to see what'd happened. That's because the door to the Hummer eased open just a fraction, a rifle barrel jutted out, and a bullet came zinging their way. It slammed into the wall behind them.

Gage sent a shot directly at the rifle.

He'd been right about the bulletproof part. His shot

collided into the glass, but it didn't penetrate. That meant he had to draw Dalvetti out of the vehicle.

Dalvetti fired again, and Gage had no choice but to get down as well. He tried to use his body to shield Lynette, but there was always a possibility that a bullet could go through him and hit her.

And the baby.

That sickened and riled him. This was the last thing he'd wanted for Lynette and the child.

Behind the Hummer, Gage could see Nate and Kade making their way up the steps. Both had their weapons drawn, and that meant Dalvetti was trapped.

Or maybe not.

The man fired off two more shots with his rifle, and Gage heard him hit the accelerator. Dalvetti was about to attempt an escape, and he just might get away with it. That couldn't happen. It would only give him a chance to regroup and come back again for another attack.

"Get out of the way!" Gage shouted to Nate and Kade.

They did. His brothers dived to the side just as the Hummer jolted backward.

Gage kept his gun aimed and was ready to race down the stairs after him, but the edge of the Hummer's door caught on to what was left of the courthouse entrance. The door flew open.

And Gage saw Dalvetti behind the wheel.

The look that passed between them only lasted a split second, but it was enough for Gage to see the awareness of his situation register in the man's murderous eyes.

Awareness and something else he didn't have the time to figure out.

Gage pulled the trigger.

Not once. But twice. And he sent two shots directly into Dalvetti's head.

It was never easy to kill a man, *never,* but Gage couldn't regret this one. Dalvetti would have murdered them all if Gage hadn't ended this now.

Except it hadn't ended.

Dalvetti hadn't been the only killer in the building. Gage swung in Dade's direction just as one of Ford's henchmen took aim again at his brother. Gage aimed, too, but the shots came from the front of the building.

From Kade and Nate.

Each of them took out Ford's men.

"We have to get out of here," Gage immediately told Lynette. Because while three men were dead, the most dangerous one of the lot was still missing. Plus, there was the possibility that Ford wasn't alone. Either Nicole or Patrick could be inside or nearby waiting to help Ford out.

Gage would have to postpone that fight.

After he had Lynette far away from this place.

"We can use the Hummer," Gage instructed.

He took Lynette's hand and got her moving down the stairs. That way, if Ford or someone else did start shooting, the bullets wouldn't be able to get to Lynette. Of course, that meant pulling Dalvetti's body out of the vehicle first, and it wouldn't be a pleasant task with Lynette right there to watch. Gage wished there were another way because Lynette had already seen enough death for one night.

Kade hurried to the driver's side of the Hummer, and he looked in. His brother cursed. "Get away from the vehicle!" he shouted. "Now!"

Gage didn't ask why, and neither did his other brothers. All of them started to run.

Nate and Kade raced back outside and Dade ran deeper

into the hall. Gage headed back upstairs with Lynette and
braced himself for whatever the hell was about to happen.
Behind them, the Hummer burst into flames.

Chapter Eighteen

Lynette caught just a glimpse of the fire before Gage put her back down on the steps and flattened himself over her.

"Dalvetti rigged the fire," she heard Gage say.

So, that's why it had simply burst into flames. Maybe the man had done that to destroy evidence. Or considering it was Dalvetti's vehicle, maybe it was meant to kill them. A way to reach out from beyond death and make sure they all died with him.

If they'd gotten inside, it might have done just that.

"The gas tank could explode," Gage told her.

Lynette hadn't exactly started to breathe easier, but she had thought for a moment that at least one threat was gone.

Apparently not.

Gage caught on to her again, pulling her to her feet, and they raced up the remainder of the steps together. She had just a glimpse of Nate and Kade, both outside, and both were hurrying across the parking lot and away from the Hummer time bomb. She couldn't see Dade, but she prayed he was doing the same.

When they reached the top, Gage slowed and looked around. First at the long stretch of offices just behind the balcony to their right and then at the equally long corridor on their left. Both were pitch-black, and he pushed up the light switch on the wall.

Nothing happened.

Lynette wanted to curse. "Someone's cut the power," she whispered.

Maybe Dalvetti or one of his men was responsible. Maybe her father. But she doubted it was a power outage. No. Someone had done this to give him or her an advantage for either escape or attack.

She figured with their luck, it was the latter.

"We have to find a way out," Gage insisted. "Keep watch behind us."

She managed a nod. Managed to make brief eye contact with him, too. Gage was focused on the situation, on getting them out of there, but he took a second to brush a kiss on her cheek. Then, he was all cowboy secret agent again.

Behind them, at the bottom of the stairs, there was a thick blast, a lot louder than the one that'd disabled the cruiser. It rumbled through the building, shaking every inch of it.

Oh, mercy.

Lynette had braced herself for the gas tank to explode, but she'd had no idea that it would be that loud. Framed pictures tumbled from the walls and crashed to the floor, and bits of the acoustic ceiling hailed down on them. But the walls held.

Thank God.

Now, she only hoped that Gage's brothers had gotten far enough away from the blast so they weren't injured. She hated every moment of this. The fear. The worry. The realization that Gage and his brothers could die because of her. Because of her father.

"There's a fire escape at the back of the building," she let Gage know.

Basically, it was a metal landing with stairs leading down to the ground. Maybe Ford hadn't managed to block it somehow. Also maybe the fire department was already on the way because she was certain that by now someone had called them. Especially since the gas tank explosion had no doubt started a fire.

The back of the building wasn't really that far. Only about sixty feet. But between the fire escape and them were offices.

Lots of them.

Plenty of places for someone to hide.

Lynette prayed that all of Dalvetti's men were gone or dead, and she added to her prayer that her father had retreated, as well. Of course, that left Patrick or Nicole. Her father could have told one or both about this meeting. In fact, he could have arranged the get-together so that either Patrick or Nicole would be the triggerman to kill Gage.

That way, her father could get someone else to do his dirty work.

The anger slammed through her, along with the fear that they were still in danger. Always would be. As long as her father drew breath. Because even though he'd failed tonight didn't mean there wouldn't be another episode.

When the black smoke began to coil its way up the stairs, Gage and she picked up the pace and started down the hall. Lynette put her back to Gage and kept her gun ready. Even though she'd missed the henchman when she'd fired, she tried to keep her hand steady. Tried to be ready for anything.

They passed the first office. The door was closed, and she checked to make sure it was locked.

It was.

Of course, someone could have locked it from inside, but at least she might be able to hear the person when or if they tried to open the door and attack.

She repeated the process with the next office. And the next. Until they'd made it nearly halfway down the hall.

The sound stopped both Gage and her.

She lifted her head, listening.

Was it the crackling noise from the fire? Yet something else falling from the blast?

Or was it something worse?

There were a lot of things that could fit into that *something worse* category.

"See anything?" Gage whispered.

Lynette looked around, but it was too dark to see much. There was smoke, thready streams near the stairs, but she didn't see anything else. However, she did hear something.

Sirens.

The fire department was on the way, though they might not just go bursting into the building until they'd assessed the situation. It was also possible they couldn't get in the building and might have to try to extinguish the fire from outside.

"Let's go," Gage insisted, and he started to move again.

An icy chill went through her, and even though she hadn't seen anything, Lynette sensed that something was wrong.

She heard the soft click on her left and pivoted in that direction.

But it was already too late.

Someone threw open one of those office doors and knocked the weapon from her hand. It clattered onto the floor.

And before she could retrieve it, there was someone pointing a gun right at her.

GAGE DIDN'T MISS the small gasp that Lynette made.

He turned just in time to see her gun go flying. He also saw the person who'd caused the gasp and the fallen gun.

Ford.

But while Lynette was no longer armed, her father sure was. And he had his firearm aimed at Lynette. And not just *at* her. Toward her stomach.

Hell.

This was about to get ugly fast. Especially since his brothers were no doubt trying to make their way to Lynette and him. There were a lot of possibilities for mistakes, distractions and especially bullets.

"Drop your gun," Gage warned the man, and he went closer, even though he knew he didn't have much bargaining power with that gun pointed at Lynette.

"You move another foot, and there'll be no more baby," Ford warned right back.

Lynette shook her head, motioning for Gage to stop. He did. But he couldn't stop the rage at this monster threatening an unborn child.

It took a special piece of slime to do that.

"I guess this means no more stalemate," Ford said with victory in his voice. "Well, there won't be after you drop your weapons. And you will drop them. Put them on the floor and slide them against the wall."

Gage debated it. He hated to surrender both of his guns, but he couldn't risk Ford shooting Lynette. Of course, once Gage was unarmed, he would try to shoot her anyway.

Well, maybe.

Lynette lowered her hand to her pocket. Ford reacted. Man, did he. He shoved the gun closer to her.

"You said put down the weapons," Lynette clarified.

She fished around in her pocket and came out with a

small police-issue handgun. No doubt something one of his brothers had given her. She eased it onto the floor and kicked it away from her.

Too bad she hadn't held on to it.

Because they might need it before this was over.

Whatever *this* was.

Outside, he heard the fire engines screech to a stop. Good. They'd put out that fire, but it would be a while—too long—before they could climb up those stairs. That meant Gage had to buy them some time.

"What's this all about?" Gage demanded, looking straight at Ford. "Are you working with Patrick or Nicole?"

Ford made a mock huffing sound. "No. Neither of them knows anything about this. They were just convenient tools. Or so I thought. I told them Lynette had found something incriminating, but sadly they didn't do anything about it except make threats and get angry."

"You thought you'd incite one of them to kill me," Lynette said. Her voice was surprisingly strong, and there was rage in it.

Not good.

Rage usually meant a person was willing to do something risky. Gage didn't want her taking any more risks.

"I thought Patrick and Nicole would *scare* you," Ford corrected. "So that you'd come to me for help."

"To you for help?" Lynette questioned. "And why would I do that?"

"I was your last resort. Well, after Gage. But I'd planned on Dalvetti getting him out of the picture tonight. You just can't get good help these days, not even when they're so-called bloodthirsty drug lords out for revenge. That idiot made a mess of things downstairs."

Gage had to fight back rage, too. How dare this SOB

act so cavalierly about something so deadly. He wished he could beat Ford to a pulp. And he just might before this was over.

"Your guns," Ford reminded Gage. "Put them on the floor now."

Gage laid down his primary and kicked it in the direction of Lynette's gun, but he took his time taking out the weapon from his slide holster in the back of his jeans. What he needed was a way out of this, and he wanted to hang on to his weapon as long as possible to make that happen.

"Are you saying you had no plans to kill Lynette?" Gage asked. Yeah, it was a distraction question, but he really did want to know what was going on inside that sick mind.

"No plans for that," Ford assured him. "Still don't have any. The hit man was just supposed to fire shots at her, that's all."

"He didn't listen," Gage said through clenched teeth. "He fired into her dark bedroom."

Ford shrugged. "Disappointing, yes. But you took care of him for me. And Lynette. I appreciate that."

"Thanks," Gage growled. But he damn sure hadn't saved Lynette so he could hand her over to Ford like this. "What happens now? How are you *not* going to kill Lynette this time?"

"Easy. When we're done here, she'll go back to the mental institution in Mexico for some experimental drug therapy. I've heard it does wonders for personality adjustment…and some memory loss. In a few months she might be ready for a return trip home."

Gage nearly broke his fingers with the hard grip he had on his backup weapon. He judged the angle, hoping he had a shot, but he didn't. Ford had moved so that Lynette was essentially his human shield.

"You're going to brainwash me," Lynette concluded.

Ford lifted his shoulder. "I suppose you could call it that."

Yeah, it would be exactly that. God knows what those drugs would do to Lynette's mind and the baby. Plus, Lynette wasn't just going to submit. She'd fight back.

And lose.

Downstairs, Gage could hear the firemen entering the building. If that made Ford nervous, he darn sure didn't show it. The man was cool and unruffled.

"The stairs are impassable," Ford remarked. "Don't count on your firemen friends or your brothers to get up here to help you out."

Oh, but they would.

But Gage rethought that when he studied the hallway and Ford made a sound deep within his throat. It sounded smug, or something.

"What did you do?" Gage demanded.

"I blocked the fire escape. No one's coming in that way any time soon."

Gage didn't bother cursing out loud, but that was not good news. Still, his brothers were resourceful, and they'd figure out a way to get in eventually. Gage got busy with some time-buying.

"We're really supposed to believe you don't want Lynette dead?" Gage asked.

"A shot to my stomach could kill me," Lynette pointed out.

Oh, man. She was shaking all over now, including her voice, and not from fear, either. If Gage didn't do something soon, she was going to launch herself right at her father.

"Then don't take the risk," Ford warned her. He used the barrel of his weapon to motion at Gage again. "Your gun, on the floor. If I have to repeat it again, Agent Ryland, I will pull this trigger."

Gage didn't doubt it. And that meant he had just one shot at this. He would lean down. To the side. So that Lynette was no longer in his line of fire. Gage would pretend to put the gun on the floor.

Then, he could yell for Lynette to get down.

And Gage would fire.

The plan sucked, and there were so many things that could go wrong. Too many. But their odds weren't so hot with Ford calling the shots, either.

"Can I say goodbye to Lynette?" Gage asked the man. It would be a fake goodbye, but he wanted to say it anyway. Every word might buy them some time, because he might be able to distract Ford.

Or goad him into doing something he hadn't planned— like aiming that gun at Gage instead of Lynette.

If that happened, Ford was a dead man.

Ford hesitated. "Make your goodbye quick."

Lynette's back was to him, but she looked over her shoulder at him.

"I'm glad I had you in my bed tonight," Gage said. Words meant to set Ford's teeth on edge. "It was like old times."

Lynette smiled. A forced one. But hey, if Ford could see it, it would still get to dear ol' dad. "Gage, you're the only man I've ever loved."

Okay.

That didn't sound like words for Ford. But for Gage.

Years ago, she'd told him that she loved him. Too many times to count. But that was *years ago*. Before they'd broken each other's heart and gone their separate ways. Before her father had ripped them apart.

Something he was still trying his damnedest to do.

Lynette's fake smile faded, and even though he couldn't see them, Gage thought there might be tears in her eyes. "And I'll love you and this baby until the day I die."

Ford made a sound of utter disgust.

Gage still had hold of his gun, but he wasn't in position to fire because Lynette was in front of her father.

But time had run out.

The risk of staying put was far greater than the risk of doing what he had to do. Gage pushed Lynette out of the way and came up ready to fire. He did.

So did Ford.

Both shots blasted through the air.

Chapter Nineteen

Lynette shouted for her father to stop. But she knew it wouldn't do any good.

He fired at Gage anyway.

It missed, thank God.

The shot slammed into the wall next to Gage.

But her father immediately ducked into the dark office, and he reaimed. Fired.

She watched the whole nightmare unfold. In slow motion. As she tumbled to the floor. Helpless to do anything to stop another bullet from slamming into Gage.

And it did.

The bullet tore through Gage's right arm.

Lynette landed hard on her shoulder, out of harm's way. But not Gage. He was in the worst place possible—out in the open and in a direct line of fire. Her father was ready to pull the trigger again.

And she couldn't let that happen.

Heaven knows how badly Gage was already hurt, and she couldn't risk another shot.

She kicked at her father and barely made contact with his shin. It was just enough to distract him. He looked down. Her father aimed the gun.

At her.

Gage made a feral sound, and despite his gunshot

wound, he dived right at Ford. They collided and went flying back deeper into the office.

Lynette didn't know if her father had managed to hang on to his gun, but if he had, it was only a matter of time before he'd fire it again. She scurried across the floor and retrieved the handgun that Dade had given her before they left the sheriff's office.

She took aim.

But couldn't shoot.

The darkness was only part of the problem. Her father and Gage were in a fight for their lives, their bodies tangled around each other, and it would be impossible to fire and not risk hitting Gage.

She saw Gage's fist slam against her father's face. But she also saw something else.

The gun in her father's hand.

Her heart sank. Because his finger was still on the trigger.

She wanted to shout to Gage to be careful, but at this point, her warning would only be an unnecessary distraction. Lynette tried to remind herself that he was a trained federal agent. He'd no doubt been in situations like this. But he was hurt and unarmed.

He needed her help.

Lynette inched forward, waiting and looking for any chance to kick her father or even shoot. The chance didn't come. Ford angled the gun.

Fired again.

And Lynette watched in horror as the bullet slammed into Gage's chest. He flew back, gasping for air.

Maybe dying.

He couldn't die. He just couldn't.

The tears burned her eyes. The fear had her by the

throat. But she forced herself to move. She didn't know how because everything was on autopilot now.

Ford lifted the gun, took aim at Gage again, but Lynette shouted, "No!"

Her father looked at her, just a split second, and she kicked at the gun. To her surprise, he stopped. Well, for just that second. And then he whipped out another gun from his pocket.

He aimed one gun at her.

And one at Gage.

She glanced at Gage. He was still gasping. And he ripped open his shirt so she could see the Kevlar vest. Like the one she was wearing.

The relief flooded through her.

He wasn't dead. He hadn't been shot in the chest. But he was injured, and she had no idea how badly. She only knew she had to get him to the hospital. Hopefully, there was already an ambulance on the way. But she seriously doubted that her father planned to let Gage get the help he needed.

"Put down that gun," Ford ordered her.

"No." And Lynette didn't hesitate.

Her father made a sound of amusement. "I killed the last woman who told me that."

"My mother?" Though she already knew the answer.

"Your mother," he verified, volleying glances between Gage and her. Gage was doing the same while fighting for air and clutching his chest. He was also inching his hand toward his gun that had fallen on the floor.

"You drowned her because she said no to you?" Lynette asked, and she didn't bother to tone down the hatred. She wanted her father's full attention on her so that Gage could get that gun.

"Of course. She was a tramp, you know. She refused to

stop seeing her lover." He laughed. It was hollow and cold. "You should have seen her face when I told her that Sheriff Chet McLaurin was dead. She fell apart, dropped down on her knees, sobbing. Killing her was easy after that."

Every detail turned her stomach and made her want to pull the trigger. But she couldn't risk that, not while her father still had that weapon aimed at Gage.

From the corner of her eye, she saw Gage ease his hand over the gun.

"That's what will happen to you when I kill Gage," Ford warned. "You'll fall apart. You'll need the asylum after that."

Lynette shook her head. "I'm not letting you kill Gage. I didn't stand up to you ten years ago, but I'm doing it now."

He laughed again. "You can't shoot me. You're not a killer, Lynette."

No. She wasn't. But she would do whatever was necessary to protect the man she loved.

She waited until Gage had the gun in his hand before she asked her father a final question. "You think you'll get away with murder again?" she pushed.

"Of course. I'm a man of money and resources. With Gage dead, and you committed to the asylum, there'll be no witnesses. No one to tell the story of what happened here tonight."

She looked him straight in the eyes. "Don't be so sure of that." Lynette paused. "I have a tape recorder in my pocket, and I turned it on when I took out the handgun. I've got your confession to two murders and the attempted murder of a federal agent."

Because she was staring at him, she saw her father's eyes widen. Heard the jolt of breath. He opened his mouth, probably to say she was lying.

She wasn't.

And her expression must have let him know that.

Lynette heard the footsteps in the hall. Someone was running toward them. The Rylands, no doubt. They'd finally made it through the barricade on the fire escape.

"Soon, this room will be filled with lawmen, and one of them will cuff you. Read your rights. And haul you off to jail." She kept her attention nailed to her father. "I'll be there when you're convicted of murder. When you're disgraced and the talk of every gossip in the state."

Gage shook his head. "Stay back, Lynette." She did, but she didn't stop staring at her father. "And I'll also be there when they shove a needle into your arm." Her chin came up. "I got you, you bastard."

Ford moved so fast that even though she was tuned in to his every move, she still didn't see it coming. His hand flexed. Ready to pull the trigger.

But he didn't shoot at her. Or Gage.

Senator Ford Herrington turned the gun on himself. And fired.

Chapter Twenty

Gage felt as if he'd been kicked in the chest by an ornery rodeo bull. His arm where he'd been shot wasn't feeling too good, either. But he was alive and nearly in one piece. And the best part?

Lynette didn't have a scratch on her.

How she'd come out of that nightmare unscathed was nothing short of a miracle, but it was a miracle that Gage would take. But he rethought that. No injuries, but she looked on the verge of losing it as Mason and Kade helped Gage into the emergency room. Nate and Dade were right behind them.

"He's been shot," Lynette called out to the entire E.R.

And the place wasn't exactly empty. Grayson and his brothers' wives were all there: Darcy, Kayla and Bree. The kids, too. Three of them, Robbie, Noah and Kimmie, were toddling around while Darcy and Kayla held twin baby girls who looked to be a couple of months old. Kade and Bree's, no doubt.

"Are we having a family reunion?" Gage asked.

But his joke went over like a lead balloon because the women turned pasty-white, and Darcy immediately motioned for a medic.

"He needs help *now*," Lynette insisted.

Actually, he didn't, but Gage figured that wasn't an

argument he was going to win when it came to the *now* part. The bleeding had stopped. He could breathe without writhing in pain. And he was more than a little pleased that Lynette and his baby were no longer in danger. A bit of pain and blood were a small price to pay for that.

"This way," a medic said, hurrying toward them. He grabbed a wheelchair, put Gage in it, and without stopping, he wheeled him into the examining room.

"You can wait outside," the medic said when Lynette followed.

"No. I can't," she insisted right back.

Most of the others came, too, all of them peering at Gage and his injuries. Only Kayla stayed back with the three toddlers, probably because she didn't want them to see the blood on Gage's arm.

Gage didn't want them to see that, either.

He hadn't been able to shield his family from the danger, but there was no reason to add to the trauma that'd just happened.

"How badly are you hurt?" Darcy asked, handing the baby girl to Kade.

Gage was about to say *"not bad,"* but Lynette answered for him. "He has a gunshot wound to the arm. He's wearing Kevlar, but he took a direct shot to the chest."

All the lawmen and Bree winced. Probably because they knew how it felt.

"Yeah, it hurts all right," Gage complained but then hated that it only caused Lynette to look even more concerned. Soon, he would have to do something to get that concerned, pained look off her face.

He'd have to do some fence-mending with his family, too.

Gage glanced at each member of his Ryland clan. Even

with the pain, it was good to be here. Even better to be surrounded by blood who had his back.

"You a dad yet?" Gage asked Grayson while the medic started easing off Gage's shirt.

"I am." Grayson smiled from ear to ear. "A boy. Eight pounds, nine ounces."

"He's a big one," Darcy added. "But Eve's doing great. We were with them when we got Dade's call that you were coming in to the E.R."

"The baby's a Ryland through and through," Grayson went on. "Dark hair. Our gray eyes. Built like a cowboy. We've named him Chet David."

After their grandfather. It was a good legacy to continue. It was also reminder that in about seven and a half months, Lynette and he would have their own little cowboy or cowgirl. Gender didn't matter to him. Gage was just thankful this baby could have a safe, normal life. Especially after the unsafe, nonnormal start.

Gage looked at Lynette again to see how she was dealing with all of this and her father's death, but she had her attention fastened on him.

"I'm so sorry I couldn't stop this from happening," she whispered.

He caught on to her hand, even though the movement hurt, and he eased her closer. "You stopped it just fine. Later though, I'll be riled at you for going to the courthouse in the first place."

Riled, for at least five seconds.

Gage pulled her down for a kiss that was probably too long and too hot considering they had an audience.

"Told you they were back together," Mason mumbled.

"I don't think they were ever apart," Kade corrected. "Never could keep their hands off each other."

Gage was amused at this speculation about his personal

life, but not so amused that Lynette still looked ready to drop. He had her sit on the edge of the examining table while the medic kept on working, kept on clearing away the blood on his wound.

"We left Mel and Luis at the courthouse," Dade relayed to Grayson.

The other deputies, Gage recalled. He felt sorry for them. Working that crime scene was going to be a bear. Dead bodies always were.

"I'll go back in a few minutes and check on things," Dade added. "It won't be long before the press gets wind of this."

Dade was right. A senator's suicide would make the front page for a while. Maybe he could talk Lynette into staying away from a newspaper and a television for the next couple of weeks. Even her own newspaper. He didn't want her reliving that even if he couldn't completely shield her from the necessary follow-up that Grayson would have to do.

"I have something for your investigation," Lynette volunteered. She reached in her pocket, took out the tape recorder and handed it to Grayson.

So, it hadn't been a bluff after all. She had finally gotten the evidence to prove that her father was a cold-blooded killer. And a coward, of course.

"My father made a confession of sorts before he killed himself," Lynette added. She looked back at Gage.

And he finished for her. "Ford murdered Lynette's mother and Granddaddy Chet."

The silence slipped through the room, and even the young medic stopped and volleyed glances at all of them. There probably wasn't a person in Silver Creek who hadn't heard of their grandfather's murder, the way he'd been gunned down by an unknown assailant.

The gossip had never stopped.

Neither had the family's pain.

Some folks had even whispered that Gage's father, Boone, had been the one to pull the trigger. Or maybe Gage's mother. Perhaps Lynette's mother, too, since there had also been gossip about the affair between Chet and her. But Ford's reputation hadn't made him a top-list suspect. Well, except in Gage's and Lynette's minds.

Later, each of his brothers would have to deal with the loss in their own way.

But it wasn't a wound that would completely heal.

Ever.

Gage didn't have any training in psychology, but it didn't take a shrink to know they were all in law enforcement because of their grandfather. Chet McLaurin had made them all the men they were today.

And his murder had sealed their fates.

Gage mentally shrugged. There were much worse fates and paths that could have been sealed. At least they were all on the good side of the law.

Mason's favorite saying was right. *Justice isn't just coming—it's already here.*

"I can take over," Gage heard someone say, the voice cutting through the silence.

Dr. Mickelson shoved back the green curtain and stepped around the others. Gage had known the lanky doc his entire life. Heck, the man had delivered him, but apparently he was still going strong.

"Welcome home, Gage," the doctor greeted. "You Ryland boys are keeping me in business with these gunshot wounds. And babies." He gave one of the twin's toes a playful jiggle. "I don't guess it'd do any good to ask y'all to go in the waiting room?"

No one budged.

"Didn't think so." The doctor flexed his eyebrows. "Well, if you're squeamish or prone to puking, look away, because a gunshot wound isn't pretty."

Dr. Mickelson peeled off the rest of Gage's shirt, and Lynette went pale again.

"It's not that bad, Lynette," the doctor assured her, even though he hadn't done more than glance at her. The doctor had delivered her, too. "Looks like the bullet went through and through."

The medic unstrapped the Kevlar vest, and Gage saw the makings of an ugly bruise near the center of his chest. Ford might have been a coward, but he was clearly a good shot. If Gage hadn't been wearing the vest, the bullet would have gone through his heart.

"You'll need that wound dressed," the doctor continued. "And a chest X-ray to make sure your ribs aren't cracked. Your family and Lynette can't be there for that."

"Lynette is my family," Gage corrected. "She's my wife."

The doc flexed his eyebrows again, made a sound of approval and turned to her. "We'll get Gage all stitched up and then check you out, too. You're looking a little peaked there."

"I'm pregnant," she confessed, never taking her attention off Gage.

Dr. Mickelson made another sound of approval. Darcy and Nate made a sound of a different kind. Surprised ones.

"When are you due?" Nate asked.

"Early May," Lynette answered.

"Me, too," Darcy said, explaining the reason for the surprised sounds.

Mason just groaned. "None of you better expect me

to change diapers. Or babysit." He took the tape recorder from Grayson. "I'll get started on the paperwork."

Mason gave Lynette and him a glance that Gage decided to interpret as brotherly affection. Coming from Mason, it was practically warm and fuzzy.

The others weren't so subtle. They came forward in a wave to hug Lynette and offer congrats and good wishes. It wasn't quiet, but the doctor tolerated it for several moments before he hitched his thumb to the waiting room.

"The sooner I do this, the sooner you can take him home," Dr. Mickelson said.

That sent them all scattering. All but Lynette. And she still had that terrified look in her eyes. Gage decided this couldn't wait for X-rays and stitches.

"Could you give us a minute?" he asked the doctor and the medic.

The doctor mumbled something about Rylands, bullets and babies and strolled out. The medic went with him. And Gage turned to Lynette to get this show on the road.

"You're not leaving me," she blurted out. But then she shook her head. "I mean, you're not leaving me, are you?"

Gage hated that she'd spent one second worrying about that. He stood. Or rather tried to. But Lynette grabbed his good arm and had him sit on the examining table.

"I'm not leaving," he verified. "In fact, I'm not going back to the CIA. I'm staying here in Silver Creek. Maybe I'll even apply for a deputy job so I can spend more time with you and the baby."

Finally, he saw the relief on Lynette's face, and her breath just swooshed out. It was Gage's turn to catch on to her, and he eased her closer so that he had hold of her and she was standing between his legs. Since they were already halfway to a hug anyway, he pulled her even closer.

Yes, there was pain, but he didn't care.

Especially when he kissed her.

One taste of her mouth, and the last thing he felt was pain. Lynette did some floating, too, and made a silky little moan right before she melted against him.

"Your mouth can stir a lot of things inside me," she whispered. And then she did something amazing.

She smiled.

Her entire face lit up.

That put everything in his head and his body in their right places. Lynette was okay. His baby, too.

"I always thought you deserved better," he let her know, sliding his hand over her stomach.

"Then you should change your name to *better,* because you're what I want. What I've always wanted." Her breath broke on the last word, and tears watered her eyes.

He shook his head. "I have no idea why."

"Let me remind you." And she kissed the breath right out of him.

As reminders went, it was a darn good one. Even though Gage wasn't in any shape to drag her off to bed, he sure as heck could fantasize about it.

Later, he'd do more than fantasize.

She kissed him again and then stepped back. "You need that X-ray."

Gage didn't let her go. He snagged her hand. "I'm in love with you. You know that, right?"

More tears came, but she nodded. "I suspected as much. But it's good to have the words."

Then he would say them to her often. Daily, in fact.

"I'm in love with you, too," she added. "You know that, right?"

Now, it was his turn to feel the relief. "I suspected as much when you told me you hadn't had sex in ten years."

Gage kissed her again. "I think we need to make up for all that lost time."

She put her mouth against his ear. "I'll respect you in the morning."

He gave her his best devilish smile. "It's not respect I'm aiming for, darlin'."

Lynette laughed, and he realized it'd been way too long since he'd heard that. Another note.

Make her laugh daily.

"Will you marry me?" he asked.

"We're already married. Ten years now," Lynette reminded him.

Man, he had some anniversary gifts to make up for. He was ready to spend some serious time shopping and keeping Lynette happy.

"Then, marry me again?" Gage asked. "Go on a honeymoon with me so we can stay in bed for a week. Make that two," he corrected. "And we'll promise to love each other for the rest of our lives."

Her mouth hovered over his. "Deal."

Now, that was a word he'd wanted to hear. Gage hauled Lynette to him and he kissed her.

* * * * *

"Who's the gunman?" he asked.

She shook her head. "I don't know."

"And you thought it was okay to bring this kind of danger to the ranch without warning anyone? Someone other than you could have been killed tonight."

He knew that sounded gruff, insensitive even. But no one had ever accused him of putting sensitivity first. Still, he felt…something. Something he cursed, too. Because Mason hated the fear in Abbie's voice. Hated even more the vulnerability he saw in her eyes.

Oh, man.

This was a damsel-in-distress reaction. He could face down a cold-blooded killer and not flinch. But a woman in pain was something he had a hard time stomaching. Especially this woman.

He blamed that on her flimsy gown. And cursed again.

MASON

BY
DELORES FOSSEN

First published in Great Britain 2013
by Mills & Boon, an imprint of Harlequin (UK) Limited,
Eton House, 18-24 Paradise Road, Richmond, Surrey TW9 1SR

© Delores Fossen 2012

ISBN: 978 0 263 90348 5
ebook ISBN: 978 1 472 00700 1

46-0313

Harlequin (UK) policy is to use papers that are natural, renewable and recyclable products and made from wood grown in sustainable forests. The logging and manufacturing processes conform to the legal environmental regulations of the country of origin.

Printed and bound in Spain
by Blackprint CPI, Barcelona

Imagine a family tree that includes Texas cowboys, Choctaw and Cherokee Indians, a Louisiana pirate and a Scottish rebel who battled side by side with William Wallace. With ancestors like that, it's easy to understand why *USA TODAY* bestselling author and former air force captain **Delores Fossen** feels as if she were genetically predisposed to writing romances. Along the way to fulfilling her DNA destiny, Delores married an air force top gun who just happens to be of Viking descent. With all those romantic bases covered, she doesn't have to look too far for inspiration.

Chapter One

The scream woke Deputy Mason Ryland.

His eyes flew open, and Mason stumbled from the sofa in his office where he'd fallen asleep. He reached for his shirt but couldn't find it. He had better luck with the Smith & Wesson handgun that he'd left on his desk.

He threw open his office door and caught the scent of something he darn sure didn't want to smell on the grounds of his family's ranch.

Smoke.

The wispy gray streaks coiled around him, quickly followed by a second scream and a loud cry for help.

Mason went in the direction of both the smoke and the voice, racing out into the chilly October night air. He wasn't the only one who'd been alerted. A handful of his ranch hands were running toward the cabin-style guesthouse about a hundred yards away. It was on fire, the orangey flames licking their way up the sides and roof. And the place wasn't empty.

His newly hired horse trainer, Abbie Baker, was staying there.

That got Mason running even harder. So did another shout for help. Oh, yeah, that shout was coming from the guesthouse all right.

"Call the fire department," he yelled to one of the ranch hands.

Mason also shouted out for someone to call his brothers as well even though they would soon know anyway. All five of them, their wives and their children lived in the family home or on the grounds of the ranch.

Mason made it to the guesthouse ahead of the others, and he tried to pick through the smoke and the embers flicking through the night air. He hurried to the sound of his trainer's pleas for help.

And he cursed when he saw her.

Abbie was in the doorway, her body half in and half out of the house, and what was left of the door was on her back, anchoring her in place.

The smoke was thick and black, and the area was already hot from the flames, but Mason fought his way through just as one of the ranch hands caught up with him. Rusty Burke. Together, they latched on to the door and started to drag it off Abbie. Not easily. It was heavy and bulky, and it didn't help that the flames were snapping at them.

Mason didn't usually think in terms of worst-case scenarios, but he had a split-second thought that his new trainer might burn to death. The possibility gave him a much-needed jolt of adrenaline, and Rusty and he threw the door off her. In the same motion, Mason latched on to her arm and dragged her away from the guesthouse.

"I couldn't get out," she said, her voice clogged with smoke and fear.

"You're out now," he let her know.

Out but not necessarily safe. The ranch hands were already there with the hoses, but he doubted the house would stand much longer. If it collapsed, Abbie could still be burned or hurt from the flying debris.

CHOICE OF **TWO** GIFTS!

A **treat** from us to **thank you** for reading our books!

Turn over *now* to find out more

Thanks for reading!

We're treating you to **TWO** fabulous offers...

2 FREE BOOKS

from your favourite Mills & Boon series plus have books delivered to your door every month!

Find out more and claim your free books at
www.millsandboon.co.uk/bookclub

or call 020 8288 2888 and
quote BOOKCLUB today!

Plus ## 15% OFF **

Your next order online with code
THANKSMAR at **www.millsandboon.co.uk**

MILLS & BOON

"Are the horses okay?" she asked. Mason was more than a little surprised that she'd think of the animals at a time like this.

"They're fine." At least he was pretty sure of that. "This is the only building on fire."

Mason scooped her up, and she looked at him. It was pitch-dark, probably two or three in the morning, but thanks to the flames and the hunter's moon, he saw her eyes widen. A single word left her mouth.

"No."

Mason didn't have time to question that *no* before she started struggling. She wasn't a large woman, five-five at the most and on the lean side, but she managed to pack a punch when she rammed her elbow against his bare chest. He cursed and put her in a death grip so she couldn't fight her way out of his arms.

"I'm trying to save you," he reminded her, and he added more profanity when she didn't stop fighting.

Abbie was probably still caught up in the fear and the adrenaline, but Mason was finding it a little hard to be sympathetic with the cold rocky ground biting into his bare feet and with her arms and legs waggling around.

"We have to get away from the fire," he snarled.

Those wide frightened eyes looked at the flames, and she stopped struggling just long enough for Mason to get a better grip on her.

He started running toward the ranch office where lately he'd been spending most of his days and nights because of the heavy workload. He could deposit Abbie there and hurry back to see if the guesthouse could be saved. He wasn't hopeful, especially because the ranch wasn't exactly in city limits. It would take the fire department a good twenty minutes to reach them.

The door to his office and quarters was still open, and

he hurried inside, flipped on the lights with his elbow and placed her on the sofa. Mason looked down at her, to make sure she wasn't injured.

She didn't appear to be.

Visibly shaken, yes. Trembling, too. Pale and breathing way too fast. All normal responses under the circumstances.

Her eyes met his again, and Mason saw the fear that was still there. And maybe something else that he couldn't quite put his finger on.

"Did you try to kill me?" she asked.

That single question seemed to be all she could muster because she groaned, closed her eyes, and the back of her head dropped against the sofa.

Mason huffed. That definitely wasn't something he expected to hear her say. He'd been a deputy for fifteen years, and his employee no doubt knew it. Even though most people were leery of him because…well, because he wasn't a friendly sort, they didn't usually accuse him of arson or attempted murder.

"Why would I set this fire?" he demanded.

Abbie opened her mouth, closed it and shook her head. She also dodged his gaze. "I'm not sure what I'm saying right now. I thought I was going to die."

Mason guessed that was a normal response, but he was beginning to get a bad feeling about this. "How did the fire start?"

Abbie shook her head again. "I'm not sure. I woke up, and there was smoke all around me. I tried to get to the door, but I started coughing and couldn't see." She paused, shivered. "When I got to the door and opened it, it fell on me." Another pause. "Or something."

"Or something?" he pushed.

Oh, man. The bad feeling was getting worse, and Mason

blamed it on that stupid question. Was there a nonstupid reason that she thought someone had tried to kill her, or was this the ramblings of a woman whose mind had been clouded with fear and adrenaline?

"Or something," she repeated.

Abbie pushed her light brown hair from her face. Long hair, he noticed. Something he hadn't realized because she always wore it tucked beneath a baseball cap. In fact, he'd thought of her as tomboyish, but there wasn't anything boyish or tom about the person lying on his sofa. In that paper-thin pale blue gown, she looked like a woman.

An attractive one.

Something Mason wished like the devil he hadn't noticed. She worked for him, and he didn't tread down that path. Business and sex never sat well with him.

"Did you leave the stove on?" he pressed.

But all he got was another head shake—something else that didn't please him. He wanted some answers here, and he wanted something to tamp down that bad feeling in his gut. However, the knock on his already-open door had him shifting in that direction.

It was his ranch hand Rusty. The lanky young man was out of breath and looked on the verge of blurting something out before his attention landed on Abbie. He motioned for Mason to meet him outside.

Mason looked at Abbie. "I'll be right back." Yeah, it sounded like a warning and it was. By God, he was going to get those answers and settle this uneasy feeling. He would find out why she'd thought he had tried to kill her.

He stepped outside with Rusty, and when he got a better look at Rusty's face, he pulled the door shut. "More bad news?" But it wasn't exactly a question. Mason could already tell there was.

Rusty nodded. "The guesthouse collapsed. Nothing left to save."

Well, heck. That didn't please Mason, but it could have been much worse. His trainer could have gotten killed.

Abbie could have gotten killed, he mentally corrected.

And he cursed himself for thinking of her that way. Mason blamed it on that blasted thin gown and those frightened vulnerable brown eyes.

"There's more," Rusty went on, grabbing Mason's attention.

Mason took a deep breath, ready to hear the news he probably didn't want to hear, but before Rusty could spill it, he saw his brother Grayson hurrying toward them.

Like Mason, his brother was half-dressed. Jeans that he'd probably just pulled on and no shirt. Even half-dressed, Grayson still managed to look as if he were in charge.

And he was.

As the eldest of his five brothers and the Silver Creek town sheriff, Grayson had a way of being in charge just by being there.

"How's the trainer?" Grayson immediately asked.

"Alive," Mason provided. He didn't add the customary *and well* part to that because he wasn't sure that was true. He should probably look to see if she'd had a blow to the head. After all, the door could have hit her when it became unhinged. She might even have a broken bone or two.

"The EMTs are on the way," Grayson explained. He looked at Mason. "Rusty told you about the guesthouse?"

Mason nodded. "It's gone."

Grayson stopped next to him, his breath gusting. Probably because he'd run all the way from the main ranch house. "Yeah. And there was a gas can by the back porch. Rusty managed to pull it out of there before the flames took over."

What the devil? Mason mentally went through the reasons why Abbie would have had a gas can on the porch, and he couldn't immediately think of one. She trained his cutting horses and didn't have anything to do with any ranch equipment that required gasoline.

"Looks like someone could have set the fire," Grayson concluded.

Arson. On the ranch.

The anger slammed through Mason. Even though he had five brothers who were equal owners of the land, the ranch was *his* domain. He ran it. It was what he loved, more than a badge, more than just about anything. And if someone had intentionally burned down the guesthouse with Abbie inside, then that someone was going to pay and pay *hard*.

"It could have been worse," Rusty went on, turning to Grayson. "Mason barely got Abbie out of there in time."

That was true. And Mason went back to Abbie's stupid question.

Did you try to kill me?

Had she seen something or someone? Maybe. And Mason changed that *maybe* to a *probably* after remembering the way she'd looked at him. He was accustomed to people shying out of his way. Used to the uneasiness that he caused with his steely exterior, but Abbie's fear had twisted something inside of him that he hadn't felt before.

The sound of sirens sliced through his anger and thoughts, and all three of them looked in the direction of the road where there were swirls of red-and-blue lights approaching. The fire department, an ambulance and a sheriff's cruiser. Could be one of his brothers, Dade or Gage, in the cruiser, because they were both deputies.

"I'll talk to them," Grayson volunteered. "You stay with the trainer until the EMTs have checked her out."

He would, but while he was doing that, Mason could ask some questions that might help them get to the bottom of all of this.

Grayson and Rusty headed out in the direction of the approaching emergency responders, and Mason threw open his office door. His attention zoomed right to the sofa where he'd left Abbie.

She wasn't there.

Mason looked at the adjoining bathroom. Door closed. And that's probably where she was—maybe crying or falling apart from the inevitable adrenaline crash.

He took a moment to pull on his boots, but when he still couldn't find his shirt, he crossed the large working space and knocked on the bathroom door.

No answer.

So he knocked again, harder this time. "You okay in there?"

Still no answer.

He rethought that crying or falling-apart theory and moved on to one that caused his concern to spike through the roof. Maybe she was unconscious from an injury he hadn't noticed.

No knock this time. Mason kicked down the door and was thankful when it didn't hit her. He looked at the sink first. Not there. Then, the separate toilet area. Not there either. And she darn sure wasn't in the shower.

That's when he noticed the bathroom window was wide-open.

What the devil was going on?

He hurried to the window and looked out. Thanks to that hunter's moon, he saw her. Barely. She was at least thirty yards away, her pale blue gown fluttering in the wind.

Abbie was running as if her life depended on it.

Chapter Two

Abbie didn't take the time to tell herself that it'd been a really bad idea to come to the Ryland ranch. But that's what she would do later. For now, she just had to get out of there as fast as she could and hope that she could somehow make it to safety.

Safety with no car, no money, no shoes.

Clearly, she had some big strikes against her.

Abbie glanced over her shoulder and saw one of the biggest strikes of all. Mason Ryland. Her boss and perhaps the person who wanted her dead.

She'd been a fool to come here, and that foolishness might soon get her killed.

With Mason's footsteps bearing down on her, Abbie didn't give up. She ran, praying that she would make it to the fence before he could grab her. The fence wasn't a sure thing. First, she'd have to scale it and then try to disappear into the thick woods that surrounded the sprawling ranch. But just reaching the fence was her next obstacle.

"Stop!" Mason yelled.

His angry voice tore through the darkness, through her, and she had a terrifying thought.

What if he shot her?

After all, he had a gun. Abbie had seen it when Rusty and he had pulled the door off her. The sight of that weapon and his fierce take-no-prisoners expression had caused her heart to skip a beat or two.

She kept running, her lungs already starved for air, but she wasn't fast enough. With the fence still yards away, Mason grabbed her shoulder and dragged her to a stop before he whirled her around to face him.

"What the hell do you think you're doing?" Mason demanded.

Abbie wanted to demand the same thing, but she couldn't gather enough breath to speak. Mercy, her teeth were chattering from the chilly night air and the fear.

"Well?" he pushed. He looked down at her. At her face. At her gown. At the garment she was wearing over her gown. "And why did you steal my shirt?"

"I borrowed it," Abbie managed to say. She would have done the same to a pair of shoes if she could have found them. She hadn't. So she'd run out of his office barefoot.

He mumbled some more profanity and stared at her as if she'd lost her mind. Maybe she had. But thankfully he didn't shoot her or threaten to do it. That reprieve meant she had a chance to try to talk him out of whatever he was planning to do to her.

"Look, I'll just go," she managed to say after sucking in some more air.

"To heck you will." He kept a punishing grip on her arm. "First, you'll tell me about that fire and why you ran. After that, I can decide if I'll arrest you for arson."

That put some air back in her lungs. "What? Arrest me? I didn't do anything wrong."

Mason gave her another you've-lost-your-mind glare, and those ice-gray eyes drilled into her. Abbie couldn't see the color of his eyes in the darkness, but she knew them well enough from her job interview. Not that he'd given

her more than a passing glance in the three days she'd
worked for him.

Well, he was doing more than glancing now.

In addition to the glare he'd aimed at her, his gaze kept
dropping to her cotton nightgown. It wasn't a garment
meant to be provocative, but she felt exposed with Mason's attention on her.

Mason had a way of doing that, she'd learned.

Tall, dark and dangerous with his black hair and hard
face. His brothers had those same Ryland looks, but they
were softened on their faces and bodies. Not Mason. He
looked like an ornery vampire.

Without a shirt.

Added to that were those gunmetal-gray cop's eyes that
saw, and had seen, way too much.

Abbie slid her left hand over her chest. Over the silver chain that veed down into her gown and in between
her breasts. She couldn't let Mason see the pendant at the
end of the chain. If he did, the anger and questions would
come at her full blast.

"We can stand out here and freeze our butts off," he
continued, "or you can tell me what happened."

Because she couldn't tear out of his grip and because
he had that gun, Abbie knew she had to give him some
kind of answer. The truth?

Probably not.

Not until she was sure she could trust him, and so far
Mason hadn't done anything to make her believe she could.
Well, except pull her out of the burning house, but she
wasn't sure yet why he'd done that. Maybe her shouts for
help had drawn so much attention that he felt he had no
choice but to make a show of rescuing her. He probably
wouldn't have wanted anyone saying he'd let his trainer

burn to death. Even if maybe that's what he'd wanted to happen.

"I already told you I'm not an arsonist," she explained. "I woke up, and the place was already on fire. I tried to get out, but when I made it to the front door, someone pushed me to the ground and shoved the door on me."

"What *someone?*" he challenged.

Abbie shook her head. "I didn't see his face."

He studied her, his glare getting even harder. "So why accuse me then?"

Now, here's where she had to lie. "I was scared. Talking out of my head. I've never come that close to dying."

And that, too, was a lie. A whopper, actually.

Oh, she'd come close all right.

The seconds crawled by, and even though her teeth were still chattering and the goose bumps were crawling all up and down her, that didn't seem to give Mason any urgency. Even though he was no doubt cold, too.

That no-shirt part caught her attention again.

She didn't want to look at him. Okay, she did. Once more she was intrigued by how the Ryland genes could have created this puzzling mix of danger and hotness. Under different circumstances, she might have been attracted to Mason Ryland.

Abbie mentally groaned at that thought. Not good. Thoughts like that could only make this situation worse. And she was already at *worse*. The trick now would be to stop the damage from escalating into a full-blown nightmare.

"I have to get out of here," she blurted out. "I can't stay."

Still no urgency from Mason, and when she tried to move, he snapped her back in place. "You honestly believe someone tried to kill you tonight?"

Abbie thought about her answer. "Yes," she said, even

though she dreaded what he would ask next. She didn't have to wait long.

"Why would someone want to kill you?"

Mason's question hung in the air and was just as smothering and as potentially lethal as the fire and smoke had been. Abbie tried to shrug. "Since I've been here at the ranch, I've had the feeling someone's watching me."

Also the truth.

Without warning, Mason released the grip on her, but he continued that ruthless stare. "Did you tell anyone about this?"

Abbie settled for a head shake.

"Well, you should have," he growled. "We have surveillance cameras all over the ranch, but they're not monitored unless I'm aware there's a problem. I wasn't aware. Plus, there's the part about me being a deputy sheriff. I would have been very interested in knowing that you thought someone might be watching you."

"I'm sorry," Abbie mumbled. But there's no way she could have told him about her suspicions without making Mason and his brothers suspicious. "I'll pack my things…" Except her things had all burned. She was literally wearing everything she owned. "I have to leave," she repeated.

"Not a chance. If the fire was arson, there'll be an investigation. Grayson will need to interview you. There will be paperwork. And I hate paperwork," he added in a gruff mumble.

Grayson, the sheriff. Another set of cop's eyes. Just what she didn't need right now. But she couldn't very well break into a run and expect to get away.

No.

Her best bet was to pretend to cooperate so she could get out of there as fast as possible. Then she could regroup and figure out what to do.

Abbie glanced down at her gown to make sure the pendant was still hidden. It was. "Could I maybe borrow some clothes?"

Mason didn't jump right on that with a resounding yes, but he finally grumbled one under his breath. What he didn't do was stop the staring, and he sure as heck didn't move.

"For the record, I think you're lying about something," he informed her. "Don't know what yet, but I *will* find out. And if you set that fire, so help me—"

"I didn't set it," Abbie snarled back.

"You're willing to have your hands and clothes analyzed for traces of gasoline or some other accelerant?" he snapped.

The question stopped her cold. Under normal circumstances, no, she wouldn't mind. She would even volunteer. But these were far from normal circumstances. She obviously needed to get out of there.

Still, Abbie nodded. "Of course."

Mason stared at her. And stared. Before he finally hitched his shoulder in the direction of the fire and the other ranch buildings. "Come on."

Not exactly a warm and fuzzy invitation, but Abbie was thankful they were walking. Not easily and not very quickly. After all, she was barefoot, and Mason seemed to be as uncomfortable as she was.

"Tell me why you came here," Mason tossed out. A demand that almost caused her heart to stop. Until he added, "Why did you want to work at the Ryland ranch?"

"You asked that in the interview," she reminded him, but Abbie paraphrased the lie to refresh his memory. "You have one of the best track records in the state for cutting horses. I wanted to be part of that."

Mercy, it sounded rehearsed.

He made a gruff sound to indicate he was giving that
some thought. Thought smothered with suspicion. "You
knew a lot about the ranch before you applied for the job?"

Abbie nodded—cautiously. The man had a way of completely unnerving her. "Sure. I did a lot of reading about
it on the internet."

"Like what?" he fired back.

She swallowed hard and hoped her voice didn't crack.
"Well, I read the ranch has a solid reputation. Your father,
Boone Ryland, started it forty years ago when he was in
his early twenties."

Mason stopped and whirled around so quickly that it
startled her. He aimed his index finger at her as if he were
about to use it to blast her into another county. Then, he
turned and started walking again.

"My *father*," he spat out like profanity, "bought the
place. That's it. He didn't even have it paid off before he
hightailed it out of here, leaving his wife and six sons. A
wife who committed suicide because he broke her spirit
and cut her to the core. He was a sorry SOB and doesn't
deserve to have his name associated with *my* ranch that
I've worked hard to build."

The venom stung, even though Abbie had known it was
there. She just hadn't known it would hurt this much to
hear it said aloud and aimed at her.

"You don't look as much like your father as your
brothers do," she mumbled. And before the last word had
left her mouth, Abbie knew it had been a Texas-sized mistake.

Mason stopped again, so quickly that she ran right into
him. It was like hitting a brick wall. An angry one.

"How the hell would you know that?" Mason demanded.

Oh, mercy.

Think, Abbie, think.

"I saw your father's picture," she settled for saying.

The staring started again. Followed by his glare that even the darkness couldn't conceal. "What picture?" he asked, enunciating each word.

Abbie shook her head and started walking. Or rather, she tried to do that. But Mason caught onto her arm and slung her around to face him.

"What picture?" he repeated.

She searched for a lie he'd believe, one that could get her out of this nightmare that she'd created. But before she could say anything, Mason's gaze snapped to the side.

And he lifted his gun in that direction.

For one horrifying moment, Abbie thought he was going to turn that gun on her, but his attention was focused on a cluster of trees in the distance. The trees were near the fence that Abbie had fought so hard to reach.

Mason stepped in front of her so quickly, she hadn't sensed it coming. He put himself between her and those trees.

"What's wrong?" she asked.

"Shh," he answered, and like the rest of this conversation, he sounded rough and angry.

Mason was a lot taller than she was, at least six foot three, so Abbie came up on her toes to look over his shoulder. She saw nothing. Just the darkness and the trees. Still, that nothing got her heart racing.

Because someone had set that fire.

In her attempts to evade Mason, Abbie had failed to realize that if Mason wasn't on to her, if he didn't know why she'd really come to the ranch, then someone else had set that fire.

Someone else had tried to scare her. Or worse.

Hurt her.

"You think someone's out there?" she asked.

But Mason only issued another *shh* and looked around as if he expected them to be ambushed at any moment.

Abbie stayed on her toes, although the arches of her feet were cramping. She ignored the pain and watched.

She didn't have to watch long.

There.

In the center of that tree cluster. She saw the movement. So slight that at first she thought maybe it was a shadow created by the low-hanging branches swaying in the wind. But then, the shadow ducked out of sight.

"I'm Deputy Mason Ryland," Mason shouted. "Identify yourself."

Silence. Well, except for her own heartbeat drumming in her ears. Who was out there? The person who'd set the fire? Or was this something worse?

"Get down on the ground," Mason said to her. "I'm going closer."

Abbie wanted to shout no, that it could be too dangerous to do that, but Mason caught onto her arm and pushed her to the ground. "Stay put," he warned. And he started in the direction of those trees.

With each step he took, her heart pounded harder, so hard that Abbie thought it might crack her ribs. But she didn't move, didn't dare do anything that might distract Mason.

He kept his gun aimed. Ready. Kept his focus on the trees. When he was about fifteen yards away, there was more movement. Abbie got a better look then—at the person dressed head to toe in black.

Including the gun.

The moonlight flickered off the silver barrel.

"Watch out!" Abbie yelled to Mason.

But it was already too late. The person in black pointed the gun right at Mason.

Chapter Three

Mason dived to the ground and hoped Abbie had done the same. He braced himself for the shot.

It came all right.

The bullet blasted through the night air, the sound tearing through him. Mason took aim and returned fire. The gunman ducked just in time, and Mason's shot slammed into the tree and sent a spray of splinters everywhere.

And that's when it hit Mason. The gunman hadn't fired at him.

But at Abbie.

Mason glanced over his shoulder to make sure she was okay. She seemed to be. She had stayed put on the ground with her hands covering her head. Good. But her hands wouldn't stop a bullet.

What the devil was going on?

First the fire, now this. It wasn't the first time danger had come to the ranch, but it was a first attack on one of his employees.

An employee who had plenty of questions to answer.

After Mason took care of this gunman, he would ask Abbie those questions. First, he wanted this shooter alive to answer some, too, but he had no trouble taking this guy out if it came down to it.

Mason kept watch on the spot where he'd last seen the

gunman, and he lifted his head slightly so he could have a better chance of hearing any kind of movement. He heard some all right.

Footsteps.

Mason cursed. The gunman was running.

Escaping.

Mason fired another shot into the trees and hoped it would cause the guy to stop. It didn't. Once the sound of the blast cleared, Mason heard the footsteps again and knew the shooter was headed for the fence. He would make it there, too, because it wasn't that far away, and once he scaled it, he could disappear into the woods.

That wouldn't give Mason those answers he wanted.

Mason got to a crouching position and watched the fence, hoping that he would be able to see the shooter and wound him enough to make him stop. But when the sound of the footsteps stopped, the guy was nowhere in sight.

"Don't get up," Mason barked to Abbie.

But that's exactly what *he* did. He kept his gun ready, but he started running and made a beeline to the fence. Mason ran as fast as he could. However, it wasn't fast enough. He heard the gunman drop to the other side of the fence.

Mason considered climbing the fence and going after him. That's what the rancher in him wanted to do anyway. But his cop's training and instincts reminded him that that would be a quick way to get himself killed.

Maybe Abbie, too.

The gunman could be there waiting for Mason to appear and could shoot him, and then go after Abbie. His brothers and some of the ranch hands were no doubt on the way to help, but they might not arrive in time to save her.

So Mason waited and stewed. Whoever had set that fire and shot at Abbie would pay for this.

When he was certain they weren't about to be gunned down, Mason stood. He kept his attention and gun on the fence and backed his way to Abbie.

"Let's get out of here," he ordered.

Mason didn't have to tell her twice. She sprang to her bare feet and started toward the ranch—backward, as Mason was doing.

"Why did he try to kill you?" he asked her without taking his attention off the fence.

Abbie didn't jump to deny it, but she didn't volunteer anything either. She was definitely hesitating, and Mason didn't like that.

"Why?" he pressed.

"I'm in the Federal Witness Protection Program," she finally said.

Of all the things Mason had expected to hear, that wasn't on his list. But his list now included a whole barnyard of questions.

"Who's the gunman?" he asked.

She shook her head. "I don't know."

Mason couldn't help it. He cursed again. "And you thought it was okay to bring this kind of danger to the ranch without warning anyone? Someone other than you could have been killed tonight."

He knew that sounded gruff. Insensitive even. But no one had ever accused him of putting sensitivity first. Still, he felt…something. Something he cursed, too. Because Mason hated the fear in Abbie's voice. Hated even more the vulnerability he saw in her eyes.

Oh, man.

This was a damsel-in-distress reaction. He could face down a cold-blooded killer and not flinch. But a woman in pain was something he had a hard time stomaching. Especially this woman.

He blamed that on the flimsy gown. And cursed again.

"I need details," he demanded. "Why are you in witness protection, and why would someone want you dead?"

She opened her mouth to answer, but before she could say anything, Mason heard Grayson call out to them. "Are you two okay?"

Mason was, but Abbie looked ready to keel over. "We're not hurt," he shouted to his brother. Because the gunman was probably long gone, Mason turned in Grayson's direction so he could get to him faster. "The guy shot at Abbie."

"Abbie?" Grayson questioned. Like the other half dozen or so ranch hands with him, he was armed.

"She's the new cutting-horse trainer I hired," Mason explained. "And she's in witness protection."

The news seemed to surprise Grayson as much as it had him.

"I don't know who tried to kill me," Abbie volunteered.

Her voice wasn't just shaky, it was all breath and nerves. She let out a small yelp when she stumbled. Probably landed on a rock, because there were plenty enough to step on. That did it. Mason put his gun in the back waist of his jeans and scooped her up. He didn't forget that it was the second time tonight he'd had her in his arms—and neither circumstance had been very good.

Too bad *she* felt good.

She smelled good, too, even though he could pick up traces of the smoke. Her scent, the feel of her, stirred things he had no intentions of feeling, so he told those feelings to back off. Way off. He wasn't going there with Abbie.

Then he looked down at her. Saw the shiny tears in her eyes. Heard the slight hitch in her breath when she tried to choke back those tears.

"I've been in witness protection for twenty-one years," she whispered.

Mason did the math. If he remembered correctly, Abbie was thirty-two. That meant she'd entered the program at age eleven. A kid.

"And nothing like this has ever happened to you?" Grayson asked, sounding a little too much like a hard-nosed cop for Mason's liking.

That was a big red flag, because Mason remembered that it was a question he should have asked. No. He should have *demanded*. He forced himself to remember that he was a deputy sheriff and that Abbie had put them all in danger.

Still, he felt that twinge of something he rarely felt. Or rarely acknowledged anyway.

Sympathy.

He'd rather feel actual pain.

"Years ago, someone tried to kill me," Abbie answered. And she paused for a long time. "Not long after my mom and I entered witness protection, someone fired shots at me." Another pause. "They killed my mother."

Oh, hell.

Nothing could have stopped that slam of sympathy. *Nothing.*

Mason and his brother exchanged glances, and Mason knew there'd be more questions. Had to be. Grayson would need to investigate the fire and shooting. One of them would also need to contact the U.S. Marshals who ran witness protection and let them know that Abbie's identity had been compromised.

Still, twenty-one years was a long time to go without a *compromise*. And Mason considered something else. Why had it happened now, only three days after Abbie had arrived at the Ryland ranch?

A coincidence?

His gut was telling him no.

Mason kept that to himself and trudged the last leg of
the distance to the ranch. He headed straight for his office, and this time he didn't intend to let Abbie run away.

The first thing Mason did was place her on the sofa
again, and despite all the sympathy he was feeling, he
gave her a warning glance to stay put. Grayson followed
him inside, no doubt ready to question Abbie, but Mason
didn't plan to start until he'd located a few things. First,
he got Abbie a blanket and then he found her some socks.

"Who killed your mother?" Grayson started. "And
why?"

Abbie put on the socks, mumbled a thanks and pulled
the blanket around her.

Her sigh was long and weary. "My mother and I went
into witness protection after she testified against her boss,
Vernon Ferguson, a corrupt San Antonio cop." Her voice
was as shaky as the rest of her. "Ferguson got off on a
technicality, and shortly afterward he sent a hired gun
named Hank Tinsley after us. Tinsley turned up dead a
few days later."

Mason figured there were plenty of details to go along
with that sterile explanation. The stuff of nightmares.
Something he knew a little about because his grandfather Chet had been shot and left to die. Mason had been
seventeen, and even though nearly twenty-one years had
passed, the wound still felt fresh and raw.

Always would.

Not just for him but for all his brothers.

That wound had deepened to something incapable of
being healed when his father had left just weeks later. And
then his mother had committed suicide.

Oh, yeah. He could sympathize with Abbie.

But sympathy wasn't going to keep her safe.

"You think this Vernon Ferguson came after you to-night?" Mason asked. He stood over her, side by side with Grayson.

Abbie shook her head. "Maybe."

It was a puzzling answer, and Grayson jumped on it. "You have somebody else other than Ferguson trying to kill you?"

"I don't know. Over the past twenty years, Ferguson has managed to find me two other times, and both times he sent hired guns. Nothing recent, though. Mainly because we've been very careful."

Mason didn't miss the *we,* and later he would ask who this person was in her life. Because it might be important to the investigation. Not because he was thinking she had a boyfriend stashed away. On her job application she had said she was single, but that didn't mean she wasn't in love with someone.

And for some reason, a reason Mason didn't want to consider, that riled him a little.

Abbie closed her eyes a moment and when she opened her eyes, she turned them on Mason. "My caseworker is Deputy U.S. Marshal Harlan McKinney over in Maverick County. He'll need to know about this."

Mason nodded, but it was Grayson who reacted. "I'll call him. And check in with the fire chief." Grayson glanced at her shoeless feet peeking out from the blanket. "I'll also ask my wife about getting you some clothes."

"Thank you," she said in a whisper. Abbie didn't move until Grayson was out of the office and had shut the door. Then she sat up as if ready to leave.

"You're not going anywhere," Mason reminded her.

She blinked. "But I figured you'd demand that I leave. It's not safe for any of you with me here."

"That's probably true, but you're still not going anywhere." In case she'd forgotten, he took his badge from his desk and clipped it to the waist of his jeans. "You've got six lawmen on this ranch."

Her gaze came to his again. "And yet someone still got to me."

Yeah, and that meant whoever had done this was as bold as brass, stupid or desperate. Mason didn't like any of those scenarios.

"Why would Ferguson still want you dead if he got off on the charges with a technicality?" Mason asked. He located a black T-shirt in the closet and pulled it on. He grabbed his black Stetson, too.

"Maybe he still considers me a loose end." But she didn't sound convinced.

And that only reinforced the fact that something just wasn't right here.

Mason pulled his chair over to the sofa and sat so that he'd be more at her eye level. Abbie adjusted her position, too, easing away from him, and in the process the blanket slid off her.

Great.

He felt another punch of, well, something stirring below the belt when he got another look at the gown. And at her breasts barely concealed beneath the fabric. Not a good combination with that vulnerable face and her honey-brown eyes.

"I swear, I didn't mean for this to happen," she said. "I didn't know Ferguson could find me. I've always been careful."

Mason made a heavy sigh and reached out. He doubted his touch would give her much comfort, but he had to do something. He put his fingertips against her arm. Rubbed gently.

And he felt that blasted below-the-belt pull happen again.

Their gazes met, and the corner of her mouth lifted. Not a smile but more of a baffled expression. Either she figured out he was going nuts or else she was feeling something, too.

"For the record, I didn't think you'd be like this," she said.

The cryptic remark got his attention, and Mason would have asked what she meant. If her gown hadn't shifted. Yeah, he saw her breasts. The tops of them anyway. And while they snagged his attention in a bad way, it was what was between her breasts that snagged it even more.

The pendant.

Or rather, the silver concho.

He instantly recognized it because he had one just like it. All of his brothers did. A custom-made gift from their father with their initials on the back. A blood gift he'd given them all just days before he'd run out on them.

Abbie gasped when she followed Mason's gaze, and she slapped her hand over the concho. Mason just shoved her hand away and had a better look at the front of it.

And there it was.

The back-to-back *R*s for the Ryland ranch. This wasn't a new piece either. It was weathered and battered, showing every day of its twenty-one years.

Abbie tried again to push his hand away, but Mason grabbed both her wrists. He turned the concho over, even though it meant touching her breasts. But it wasn't her breasts that held his attention right now. It was the other initials on the back.

B.R.

For his father, Boone Ryland.

Mason let go of the concho, leaned down and got right

in Abbie's face, but it took him a moment to get his teeth
unclenched so he could ask her the mother of all questions.

"Who the hell are you?"

Chapter Four

Abbie knew her situation had just gone from bad to worse. She also knew that Mason wasn't just going to let her run out of there again. Not that she could.

Not now.

Not after the gunman's attack.

She'd opened this dangerous Pandora's box and had to stay around long enough to close it. If she could. But closing it meant first answering the Texas-sized question that Mason had just asked.

Who the hell are you?

"I'm Abbie Baker," she said, knowing that didn't clarify anything, especially because it was a name given to her twenty-one years ago by the U.S. Marshals when she and her mom had entered witness protection.

Her real name was Madelyn Turner. Maddie. But she no longer thought of herself as that little girl who'd nearly died from a hired gun's bullet.

She was Abbie Baker now.

And she had a thoroughly riled, confused cowboy lawman looming over her. He was waiting for answers that didn't involve her real name or anything else so mundane. Mason's attention and narrowed glare were on the concho.

"Where did you get it?" he asked.

Abbie considered another lie. She'd gotten so good at

them over the years, but no one was *that* good. There was no way she could convince Mason that she'd found the concho and then had coincidentally applied for a job at the Ryland ranch.

There was nothing chance about it, and now she might have endangered not just Mason but also his entire family. Someone had come after her tonight, and she had to get to the bottom of that—fast.

First, though, she had to get past Mason, literally. And that meant giving him enough information to satisfy him but not so much that he would have a major meltdown.

"Where did you get the concho?" he repeated.

Abbie tried not to look as frightened as she felt, but she figured she wasn't very successful. "Your father gave it to me."

She saw the surprise go through his eyes. Maybe Mason had thought she'd stolen it or something.

"My *father?*" he snapped.

Abbie settled for a nod, knowing she would have to add details. But the devil was in those details, and once Mason heard them, he might physically toss her off the ranch. That couldn't happen at this exact moment.

"When?" he pressed. "Why?"

She had no choice but to clear her throat so she could answer. "When I turned sixteen. He said it was a good-luck charm."

That was a lie. Actually, Boone had said he wanted her to have it because it was his most valuable possession. Something he'd reserved for his own children.

Nothing about his severe expression changed. Mason's wintry eyes stayed narrowed to slits. His jaw muscles stirred. He continued to glare at her. For several snail-crawling seconds anyway. Then he cursed. One really bad word. Before he turned and scrubbed his hands over his

face. It seemed to take him another couple of moments to
get his jaw unclenched.

"So Boone is alive," he mumbled. "Or at least he was
when you were sixteen."

"He still is alive," Abbie confirmed. "I talked to him
on the phone before I went to bed." She chose her words
carefully. "He met my mother and me about four months
before she was killed."

"Where?" he barked.

"Maverick County. But we've lived plenty of other
places since then." She paused because she had to gather
her breath. "We move a lot, finding work at ranches all
over the Southwest. He's always worried that Vernon Ferguson will find me." And finish what he'd started.

Mason's eyes narrowed even more. "Boone lived with
you?"

"He raised me," Abbie corrected.

That didn't improve Mason's ornery mood. More profanity, and the corner of his mouth lifted in a dry smile
that held no humor at all.

"He raised you." And he repeated it. "He couldn't raise
his own sons or be a husband to his wife, but yet he took
you in. Why?"

Abbie had asked herself that a thousand times and still
didn't have the answer. "It was either that or I would have
had to go into foster care. There weren't many options for
a kid in witness protection."

"You would have been better off in foster care," Mason
mumbled. "I figured the SOB was dead." He held up his
hand in a stop gesture when she started to speak. "He
should be dead."

That sent a chill through her. That chill got signifi-
cantly worse when Mason grabbed her arm and pulled
her to her feet.

"He sent you here," Mason accused. "Why? He wants to mend fences with us after all these years?"

Abbie didn't get a chance to deny it.

His grip was hard and punishing. "Well, you can just go back to Maverick County and tell the bastard that he's not welcome here. Neither is his lackey. Consider yourself officially fired."

"He didn't send me," Abbie managed to say.

Mason no doubt heard her, but he didn't respond except to haul her toward the door. Abbie dug in her heels. Or rather, tried. It was like wrestling with an angry bear. She wasn't a weakling, and her work with the cutting horses had honed some muscles that most women didn't have, but she was no physical match for the likes of Mason.

Still, she had to make him understand.

"Boone didn't send me," she repeated. "In fact, he wouldn't be happy if he knew I was here." And that was a massive understatement.

That stopped Mason, finally, even though they were just inches from the door.

"Boone knows how much you hate him," she added.

Oh, that put some fire into those ice-gray eyes. "He can't begin to imagine how much I hate him." His attention dropped back to the concho. "I put a bullet through mine and then nailed it to my bedroom wall so it's the first thing I see when I wake up. That way, I can remember that the man who fathered me is a worthless piece of dirt."

Abbie had expected anger, but she hadn't quite braced herself enough for this outright rage. Boone had been right. He had done the unforgivable when he'd walked out on his family. At least it was unforgivable in Mason's eyes, and she wondered if she stood a better chance pleading her case to one of his brothers. The problem was, she might not get the chance to do that.

Mason started moving again, toward the door.

"Why did Boone leave Silver Creek?" she asked.

Again, that stopped him. Well, sort of. Mason didn't open the door, but he put her back right against it, and he kept his grip hard and tight on her shoulders. She was trapped, and Boone's warning came flying through her head.

Mason isn't the forgive-or-forget sort.

It was one of the few times Boone had talked about his sons, about the life he'd left behind here in Silver Creek. Boone wouldn't have wanted her to come here, but she'd had no choice. This was her best bet at finding the answers to why Boone had been so secretive lately. He was definitely keeping something from her, and Abbie was scared that the *something* meant he was in serious danger.

"You tell me why he ran off," Mason challenged.

She shook her head. Actually, her whole body was shaking, maybe from the adrenaline. Maybe the cold.

Maybe Mason.

She glanced down between them, at the fact that their bodies were pressed against each other. Not good. After all, despite the anger and Boone's warning about this particular Ryland, Mason was a man, and she was a woman.

Mason must have realized it, too, because while still scowling and cursing, he stepped back. "Why did Boone leave?" he repeated.

Abbie had to shake her head again. "I don't know." It was the truth, but she wished she had the answer because it would no doubt clear up a lot of other questions she had. "He wouldn't say. But for what it's worth, he was a good surrogate father to me."

Mason made a skeptical sound and threw open the door. However, he didn't toss her out. That's because his oldest brother, Grayson, was standing in the way. He had an armful of clothes, a concerned look on his face and the same cop's eyes as Mason. And he eyed the grip that Mason had on her.

"A problem?" Grayson asked, suspicion dripping from his voice. He waited until Mason let go of her before he handed her the clothes from his wife.

"Yeah, there's a problem," Mason verified. "Boone sent her."

"He didn't," Abbie answered as fast as she could, and she was getting darn tired of that broken-record accusation.

Grayson looked first at Mason. Then her. "Is that why you're here at the ranch, because of Boone?"

"No," Abbie said at the exact moment that Mason said, "Yes."

Grayson gave them a raised eyebrow. "Well, which is it?"

Both Rylands stared at her, waiting. "Boone doesn't know I'm here, and he didn't send me," Abbie insisted. "He believes he doesn't stand a chance of reconciling with any of you."

"He's right," Mason jumped to answer.

Grayson didn't voice an opinion, but his expression made it clear that Mason and he were of a like mind. And that meant Abbie was wasting her time and putting them in future danger for no reason. Well, except that she might get some answers from Grayson that she hadn't managed to get from his brother.

Abbie hugged the clothes to her chest and looked Grayson in the eyes. "Boone never talked much about all of you, so I don't know why he left."

Mason cursed.

Grayson lifted his shoulder. "Does it matter why?" he asked.

Unlike Mason, he actually waited for her to answer. "Maybe." That required a deep breath. "Something's wrong."

"If he's dying, then you'd better break the news to someone who gives a flying fig," Mason grumbled.

Abbie was about to tell him that Boone wasn't dying, but she had no idea if that was true. And that made her sick to her stomach. Yes, Mason had a right to be this enraged, but she was already getting tired of it. He was aiming that venom not just at her but also at the man who'd raised her. A man she loved like a father.

"Get dressed," Mason said again. This time it was an order, and he grabbed on to the concho and shoved it back into her gown so that it was out of sight. "I'll drive you into town so you can leave Silver Creek."

Grayson had a different reaction. He flexed those previously raised eyebrows. "Someone just tried to kill her," he reminded Mason. "And that someone likely set fire to the guesthouse with her in it. As the sheriff, I think I'd like to get to the bottom of that first before she leaves."

"Boone sent her," Mason argued.

"And we can send her back. After the doc checks her out and she answers a few questions." Because Mason was clearly gearing up for an argument, Grayson tipped his head to the clothes. "Go ahead and change."

Abbie considered staying put, considered trying to convince them that she wasn't there on a mission of peacemaking, but it was obviously an argument she'd lose. On a huff she headed to the bathroom but didn't shut the door all the way. She needed to hear what the Ryland brothers were planning to do with her. Too bad she couldn't quite manage that because both lowered their voices to whispers.

Angry ones.

Mason was still no doubt insisting that she leave im-

mediately. Grayson had the more level head, and she remembered Boone calling him an old soul.

Abbie hurriedly changed into loose pants and oversized
denim shirt. No underwear, but the flat slipper-type shoes
fit. She was ready to face down the enemy, or rather her
former employer, until she caught sight of herself in the
mirror. Mercy. There was soot on her face. Her hair was a
tangled mess, and there were dark circles under her eyes.
And then she wondered why she cared.

Oh, yes. She remembered.

Mason, and that body-to-body contact. Abbie cursed
him. Cursed herself. She didn't let men get under her skin,
and she wasn't about to start now.

Steeled with that reminder, Abbie walked back into the
main room, only to have both Ryland men stop their whispered conversation and stare at her.

"So, what's the verdict?" she came right out and asked.
Of course, Mason scowled at her and mumbled something
she probably didn't want to hear anyway.

"Our other brothers Dade and Nate are out looking for
the man who took shots at you," Grayson informed her.
He was all cop now. "Any idea who he was?"

She shook her head. "It was too dark to see his face."

Mason swung his attention in her direction. "What
about the man who set the fire? Too dark to see him, too?"

Abbie ignored the skeptical, snarky tone. "I didn't see
him," she verified. "In fact, I didn't see anyone. I only
sensed someone was there."

"Your senses are good," Grayson volunteered. "Because
I looked at the door that Mason pulled off you. It'd been
torn from its hinges. If you didn't do that—"

"I didn't."

Grayson lifted his shoulder. "Then someone else did.
I'm guessing it was the same man who fired those shots."

She guessed the same. Abbie also guessed that his brothers would give it their best efforts in searching for the man. But she also knew there were miles and miles of wooded area surrounding the Ryland ranch. The odds weren't good. And that put a hard knot back in her stomach.

"He'll be back," she said before she could stop herself. Abbie instantly regretted the admission, but it didn't surprise Grayson. Perhaps not Mason either. It was hard to tell because his face seemed to be frozen in that permanent glare.

"Boone didn't send me," she reiterated. "And I'm sorry that you're riled because someone tried to kill me on *your* ranch."

"I'm not riled because of that." That got rid of the glare. Judging from his annoyed huff, Mason hadn't intended to ditch the glare, raise his voice. Or show even a smidgen of what had to be a bad temper to go along with that gruff exterior.

But Abbie hadn't intended to go the snark route either. "Look, I'm frustrated. Scared. And feeling a dozen other things that you clearly don't want me to feel. I'm sorry."

"Quit apologizing," Mason snapped. He stared at her. And stared. Then cursed again. "Quit apologizing," he repeated.

Like the little arm rub he'd given her earlier, before he'd seen the concho, it sounded, well, human.

Grayson gave them both a stern glance, especially his brother. "Are you two sleeping together or something?"

"No!" Mason and she said in unison. Mason shot his brother a look that could have frozen Hades.

Grayson did some more staring and then made a sound of disbelief. "Then maybe we can concentrate on finding the man who tried to kill you." He waited until he had their

attention before he continued. "I've already made a call to
Marshal Harlan McKinney to let him know what's going
on, and I've put out feelers to find out if Vernon Ferguson's connected to this."

She gave a weary sigh and pushed her hair from her
face. "You won't find a connection," Abbie assured him.
"Ferguson's too smart for that." And that reminder caused
her to go still. "Ferguson found me awfully fast. I've been
here at the ranch only three days."

"Maybe Boone told him," Mason instantly suggested.

Abbie didn't even have to consider it. "Boone doesn't
know I'm here. That's the truth. I told him I was visiting
a friend in Austin."

Mason gave her a flat stare. "So you're telling us the
truth, but you lied to him?"

"Yes." She ignored his sarcasm and turned toward
Mason. "Did you do some kind of background check on
me?"

Mason probably would have preferred to continue the
sniping match, but she saw the moment that he turned
from an angry son to a concerned rancher and lawman.
"Of course. I use a P.I. agency in San Antonio to screen
potential employees." He paused. "I don't have the report
back on you yet."

Later, she would curse herself for not realizing that
Mason would run such a check. She didn't have an arrest
record. In fact, not many records at all, and that would
have perhaps flagged a P.I.'s interest.

It had probably flagged Marshal McKinney, too, but
Abbie had called him right before she applied for the job
at the ranch to tell him she might be working there for a
short period of time. She'd also asked the marshal not to
tell Boone, and McKinney must have complied because

Boone hadn't tried to stop her. And he would have if he'd known she was anywhere near Silver Creek.

Abbie shook her head and stared at Mason. "So why did you hire me before you got the report?"

"Because he needed a cutter," Grayson jumped to answer. "He goes through five or six cutting-horse trainers a year."

The muscles in Mason's jaw tightened. "Because most aren't worth spit." Another pause, and he tipped his head toward her. "She seemed to know what she was doing."

"Thanks. Your father trained me," she added, knowing it would cause his glare to return. It did. Not just from Mason, but his brother, too.

She huffed but regretted that little jab. It was clear she wasn't going to win them over to her side, so it was best to tell them the truth and hope they'd be willing to do something to help her.

Abbie took a deep breath before she started. "Something happened about a month ago. I'm not sure what," she added because it looked as if both Rylands were about to interrupt her. "I know it started when Boone heard the news reports about the senator who committed suicide here in Silver Creek."

"Ford Herrington," Grayson supplied.

Abbie waited for them to add more. They didn't. But she'd done her own reading about the senator. He'd confessed to murdering his wife and the Ryland sons' grandfather Chet McLaurin, before taking his own life.

"What connection did Boone have to Senator Herrington?" Abbie asked.

"You mean other than Herrington murdering Boone's father-in-law?" Mason asked. He was back to being a cowboy cop again.

She nodded. "Is there something more?"

Mason shook his head, huffed. "According to Ford, our grandfather was having an affair with Ford's wife."

"Was he?" she pressed, though she still couldn't see the connection with Boone.

"Maybe." And when Mason paused, Grayson took up the explanation. "His wife was having an affair with someone. Ford's daughter, Lynette, confirmed that. She overheard her mother talking about it before she was killed, and Lynette has no reason to lie, because she's our sister-in-law."

So maybe that was the connection she'd been searching for. But why would a decades-old affair between a senator's wife and Boone's father-in-law have such an impact now? Especially because everyone seemed to know about it.

"Is it possible that the senator's wife got pregnant and had your grandfather's baby?" Yes, she was grasping at straws, but she had to find what had set all of this in motion.

Mason lifted his shoulder. "I suppose she could have gotten pregnant, but she didn't give birth. No time for that. From the time line we've been able to come up with, Ford killed her only about a month after the affair started."

Well, there went her secret-baby theory.

"Boone got upset when he saw the news reports about the senator's suicide," she added. "And he followed the story like a hawk. I'd never seen him like that, and since then he's been secretive. Agitated. He even hired a P.I., and he won't tell me why."

The brothers exchanged concerned glances. "What's your theory?"

Abbie had to take a deep breath. "I suspect something bad happened to Boone all those years ago. Something bad enough to cause him to walk out on his family."

"And what would that be?" Mason's tone wasn't quite as lawmanlike as it had been for his other questions. The emotion and old pain were seeping through.

"I'm not sure," Abbie admitted. "But a week ago I heard him talking to someone on the phone. I don't know who, but it could have been the P.I. I only caught pieces of the conversation, but Boone mentioned the ranch. And all of you."

"Us?" Mason challenged.

She nodded. "I think he was worried about your safety." Mercy, she wished she'd heard more of that call. "He also said something else."

"What?" Mason pressed when she paused.

Abbie tried to repeat this part verbatim. "Boone said the past was catching up with him and that it wouldn't be long before someone came to kill him."

Chapter Five

Mason listened to every word that Abbie said, but it took a moment for her bombshell to sink in.

"Who wants Boone dead?" Mason asked. "Other than me, that is."

There was a flash of annoyance in her eyes. Probably because she felt he was being too hard on her surrogate daddy. He wasn't. There wasn't such a thing as too hard when it came to Boone Ryland.

"I don't know who wants him dead," she insisted. "But I could tell from his voice and body language that the threat was real."

Hell. This was not a turn that Mason wanted. It might not even be true, but just the fact that Abbie had tossed it out there meant it would have be investigated. Not by him. Well, not unless he learned that Boone had been the one to cause the fire and the gunman.

Then Boone would have to *answer* for it.

Grayson shook his head. "If Boone thought someone was trying to kill him, why would he let you out of his sight?"

It was a good question, especially considering Boone had chosen to raise this woman and she seemingly had such a high opinion of him. Mason only wished he'd thought of the question first. He couldn't let the past and Abbie's vulnerable eyes cloud his head.

Too late, the little voice inside him mumbled.

Mason would make it his mission to prove that little voice wrong.

"Like I said, I lied to him," Abbie explained. "Boone thought it would be a good idea if I disappeared for a while and put some distance between him and me. He wouldn't say why," she quickly added. "He seemed relieved when I told him I was going to Austin for a month, but I didn't dare tell him I was coming here, or he would have tried to stop me. He knows none of you want contact with him, directly or otherwise. I just wanted to find out why he might be in danger."

So if Abbie was telling the truth, and Mason thought she might be—about this anyway—then Boone was in some kind of danger and he didn't want that spilling onto her. Clearly, he loved his foster daughter a heck of a lot more than he'd loved his sons.

But that didn't surprise Mason.

"I need to do some checking," Grayson finally said. "If the fire and the gunman are connected to Boone, then I'll have to ask him some questions."

Mason waited for Abbie to object. She didn't. Strange. Mason had thought she might try to come up with a good reason why Grayson shouldn't do that. Mason was certainly trying to come up with one. He didn't want Grayson or anyone else in the family to have any contact with the man.

However, the alternative to questioning Boone wasn't a good one: the possibility of continued danger and threats on the ranch.

Grayson looked at him. "I need to wrap up some things with the fire chief and check on Nate and Dade."

Good plan, but Mason knew if his brothers had found the gunman, they would have called.

"Why don't you go ahead and take Abbie to the main house? The doctor will be here soon," Grayson suggested. Mason wasn't sure what Grayson saw in his expression, but it caused him to add, "She's just the messenger, Mason. She didn't cause Boone to walk out on us all those years ago."

Abbie looked both uncomfortable with that reminder and a little relieved. Of course, if she was telling the truth about all of this, she would no doubt want them to leap headfirst into saving Boone.

That wasn't going to happen.

Unless…saving his sorry butt would mean keeping the family safe. But Mason was a long way from believing that.

"Come on," Mason told Abbie, and he started out of his office and toward the main house. He kept his gun ready, just in case, but he doubted the gunman would make a repeat appearance tonight.

"You think this is a smart move?" Abbie asked, catching up with him. "I don't want the gunman coming to the house."

"Neither do I," Mason assured her. "It's the safest place on the ranch. It has a security system with surveillance cameras."

And some areas of the grounds had cameras, too. As soon as he had Abbie tucked away in one of the guest rooms, she could wait for the doctor and he'd check the surveillance feed to see what he could find out about the gunman.

About Abbie, too.

"Your family isn't going to like my being there," she mumbled. She followed him along the crushed-limestone walking path that would take them directly to the back porch.

Mason couldn't disagree with that. They wouldn't like it. But they wouldn't turn her out. Not tonight anyway. If he found out she'd told him another lie, even a single one, then he would toss her out himself.

"I didn't mean for any of this to happen," Abbie added. "I figured I'd come here, get some answers to save Boone and then leave."

"Guess you figured wrong, huh?"

But Mason immediately regretted that dig. Yeah, they'd been jabbing at each other since she'd spilled the beans about Boone, but it wasn't helping matters. There was no way Abbie could ever understand how Boone had ripped his sons to pieces and then turned his back on them. And that led him back full circle to a question he just had to ask.

"Boone knew about my mother's suicide?"

There was enough illumination from the security lights and the house that Mason could see the answer on Abbie's suddenly stark face. "He knew. He didn't talk about it, but I heard him mention it once to my mother."

Her mother. Probably the woman Boone had bedded down with while still a married man. Mason didn't intend to ask about that or anything else that wasn't directly relevant to the investigation into the fire and gunman. The less he knew about Boone, the better. The man was like battery acid, eating away at the people he'd once claimed to love.

"I think Boone kept up with all of you as best he could," she continued. "But he always did it in a way not to draw attention to himself."

Yeah, so that no one could find him after he'd run out.

But something about that didn't sit right. Not now, not after meeting Abbie. Maybe Boone had lain low for her sake. To keep the corrupt ex-cop, Ferguson, from finding her.

More battery acid.

Boone had protected Abbie, but he hadn't cared a rat's you-know-what about his own blood kin for the past two decades.

Mason walked ahead of her onto the porch and punched in the code to unlock the door. Yet another recently added security measure. After a couple of intruders and even attacks on the grounds, Mason had taken a lot of measures that he hoped would keep everyone safe.

When he stepped into the kitchen ahead of Abbie, Mason slid his gun into the waist of his jeans, but he nearly drew it again when he heard the movement.

"It's just me," his kid brother Kade greeted. "Grayson called, said there was a problem, so I turned off the lights."

Mason kept them off, but he could still see because of the outside lights. Kade was at the table feeding a bottle to one of his twin girls. Mason didn't have a clue which one because Leah and Mia were identical.

"Everything okay?" Kade asked. "Did they find the gunman?"

"Not yet." When Abbie didn't come inside, Mason took her arm again and urged her in. Best to minimize her time outside because the gunman was still at large.

Kade's attention landed on Abbie. "It's true? She's been with Boone all these years?"

"Pretty much." Well, unless she was lying, but Mason couldn't think of a good reason for her to do that—yet. Still it didn't make sense to lie about something that was going to make her an outcast.

And that's exactly what it had done.

Kade didn't sound any happier about this situation than Mason was.

"I'm sorry for all the trouble," Abbie mumbled. She inched closer when Kade put the baby against his chest to burp her. Even in the dim light, Mason could see Abbie smile at the infant. "How many grandchildren does Boone have?"

Mason wanted to answer *none* because the man would have to be a father first before he became a grandfather. Boone wasn't anywhere close to being a father.

"Six," Kade answered, still staring at her.

Abbie's smile dissolved, probably because of Kade's less-than-warm tone. That was Mason's cue to get her out of there.

"This way," Mason instructed, and he led her out of the kitchen, into the foyer and up the stairs. It wasn't a short walk. The three-story house was huge, and it was getting bigger now that Kade and his wife were building another addition so they'd have private quarters.

He heard Abbie's breath racing by the time they made it to the top of the stairs. She was winded, he was betting. This was part of the adrenaline crash. Soon, she'd be too exhausted to stand.

Mason led her to the room directly across from his. Part of him wanted to put her as far away as possible, but the danger wasn't over. Plus, he wasn't sure he could trust her. He didn't want her sneaking out before they got the answers needed for their investigation.

"The guest room," he let her know, throwing open the door. "The doctor will be here soon to make sure you're okay. If you need anything, I'll be in there." He pointed to his own suite.

She nodded, pushed her hair from her face, but she didn't go inside. "In the morning I'll need to go to the bank so I can get some money to leave. All my cash burned in the guesthouse, and I don't have a credit card."

Mason hadn't forgotten about the fire, but for the first time he realized all of Abbie's belongings had been inside. "I owe you some wages, and if it's not enough, I'll lend you the money."

She managed another of those awkward smiles. "You're really anxious to get me out of here."

"Can you blame me?"

"No." She shook her head.

Mason didn't miss the slight tremble in her voice. She was trembling again, too. "You think it's safe for you to go?"

"It's never safe." Her gaze came back to his. "If I don't get a chance to tell you tomorrow, thank you for saving me not once but twice. And for hiring me. I'm thirty-two, but it's the first time I've gotten a job without Boone's help."

For some reason that admission and the trembling bothered him. "You don't need his help for a job. I watched you with the horses yesterday, and you know what you're doing."

"That's high praise coming from you." She paused. "It wasn't a lie, you know. I really did read about the ranch, about what you've accomplished here. You've done a good job, Mason."

He didn't want to be flattered, but he was the ranch. It was his baby. He was as married to it as his brothers were to their spouses and badges. Yeah, he had a badge, too, but it would never mean as much as this place did.

"Good night," Abbie mumbled. She turned and stumbled right smack-dab into the door.

Mason automatically reached out and caught her. He didn't pull her into his arms or pick her up as he'd done before. The less contact, the better.

"You just need some rest," he assured her, but he didn't let go of her.

Abbie made a sound to indicate she didn't believe him. And with good reason. It was a lie. Unless she had nerves of steel, she was going to be dealing with the fire and attack for a while. The stuff of nightmares, which she'd no doubt have the moment she fell asleep.

When the trembling kept up, Mason mumbled some profanity, slipped his arm around her waist and led her to the bed. He didn't dawdle. Every moment he was next to Abbie like this was a moment of discomfort and only gave more thoughts of why he didn't want to think about the discomfort.

He deposited her on the bed, issued a hasty good-night and headed for the door.

Oh, man.

What the heck was going on inside his head? Except he was pretty sure his head wasn't in on these particular feelings. No. This was a behind-the-zipper, below-the-belt kind of reaction and a slap-in-the-face reminder that he really needed to take the time to be with a woman. *Soon.*

Not Abbie, of course.

She might put a strain on his Wranglers, but she was hands-off. There was no way he'd get past her association with Boone. Or the danger. The lies, too.

Hell, she had a whole state of strikes against her. No use spelling them all out again.

Mentally kicking himself, he headed to his room, took off his Stetson, slapped on the lights and made a beeline for his laptop in the sitting room–office area. Mostly office. There were files, memos and notes stacked high but neatly on the desk. Bessie's doing. He'd need to remember to thank the housekeeper-caregiver for digging out the place—again.

Once the laptop booted up, Mason sank down in the chair and clicked on the security camera icon. The images immediately popped onto the screen, and he saw the fire department still at work next to what was left of the guest cottage. Grayson was talking to Dade and Nate, which meant his brothers hadn't found the gunman.

Soon, Mason would get a call from one of them to let him know that and inform him of any other update on the search, but for now Mason tapped into the stored security feed, and he backtracked an hour.

No flames in the cottage then. No one lurking around either. But he kept watching, and he finally saw the shadowy figure near the back porch area. There were no security cameras there.

Had the guy known that?

Maybe. And it meant Mason had some modifications to make. He wanted that and all areas of the ranch covered even if it was too little, too late.

The person on the screen moved quickly, opening a gas can and dousing the porch with the liquid, but he didn't light it. He disappeared from sight. The seconds ticked away on the camera clock, a full minute passing before the front door of the cottage popped open. But it wasn't Abbie.

The arsonist again.

He'd obviously broken in or gone through the back to the front of the house. It was a man wearing dark clothes and a baseball cap slung low on his forehead. He had some kind of tool in his hand that he used to unhinge the door, and he propped it in place before he hurried back to the gas can. He lit it with the flick of a match.

Mason saw the flames burst around the back of the cottage, and he tried not to imagine Abbie being inside. She probably hadn't smelled the smoke at this point. Probably didn't know she was a thread away from dying.

The smoke and fire billowed from the cottage, and even though there was no audio, he saw the shadowy figure move behind a tree. He put away the tool that he'd used to unhinge the door and took something else from his pocket. Mason couldn't see what, but he copied the still frame and would send it for analysis.

Moments later on the screen, Mason saw Abbie throw open the door and yell for help. She was staggering, probably because of the smoke, and that was maybe why she hadn't realized the door was falling on her. She was too late to get out of the way. It slammed right into her back, knocking her to the ground.

Mason switched camera angles, going back to the arsonist. The guy stayed there behind the tree, watching and holding whatever was in his hand. He didn't budge until Mason came running toward the cottage and toward Abbie.

He didn't stay on that camera angle. Mason switched to the others, looking for the arsonist. Finally, he went to the camera near the fence.

Bingo.

The guy was hiding behind another tree. Waiting to gun down Abbie, no doubt. Mason zoomed in on his face, adjusting the feed until he captured the image. He copied it and immediately emailed it to his brother Gage at the Silver Creek sheriff's office. He also grabbed the phone and called him.

Gage answered on the first ring. "That's our intruder?" he asked Mason.

"He is. Can you run it through the facial recognition software? I also need to see if you can identify what he's holding in the first photo."

"Doing that now," Gage assured him, and Mason heard him typing something on the keyboard. "Everything else okay at the house?"

"The wives and kids are all safe, including your better

half." Mason waited for the rest of Gage's question. He didn't have to wait long.

"Boone's not trying to worm his way back into the family, is he?" Gage asked.

"I don't think so, but it doesn't matter. He's not stepping foot on this ranch."

"Good," Gage growled. He paused. "What about your horse trainer?"

"Abbie Baker," Mason provided. "She'll be leaving in the morning." And his Wranglers or his knee-jerk reaction to her situation weren't going to have a say in it.

"When Grayson called earlier, he said she believes someone wants to kill Boone," Gage went on. "*Get in line,* right?"

"Yeah." But the agreement didn't feel as right as Mason wanted it to feel. "She said something happened last month, that Boone started getting nervous."

Last month had significant meaning to Gage because Senator Ford Herrington, the man who'd murdered their grandfather, had also been Gage's father-in-law. And one month ago, Ford had committed suicide.

"Ford was as dirty as they came," Gage verified, "but he's dead. He's not a threat to any of us, including Boone."

Mason was about to agree with that as well, but Gage spoke before he could say anything. Well, he didn't speak, exactly.

Gage cursed.

"I got an immediate hit with the facial recognition software," Gage said. "We got some major trouble, brother. Lock up the ranch. I'll get there as fast as I can."

Chapter Six

Abbie eased open the guest room door and peered out into the hall. Empty.

Thank goodness.

She had no choice but to see Mason this morning so he could usher her off the ranch as fast as humanly possible, especially since the doctor had given her the all-clear when he'd examined her. But she hadn't wanted to run into any other Rylands. Not after the frosty reception she'd gotten from Grayson and Kade. It was clear she wasn't wanted here, and after the fire and the gunman, Abbie was ready to go home and regroup.

But she rethought that.

Maybe she shouldn't go back to Eagle Pass to the house that she shared with Boone. If by some chance the gunman managed to follow her, she could end up putting Boone in danger. She didn't want that. She'd already put enough people at risk, including herself, by trying to uncover a truth that Boone obviously didn't want her to.

Before Abbie could decide where she could go, she heard the sounds coming from Mason's room across the hall. Sounds she hadn't expected to hear.

Laughter.

The door to his suite was ajar, so Abbie went closer and had a peek inside. Mason was at his desk, a laptop and a breakfast tray positioned in front of him, but he wasn't alone. There was a red-haired toddler running circles around his desk, and each time the little girl reached his chair, Mason would goose her in the stomach. Both of them laughed with each round.

It was eavesdropping, plain and simple, but Abbie couldn't stop herself. She'd never seen this side of Mason. He certainly wasn't the gruff rancher or cowboy cop she'd encountered during her interview and her handful of workdays.

Abbie watched when the toddler smacked into the side of the desk and tumbled to the floor. No more laughter. She started to cry, and Mason sprang from his chair to pick her up. Abbie knew how it felt to be in his arms, and it had a similar soothing effect on the child. She stopped crying.

"Gotta be careful, Curly Locks," he said to her, and he brushed a kiss on her forehead. But the words had no sooner left his mouth, when his attention zoomed across the room and landed on Abbie.

"Are you coming in, or do you plan to stand out there all morning?" he asked.

Abbie felt her cheeks redden, and she hoped he hadn't realized just how long she'd been watching him. She stepped inside, Mason's gaze sliding over her from head to toe. She'd tried to look presentable in her borrowed clothes and with the toiletries she'd found in the bathroom. Abbie doubted that she did.

Mason, on the other hand, looked more than presentable in his well-worn jeans, black shirt and cowboy boots. Actually, he looked hot, something she wished she hadn't noticed. Worse, he no doubt noticed that she noticed.

Oh, mercy.

Focus, Abbie.

She was about to ask who would be driving her into Silver Creek, but Mason spoke before she could.

"This is Kimmie. Kimberly Ellen," he corrected, kissing the toddler's forehead again. "Her stepmom, Darcy, is hugging the toilet. Morning sickness. Her dad, Nate, is working. And the nannies are tied up with the twins, my two other nephews and Grayson's newborn, so Kimmie and I are hanging out."

"So many babies," she mumbled. All of them Boone's grandchildren, something she wouldn't mention again. "I've never been around children. I'm more comfortable with horses," she confessed.

"Yeah. Me, too." But then he shrugged and grinned at Kimmie when she returned the kiss to his cheek.

"Nunk," the little girl said, and she dropped her head onto his shoulder.

"That's Kimmie's version of uncle," Mason explained. He eased her back to a standing position, and Kimmie ran to the toy chest next to a leather sofa. Everything in the room was masculine except for that toy chest that was stuffed to the brim.

Mason took his gaze off his niece and turned it back on Abbie. No glare this morning. His face could never be considered soft, but she thought she could see sympathy or something in his eyes. Well, she thought that until his gaze slid over her again.

Abbie checked to make sure the concho was hidden. It was. She nearly asked if something else was wrong, but then she saw it. Not anger or even disapproval. He was looking at her the way a man looked at a woman.

Oh. *That.*

The look didn't last long, and he shifted his attention to the laptop.

"Did anyone have time to check on the horses to make

sure they're okay?" she asked. It sickened her to think that the gunman who'd attacked them would go after the helpless animals.

"All of them are fine." He paused. "I'll move the ones you were training back to the pasture until I can hire someone else."

That sickened her a little, too, but there was nothing she could do about it. After what had happened, she couldn't stay.

Because her hands suddenly felt shaky, Abbie crammed them in her back pockets. "You'll be driving me into town?"

He got another look. Not one grounded in attraction this time. His forehead bunched up.

Mason tipped his head to the breakfast tray. "Why don't you pour yourself a cup of coffee while we talk."

Uh-oh. This couldn't be good, and Abbie doubted that coffee would help. Although it did smell good, and her head was throbbing from lack of both sleep and caffeine.

She went closer, poured herself a cup. "What happened?"

He motioned for her to sit in the chair next to his desk, but she shook her head. Sipped her coffee. And waited.

"The man who set the fire and shot at us is Ace Chapman," Mason let her know. "He's a hired gun and not small potatoes either. The FBI has had tabs on him for years and hasn't been able to nail him, but they estimate that he's killed more than a dozen people."

Abbie had tried to brace herself for this, but she hadn't expected it to be this bad. Not just an assassin but one with a deadly résumé. "How did this monster know I was here at the ranch?"

Mason shook his head. "I haven't figured that out yet. The P.I. agency I use for background checks is making sure nothing was leaked. But there's a possibility that someone at the agency made your photo available to the wrong person."

"How?" she wanted to know. Her heart was starting to race now, and the coffee wasn't going down easily. Her stomach was churning.

He paused a moment. "When I interviewed you for the job, the security cameras were on. I copied an image from it and sent it to the P.I. agency along with the background request."

Oh, mercy. "You always do that?"

"Always." And he didn't sound exactly apologetic either. "I don't like to take risks with the ranch, and you'd be surprised how many lowlifes apply for jobs."

No, she wouldn't. She didn't consider Boone and herself lowlifes, but they'd often given false names and information when asking for work.

Not for this job, though.

Because she'd figured Mason would do some checking, she had given her legal name, Abbie Baker, so she could use her own social security number and provide Mason with some references. Of course, she'd only given him references that weren't likely to get back to Boone. One of them had been Marshal McKinney's own stepfather, and the other, the marshal's brother. Abbie had listed them on the job application because she'd known they wouldn't leak anything to Ferguson, and besides, she'd done good work for both.

"What did the P.I. do with my picture?" she wanted to know.

"That's what I'm checking, but as a minimum he or she would have run it past law enforcement so they could check for any priors under a different name."

Great. Ferguson no doubt still had contacts with the

cops. In fact, as badly as he wanted to find her, he'd probably paid off someone to look for any information that would lead him to her.

And it had obviously worked.

Mason checked his watch. "Vernon Ferguson should be arriving at the sheriff's office soon. Grayson wants to question him."

"So do I," Abbie jumped to say.

He shook his head. "Not a good idea."

"Ferguson already knows I'm here," she pointed out. "And he might slip and say something."

Mason gave her a flat look to remind her that wasn't likely to happen. "I can arrange for you to watch the interview. You can even give Grayson some questions to ask, but I don't want you in the same room with him. If we get lucky and are able to make an arrest, Ferguson's lawyers could toss out anything he says because of the impropriety of having you in the interrogation room."

Abbie considered that, nodded and thought back through what Mason had just told her. "Are there any solid connections between this Ace Chapman and Ferguson?"

"No." He paused, checked on Kimmie and then looked at Abbie again. "But something's not adding up."

Abbie wasn't sure where this was leading, and she didn't get a chance to ask. That's because a tall, silver-haired woman came rushing into the room.

"I can take Kimmie now so you can drive into town," she said to Mason before her attention landed on Abbie. She made a slight hmmmp sound. "This is the girl Boone's been raising?"

Mason nodded. "Abbie, this is Bessie Watkins. She takes care of the place."

"And I take care of all the Rylands, too," Bessie provided. She scooped up Kimmie but kept her weathered gaze plastered to Abbie. "So how is Boone these days?"

"He's been better," Abbie settled for saying.

It looked as if Bessie wanted to say more, maybe she even wanted Abbie to send Boone a scathing message for her, but the woman simply shrugged and patted Abbie's arm. It was the closest thing she'd gotten to a friendly welcome since the Rylands had learned of her association with Boone.

"We need to leave now, but you can bring your coffee with you," Mason said and started for the door.

That was Abbie's cue to follow him, but first she deposited the coffee cup back on his desk. Despite her need for caffeine, she couldn't finish it, not with her stomach churning over the thought of Ace Chapman and Ferguson.

Mason said goodbye to Bessie and Kimmie before he walked out and down the stairs. Abbie was right behind him, waiting for him to spill whatever he'd been about to say before Bessie came into the room.

He grabbed a black Stetson from the hooks on the wall near the door and led her outside to the truck parked at the side of the house. Not a flashy late-model vehicle. It was at least twenty years old, and the once-red paint was now scabbed with rust spots. She'd heard the ranch hands making fun of Mason's ride, and she had to wonder why a man worth millions hadn't bought something better.

She climbed inside and was surprised that the interior was spotless.

"It belonged to my granddaddy," Mason said as if he knew exactly what she was thinking. And with that meager explanation, he drove away from the ranch.

His grandfather, the one who was murdered by the senator. Abbie was certain there was more to the story than she'd heard, and she wondered if it was connected to Boone.

Or to her.

"You said something didn't add up about Ace Chapman," she reminded him.

He nodded, paused. "Chapman isn't the sort of killer who'd try to burn his victim. He's a shooter. I watched the feed from the security cameras, and he broke into the cottage before he set the fire."

Oh, God. Abbie pressed her hand to her chest to try and steady her heart. "He was inside when I was sleeping?"

"Yeah." And that's all Mason said for several moments. "He could have just killed you then. Shot you in bed. You would have never known what hit you."

That chilled her to the bone, and her breath stalled in her throat. All Abbie could do was watch the Texas landscape fly by, and of course, at that moment when she was breathless and scared beyond belief, they passed a cemetery. A reminder of death that she didn't need.

"On the security feed, I saw that Ace was holding something, and I had my brother Gage analyze it," Mason continued. "Ace was filming you as you ran from the burning cottage."

That took away the rest of her breath. Abbie turned and stared at him. "Why would he do that?"

Mason mumbled something, shook his head. "At first, before I knew he had a camera, I thought maybe he burned the cottage because there was something in it that he wanted destroyed. Something other than you. Was there?"

Abbie wasn't so quick to answer *no*. She tried to think. "Just my personal items. Clothes. My cell phone."

"Anything from or related to Boone?" he pressed.

The thoughts were jumping through her head. But so was the fear. "I had a photo of Boone and me in my wallet."

Abbie couldn't think of anything else. "Maybe this assassin just wanted to make sure there was nothing inside that could be used to link him to Boone or Vernon Ferguson."

"Maybe." But Mason didn't sound convinced. "There's another reason he could have filmed it." His pause was longer this time. Definitely a hesitation. "Maybe Ace was supposed to send the film to someone."

Abbie didn't have to think about this part. "To prove to the person who hired him that I was really dead."

Mason lifted his shoulder. "But if he'd only needed to prove you were dead, he could have set up the camera in your bedroom and shot you."

There was a chill again, and Abbie hated that her hands were trembling more with each passing moment. "What are you getting at?"

He glanced at her. "Maybe Ace was supposed to make you suffer. A fire would do that. And he would have proof of that suffering. Proof that he'd done the job someone paid him to do."

She was shaking her head before he finished, but then the head shaking came to a screeching halt. "You think Ace maybe filmed it so he could show it to someone? To torment them?" And there was only person who fit that particular bill. "Boone."

Mason made a sound of agreement, but it was somewhat lukewarm. "But why would Ferguson hire Ace to kill you and show it to Boone?"

"He wouldn't," Abbie mumbled. "If anything, Ferguson would do it the other way around. He would kill Boone to get to me. I'm the one he wants." And that caused her heart to start pounding.

This wasn't making any sense.

Unless…

She thought back to the past few weeks. Boone had

been so strange. Frightened, even. Did that have anything
to do with Ace and Ferguson? Maybe. But even so, she
was still the primary target. One or both was willing to
kill her and then use her death in some way. Perhaps to
get back at Boone.

But for what?

Was this the reason Boone had said the past was catching up with him?

Abbie's gaze flew to Mason. "I have to warn Boone
about what's going on."

"I called Marshal Harlan McKinney this morning,"
Mason explained. "He's aware of the possible danger and
will contact Boone. In fact, he's probably doing that right
now."

The relief was instantaneous. And short-lived. Yes,
Marshal McKinney knew how to get in touch with Boone,
but would it be in time? And would it be enough?

"For now, just focus on you," Mason instructed. "Let's
get past the interview with Ferguson, find Ace and then
you can get back to Boone."

She nodded, knew that he was right, but Abbie couldn't
stop the blasted tears from burning in her eyes. Nor could
she stop the hoarse sob that escaped her throat. It was bad
enough that she was in danger, but now she had Boone and
the entire Ryland clan in an assassin's path.

"I need to make some kind of deal with Ferguson,"
she said, thinking out loud. "I have to do something to
stop him."

Mason cursed and dragged her across the seat toward
him. Abbie landed right against him.

"Use my shoulder," he insisted. "Go ahead and have
yourself a good cry before we get to the sheriff's office.
But any talk about making deals with Ferguson stops. I

read the man's file, and you'd be safer dealing with the devil himself."

She wanted to say that the danger would stop if she were dead, but that might not be true. Abbie no longer had any idea what would keep everyone safe. And that tore through her heart. The tears came, despite her squeezing her eyes shut, and she wiped them away as fast as she could.

"Don't say you're sorry again," Mason grumbled when she looked up at him. "Got that?"

Because that was exactly what she was about to do, Abbie stayed quiet. She stayed put, too, even though she knew this close contact was wrong. It didn't make sense. In the middle of all of this, she shouldn't be feeling all tingly because of Mason. He hated her. And the only thing that could result from this was more trouble added to the heap of it she already had.

Abbie eased away from him.

"Those weren't many tears," he pointed out. "Or maybe it's the shoulder you object to?"

"The shoulder," she readily confirmed. She risked glancing at him. "Thanks for the offer, but leaning on your shoulder comes with a high price."

He didn't deny it. Mason just kept driving, his attention on the road ahead as they entered Silver Creek. "Yeah." And that was all he said. "I guess it's true. Opposites do attract. But in our case, it can't."

Abbie couldn't agree more. They had too much bad stuff in the way to even think about something as mundane as a kiss.

But still she thought about it.

Felt it, too. In fact, just thinking about Mason's kiss rid her of the rest of that chill. And that's the reason she moved all the way back to her side of the seat. The timing was perfect because Mason turned into the parking lot of the sheriff's office and came to a stop.

Considering the awkwardness simmering between them, Abbie would have jumped from the truck, but Mason held her back and looked around. Not an ordinary look, but a cop doing surveillance of an area where an assassin might be hiding. Abbie cursed herself for not thinking of that on her own. She'd kept herself safe for twenty-one years, and it was as if she had forgotten everything Boone had ever taught her.

"Let's go," Mason insisted when he had finished checking out the area.

He led her through the back entrance and into a hall, and they'd barely managed to make it inside when a man stepped out from one of the open doors. Judging from his appearance, this was another of Boone's sons. Also judging from the shiny badge clipped to his belt, he was a deputy sheriff.

The man's attention landed on her, and she got a scowl. Yep, definitely a Ryland.

"Abbie, this is my brother Dade," Mason said.

Dade didn't respond. He turned his attention to Mason. "Vernon Ferguson is already here. I put him in the interview room."

"Did he bring lawyers with him?" Mason asked.

"Two." Dade gave a dry smile.

Abbie was surprised Ferguson hadn't brought more. He could certainly afford it. Because he'd resigned as a police officer twenty-one years ago, he'd managed his late father's estate and apparently added even more millions to it. She doubted all those earnings had been legal.

"Grayson and Gage will start the interview in a few minutes," Dade continued. "They were just waiting for you to get here."

"Then let's get this show on the road." Mason tipped his head toward a room just up the hall, and Abbie followed him.

So did Dade but not before aiming another scowl at her.

"Did Boone ever tell you why he hated us so much that he had to leave?" Dade tossed out there.

Like the scowl, she'd expected the question or one similar to it. "No. And he never told me why he hated himself either."

Dade flexed his eyebrows and made a slight sound of amusement. "Grayson said you were the shy-and-quiet type."

Abbie mimicked the sound of disapproval Dade had made. "He was wrong." And she left it at that.

She was shy and quiet, but not when it came to defending Boone. Apparently, she would get a lot of practice doing that as long as she was around his sons. Hopefully not much longer. The first step to making that happen was this interview.

The moment she stepped into the room with Mason, she spotted Ferguson on the other side of what appeared to be a two-way mirror. Even though she knew he couldn't see her, Abbie had to force herself not to take a step back, but it was a challenge. He sat there at the iron-gray metal table in his expensive dark blue suit, flanked on each side by lawyers in equally pricey clothes.

"How long has it been since you've seen him?" Mason asked.

Unfortunately, Abbie didn't even have to think about her answer. "Five years, three months." She paused, gathered her breath. "Boone and I were working a ranch down in Laredo, and he showed up."

"Did he try to kill you?"

"I wish." But she waved that off. "It's just, if he had,

we could have had him arrested. But no. He was there to remind me that he could get to me anytime he wants. And he can. From time to time he sends me flowers. Notes. Anything to let me know I'm not safe and never will be."

Mason made another of those sounds that could have meant nothing or anything, and she watched as Grayson and his brother Gage entered the room.

"Ferguson is going through a lot of trouble to keep tabs on you," Mason commented. "Especially considering his fight was with your mother."

Abbie nodded. "He probably thinks she told me some things about him. She didn't. And if she had, I would have already gone to the cops with it."

Mason stayed quiet a moment. "Because he's obviously a warped man, maybe Ferguson wants to get back at Boone for helping you."

That made the chill in her blood even worse. Because it was exactly something that Ferguson would do. The chill quickly turned to anger, and she hated Ferguson for going after the man who'd literally saved her life.

At that exact moment, Ferguson's gaze lifted toward the mirror, and it seemed as if he knew she was there. Watching him. He smiled that oily smile she saw in her nightmares. Before she could stop herself, Abbie stepped back and tried to level her breathing.

"Marshal McKinney will offer Boone protection," Mason explained. His voice and body language didn't change, but he'd no doubt noticed her little defensive maneuver. "And he's already arranging a new identity for you. Probably not in Texas this time."

No. Not in Texas. Which meant she'd have to leave her home and her career because Ferguson would trace her that way. She might have to leave Boone, too. That might be her only chance to keep him safe if Ferguson truly had him in his sights.

And that broke her heart.

Mason adjusted the audio so they could hear Grayson explaining the reason for the interview. However, he didn't even finish before Dade appeared in the doorway of the observation room.

"We found Ace Chapman," Dade said to Mason. He had his phone sandwiched between his shoulder and his ear.

Abbie pulled in her breath. She hadn't forgotten about the hit man, of course, but Ferguson had distracted and unnerved her.

"Where?" Mason asked.

Dade lifted his index finger in a wait-a-second gesture and repeated the question to the person on the other end of the line.

A moment later, Dade cursed and drew his gun. "Ace Chapman is less than a block from here and headed this way."

Chapter Seven

Mason forced Abbie to sit down in the sole chair in the observation room. Not that it would help, but the way she was trembling, he didn't want her to fall on her face. And the chair was better than pulling her back into his arms. He wanted his arms and hands free in case Ace decided to do something stupid and storm the sheriff's office.

"Mel and I will go after Ace," Dade insisted. "You stay here with Abbie."

Mel was Deputy Melissa Garza, and between Dade and her, they had enough firepower and experience to bring down the assassin. Mason would have preferred to be in on the fight himself, especially because this was the bastard who'd fired at Abbie and him, but he couldn't take the risk. Instead, he shut the door the second Dade left. And he pulled his gun.

Pulling his gun didn't help Abbie's breathing and neither did the text he sent to Grayson to let him know what was going on. Abbie was able to see his brother's reaction and Gage's, too, when Grayson whispered the news to him.

"We have to reschedule this," Grayson informed Ferguson and his lawyers. That sent a flurry of questions and complaints from the lawyers, but Ferguson himself just smugly sat there as if he'd accomplished the chaos that he'd wanted.

"Is there a problem?" Ferguson asked Grayson when Gage got up and left. No doubt going to assist Dade and Mel.

"You tell me," Grayson fired back. "Is there?"

Ferguson lifted his shoulder in a casual shrug. "No problem that I'm aware of. I'm just doing my civic duty by voluntarily coming here to answer questions. Questions that you implied were urgent." Another shoulder lift. "Apparently, they're not so urgent after all if they can be rescheduled."

Mason wished he could muck out the stables with that arrogant face. But beside him, Abbie was having a different reaction.

"Ferguson knows what this is doing to me," she mumbled.

No doubt. Well, it was no doubt *if* Ferguson had been the one to hire Ace. Mason wasn't completely convinced that he had, and he hoped Marshal McKinney could get some answers from Boone. And getting answers from Boone was something Mason thought he'd never hear himself want.

On the other side of the glass, Ferguson checked his watch. "Well, I'm disappointed with the change in plans. I'd hoped to see Maddie this morning." He made a show of looking embarrassed, because Mason doubted it was genuine. "Oops, make that Abbie. That's what she's calling herself these days. She is here, isn't she?"

Grayson didn't answer that. "Why did you want to see her?"

Ferguson huffed as if the answer were obvious. "To give her my sympathies, of course. I heard about the fire and the shooting at your family's ranch where she's working. It's all over town. Gossips," he added in mock disgust. "I just wanted to assure her that I would do everything in my power to make certain she's safe."

That put a knot in Mason's stomach. What kind of sick game was this nutjob playing?

"You want to keep her safe?" Grayson added a flat look to go along with the question.

"I do." More mock disgust, but Mason could see the edges of a smile. "She was just a child when her mother was killed. That wasn't my fault, but you cops and the press blamed me for it." He shrugged, scraped one thumbnail with another. "Still, I can't blame Abbie for the mistakes of law enforcement."

"So you don't want her dead?" Grayson asked.

"No," Ferguson jumped to answer. "All a misunderstanding on her part. I want Abbie to be safe and happy." He turned his gaze back to the mirror. To Abbie. "I want her to be able to order white daisies for her mother's grave without having to look over her shoulder."

Abbie gasped and got to her feet. She would have started for the door if Mason hadn't latched on to her.

"He saw me. He watched me." The words rushed out with her breath. "Yesterday morning I came into town to get supplies with one of the ranch hands. I stopped by the florist to order flowers for my mother's grave. White daisies. Today would have been her birthday."

Hell. Mason made a mental note to call the P.I. agency again and see if someone there had leaked Abbie's location.

"Ferguson was stupid to admit that he knew you were in town. That means he had both motive and opportunity to send Ace after you." Even though that would be hard to prove, and Abbie's rattled sigh let him know that she was on the same page.

"I do have other appointments in town," Ferguson said after another check of his watch. "I suppose if your urgent questions haven't been answered by someone else, I could return in an hour or two."

His lawyers objected again, saying that he'd gone above and beyond to cooperate with the Silver Creek sheriff's office. They made it sound like something lower than hoof grit.

Ferguson stood, aimed another smile at Abbie. Mason put his hand on her shoulder to steady her and kept watching.

"I'm meeting with Rodney Stone and Nicole Manning at the Saddle and Spur Café," Ferguson said. "It's just up the street from here, right, Sheriff?"

Abbie could no doubt tell from Grayson's reaction that the question was a shocker. "Who are those people?" she asked Mason.

"They're connected to the late Senator Ford Herrington. Stone was his personal attorney and friend. Nicole, his longtime lover and campaign manager."

She shook her head. "Why would Ferguson be meeting with them, and why mention it to Grayson?"

"I'm not sure." Mason moved closer to the mirror and waited for Grayson to ask the question that Mason was also wondering.

Grayson didn't make him wait several seconds. "How do you know Rodney Stone and Nicole Manning?"

"You don't have to answer that," one of his lawyers advised.

But Mason could see the return of the smugness on Ferguson's slimy face. "No reason not to tell the sheriff that I contributed rather large sums of money to Senator Harrington's reelection campaigns. Ford introduced me to both of them, and we've seen each other at social engagements from time to time."

Mason didn't know why that surprised him. Both men

were rotten to the core, so, in a warped way, it seemed logical that they would have an association of some kind. Maybe they were even friends.

"Why are you meeting with the senator's former business associates?" Grayson pressed.

Ferguson smiled again. "Nicole has a book deal, one of those pillow talk, tell-all biographies, and Stone is representing her. I just want to make sure that my association with the senator will be portrayed in a good light."

Something was up, and considering this was Ferguson, it was something bad.

Ferguson snapped his fingers in an aha gesture. "You know, you Rylands should meet with Stone and Nicole, too. I mean, just to make sure she has the correct details."

"Details for what?" Grayson asked.

It was a good question considering that Mason and all his lawmen brothers were involved in the shootout that had ended with Ford's suicide. Also, considering that Nicole was dirty like her late boss and lover, there was no telling what she might say.

Ferguson smiled again. "About the affair Ford's wife had."

Oh, man. Nicole was bringing Granddaddy Chet into this? But Mason didn't have time for the anger to settle in.

"My grandfather's been dead for over twenty years," Grayson remarked. He seemed cool enough on the surface, but Mason knew he was riled underneath that lawman's exterior. "And Ford confessed to his murder. That's old news. Nothing for Nicole to rehash."

Ferguson made a sound of exaggerated surprise. "Oh, I can see you're not in the information loop. You should probably ask Nicole about this."

Grayson stood and met Ferguson eye to eye. "I'm asking *you*."

If Ferguson was the least bit intimidated by Grayson's stance or tone, he didn't show it. "It's not my secret to tell, but I'm sure Nicole will share all the bits and pieces with you." He reached across the table and extended his hand for Grayson to shake.

Grayson ignored him and strolled out ahead of Ferguson and his lawyers. His brother entered the observation room and he shut the door.

"What's the word on Ace Chapman?" Grayson said immediately.

"Nothing yet. Mel, Gage and Dade are out there." Mason watched as Ferguson left with his attorneys in tow. "What was all that about Nicole Manning and Rodney Stone?"

Grayson shook his head and looked at Abbie. "I was hoping you could tell me."

"No," Abbie quickly answered. "Mason told me about your grandfather's murder. And about the affair he had with the senator's wife. But I don't know how or if it relates to anything else."

Grayson gave him a look, and Mason groaned. Someone would have to go digging back through that old baggage. All of the painful memories, including those of Boone. And that *someone* was Mason.

There was a sharp knock at the door, and Mason automatically moved Abbie behind him. Just in case Ferguson was making a surprise visit. But it was Dade, and he shook his head the moment he opened the door.

"Ace Chapman got away," Dade said, causing the rest of them to groan. "Mel and Gage are still out there, and we've asked the Rangers to set up a roadblock. We might get lucky."

"Might," Abbie repeated, and Mason knew what she was thinking. As long as Ace was out there, she was in

grave danger. He'd already tried to kill her twice with the fire and the shots, and he wouldn't hesitate to try again.

Grayson moved closer to her and made eye contact. "It's your choice, but it'd be smart for you to stay here awhile, in our protective custody."

It was an offer he would make to anyone in danger. It was no different with Abbie, but Mason knew this wouldn't be easy for any of them.

"Come on," Mason insisted, and he tightened the grip he had on her arm. She was looking wobbly again. "We'll go to my office. I need to make some calls."

And calm Abbie down.

Grayson and Dade went in one direction, and Mason and Abbie headed up the hall. He got her inside as fast as he could but didn't shut the door, because he wanted to hear if anyone came into the building. Especially Ace. He doubted the hit man would make a stand in the sheriff's office, but he wasn't taking any chances.

"Ferguson's been watching me," she repeated. "Why didn't he just kill me when he saw me at the florist?"

Mason tried to make her sit, but she started to pace.

"My guess? Ferguson's not the sort to do the dirty work himself. He probably found you and then called Ace. And maybe he doesn't really want you dead. In his own sick way he might want you alive so he can torture you."

She gave a shaky nod and scrubbed her hands down her arms. "But how did he find me?"

Yes, that was the big question, and because Mason still didn't have an answer, he took out his phone and scrolled through the numbers until he got to Sentron, the P.I. agency in San Antonio. He put the call on Speaker, hoping that whatever he heard wouldn't make matters worse for Abbie, and when the receptionist answered, Mason asked to speak to the owner, Burke Dennison.

"Tell me what you've learned about the background check on Abbie Baker," Mason demanded.

"Well, it's not good," Burke said, making Mason groan.

Yeah. This would make matters worse for Abbie, but Mason was positive she wasn't going to let him take the call off Speaker. Besides, she had a right to know, and he'd deal with the fallout later.

"The agent who handled the background check is Shelley Martin," Burke explained, "and when she didn't get any of the usual info in her initial run, Shelley sent out the picture to San Antonio P.D. and to other P.I. agencies around town."

Mason would have groaned louder if it would help.

"Shelley figured this Abbie Baker was hiding something, and she was just doing her job," Burke added.

Oh, she was hiding something all right. Hiding from a killer.

"One of the other P.I.s thought Abbie looked familiar so he did some digging, made some calls and figured out that she's really Madelyn Turner."

And all that digging could and would have alerted Ferguson.

"I take it this created some problems?" Burke asked.

"You bet it did. We'll talk later." Mason would blast Burke in a private conversation, but doing that now would only add to Abbie's anxiety. For now, he hung up.

Abbie pushed her hair from her face and leaned against the wall. "Too bad I'm not at the ranch so I could go for a ride. It might work off some of this jitteriness."

Mason understood. It's how he burned off dangerous energy. And he was feeling a lot of that now, especially because he was partly responsible for Ferguson finding Abbie.

He slipped his phone back in his pocket and walked

closer. What he didn't do was close the door, even though she might like some privacy when she fell apart. There was that dangerous energy in the mix now, and privacy would only fuel things that shouldn't be fueled.

Still, he went closer and stopped right in front of her. "I'm sorry," he told her. And he wondered if she realized just how rare it was for him to apologize.

Apparently she did, because Abbie managed a weary smile before her breath broke, and a sob made its way from her throat. "I only made things worse by coming to Silver Creek."

He couldn't argue with that, but most of this wasn't her fault. Of course, all of this had started with her lie about who she really was, but considering how quickly Ferguson had found her, it was a warranted lie.

Well, for the most part.

And it was that *most part* and the sob that had Mason moving even closer. He slid his arm around her waist. The warning in his head came almost immediately. *Danger ahead*. But the rest of him pretty much ignored that, and he stayed put.

Abbie looked up at him, her eyes shiny with fresh tears. "It's harder when you're nice to me," she whispered.

Mason smiled before he could stop himself. Then frowned. Then scowled, but the scowl wasn't for Abbie. It was for him. What the heck was he doing?

Apparently, he was making a mistake.

That's because he leaned in, lowered his head and brushed a kiss on her cheek. In the back of his mind, he rationalized that this was the kind of comfort they both needed. But that was a lie. Kissing her, even a cheek kiss wasn't for comfort. It was to appease this blasted attraction.

Abbie made a sound. Not a sob. But a soft murmur that sounded like a pleasure reaction. Mason tested that theory with another brush kiss. This time, though, his mouth moved to hers.

Oh, yeah.

It was pleasure all right. And bad. Very bad. That's because he didn't move, and he didn't stop with just a simple touch. He pressed harder. Moved closer. Touching her body with his. And taking the kiss of comfort to a whole new level.

Man, she tasted good.

Like something he'd searched for his entire life. And he couldn't feel that way, especially not about Abbie.

Did that stop him?

No.

Nor did the fact that his office door was wide-open, and one of his brothers could come walking in at any moment.

But Abbie thankfully had some sense left. She pulled back, met his gaze. "We should rethink this," she whispered. And then she did something that caused his body to clench, and beg. She ran her tongue over her bottom lip and made that sound of pleasure again.

He was toast.

Mason was ready to go back for a second kiss, but the jangling sound stopped him cold. Even through the hot haze in his head, he knew the sound meant that someone had just come through the front door of the sheriff's office.

He hoped like heck that it wasn't Ace Chapman.

Abbie no doubt thought the same thing because the fear, and some embarrassment, flashed through her eyes.

"Stay put," Mason warned her, and with his gun ready, he stepped into the hall, bracing himself for a showdown with a hit man.

But it wasn't Ace Chapman who had just stepped in.

Mason saw the man, and his stomach went to his knees.

Boone Ryland was back.

Chapter Eight

Abbie held her breath, waiting. But Mason didn't shoot at the person who had captured his attention. In fact, no one shot, but the building suddenly went silent.

She inched closer to Mason, looked around him, and she cursed when she spotted Boone. What the heck was he doing here?

"You asked him to come?" Mason wanted to know. Except it wasn't a question. It was a demand. And what was left of the heat from the kiss turned ice-cold. In fact, it felt as if the temperature in the entire place had dropped.

"No, I didn't ask him to come here." In fact, this was the last place Abbie wanted to see Boone, and his sons no doubt felt the same. Of course, she had a different reason. She loved him, and Silver Creek was not a safe place right now.

Abbie maneuvered around Mason. Then Dade. And finally around Grayson before she made it to the front where the petite brunette dispatcher sat with her mouth wide-open. Abbie had braced herself for a confrontation with Ace, but in some ways this might be worse.

The three brothers came forward, a united force, standing in the hall behind her.

"You shouldn't have come back," Dade tossed out to

Boone. But she figured any of them could have voiced that particular sentiment.

Boone didn't look hurt by the remark. Just resigned. But he did take a moment to study each of his sons. Because Abbie knew him so well, she saw the pride. The pain. And the swirl of emotions that Boone had tried to bury for the past two decades.

"Are you okay?" Boone asked, his attention returning to her.

"I'm fine," she lied. Even though she knew it would upset the others, she went around the reception desk and gave him a hug. Yes, it would cause more friction, if that was possible, but she needed that hug. Apparently, Boone did, too.

"Funny that you're concerned about her safety." Dade, again.

"Not funny," Boone assured him. "I'm concerned about your safety, too. About all of you."

Judging from the sound Dade made, he didn't believe him.

"Why are you here?" she whispered to Boone.

"Why are you here?" Boone repeated. "You said you were going to Austin. You lied to me."

She nodded. "I'm sorry. Believe it or not, I was trying to help."

"You should have talked to me first." He cocked his eyebrow in a gesture that reminded her of Grayson. "I heard about the fire and the shooting."

"We're investigating it," Grayson explained. "And we don't need or want your help."

She glanced back at Mason to see if he would add anything, but he just stood there glaring.

"Have you found the man Vernon Ferguson hired to kill Abbie?" Boone asked. He volleyed glances at all three of his sons.

It was Grayson who stepped forward to answer. "We're still looking for him." He paused. "You have proof that Ferguson is the one who hired the gunman?"

Boone shook his head. "No, but he's come after her before. And he had her mother gunned down right in front of her."

Even though that'd happened ages ago, it still required Abbie to take a deep breath. "Ferguson was in here earlier," she told Boone. "And he insinuated that this might be connected to Senator Herrington's suicide and the affair his wife had with your late father-in-law."

"You remember that?" Dade spoke up. "Of course you do. You ran out on us shortly thereafter. Bad timing." Dade jabbed his index finger in Boone's direction. "And if you think for one minute that we'll forgive you for that, for losing our mother, then think again."

Boone shook his head, and a weary breath left his mouth. "No. I know you won't forgive me. I didn't come for that. I came to get Abbie out of here before Ferguson tries to kill her again." He tipped his head toward the door. "We need to go."

"Not a smart move." Mason's voice sliced through the thick silence that followed Boone's request. "The hit man, Ace Chapman, is still out there."

"Men like him are always out there," Boone answered. "I've kept her safe for over twenty years."

"Have you?" Mason challenged. He walked past his brothers. "Because just last night someone tried to kill her. Twice."

Boone flinched, just a little, probably not enough for his sons to notice. But Abbie noticed.

"She shouldn't have come to Silver Creek," Boone said. A father's warning. Abbie had heard it often enough when she was a kid.

"I was worried about you," she explained.

Boone stared at her. "Well, now we're even because I'm worried about you. It's time to leave."

"She can't leave." Mason didn't raise his voice, didn't change his tone, but it got everyone's attention. "Abbie's at the center of an attempted murder and an arson investigation. She's not just the victim, she's also a witness, and I haven't even taken her statement yet."

"Then take it," Boone said on a huff. "I need to put some distance between her and Ferguson."

Mason came closer, put his hands on his hips. He also continued to scowl at his father. "Once she gives her statement, she'll need to be in protective custody. Not with you. But with me."

"You hardly know her," Boone fired back. "I can protect her as well as you can."

Because this could turn into a full-scale argument, Abbie huffed and held up her hands. "I'm standing right here and don't appreciate not being part of this discussion."

"It's not a discussion," Mason let her know. "It's an investigation, and it's not up to your foster father to determine how best to keep you safe."

Abbie wanted that, to be safe, but she didn't want to pit Mason against Boone. She turned to Boone, trying to figure out a way to calm some of his fears, but Mason's profanity stopped her cold.

"Not this," Mason grumbled. "Not now."

She followed his gaze to the front glass and spotted the couple making a beeline for the sheriff's office. The woman was tall, curvy and had perfectly styled honey-blond hair. The fifty-something man was wearing a business suit and carrying a briefcase.

Mason moved quickly. He came to the front of the reception desk, latched on to Abbie and yanked her behind him. Dade and Grayson came forward, too, and they created a human shield in front of her.

"What's wrong?" Abbie managed to ask.

"That's Rodney Stone and Nicole Manning," Mason said just as the couple stepped inside.

Abbie knew the names, of course. Ferguson had mentioned them earlier, and they were former associates of the late Senator Ford Herrington.

Nicole looked at the protective stance of the three lawmen, smiled, and her smile widened when her attention landed on Boone.

"The patriarch returns home," Nicole said, her voice an annoying purr.

"Just visiting," Boone insisted. "What brings you here?"

"Just visiting," Stone repeated. His voice wasn't a purr, more like a growl, and he wasn't smiling either.

"You know them?" Abbie whispered to Boone.

He nodded.

"Boone and I go way back," Nicole provided. She paused and dropped the smile when she turned to Grayson. She glanced behind him at Abbie. "So this is the woman you're trying to protect?"

"Not trying," Mason snapped. "We *are* protecting her."

"Good luck with that," Nicole mumbled. "We're here to see Vernon Ferguson."

Grayson lifted his shoulder. "He's gone, said he was meeting you two at the Saddle and Spur."

"He didn't show," Stone barked. "He's late, and I'm tired of waiting for him."

"That sounds like a personal problem to me," Mason replied. "But because you're here, maybe you wouldn't mind answering some questions. Ferguson said you plan to reveal some *secrets* in your book."

"A few," Nicole smugly volunteered.

"She's playing with fire," Stone interrupted, and he shot her a glare. "Sometimes, secrets are best kept that way." He checked his watch. "I have to go."

"What secrets?" Abbie asked when Stone reached for the door. She stepped out from behind Mason, something he obviously didn't like because he tried to block her again.

"Oh, don't worry. They don't pertain to you. Well, not directly." Nicole aimed her sick, secretive smile at Boone.

"If you have something to say to me, just come out and say it," Boone told her.

"No, thanks." Yet another dose of smugness. "You'll have to wait for the book."

"While this conversation is riveting," Stone said with sarcasm dripping from his voice, "I'm done here. If Ferguson shows, tell him to call me." And with that order she doubted the Rylands would relay, he turned and walked out.

"You'll have to excuse him," Nicole said. "Stone's a bit of a sourpuss these days. I think there are some legal issues with Ford's will. Something's making him testy."

And Abbie couldn't help but wonder if this was connected to Ace and the fire. All of it was certainly connected to the Rylands, and Boone was especially uncomfortable.

Nicole checked her own watch. "Must run. Sorry to have bothered you." She fluttered her perfectly manicured nails at them in a goodbye gesture and walked out.

"What the hell was that all about?" Mason asked, turning his attention directly to Boone.

Abbie was about to assure Mason that Boone had nothing to do with this, but Boone's expression said otherwise.

What was going on?

However, before Abbie could ask Boone some questions of her own, the phone rang. When the dispatcher-receptionist answered it, Abbie realized they should

probably wait and have this conversation in private. She
didn't know the woman at the desk, and therefore she didn't
know if everything being said here would be blabbed all
over town.

"What's wrong, Tina?" Grayson asked the woman
who'd just answered the phone.

Abbie turned, looked at the dispatcher to see what had
prompted Grayson's question. Her face said it all. The
woman turned ashy pale.

"The caller says he's Ace Chapman," she relayed, and
she handed the phone to Grayson. "He says don't bother
trying to trace the call because he's using a prepaid cell."

Abbie's stomach knotted. Her chest became tight. And
just like that, she was taken right back to the nightmare
of nearly being killed.

Mason moved closer to Abbie, both of them with their
gazes fastened to Grayson as he put the phone to his ear.
But Grayson wasn't saying anything. He was just listening.
Several moments later, he handed the phone back to Tina.

"Was it Ace?" Mason immediately asked.

"Hard to tell, but he claims he is." He looked at Boone.
"Ace said I'm to give you a message—if you'll surrender
to him, he won't harm Abbie."

"What?" Abbie couldn't ask that fast enough. She
snapped toward Boone. "Why would he ask you to do
something like that? Do you know him?"

"No, I don't." Boone went to her and ran his hand down
the length of her arm. "But it's not a bad offer."

Abbie had to get past the gasp in her throat before she
could speak. "How can you say that?" She pushed his hand
away so she could latch on to him. "What's going on?"

Mason got right in Boone's face. "Do you know who
hired Ace?"

"I'm guessing it's Ferguson."

"A guess?" Mason challenged. He stared at his father. "Start talking. Tell us why this is happening."

"I have no way of knowing that, but I do know men like Ferguson, and he probably figures this is a way of making Abbie suffer."

"It would work," she let him know, "if you were going out there. But you aren't."

Boone gave weary sigh. "It might put an end to things with Ferguson."

"And it could get you killed!" Abbie fired back. She turned to Mason for help, figuring it was a long shot at best.

"If you know men like Ferguson, then you also know he's a liar," Mason stated. "Yeah, he might have you gunned down to hurt Abbie, but he could be doing this to get you out of the way. As you pointed out, you've kept her alive for over twenty years." Mason shrugged. "Ferguson might believe his best shot at her is to get you out of the way."

The argument was dead-on, something Abbie wished she'd thought to say. Hard to think rationally, though, when her thoughts were racing and she might be on the verge of losing the man she considered to be her father.

Boone's jaw tightened. The muscles stirred there. But he finally nodded. "So, how do we stop him?"

"There's no *we* in this." Mason met his stare with one of his own. "You leave Silver Creek, and I put Abbie in protective custody."

"Boone needs protection, too," Abbie pointed out.

That suggestion went over like a lead balloon. All but Tina scowled at her, and the woman seemed as confused and frightened as Abbie was.

Boone looked at Mason again. "Keep Abbie safe. Don't make her pay for the things I did wrong."

Mason didn't respond, other than a deepening scowl. Boone gave a nod to the others before turning to her.

Boone opened the door and glanced at her over his shoulder. "I'll be here in town when it's safe for you to leave."

She was about to nod, but without warning Mason again shoved her behind him.

"Get down!" Grayson shouted.

From the corner of her eye, Abbie saw the split second of movement next to the building across the street from the sheriff's office. It was a man, dressed all in black. And before it could even register in Abbie's mind, he fired a shot.

It slammed into the glass next to Boone's head.

Boone dived to the floor. Mason and Abbie did the same, and Mason practically crawled over her and came up ready to fire. Boone also pulled the Colt that he always carried in the back waist of his jeans.

Another shot crashed into the dispatcher's desk. Tina screamed, and there was a scurry of movement. Dade and Grayson were no doubt getting the woman out of the line of fire.

Boone aimed the Colt, pulled the trigger. Just as the shooter darted behind the building and out of sight.

"It's Ace Chapman," Mason relayed to the others.

Of course. Who else? Ferguson wasn't going to do this himself, but she wouldn't be surprised if he were close by, watching all of this.

"Stay down," Mason warned her, and he levered himself up. For a moment she thought he was only shifting position, but he moved off her. "Switch places with me," he told Boone.

"No!" Abbie managed to say. She didn't want either of them up and moving, but neither listened to her.

Another shot came crashing through the glass front

door. It was reinforced with metal wire so the glass didn't shatter, but the next shot splintered some wood on the desk.

"I'm coming up," Mason said. "Everybody else stay down."

She wanted to shout no again because whatever he had in mind had to be dangerous. Of course, being pinned down by a hit man wasn't exactly safe. Abbie reminded herself that Mason was an experienced lawman.

That didn't help.

She was just as terrified for his safety and prayed that Ace wouldn't shoot Mason or anyone else to get to her.

Mason scurried to the doorway. It happened fast but in slow motion, too. Her heart and head were pounding. Her stomach, churning. But because she wasn't armed, there was nothing she could do but lie there beside Boone and watch.

Mason was fast. He came up on one knee, and in the same motion he took aim.

He fired.

Not one shot but two, loud thick blasts that roared through the room and through her. Boone threw his arm over her, pushing her all the way to the floor so that she couldn't see what was happening.

However, she did hear Mason curse.

Oh, mercy. Something was wrong.

"Get an ambulance," Mason shouted. *"Now!"*

Chapter Nine

Mason could only stand and watch the ambulance speed away with Ace Chapman inside. The medic, Tommy Watters, had mumbled something about the man's condition "not looking good." Mason couldn't argue with that. They'd be darn lucky if the hit man pulled through this.

"You did what you had to do," Grayson reminded Mason. Again.

But it was a reminder that didn't help much. In most situations like this, Mason would have shot to kill. This time, though, he'd tried to neutralize Ace while keeping him alive.

So they would have a chance of Ace telling them who'd hired him.

That chance was slim to none right now. Ace had moved at the last second when Mason had fired, and instead of Mason's shot going into the man's shoulder, it had slammed into his chest. He'd gone down hard and fast.

"If Ace says anything, Dade will hear it," Grayson added.

Yeah, Dade might because he was riding in the ambulance and would no doubt stay at the hospital until there was some kind of update. But unless Ace regained consciousness, a confession wasn't likely.

That meant they were back to having a lot of questions and no real answers.

Mason turned and headed back into the sheriff's office to check on Abbie and the others. No one else had been shot, thank God, but one look at Abbie's face and he knew she hadn't come out of this unscathed.

She was seated in the chair across from his desk. Not alone. Boone was standing by her side with his hand stroking the back of her hair. Across the hall, Tina, the dispatcher, was having a crying meltdown in Grayson's office. His brother was on the phone rounding up the rest of the deputies to help with the investigation.

Mason stepped in the doorway of his office, and Abbie immediately got to her feet. "Did Ace say anything?" she asked with way too much hope in her voice.

He shook his head, dashing those hopes to the floor. "Dade will keep us updated." And then he slid his gaze to Boone. Mason didn't say a word, but he figured his unfriendly expression would do the trick.

It did.

"I'll be out front," Boone mumbled.

"Not outside," Abbie said. No more hope, just alarm in her tone and on her face.

"No. I'll be in reception," Boone assured her.

Mason stepped back, way back, so that Boone could get past him without getting close. He didn't even look at the man who'd fathered him. Instead, Mason kept his attention on Abbie.

"You okay?" he asked her.

She made a sound, part laughter, that had nothing to do with humor. "I should be used to this by now."

"No one should be used to this," he mumbled. Even though Texas-sized warning bells were going off in his head, Mason went to her anyway and pulled her into his arms.

The bells went silent.

Everything else in his head got louder. He knew he should back away, but he didn't.

Abbie eased back, looked up at him. "I should be used to this now, too." She glanced down at his arms wrapped around her. "You've been doing it a lot lately. Don't get me wrong," she quickly added, "I like it. In fact, I need it. But I know how much it's costing you."

Yeah, there was a price tag on it all right. Each time he was with her, his thoughts drifted to sex. Nothing permanent. He never thought past the seasons of the ranch. But even a one-night stand with Abbie meant he had to get past her relationship with Boone.

Mason shrugged.

If this heat inside him kept building, he could probably get past anything, and that wasn't good either.

"Most people are scared of me," he reminded her, hoping it would cause her to back away and put an end to this.

"I know," she mumbled. No backing away. She moved closer, resting her head against his shoulder.

Oh, mercy. Her body was warm and she practically sank into him. That warmth gave his own body some bad ideas, like taking her back to the ranch and to his bed.

"Don't worry," she whispered. "I'll be out of your life soon."

Mason made a sound of agreement, but the agreement didn't settle well in his mind. It was probably the forced camaraderie from the danger that was stirring the attraction. Not that the attraction needed anything to stir it. It was there, plain and simple, and even if his body was starting to ache for Abbie, Mason knew it wasn't wise for it to happen.

He backed away to tell her that, but his cell rang before he could get out a word. Hoping that it was an update from Dade, he looked at the screen. Not Dade. But it was someone Mason had expected to call.

"Marshal McKinney," Mason greeted. He put the call on Speaker. "Thanks for getting back to me. I have Abbie with me now."

"Good. I heard about the shooting. Was she hurt?"

"No," Mason and she answered in unison.

"Good," the marshal repeated. And added what sounded to be a breath of relief. "Abbie, I'm working on your identity reassignment now and should have everything together in a day or two. Until then, I need you to remain in Deputy Ryland's protective custody. Will there be a problem with that?"

She looked at him, and Mason could almost tell what she was thinking. Yes, it would be a problem, but the alternative was worse. Just because Ace was out of commission, it didn't mean his boss wouldn't just hire someone else.

"I can stay here," she said to the marshal, but she gave Mason a questioning stare.

He shrugged. Then nodded. Which, of course, made it seem as if he were indifferent or opposed. He wasn't. He wanted Abbie safe, especially because the photo to the P.I. had likely been the trigger that had put her in danger.

"Will Boone Ryland be relocating with you?" the marshal asked her.

"Yes." She dodged Mason's gaze. "In fact, he could be Ferguson's target now. Ace Chapman called right before he attacked, and he wanted Boone to *surrender* to him."

"Any idea why?" McKinney asked.

"No, but I'm hoping we'll find out."

"Vernon Ferguson is in town," Mason informed McKinney. "Either my brother or I will question him again, maybe put some pressure on him."

"I doubt he'll crack," the marshal said. "But it won't hurt to try."

No, it wouldn't. Well, it wouldn't as long as Mason could keep Ferguson far away from Abbie.

Mason ended the call and looked down at her. "I need to take you back to the ranch."

She didn't argue, not exactly. "I have to talk to Boone first."

Of course she did. Mason stepped aside and had her go ahead of him, but he also followed her to the front reception area where Boone was standing and looking out the broken glass door.

"You're leaving?" Boone turned and immediately asked her.

Abbie nodded. "Marshal McKinney is making arrangements for us, but in the meantime I'll be at the ranch. I just wanted to make sure you were headed someplace safe."

"I am," he promised. Boone shut the partially shattered door, hooked his arm around her and brushed a kiss on her forehead. Yet another fatherly gesture that had Mason's blood boiling.

Boone must have noticed Mason's reaction because he eased away from Abbie. Mason's temper cooled, and he reminded himself that Abbie needed a fatherly shoulder right now. Still, that didn't mean he was going to play nice when it came to Boone.

"You'll keep her safe?" Boone asked.

That pushed Mason's ornery button. Of course, anything Boone said was likely to do that. "Yeah, but not because you're asking." In case Boone had forgotten, Mason tapped the badge on his belt.

And Mason cursed himself.

Because Abbie saw the badge tap, and she looked as if he'd slugged her. Great. That kiss, the hugs and dirty thoughts were bleeding over into the job. And that could be a massive mistake.

"When things settle down," Boone said, "I'd like to visit your mother's grave."

"No." And Mason didn't hesitate. "The cemetery's too close to the ranch, and I don't want you there."

"I could use the back way and come up from the other end of the creek," Boone offered. "None of you would have to see me."

"But we'd know. Besides, it's in bad taste to visit a woman you helped put in the grave." Mason snapped toward Abbie. "Ready?" It wasn't a suggestion.

However, before she could answer or move, Boone spoke. "We need to talk. Not about the cemetery or ranch. I'll stay away like you want. But we need to talk."

Mason was about to say they had nothing to discuss, but there he was again, letting personal stuff get in the way. Truth was, they might have something to talk about.

"You're sure you don't know Ace Chapman?" Mason asked. Yeah, he'd already asked something similar, but he hadn't like the answer he'd gotten then.

Boone looked him straight in the eye. "I never met him in my life." He paused. "But there are some things I need to tell you and your brothers."

Mason held up his hand. "We're not taking a trip down memory lane here."

Boone blew out a long, weary breath. "We have to," he insisted. "I need to tell you what happened twenty years ago that caused me to leave."

"No," Mason said through clenched teeth. "None of us want to hear it."

"You need to hear it," Boone calmly said. "Because what happened then could be the reason Ace Chapman just tried to kill us."

ABBIE FROZE AND MENTALLY repeated what Boone had just said. "The attack is related to something you did?" she asked, praying the answer would be no.

But Boone didn't say no. He tipped his head to the hall. "Why don't we take this into Grayson's office?"

Her attention darted to Mason, to see how he was reacting to all of this, and he was just as shocked as she was. Except his was mixed with anger.

Mason aimed his index finger at Boone. "This better not be some trick to get us to listen to your sob story."

"It's not," Boone assured him, and he walked past them toward Grayson's office.

Mason and she followed. "You know what this is about?" Mason asked her.

"Don't have a clue." But Abbie hoped it didn't make things worse.

Boone went into Grayson's office, and Grayson looked at his brother first. "He said he's got something to say about Ace Chapman," Mason snarled.

Grayson's mouth tightened, and he ended his call and slipped his phone back in his pocket. "Then say it fast," Grayson ordered. "Because I'm busy."

Despite that hurry-up tone, Boone took his time answering. "Twenty-one years ago your granddaddy Chet started investigating Ford Herrington. Ford wasn't a senator then. He owned a couple of successful businesses in the county, and Chet thought Ford was involved in an illegal land deal to expand one of those businesses."

"Old news," Mason snarled. "I studied Ford's file, and I know all about that deal. There's no proof that Ford was personally involved. That's why neither Chet nor anybody else ever arrested him."

"The night he was killed, Chet went out to the Herrington estate to question Ford's wife, Sandra." Boone continued as if he hadn't heard Mason.

"We know that Granddaddy Chet had an affair with Sandra," Grayson interrupted. "Ford admitted that right before he killed himself."

"Ford was wrong," Boone said. That grabbed Abbie's attention and created a heavy silence in the room. "Chet wasn't having an affair with Sandra," Boone continued. "I was."

Abbie was sure she blinked. Until a month ago she hadn't even realized that Boone had known the late senator, so this was the first she was hearing about Herrington's wife.

"You had an affair?" Mason demanded. But it wasn't just a simple question. No, it was laced with suspicion and anger. Especially the anger.

Boone nodded. "It didn't last long, and it was a huge mistake. By the time Chet showed up that night, Sandra and I were already ending things."

The silence returned, and the brothers exchanged glances. "Mom knew?" Grayson asked.

"I don't think so." Boone cursed under his breath. "Chet didn't know, not until that night when he found Sandra and me together."

Abbie went closer. "What happened?"

Again, Boone took his time answering. "Chet was furious. Understandable. I was cheating on his daughter—"

"And you had six kids at home," Mason snapped.

"Yes," Boone acknowledged. Staring at Mason. "Like I said, it was a bad mistake. And it got worse." He paused. "Ford showed up at his house, too, while I still there, and he was suspicious. He said he knew that Sandra was having an affair, and rather than let Ford go to your mother and tell her, Chet lied and told Ford that he was the one who'd been seeing Sandra."

"Granddaddy Chet lied to protect you?" Mason pressed.

"And to protect your mother," Boone verified. "Ford was furious and out of control. He said he'd kill Sandra and make it look like an accident or suicide."

Mason cursed, and his brother wasn't far behind with the profanity. "You didn't bother to tell anyone this?" Grayson snarled.

"There wasn't time." Boone wearily dragged his hands over his face. "Chet told me to leave, and I did. Because I was stupid and thought he could handle things. I went to a bar, got drunk, and when I was leaving to go home two of Ford's bodyguards grabbed me and took me to a storage warehouse in San Antonio."

Abbie looked at Mason to see if he'd known any of this. Judging from his stunned expression, the answer was *no*.

"That same day Chet was gunned down in what was supposedly a botched robbery attempt," Boone went on. "And then Sandra drowned in the creek." His gaze came to Mason's again. "Neither was an accident. Ford either had them killed or he did it himself."

Mason opened his mouth, closed it. It took him several moments to speak. "You kept this to yourself?"

"I couldn't tell anyone," Boone insisted.

Mason huffed and aimed a scowl at his father. Abbie wanted to intercede; she wanted to do something to defuse the tension, but she didn't know where to start. She'd known Boone was troubled after the senator's suicide, and this might be the reason. Well, at least the beginning of the reason.

"You said Ford's bodyguards took you to a warehouse," she said to get the conversation moving again. "What did Ford do to you?"

"Everything," Boone whispered, and he repeated it. "Ford came to me and gave me an order to leave town."

"Why didn't he just kill you like he did the others?" Grayson fired back.

"Because I told him I'd recorded the conversation in which he threatened to kill Sandra and make it look like an accident. I didn't. It was a lie. A bluff," Boone corrected. "And that's when Ford threatened to kill one of you. I couldn't let that happen."

Abbie pulled in her breath. Even though this had happened over twenty years ago, she could still hear the pain, fresh and raw, in Boone's voice. However, she could also see that same pain in Grayson's and Mason's faces.

"So you worked out some kind of blood deal with Ford?" Grayson asked.

"I guess you could call it that. It benefited Ford, that's for sure. He said he'd let all of you live if I left town and the tape recording never surfaced."

Abbie's stomach dropped.

But Mason's reaction was less extreme. He gave Boone a flat look. "Again, why didn't you tell anybody this?"

"Because I didn't want any of you to die."

"Someone did die," Grayson pointed out. "Our mother committed suicide because you left."

"Your mother had battled depression most of her life." Boone mumbled something else that Abbie didn't catch. "And Ford pushed her over the edge by telling her about the affair. I didn't know that until after the fact. Ford paid me a visit and gloated about how she'd fallen apart when he told her that I'd slept with Sandra."

Oh, mercy. The color drained from Mason's face. Grayson didn't fare much better. He turned, dropped down into the chair behind his desk and buried his face in his hands.

Despite his pain, Mason faced Boone head-on. "How

did Ford find out his wife had the affair with you and not with Granddaddy Chet?"

"Sandra told him right before he killed her. That's when Ford realized he'd murdered the wrong man."

Their grandfather had died for no reason. Well, no reason other than letting Ford believe he was sleeping with Sandra Herrington.

"If you'd told someone sooner, we could have caught Ford," Mason insisted. "And you wouldn't have put the family through hell and back."

"I tried to catch him." Boone leaned against the wall and let it support him. "I tried for years, but Ford was too smart for me. He never left a trace of himself behind."

"Until he committed suicide," Abbie mumbled. She gave that some thought and shook her head. "I saw you reading the newspapers about the suicide, but you didn't seem relieved."

"I wasn't," Boone admitted.

That caused Mason to huff. "I guess because you no longer had a reason to stay gone."

"No." Boone looked away. "Because I had an even bigger reason to stay gone."

Abbie was certain she'd misheard Boone. "What do you mean?"

But Boone didn't get a chance to answer. That's because the bell over the front door jangled, and after the shooting, everyone was clearly on edge. Both Mason and Grayson drew their guns, and Boone stepped in front of her—just as Mason tried to do the same. They ended up colliding shoulders, causing Mason to shoot his father a glare.

Grayson stepped out in the hall, his attention locked on the front. And he cursed. "What are you doing here?" he asked, and it wasn't a friendly question.

"I heard you had some trouble," the visitor said.

Abbie groaned because she recognized that voice—Vernon Ferguson.

"Stay put," Mason warned her.

But he didn't and neither did Grayson and Boone. They all waltzed out of the room to deal with the man after *her*. Well, Abbie was tired of hiding out and letting them fight her battles. Tired of what this was doing to the Rylands. So despite the warning, she stepped out as well, and Ferguson snagged her gaze right away.

He gave her an oily smile. "Abbie, I'd hoped to run into to you today."

"Did you figure I'd be dead?" she fired back, earning her a first-class glare from all the Ryland males. She returned the look and elbowed her way past them to face Ferguson.

"Dead?" Ferguson made a tsk-tsk sound. "I hear an accusation coming on." He made a sweeping motion toward the bullet-riddled glass. "I suppose now you're going to ask me if I hired the person to do this?"

"You bet I am," Abbie answered.

"Abbie," Mason warned again. "You shouldn't be doing this."

"We all do a lot of things we shouldn't do." And she aimed that at Boone for keeping secrets all these years. Yes, he had a good reason for keeping things quiet—so he could protect his sons—but they wouldn't be here if it weren't for his affair with a married woman.

"I'm sure you already know the hit man's name is Ace Chapman," Abbie supplied to Ferguson. Mason caught onto her to keep her from going closer, but she threw off his grip. "So did you hire him?"

"Of course not." His light, off-the-cuff tone didn't help her suddenly surly mood.

"You're a coward, you know that? You get people to

fight your fight." Abbie didn't wait for him to respond. "My mother wasn't a coward. She stood up to you and testified against you."

Ferguson's eyes narrowed, and Mason stepped directly in front of her, cutting off her view of the reaction she'd caused in the weasel who'd tormented her for most of her life.

"And look where that got your mother," Ferguson calmly said.

Nothing could have held her back at that point. *Nothing.* Abbie came out from behind Mason and rushed around the counterlike desk that divided the entrance from the rest of the building. She made it to Ferguson with Mason right on her heels and with Boone moving in from the side, and it was Mason who stepped between them at the last second. Boone grabbed Ferguson.

"It's time for you to leave," Mason told the man while he used his brute strength to keep Abbie behind him.

Ferguson stared them both down. "Of course." There wasn't even a touch of emotion in his voice. "But I'm not the threat here." Ferguson threw off Boone's grip. "He is."

Abbie quit struggling to get past Mason, and she looked at Boone, waiting for him to deny it.

But he didn't.

Mason obviously noticed the lack of denial, too, because he stared at his father. "What's he talking about?"

"Tell them," Ferguson taunted. "Tell them that the reason Abbie was nearly killed was because of you."

Again, Boone didn't deny it, and that robbed Abbie of her breath.

"I told you the truth about that deal I cut with Ford," Boone finally said. He let that hang in the air for several seconds. "But I didn't tell you that Ford promised he would reach out from the grave to ensure I never came back to Silver Creek."

Ferguson smiled again. "What Boone is fumbling to say is that Ford left instructions to have him—and all the rest of you—murdered."

Chapter Ten

Mason hadn't thought this investigation could get any crazier, but he'd been wrong. Abbie clearly thought the same because she just stood there with a stunned look on her face. The only one who wasn't gob smacked was Ferguson, and he was enjoying this way too much.

Mason did something about that.

"You're leaving now," Mason ordered the snake who'd just delivered the latest bombshell, and he moved closer to let Ferguson know he would be tossed out if he didn't obey. Mason wanted details of this beyond-the-grave mess, and he didn't want to discuss anything else in front of the man who'd tried to kill Abbie.

Well, Ferguson was probably the one who'd hired Ace to kill her.

However, after this latest revelation, Mason had to rethink that. Boone certainly wasn't jumping to say that Ferguson's claims weren't true.

Ferguson gave them an exaggerated wave, another of those blasted smiles, and he walked out.

"Start talking," Grayson demanded the moment Ferguson was out of earshot. He had his narrowed eyes aimed at Boone, and Mason made sure his glare let Boone know that he would explain everything.

Boone nodded and gave a heavy sigh. "All those years

ago when Ford threatened to kill you and your brothers, I told him that I'd kill him first. He laughed and said it was already too late for that, if he didn't call off his goons within the next ten minutes that at least two of you would be gunned down."

That required Mason to take a deep breath. All of his brothers had been young then, especially Gage and Kade. Heck, they'd been barely eleven and twelve. Just kids. The idea of a hired gun killing them tore at him hard.

"You believed Ford?" Mason clarified.

"Oh, yeah. He'd just murdered his wife and your grandfather. I didn't think it'd be much of a stretch for him to add two of my boys to the list."

Boys. That hit hard, too. Mason had been sixteen and his father's right-hand man at the ranch. Mason had wanted to be just like him. Until Boone walked out. And then Mason had just wanted him gone and out of their lives forever.

"What about Ford leaving instructions to kill us after his death?" Mason pressed.

Boone nodded, a muscle flickering in his jaw. "The same day that Ford ran me out of town, he said I couldn't come back. *Ever.* I said I'd come back as soon as I put him in the grave."

"You threatened to kill him?" Abbie asked.

Boone met her gaze. "I would have killed him, but he showed me a letter. It was instructions that in the event of his death, me and my entire family were to be killed." He paused. "I didn't think it was a bluff."

No, not from Ford. He wasn't the bluffing type. And that meant the danger was just starting.

For all of them.

Abbie stepped closer to Mason, her arm brushing against his, and she looked up at him as if she knew exactly what this was doing to him. And what it was doing was tearing him apart. He didn't want to go through this again. Didn't want to relive the memories of the god-awful past. He just wanted to toss Boone out and go back a couple of days.

But then Mason glanced down at Abbie.

Going back would mean there'd been no rescue, no kiss. No gentle arm brush. And that was a good thing.

Okay, it wasn't, and all the lies he told himself wouldn't change that.

That caused Mason to mentally curse again. He wasn't sure why it was good to have Abbie here, but for the first time in a long while, he felt he had someone on his side. Even if having her there would complicate the heck out of an already-complicated situation.

"I don't know who Ford instructed to kill us," Boone continued. "I don't know who got that letter. That's what I've been trying to find out since the moment I heard Ford had committed suicide."

"Lynette," Grayson said, taking the name right out of Mason's mouth. "I'll call her." He turned and headed up the hall in the direction of his office.

Abbie looked at Mason again. "Lynette?"

"Ford's daughter. She's married to my brother Gage. She and her father weren't exactly close." That was a massive understatement. Right before his death, Ford had tried to kill both Gage and Lynette despite the fact that Lynette was pregnant. "Still, she might know something."

But Abbie shook her head. "Ford died nearly a month ago. Why didn't this assassin he'd hired come after all the Rylands then? He might not have been able to find Boone, but the rest of you were all here in Silver Creek."

Unfortunately, Mason had an explanation for that. "Ford's will was read just two days ago."

And shortly thereafter, there'd been the fire and then

Ace Chapman's attacks. Knowing what he'd just learned, it was hard for Mason to believe that it was all a coincidence.

But something still wasn't right here.

"If this was Ford's doing, then why set the fire that could have killed Abbie?" Mason asked.

All of them looked at each other for several moments, and it was Boone who finally spoke. "Maybe to make me suffer. If Ford found out that I'd practically raised Abbie, he might want her dead along with my sons."

"Or," Abbie said and then paused. "The fire and the attempts to kill me are all Ferguson's doing." Another pause. Her breath trembled a little. "Maybe Ford's assassin is just getting started."

Hell.

Mason couldn't discount that. There could be two forces working against all of them, but that meant that Abbie could be a target from both sides. Abbie must have realized that, too, because the color drained from her face.

"Come on." Mason caught onto her arm. "I'll get you a drink of water. I also need to see what I can find out about Ace Chapman's condition."

Mason took a step. Abbie didn't. "What about you?" she asked Boone.

He shrugged and dropped down into one of the reception chairs. "I'll wait around and see what Grayson learns from Lynette."

Abbie nodded. "I won't be long."

Mason didn't miss the loving tone she used nor the loving look Boone gave her in return. Like father and daughter. Ironic. Mason had always heard his mother say that Boone had wanted a daughter. Well, now he had one. And he'd lost all his sons in the process.

Abbie followed Mason down the hall, and they paused at Grayson's doorway. His brother was still on the phone with Lynette, so Mason went to his own office and took a bottle of water from the fridge.

"I thought you were going to rip Ferguson's eyes out," Mason said when he handed her the water. He also motioned for her to sit because she didn't look too steady on her feet.

"I thought I was, too." Abbie didn't sit, but she did look up at him. "You stopped me. I'm not sure I want to thank you for that."

Mason nearly smiled. *Nearly.* And then he remembered how the scumbag had made Abbie's life a living hell. "If he'd touched you, I would have had to shoot him. I don't want that. Not yet. Not until we're sure he's called off his dogs. It won't do us any good if he's dead and the attacks continue."

"So you do think Ferguson is behind the attacks?"

"Maybe." He rethought that. "But Ford was just as dirty, just as dangerous as Ferguson, and I wouldn't put it past him to try to get some revenge."

She groaned, shook her head. That's when Mason decided to push the sitting idea again. He took her by the arm and eased her into the chair. "Stay put, drink your water and I'll make some calls."

She nodded, but there was no agreement in her eyes. "I know it hurts when you see Boone with me."

Mason settled for a shrug.

"I know it hurts," Abbie repeated. She paused, drank some water. "All those years he wasn't happy. I never knew why, of course. And that's a roundabout way of saying that he never stopped loving any of you."

Mason wanted to believe that, but believing would mean letting go of the past. He wasn't ready for that. "Remember, I put a bullet through the silver concho he gave me."

Abbie stood, slowly, and placed the water on the edge of his desk. "I'm sorry, too, about the affair that Boone had."

That put a damper on the cozy, protective feeling he had when looking down at Abbie. "Don't apologize for him."

"I'm not," she insisted. "I'm telling *you* that I'm sorry because it must hurt, even after all these years."

"It does." And he wanted to hit himself for that too-easy but too-true confession.

Now it was Abbie who touched his arm. Not a good time for it with the air zinging, but Mason didn't stop her. "I knew their marriage wasn't perfect." And he had to pause. "My mother was on antidepressants and would go into these dark moods where she wouldn't come out of her room for days."

"I'm sorry," Abbie repeated.

"It was a long time ago," he assured her. Mason lifted his shoulder. "Still, I didn't know Boone had slept with Sandra Herrington."

Abbie made a sound of agreement. "It apparently set a lot of bad things in motion."

Mason couldn't argue with that, but he was an adult now, and even though he didn't want to give Boone an inch, he could see the situation through adult eyes. That didn't mean he could forgive Boone, but Mason knew where the bulk of the blame belonged. On Ford Herrington.

A dead man.

"You're not scowling," he heard Abbie say, and that snapped his attention back to her.

Because a glare and a scowl were his usual expressions, he had to think about that for a second or two. He certainly hadn't been thinking good thoughts, so maybe it had something to do with that arm rub.

Mason stared at her. She stared back. And it was one of those moments where he could see pretty much what she was thinking, and whether it was good or bad, Abbie was just as puzzled about him as he was about her.

She shook her head, drew back her hand so that she was no longer touching him. "Just to let you know, I don't make it a habit of doing this."

Doing what? flickered through his mind. But a flicker was all the time he had because she came up on her toes, slid her hand around the back of his neck and kissed him.

The jolt was instant. And nice. It slid through him like the blazing Texas heat, and while part of him remembered that this just wasn't a good idea, he couldn't remember why it wasn't.

Mason hooked his arm around Abbie's waist, gathered her into his arms and kissed her right back. He figured if he was going to make things worse that at least it should aim for making them feel better first. And feeling better was exactly what happened.

Yeah, there was that blasted heat that got even hotter when her breasts pressed against his chest. But there was more than heat. The taste of her, like sweet summer wine. And the feel of her mouth beneath his. She was soft in all the right places, and one place in particular made Mason hard as stone.

She pulled back, gasping a little, and looking more than stunned. Mason knew how she felt. He was pretty sure that kiss shouldn't have felt that good, and Abbie's taste shouldn't still be on his lips.

Oh, man.

And Mason just kept mentally repeating that.

The corner of her mouth lifted. "Now you're scowling."

He met her gaze. "I don't want to want you."

"Yes." She brushed her lips over his again. "I know."

Their gazes held, and Mason had no idea what he could say to cool this down, but he figured he had to say something. He didn't get that something out, however, before he heard the footsteps. They stepped away from each other. But not in time. His brother Dade appeared in the doorway and gave them a glance that quickly turned to a cop's stare.

"You want something?" Mason asked to stop his brother from asking his own question. A question that would no doubt involve what was going on between Abbie and him.

"Yeah." And that's all Dade said for several moments while he continued to look them over. "Ace is in surgery, and the hospital will call when he's out."

Mason mentally punched himself again. Ace Chapman should have been in the forefront of his mind. Not kissing Abbie. This attraction was a distraction, and it wouldn't help him get to the bottom of what was going on.

"Why is he still here?" Dade asked, hitching his thumb in Boone's direction.

Mason could go a couple of ways with this, but he took the easy road. "He's waiting for news."

Dade's lifted eyebrow was a cue for Mason to provide more, and he would have if Grayson hadn't come up the hall.

"It's Lynette," Grayson announced. "She found something." He clicked the speaker button on his phone and lifted it for them to hear.

"I went through the probate records," Mason heard his sister-in-law say on the other end of the line. "I wasn't at the reading of the will, but my father apparently left three sealed letters in a safety deposit box in San Antonio. He also left instructions with his lawyer to hand out those letters after his death."

Beside him, Abbie pulled in a hard breath. Grayson wasn't faring much better in the breath department. Because, Mason doubted that Ford had left inspirational advice or good tiding in those sealed envelopes.

"Who got the letters?" he asked.

And Mason braced himself for news that he was certain he didn't want to hear.

Chapter Eleven

"Those letters went to Rodney Stone and Nicole Manning," Abbie heard Lynette Ryland say. "And the third went to Vernon Ferguson."

Lynette paused, no doubt when she heard their collective groans and mumbles. "Is Ferguson the man you think tried to kill the horse trainer at the ranch?"

"The very one," Grayson assured her. "Any idea what was in those letters?"

"None," Lynette quickly answered. "As I said, I didn't even go to the reading of the will, but I can ask my father's former secretary. She and I are still close, and she might have typed the letters for him."

To Abbie that sounded like a long shot. Considering the possible nature of the letters, the senator would have typed them himself. Or hired someone he could eliminate. But right now long shots were all they had.

That, and Ace.

If he survived the surgery, they might be able to get him to confess the name of the person who had hired him, and if they got very lucky, maybe he would tell them what the letter had said. Of course, Ferguson had already admitted that he knew Ford had left instructions to kill them all, so maybe the letters were just that: instructions to kill.

"What about a connection between Ferguson and your

father?" Mason asked Lynette. "Did you find anything other than this letter to link the two men?"

"Nothing so far. In fact, I just searched through the computer files I have, and Ferguson's name isn't mentioned. I'll keep digging. I don't have access to all of my father's things—he disowned me a few days before he killed himself—but before he died, I copied some of his files. *Lots of them,*" she corrected. "I'll go through those now."

"Look for a connection that happened about twenty years ago," Mason added.

An uncomfortable silence went through the room, and Abbie knew why. Twenty years ago was when Boone had left and Ford had killed both Chet Ryland and Lynette's mother. The very woman who had had an affair with Boone.

It was also the year Ferguson had gunned down Abbie's own mother.

On the surface, this shouldn't be connected, but maybe she was missing something. Or someone. The only real living link to all of this was Boone himself. But certainly if Boone knew something, he would tell her, right?

But he hadn't told her about the affair. In fact, Boone had kept a lot of secrets.

Abbie quickly pushed that aside. She wouldn't doubt him, not after everything he'd done for her.

"If I find anything, I'll let you know," Lynette assured them.

"Thanks." Now it was Grayson's turn to pause. "You do know that Boone's back in Silver Creek?"

"Yes," Lynette said cautiously, as if she'd just stepped on a few eggshells. "Gage is, uh, considering what to do. I warn you, though, he's not happy about this."

The brothers exchanged uneasy glances. "Try to keep Gage away from here for a while," Grayson suggested. "A fight won't do us any good right now."

"I'll see what I can do," Lynette promised. "But Gage is, well, Gage."

Another brother. One who no doubt hated Boone as much as the others, because there was a possibility of a fight. It had already been a long morning, but it was apparently about to get a lot longer.

"We already knew that Ferguson had contact with Nicole Manning and Rodney Stone," Mason reminded them the moment Grayson ended the call. "And contact with Ford, too. It's not much of a stretch for Ford to give a lowlife like Ferguson an order to kill. Ferguson could have then hired another lowlife like Ace."

The brothers exchanged more groans. "Three letters," Dade repeated. "That means all three of the people who received them can continue to point fingers at each other."

Oh, mercy. Abbie hadn't even considered that. Maybe only one letter was a death warrant, and the other two were there just to muddy the waters. If so, it would work because no one would simply confess to conspiracy to commit murder.

Even though Abbie had never met Ford Herrington, she was getting a clearer picture of what he'd been capable of, and of course, he would attach himself to someone equally evil like Ferguson.

"I'll get Nicole and Stone back in here for questioning. Ferguson, too," Grayson insisted although he didn't sound any more optimistic than Abbie felt.

Mason looked at Abbie. "Did Ford ever contact you?"

"No." And Abbie was almost positive of that. "Twenty years is a long time. A lot of people have come in and out of our lives, but I don't remember Ford. And I think I'd remember seeing him."

Mason made a sound of understanding. *"Our,"* he mumbled.

Our as in Boone and her. Abbie wished she could take it back because the scowls returned to all of the Ryland brothers' faces.

Mason pushed past her, and with all of them following, he made his way back to the front of the building where Boone was still waiting. Boone was seated, but the moment he spotted them, he eased to a standing position.

"Something else wrong?" Boone asked. His gaze went straight to Abbie.

"Maybe." She figured this would sound better coming from her than his sons, because their scowls had returned. "You said Ford came to see you, to tell you that your wife had committed suicide. Did he see me?"

Boone scrubbed his hand over his forehead, and for a moment he looked confused. That was before the concern slashed through his eyes. "You think—" But that was as far as Boone got.

The back door flew open, the movement so abrupt that it slammed against the wall. She heard Mason mumble some profanity under his breath. Dade did, too.

And Abbie soon saw why.

It wasn't Ferguson or some gunman, but there was a threat nonetheless. She automatically stepped in front of Boone, and just as automatically, he pushed her to the side.

So he could face their visitors head-on.

MASON WATCHED AS HIS brothers walked in. First, Nate. The calm and sensible one who was also Dade's fraternal twin. Nate didn't look ready to explode. But the other two, well, that was a different story. Gage and Kade were spoiling for a fight. Lynette obviously hadn't been able to convince Gage to stay out of this.

"It's true," Gage spat out like profanity.

Mason was far from being a fan of Boone, but Abbie had already been put through too many wringers today.

That thought stopped him cold.

Since when did he react based on someone else's feelings, someone who wasn't a sibling?

Apparently now.

Because Mason maneuvered himself in front of her. In front of Boone, too, and he glared at his younger brothers—Dade included—who had already joined the battle march with the others toward the reception counter.

"I want you to leave now!" Gage punctuated that by jabbing his index finger at Boone.

"He'll leave when this investigation is over," Mason let them all know. Grayson gave a hesitant but concurring nod. "Abbie's in danger. Hell, we all are. And Boone stays put until I throw at least one dirtbag in jail for taking shots at us."

That took a little of the fighting fire out of Gage's eyes. Unlike Nate, this brother was not the calm and sensible one.

"Lynette said we could all be in danger," Gage tossed out there.

"We are," Mason verified. "Ford might have left orders to have us all killed, and Abbie might have gotten caught in the cross fire." Or she could be the reason for the cross fire, but Mason kept that to himself. This little family reunion was already complicated enough.

"I left Darcy and the kids with two of my detectives," Nate explained. "And I sent two more to stay with Lynette at the newspaper office where she's working today."

Darcy was Nate's wife and the assistant district attorney, and yeah, it didn't surprise Mason that Nate would think of them at a time like this. The Rylands were often a fiery lot, but they put their families first.

Unlike Boone.

The afterthought was still automatic, but Mason knew he was going to have to give it some thinking time. Maybe he could combine it with a cold beer and another kissing session with Abbie. Kissing her confused the heck out of things, but heaven help him, it felt good.

"Why did you come back?" Nate asked, his attention fastened on Boone. There was cool anger in his voice, but there was no mistaking the fact that it *was* anger.

Boone tipped his head to the bullet-damaged safety glass in the door. "Because of that. Because you're right about all of you being in danger." He shook his head, dipped his gaze. "I tried to stop this from happening."

His words did nothing to soothe Gage. He came closer, with Kade right on his heels. No surprise that the two were presenting a united front. Gage and Kade were the youngest of the pack and were just as much friends as they were brothers.

"Grayson called," Gage said. No coolness in his voice. "He explained what's happening."

"Ford could be behind the attack," Mason verified. He didn't owe Boone anything, but he wanted to clarify to his hotheaded brother that the person responsible for this mess wasn't in the room but rather in the grave.

"Ford," Gage repeated with even more venom. Yeah, his late father-in-law wasn't exactly a do-gooder. "That doesn't mean he should be here." Another finger jab at Boone. "He could have told us this over the phone."

Boone nodded. "I could have, but I wanted to see my sons."

Oh, man. That was *not* the right thing to say, and it

started an explosion of profanity and old-wound accusations from Dade, Gage and Kade. Mason wasn't much for a verbal brawl, especially when he looked at Abbie. She had her hands up, already posturing herself to protect Boone. But Mason noticed something else.

She was blinking back tears.

This was ripping her apart as much as it was his brothers.

"Stop," Mason said. He didn't shout. Didn't have to. For years he'd worked on his ice-man, badass facade, and times like this, it came in handy.

Everybody stopped. They stared at him. Waiting, no doubt, for some words of wisdom to make this all better. Or maybe waiting for him to toss Boone out on his ear. But wise words were Grayson's department. The tossing? Best left for Gage or Dade. Mason did what he did best. He was putting an end to this now.

"You can settle your differences with Boone later. Right now, we focus on keeping us all alive. Got that?"

They weren't pleased about it, but no brother objected. Grayson even made a sound of agreement and turned to Kade. "What about Bree and the twins? Where are they?"

Mason cursed himself for not already thinking of Kade's wife and babies. Bree was a deputy sheriff, but that didn't mean he wanted her trying to fend off an assassin by herself.

"They're okay," Kade assured him. "Bree took the twins and drove to Kayla's estate in San Antonio. Kayla has a bodyguard with them."

Good. That meant Kayla, Dade's wife, was safe, as well. Plus, the estate was more like a fortress, and they'd used it before when family members needed protection.

So that left Abbie.

Not family, exactly, but she was still in danger and

standing in front of a glass door and window where a hired gun could spot her and take aim. Ace might be out of commission, but that didn't mean Ford and/or Ferguson hadn't arranged for backup.

"I'm taking Abbie upstairs to the apartment," Mason let the others know. "She can stay there while I make some calls, check on Ace's condition, and then I'll take her back to the ranch."

As expected, that earned him a few raised eyebrows, and in return Mason's scowl deepened. He didn't bother to remind them about bullets going through glass or the tenacity of the men they were dealing with. He just took Abbie's arm and got moving.

"The apartment?" Abbie questioned, looking back at the others.

"A glorified flop room," Mason clarified. He got her past his brothers and down the hall to the back stairs. "You can get some rest there, and I'll have food brought up."

She didn't argue, which told him just how exhausted she was. He needed to make those calls fast and make sure the ranch was as secure as it could be before he drove her back out there.

They went up the stairs, and Mason threw open the door. Yeah, definitely a flop room, but once it had been the jail and storage area. Now, it was just one big room with a bed, sitting area, kitchenette and bathroom.

"Get some rest." He glanced at the bed and turned to get out of there fast. Having Abbie with him and in the vicinity of a bed wasn't a good idea.

But Abbie didn't let him leave. She stepped in front of him. "Thank you."

Mason didn't ask for any clarification because it would keep him there longer, but Abbie still didn't let him leave. She touched the seam on the sleeve of his black T-shirt and then started to run her fingers over it. Not touching *him* but still touching.

"Will you always hate me because of Boone?" she asked.

The question took him aback, not because he hadn't thought about it, but because Mason hadn't expected Abbie to come right out and ask.

"No, but I'll always *want* to hate you." He cursed, shook his head. "That's a lie. I don't want to hate you at all. I want to kiss you hard and long. And more than that, I want you in my bed."

She didn't back away, didn't stop touching his shirt. But she did dodge his gaze.

"This is the point where you want to run in the opposite direction," he suggested.

"I don't want to run." Now she looked up at him. "I want to be in your bed."

Mason cursed some more, but the profanity didn't stop the heat from just sliding hot and deep into him. Just the way he wanted to slide right into her.

"And then what?" he asked.

She gave a quick, awkward shrug. Then fought a smile. "We have sex?"

"Smart-ass," he mumbled.

But there was no anger in it. Just frustration that the bed thing couldn't happen right now. Or that it would happen despite the bad consequences. Disgusted with her, himself and this body heat, he slipped his arm around her waist and eased her to him.

That didn't help with the heat either.

"I don't usually talk this much about having sex," he snarled. "I just more or less do it."

She smiled again and, man, it was incredible. Abbie

was a knockout, and no part of him was going to let him forget it.

"I've thrown you off your game," she said, her breath making the words a whisper.

"No game," he admitted. "And that's part of the problem. It'd be easier if this could be just a one-night stand. I'm good at those."

"I'll bet you are." Her breath went even thinner, and she slipped her gaze down his chest and to the front of his Wranglers.

Mason couldn't help it. He laughed. Okay, not a laugh exactly, but it was as close as he got.

He stared at her, lifted his hand to her mouth and brushed the pad of his thumb over her bottom lip. She made a shivery sound, and her eyelids fluttered closed.

His body clenched.

Begged.

Then started to ache.

"You're overthinking this," Abbie said, melting against him until her face was cushioned right in the crook of his neck.

"Maybe you're right." He wanted her to be right. "You come to my bed tonight, and we can overthink it later." When he'd taken her hard, fast and deep.

The thought kept repeating in his head, and that was probably why he didn't hear the footsteps until they were practically right on Abbie and him. Mason swung in the direction of the doorway, automatically reaching for his gun. But it wasn't the threat that his body had prepared him for. It was just Gage. With a funny look on his face.

Mason huffed. Gage had no doubt noticed the close contact between Abbie and him, and Mason was sure he'd get an earful about it later. Heck, an earful might actually do him some good.

Might.

"What?" Mason snarled because Gage wouldn't have expected any other tone from him.

Gage hitched his thumb to the stairs. "Lynette's on the phone. And I think you'll want to hear what she has to say." Gage paused, his gaze shifting to Abbie. "She found something about *you* in her father's files."

Chapter Twelve

Abbie hated being the topic of conversation, especially when it was six lawmen doing the conversing about the memo that Lynette had found.

The memo was actually a handwritten request from Ford to the P.I. agency he used to find the identity of the "kid" living with Boone Ryland in Mesa, Texas.

That kid was Abbie.

The timing and place left no doubt about it, and it coincided with Ford's visit to tell Boone about his wife's suicide.

Now the trick would be to find something else that would prove that Ford had not only learned her identity but that he'd reported it and her location to Ferguson.

All six Ryland brothers were at the massive wood table in the family-style kitchen at the ranch with stacks of files, papers, laptops and the remainder of brisket dinner that had been served by Bessie, the cook.

"You didn't eat enough," Bessie whispered to Abbie.

No, she hadn't, but her stomach was still churning and had been since Lynette's call earlier that day. It also didn't help that Mason and the others had devoted the entire afternoon to figuring out what Lynette had found in her father's files.

"It's okay," Lynette whispered to Abbie, and gave her a sympathetic look. "They'll get to the bottom of this."

Because Lynette had said that for the past couple of hours, Abbie had her doubts. Still, the lawmen were digging through the stacks of files that Lynette had brought over.

While she and Lynette helped Bessie with the dishes, Abbie glanced at Mason, something she'd been doing a lot. Each time his attention had been fastened to the files, but for this latest round, her glance met his. Mason didn't say a word, just made a slight shift in his expression, seemingly asking if she was all right.

Abbie settled for a nod.

Lynette made a hmm-ing sound that snagged Abbie's attention. Mason's sister-in-law hadn't missed the exchange, and judging from her slight smile, she hadn't missed the heat between her and Mason.

"Is it serious?" Lynette whispered.

"No, it's just this crazy attraction." But why had she admitted that to a woman she hardly knew? And why did it feel like a lie? Yes, the attraction was there. No doubt about it. However, Abbie was afraid this was going to lead to a massive broken heart for her.

"Gage and the others won't like it," Lynette said, still keeping her voice low. "Not at first anyway. But they'll get over it."

"Will they?" Again, she didn't think before she spoke, but Abbie wasn't surprised to realize that she really wanted to know the answer.

Lynette patted her arm, smiled softly. "They will."

Abbie had known the woman for only a few hours, but she already liked her. And hoped Lynette was right. Of course, the minute that the danger was over, Mason might insist that she leave before he and his brothers had a chance to *get over it*.

Grayson's phone rang, the sound shooting through the rumble of conversation, and he put the call on speaker after glancing at the screen.

"Dr. Mickelson?" Grayson said.

Abbie automatically held her breath because this was no doubt an update about Ace Chapman.

"No change in Chapman's condition," the doctor said. "He hasn't regained consciousness since the surgery."

Mason groaned. Abbie mentally did the same. They needed him to wake up so he could tell them who had hired him.

"It's not good," Dr. Mickelson continued. "And neither are the rest of his vital signs. I think you have to brace yourself for the likelihood that he's not going to wake up."

They'd already braced themselves for that, but Abbie couldn't give up hope.

Grayson thanked the doctor, ended the call and looked around the table. "So what do we have?" he tossed out there.

"The memo Lynette found, of course," Gage volunteered. "And confirmation that Ford paid the P.I. agency for eleven hours of work to identify the *minor child*."

"The eleven hours is proof they did just that," Mason stated. He looked at her. "Because if they hadn't, the P.I.s would have been on the assignment a lot longer."

Yes, she hadn't considered that. So Ford had learned who she was.

"Two days after the P.I.s were paid, there was another attempt to kill Abbie," Mason continued. "There's no proof that Ferguson was behind that, but…"

"There's proof," Abbie interrupted. "Ferguson left some kind of message on our answering machine."

"Message?" Gage and Mason questioned in unison.

Abbie shook her head. "Boone erased it. I heard him listening to it and I recognized Ferguson's voice. That afternoon as Boone and I were trying to leave, someone tried to kill me."

The brothers exchanged uneasy glances. "Why would Boone erase it?" Mason asked.

But Abbie had to shake her head again. "Boone must have realized there was a threat because he was trying to get me out of there fast." Then she paused. "But why would Ferguson leave a threat that would implicate him in another attempt to kill me?"

The question didn't earn her any nods or answers, but it did create some scowls and under-the-breath mumbles. Probably because this meant one of them was going to have to have a conversation with Boone. He was still in town at the hotel near the sheriff's office, but they no doubt wanted to avoid him.

"I can call him now and ask him about the message," Abbie let them know.

"No," Grayson insisted. But he didn't say anything else and that uncomfortable silence returned.

"The question should be asked during an interview," Mason finally said. "If you alert him that we know about the erased message, then it might give him time to come up with an answer."

Abbie blinked. "An answer that isn't the truth," she concluded. Now she was the one to groan.

Mason stood, sliding the papers he'd held back onto the table. "It wouldn't be the first time Boone has lied. And I know you think highly of him—"

"And I know you don't," Abbie interrupted. It took her a moment to get control of her voice. "Boone wouldn't lie about something like this, about something that could affect our safety."

None of them agreed with her. The best she got was a so-so shrug from Bessie. The coldest response was from Mason, and that's when it hit her. Lynette had been wrong. The Rylands were never going to get past this.

Never.

That little fantasy she'd been weaving in her head about Mason turned to dust. It felt as if her legs had, too.

"I think I'll turn in for the night," Abbie managed to say around the lump in her throat.

It was way too early for bed, but she figured none of them would mention that. They didn't. So Abbie got out of there as fast as she could. She mumbled a thanks to Bessie for the dinner and hurried up the stairs to the guest room where she'd slept the night before.

Abbie made a beeline for the bathroom and the shower, and she stripped off her shoes, shirt and pants. Tossed them on the floor. Just as Mason threw open the door.

He froze.

So did Abbie.

And she followed his gaze as it slid down her body. First to the silver concho pendant that must have riled every bone in his body. Then to her bra and panties.

No riled look for those.

Heat sizzled in those cool gray eyes.

"I stormed out of the kitchen," she reminded him. Abbie picked up the shirt and held it in front of her like a shield. "I figured you'd let me stew awhile."

He flexed his eyebrows, eased the door shut and leaned back against it. "If I'd let you stew much longer, I would have found you naked."

True. And the possibilities of that left her a little embarrassed—and aroused.

"Boone won't lie about the message he erased," she re-stated, just to get that out of the way.

He nodded, made a sound of agreement that came from deep within his throat. A husky male rumbling that shook her body and blood.

Abbie tried to hang on to the anger, she really tried, but it was hard to do while standing there in her borrowed ill-fitting underwear. And with Mason in the room. Especially with Mason. Every riled bone in her own body was attracted to him.

"Damn you," she grumbled.

The corner of his mouth lifted. "I feel the same way about you." He reached behind his back, locked the door and pushed himself away from it.

It was the sound of the lock clicking that caused her heart to slam against her chest, but when he made it to her, when he hooked his arm around her and hauled her to him, that robbed her of her breath.

Mason kissed her.

This wasn't the gentle kisses he'd doled out earlier. No, it was as if something dark and dangerous had been unleashed, and he took full control. He anchored her to him with that hooked right arm, and his left hand went to the back of her neck. He angled her head so he could deepen the kiss.

Yes! That was the thought that went through her mind. The only thought that had time to form because Mason continued the assault on her mouth until thinking was next to impossible.

He dropped his hand from her neck, sliding it between them. And over her breasts. The breath she'd managed to catch vanished again, and Abbie only felt the heat. The need.

She only felt Mason.

He unclipped the front hook of her bra, and her breasts spilled out into his hands. His touch there alone was enough to make her legs go weak, but then he shoved aside the concho, lowered his head and took her right nipple into his mouth.

Abbie made a shivery sound and sagged against him. The only thing she could do was hold on for this wild ride.

He lifted her, and Abbie wrapped her legs around him to bring the center of her body right against his. The pleasure slammed through her, instant and hot, and she had no doubt that this was what she wanted. Mason wanted it, too, because he carried her to the bed and let her drop onto the soft mattress. He followed until he was on top of her and settled right between her legs.

Abbie couldn't process everything. It was coming at her so fast that all she could do was feel and let Mason take her anywhere he wanted to go.

He caught his thumb on the elastic top of her panties and shimmied them off her body. She was naked now. Not a stitch of clothing. But Mason was fully dressed, and she wanted to do something about that. She fought with his shirt while he fought to get his boots off. It was working until his hand went lower. And lower. Until he slid his fingers into her.

Abbie gasped.

The heat soared too hot, too much, too fast. The climax hit her before she had a chance to say anything. She'd expected something amazing with Mason.

But she hadn't expected *this*.

She hadn't expected for it to feel as if he'd shattered her body into a thousand pieces of light and fire.

It took her a moment to open her eyes. Another moment to catch her breath. And yet another moment to see the look on Mason's face. He wasn't touching her now. His hand had frozen in place. His mouth was slightly open. And he was staring at her, waiting.

Abbie knew exactly what he was waiting for.

"It's my first time," she managed to say.

His mouth was still open. He still had that poleaxed expression on his face, but it took a while to speak. "You're a virgin." And it wasn't a question.

She nodded. Swallowed hard. "Please tell me it doesn't make a difference." Abbie reached for him, to hold him in place so they could finish what they'd started.

But Mason moved off her and stepped away from the bed. Mumbling something that she couldn't quite catch, he started to pace.

"It doesn't make a difference," she insisted.

"To hell it doesn't." He tossed his hands in the air, palms up. "Trust me, it makes a difference."

She groaned, already anticipating the discussion—no, make that an argument—they were about to have. She got to her feet, righted her bra and put her panties back on. "It wasn't as if I planned it this way. I've been in witness protection since I was eleven. Not many opportunities came up for me to trust someone enough to hop into bed with them."

He aimed a scowl at her. "You should have told me before I ever kissed you."

Now it was her turn to scowl. "And just how would I have worked that into the conversation, huh? If I'd said I was a virgin, you would have thought I was some innocent naive woman that you couldn't touch."

"Yeah, I would have." His hands went in the air again. "And I darn sure wouldn't have kissed you, got that?"

Yes, she *got that*. On some level Abbie had known what

his reaction would be, and maybe that's why she hadn't told him. She'd wanted that kiss. She'd wanted to know what it would feel like to be with Mason—in his arms and in his bed.

Frustrated with herself and with Mason, Abbie snatched her clothes from the floor and started putting them back on. "You think having sex with me will mean a commitment."

He stared at her, gave her a flat *duh* look.

"It doesn't have to be," she assured him.

"Yeah, it does."

She caught onto his arm when he started to walk away. "Why? Because you'd be my first? Get over yourself, Mason. I'm thirty-two years old. How many women my age do you think stayed with their first lovers?"

He paused, moved in closer. "It doesn't matter." His thumb landed against his chest, and he spoke through clenched teeth. "*I* don't sleep with virgins."

She wanted to ask if that was true, if he'd ever had a virgin for a lover, but Abbie knew he wasn't lying. Mason had lived his life keeping people at arm's length, at creating this dark and brooding facade that frightened people. Virgins steered clear of him, and he did the same to them.

"Sex is simpler if there are no strings attached," Abbie mumbled.

Mason certainly didn't deny that. "And you come with plenty of strings."

Again, she could only nod and try to push aside the dull ache still burning in her body. Yes, he'd made her climax, but it didn't seem nearly enough when she was lusting after every inch of him.

Mason cursed again, making her believe that he was still doing some lusting of his own. He moved away from her, sank down onto the foot of the bed and cursed some more.

"A virgin," he said, and he repeated it. "I wouldn't have guessed."

"Then maybe I should have let you find out the hard way." Abbie gave him a flat look so that he'd know she was joking.

Well, maybe.

Mason returned the flat look. "Do I need to give you the talk about your first time being with someone special?"

"You *are* special." Abbie said it fast, like ripping off a bandage. Besides, fast meant he couldn't add anything else—like making it special with someone she loved.

The *L* word would send Mason running.

She huffed. Heck, he already was running.

Abbie went to him, despite the warning glare he gave her, and she slid her hand through his hair, tilting his head slightly so they made direct eye contact.

"I don't want you to be special. I don't want to feel this way about you. Because I know my strings complicate things." Abbie didn't back down, although this wasn't easy. "But I can't help it. I want you, and I'm possibly falling in love with you."

Let the running begin.

He huffed, stood and brushed a very chaste kiss on her cheek. "I'm not the right man for you." And with that, he started for the door. Not exactly running but close.

"Who says you're not?" she fired back.

Mason stopped, kept his back to her. "Anyone who knows me."

Abbie's hands went to her hips. "I'll venture a guess that no one knows you because you haven't let anyone in since you were seventeen."

He glanced at her over his shoulder. No scowl or glare

this time, but amusement danced through his eyes. "Analyzing me?"

The moment called for some levity. "Seducing you, but obviously failing."

Mason laughed in that low husky way that always made her melt. Oh, yeah. She was possibly falling in love with him.

He opened his mouth, but the sound stopped him from saying anything. Abbie was so focused on him that it took her a moment to realize his cell was ringing. Mason took it from his pocket, cursed.

"It's Rodney Stone," he relayed to her and answered it by putting the call on Speaker.

"I went by the sheriff's office, but none of you were there, just the night deputy, and I don't want to talk to her. She gave me your cell number."

"What do you want?" Mason demanded, the impatience evident in his voice. Abbie was right there with them. She'd had enough of all their suspects for one day.

"I want you and your brothers to investigate Nicole Manning," Stone insisted.

"We are. And you, too. In fact, we want to know what was in the letter that you got from Ford Herrington."

Silence for several moments. "The letter's not important. It was just to thank me for all my years of service."

"Admirable." Sarcasm replaced the impatience. "But I'll want to read it."

"Fine," Stone snapped. "Read it and then do your job. Investigate Nicole."

"Anything specific or are you just slinging mud?" Mason asked.

"No mud. Be at the sheriff's office tomorrow morning, and I'll bring proof."

"Proof of what?" Mason pressed when Stone didn't continue.

He made that smug sound that Abbie had heard him make earlier. "Proof that Nicole is the one who's trying to kill all of you."

Chapter Thirteen

Mason gulped his third cup of coffee while he finished up the paperwork for the arson and shooting incident at the ranch. Later, he'd have to do the same for Ace Chapman's second attack and then the reports that would come when Rodney Stone arrived with his so-called evidence. He hated paperwork and hated even more when he couldn't get his mind centered on it. And Mason knew the exact reason for his lack of focus.

Abbie.

Man, fate was laughing its butt off right about now. In high school other guys had wanted virgin trophies, but not him. He preferred his women with some baggage. Women who didn't want a commitment any more than he did. He'd steered clear of virgins, Goody Two-shoes and anyone with marrying potential.

Until now.

And he could still steer clear, he reminded himself. Maybe Ace would regain consciousness and spill all the details about who hired him. Maybe Stone could give them something to arrest Nicole. Or vice versa. Mason didn't care who was responsible, only that he wanted that person out of commission and facing down some justice. Then he could give some serious thought to this emotional mess with Abbie.

A virgin!

Well, it ruled out a one-night stand, that's for sure. Of course, that didn't stop him from wanting both her and that single encounter in bed. He huffed. No, it didn't rule out anything except he was going to have to figure out a way to keep his hands off her.

That resolution lasted about a second.

Carrying a bag from Tip Top Diner, Abbie stepped into the doorway of his office, and she looked far better than any woman had a right to look. Snug jeans that she'd borrowed from Dade's wife, Kayla. Mason never remembered those jeans looking that great on his sister-in-law. The borrowed sapphire-blue top was in the same category.

Hot.

And *hot* and *virgin* didn't go together. Not for him.

Abbie had pulled her hair back into a ponytail, something she'd likely done for comfort and not to make him notice her neck.

"Dade got us cinnamon rolls," she announced, smiling. Damn. That smile was working a number on him, too.

Abbie opened the bag, deposited one of the wrapped heavenly smelling pastries on his desk and then took out one for herself. She made an mmm-ing sound when she bit into it.

Mason's body started to beg when she licked her fingers.

Oh, this is going great.

"You're in a good mood," he settled for saying, and his tone let her know that he didn't share that mood with her. He was frustrated, ornery and in need of sex.

Hell.

He was in need of Abbie, and that only made his mood worse.

"I'm optimistic," she explained, glancing at the clock.

"Stone is due here any minute now. By lunch, we could all be out of danger."

Maybe. Mason didn't have a lot of faith in Stone. Nor their other suspects—Nicole and Ferguson. He had to add Boone's name to that list, as well. He didn't think for a minute that Boone had hired anyone to shoot at Abbie, but Mason had to ask him about that phone message that he'd erased. Boone could be some kind of unwilling or unknowing accomplice.

"Marshal McKinney called a few minutes ago," Mason filled her in. "He's still working on a new identity and location for you. He might have something ready by the end of the day and wants you to stay in my protective custody until then."

Abbie studied him a moment. "Are you scowling because of that or because of last night?"

"I always scowl," he reminded her, and he definitely didn't want to talk about *last night*.

"Not always. Sometimes, you have a back-off expression that looks like a scowl. But this one is the real deal." She didn't wait for him to comment on that observation. "So are you regretting that you didn't sleep with me, or are you just upset that things got as far as they did?"

Mason was sure he didn't want to answer that either, and that certainty went up a notch when he realized Dade was standing in the doorway. Ah, heck. He'd let Abbie's questions, tight jeans and finger licking distract him, and now his brother had overheard the questions that Mason would have preferred to keep private.

And unanswered.

Dade's eyebrow hiked up. So did the corner of his mouth. Yeah, Dade was enjoying this, and if kept enjoying it, he was about to be a dead man.

Abbie's face turned red, and she dodged Dade's gaze.

"You'd better not have anything to say. Got that?" Mason dared his brother.

Dade held his hands up in mock surrender, and he looked at Abbie. "He likes to say *got that* a lot. Have you noticed?"

She nodded. "I've been on the receiving end of a few of them. It means shut up and don't argue."

Mason didn't contradict her. That's exactly what it meant, and Dade better not press it.

But Dade only gave him a smug look. "I thought you'd like to know that Stone just walked in." The levity faded. "And Boone. Grayson's not here yet. His baby's running a slight temp, and they might have to take him to the doctor."

They would take him to the doctor, Mason mentally corrected. The baby, Chet David, was only a month old, and there was no way his big brother would put an interrogation above his baby boy.

Mason got to his feet. "Put Stone in the interview room. I'll talk to Boone here in my office." Because he didn't want another go-round in reception. Abbie would no doubt want to follow him there, and Mason didn't want her near all that glass.

"I'll send Boone back," Dade mumbled.

Abbie ditched the rest of her cinnamon roll, shoving it back into the bag, and she stood, as well. No doubt waiting for Mason to send her out of the room so he could conduct an official interview with Boone.

"You can stay," he let her know, "but I ask the questions."

She nodded and looked as if she wanted to say something. Mason only hoped it didn't have anything to do with the incident on the bed. But then she shook her head and turned toward the sound of approaching footsteps. A moment later Boone appeared in the doorway.

"Mason," he greeted. "Abbie." He didn't exactly give them the raised eyebrow as Dade had, but his forehead bunched up. Was he wondering why the two of them were together—again? No doubt. His father wasn't trustworthy, wasn't worthy of being called a father, but he wasn't stupid.

"How soon are the marshals getting Abbie out of here?" Boone asked him.

"Soon. I'm working on it. You want a lawyer present for this?"

Abbie made a slight groan, but Boone didn't look the least surprised. He just shook his head. "What's *this* about?"

Mason had no intention of soothing the concern in Boone's voice. He cut right to the chase. "When Ford visited you twenty years ago to tell you that Mom was dead, Ferguson called you shortly thereafter. You remember?"

Boone lifted his shoulder and glanced at Abbie. "What's going on?"

"You erased a message from Ferguson," she explained.

An explanation Mason didn't want her to give, but it seemed to jog Boone's memory. "Yeah, I remember." He shrugged. "Ferguson asked if Abbie was still sleeping with the lights on. Not a threat, exactly, but because he'd called the rental house, that meant he knew how to find us."

Mason felt the little twist in his stomach, and he hated that Ferguson had done things like that to Abbie. It was torture, plain and simple, and he was continuing it twenty years later.

"Any idea why Ferguson called first?" Mason asked. "If he knew where you were, why didn't he just go after Abbie without warning you?"

Boone got a pained look on his face and glanced at Abbie. "I think a man like Ferguson enjoys the hunt. And he did send someone after her. We barely made it one step out of the house when the hired gun opened fire."

"Boone had to kill the hired gun," Abbie added. "So we weren't able to prove that Ferguson hired him."

More than a twist this time. Mason's stomach turned rock hard. Abbie was alive because of Boone. No wonder she thought of him as a father.

Mason got his mind off that and back on business. "So why erase the message from Ferguson?"

"I didn't want Abbie to hear it." And Boone looked Mason straight in the eye when he answered. "Yeah, we were already in the process of leaving, but she would have taken the answering machine with us."

It was a reasonable explanation, and Mason had to remind himself that if this were any man other than Boone, he probably wouldn't have any doubts. And he had to admit that his doubts weren't even reasonable. Any fool could see that Boone loved Abbie like a daughter. So, yeah, he would have taken little steps and big ones to protect her.

Abbie gave Boone's arm a squeeze. A reassurance that she didn't share Mason's doubts.

"You two okay?" Boone asked, looking first at her and then at Mason.

She nodded. Glanced at Mason. Waiting for him to answer.

Mason figured it was a good time to change the subject. He wasn't okay. Neither was Abbie despite that nod, and he didn't want to slip into a personal conversation with a man he still hated.

"I need to question Stone. You can watch from there." Mason pointed to the room across the hall. "There's a two-way mirror."

Mason headed out fast, but before he stepped into the interview room, he took a moment to gather his thoughts and to mentally slug himself. He was lawman right now, and he had to act like one or the danger was never going to end for Abbie. With that reminder out of the way, Mason got to work.

Stone was already seated, and he had his open briefcase on the table. "Where's the sheriff?" he immediately asked.

"Busy. You get to talk to me instead." Mason spun one of the chairs around, dropped down on the seat and rested his arms on the chair back.

Stone didn't try to hide his disapproval of being relegated to an interview with a deputy, and Mason didn't attempt to hide his disapproval of a man he thought was a couple of notches below slime. Anyone who worked for Ford for two decades couldn't have stayed completely legal.

"The proof I promised." Stone took out a paper from his briefcase, reached across the table and handed it to Mason.

Mason had a good look at the *proof.* It was a lengthy email from Ford to Nicole, and the first part dealt with Ford's reelection campaign. Nothing incriminating until Mason got to the last paragraph.

"My daughter has been snooping through our old business files," Mason read. "Make sure you cover both of us. While you're at it, take care of that Ryland mess."

Mason had known that Ford's daughter, Lynette, had been looking through her father's files for proof of his wrongdoings. That fit with the date of the email—two months earlier. But Mason had to mull over what Ford had meant by the *Ryland mess.*

"Ford is telling Nicole to kill all of you, including Boone," Stone concluded.

Ford was as dirty as they came, but that interpretation was a stretch. "You have anything else?"

"Isn't that enough?" Stone howled. "Nicole is the one

behind these attacks, and she's operating on Ford's orders. He probably left her money to carry out his wishes."

That was possible, but Mason could see this from a different angle. "This might have been about the time that Ford learned my brother Gage was alive. Or he could have been referring to the fact that Lynette didn't get her marriage to Gage annulled when Ford insisted she do it."

Stone jumped to his feet. "This isn't about your brother. It's about Ford leaving instructions to have you murdered."

Mason wished that's what the email proved, but it didn't. He shook his head and dropped the paper back on the table. "I'll have Grayson look at it, but I don't think he'll come to the same conclusion you have."

Stone's hands went on his hips, and he huffed. "Somebody wants you dead, and judging from the way this investigation has stalled, that email is as close to proof as you have."

"The investigation hasn't stalled," Mason mumbled. At least he hoped not. Every passing minute meant Abbie was in danger.

Abbie. He glanced back at the mirror. She was there, watching and listening, and Mason knew it was a bad time to remember that. But each conversation about the death threats had to feel like opening old wounds, especially because this wasn't just about her. It was about all of them.

Well, not Rodney Stone.

And that brought Mason back to something else he needed to know. "What was in the letter that Ford's probate attorney gave you when the will was read?"

Stone blinked. In fact, that was his only reaction for several seconds. He obviously hadn't expected that question. "It was personal."

That wasn't the right answer. "Yeah, I bet. But considering it could be important to an attempted-murder investigation, personal doesn't count. What was in the letter?" Mason pressed.

Stone's surprise morphed into anger. "Ford thanked me for all my years of service."

Mason made a circling motion with this finger to tell Stone to keep talking.

This time Stone's eyes narrowed. "There's nothing more to add. There was no money, nothing of value. Just his thank-you for twenty-two years of putting up with him."

Okay, that little outburst seemed genuine. Of course, that could be faked. "I want to see it."

"You can't." Stone met Mason's stare. "I tore it up." He rolled his shoulders. "I was upset because I was expecting more."

"Any reason why?" Mason pressed.

"Yes!" But it took him several moments to continue. "Nicole got a letter, too, but she was grinning from ear to ear when she read hers. I'm betting Ford left her a bundle."

"Maybe. Or maybe she was grinning to rile you. If so, it worked."

Stone shook his head. "No, she was pleased about something. Maybe more orders to kill some Rylands." He cursed. "I was so mad that I ripped my letter of *thanks* into pieces and flushed it down the toilet."

"Convenient," Mason remarked.

"The truth," Stone corrected. "My letter was nothing. Less than nothing. But Nicole's, well, you should demand to see it."

Oh, Mason would, but she'd likely have the same story about getting mad and destroying it. That left Ferguson. Mason might have better luck getting a letter from a nest of rattlers.

There was a rap at the door, and a split second later, it opened. Dade stuck his head in and motioned for Mason to come into the hall. He did, bracing himself for more bad news, and he shut the door behind him.

Dade wasn't alone. Both Boone and Abbie were there, and judging from their expressions, this was going to be bad.

"Gage just called from the hospital. Ace regained consciousness," Dade immediately let Mason know.

It took a moment for the relief to set in. "Is he able to talk?"

Dade nodded. "He's not only talking but making some demands."

The feeling of relief flew right out the window. "What kind of demands?"

Dade looked at Abbie, and she was the one to answer Mason's question. "Ace told Gage that he'll speak to only Boone and me. He says if we come to the hospital, he'll tell us who hired him. *But only us.*"

"Hell," Mason mumbled, and Dade agreed. "This could be some kind of trap."

Abbie didn't argue that. "Gage said Ace is heavily sedated, and he's too weak to even get out of bed. He doesn't have a gun, and he can't hurt us."

Mason wasn't so sure of that. Maybe physically Ace couldn't do any harm, but Mason didn't trust him. If Ace was ready to confess all, then he likely had something up his sleeve.

Maybe.

Or maybe the hit man just wanted to stay alive.

"We don't have a choice," Abbie insisted.

"Yeah, we do." But Mason knew that was a lie. He wanted Abbie as far away from Ace as possible. He wanted her safe inside. Except no place was safe as long as someone wanted to kill her.

"You'll be with us," Abbie argued. "But we have to hurry. Ace said the offer is only good for fifteen minutes."

Mason cursed again. "Why the time limit?"

"Ace thinks his boss will try to kill him," Dade explained. "He wants to be moved to a more secure location ASAP."

Now, that was something Mason couldn't dispute. Ace was definitely a loose end, and the person who hired him wouldn't want him talking to anyone. Of course, getting him to a safe place wouldn't be easy.

"I'll finish up with Stone," Dade let him know. "Mel's outside in the parking lot now, just to make sure no one is out there. I'll also call Gage and have him meet you in the hospital parking lot. Kade can start working on moving Ace."

It was also his brother's way of saying for them to get to the hospital *fast*. If Ace stuck to his unreasonable condition for a confession, the minutes were literally ticking off.

Still, Mason took a moment to consider all the angles. There were some potentially bad angles in a situation like this—like the bad feeling in his gut—and it riled him to the core that he couldn't do anything about them.

"Let's go," Mason said to Abbie and Boone. He took his weapon from his shoulder holster and hurried down the hall toward the back exit. They were right behind him.

When he sided the door, he spotted Mel, the deputy, as she was canvassing the parking lot. She also had her gun drawn and gave them a thumbs-up to indicate it was safe. Well, as safe as she could make it. Mason didn't waste any time getting Boone and Abbie into his truck and out of the parking lot. Abbie slid in next to Mason, and Boone took the passenger's side.

Thankfully, Boone drew a weapon as well, his Colt, and he used the side mirror to keep watch, but he also glanced at the dash. Then at Mason. "You kept your granddaddy's truck," he commented.

"Yeah." And Mason didn't add more. It certainly wasn't the time to explain that the truck was his last thread of connection to his grandfather. It didn't mesh with the stone-hard attitude he preferred to toss back in people's faces.

Abbie leaned in a little, pressing her arm against his. "I like the truck. It suits you."

Mason frowned and wondered when the heck his choice of vehicles had become of such interest to others. But he didn't hang on to the anger long. He made the mistake of glancing down at Abbie, and he turned to dust again. That's because her eyes let him know that her truck talk was a way of calming her raw nerves.

"It'll be okay," Mason tried to assure her. He wasn't one to dole out promises he couldn't keep, but in this case he made an exception. He wanted to do something to get that worry off her face.

"What if Ace doesn't tell us what we need to know?" she asked in a whisper.

Mason lifted his shoulder, tried to look as cool and mean as possible. "Then we keep looking. Keep asking questions." Because there wasn't an alternative.

Okay, there was.

Marshal McKinney could whisk Abbie away to a new life and a new name. He could make her safe. And even though that twisted away at Mason's stomach, and even though he didn't want to explore why it was doing that, there was a bottom line here.

Abbie would be safe.

And for now, Mason would bargain with the devil to make sure that happened.

Mason pulled into the parking lot as close as he could to the entrance, and he waited until he saw Gage in the doorway before he turned off the engine. "Move fast," he told Abbie. "I don't want you outside any longer than necessary."

She nodded and followed behind him when he stepped from the truck. Mason made it just a couple of steps before he heard the sound.

And it was already too late.

A bullet slammed into his truck.

Chapter Fourteen

Abbie barely had time to react to the shot that was fired before Mason hooked his arm around her waist and dragged her to the ground.

She landed on her knees, but Mason pushed her down until she was flat against the parking lot pavement. Then he followed on top of her.

Protecting her.

Again.

"Boone?" she shouted just as another shot crashed into the window on the driver's side.

"I'm okay. Stay down!" Boone shouted back.

Abbie had no intention of doing otherwise, but she wasn't the only one in danger. Both Mason and Boone were in the line of fire, and neither would get out of that danger. And all because of her. They could die in this parking lot trying to keep her alive.

"Should I call for backup?" she asked.

Mason shook his head. "Gage will do that. Crawl underneath the truck," he ordered her.

Abbie started to do that, but the shots came at them nonstop. She also heard other shots. Not just Mason's, but ones coming from the front of the hospital where Gage was hopefully returning fire.

But who was trying to kill them this time?

It couldn't be Ace because he was in the hospital. If he'd somehow managed to escape, Gage would have told them. It wasn't Stone either, because just minutes earlier they'd left him at the sheriff's office. Of course, any of their suspects could have hired another triggerman.

Abbie rolled to the side and beneath the truck, but she still couldn't see anything because Mason adjusted his position so that he was directly in front her. She watched where he took aim and fired. Not in the parking lot or at the hospital. Mason fired the shot toward the parklike area at the back of the building.

The perfect place for a gunman to hide.

There were thick shrubs, trees and benches. So many places to lie in wait. And because the gunman had started shooting almost immediately after they'd gotten out of the truck, that meant the person had been waiting for them. Maybe that same person had used Ace's demand to put this deadly plan in motion.

"You see him?" Boone called out.

"No," Mason answered, and he sent another shot into the park. "But he's using a rifle."

Oh, mercy. So the gunman could be far enough away from them not to be spotted but still able to deliver a fatal shot.

A bullet smacked into the truck, less than an inch from where Mason had crouched.

"You need to get down!" Abbie demanded.

He didn't, of course. Mason stayed put and kept firing. Until she heard the thudding click to indicate he was out of ammunition.

"I have an extra magazine of ammo in the glove compartment," he mumbled.

Mason turned, no doubt to head in that direction, but Abbie latched on to him and pulled him back to the ground.

"Are you crazy? If the shooter's got a scope on that rifle, and he probably does, he'll pick you off the second you climb back into the truck."

Mason didn't argue. Couldn't. Because he knew she was right.

"I'm nearly out of ammo, too," Boone let them know.

That wasn't good news, but thank goodness Gage was still firing. Plus, backup should be arriving any minute.

And then Mason cursed.

Abbie's heart jumped into her throat. "What's wrong?"

"The shots are getting closer."

She listened. Hard to do with her pulse crashing in her ears, but she soon heard what Mason already had. Yes, the shots were getting closer, and that meant the gunman was moving in for the kill. But she also heard something else.

A siren.

Backup would be here soon. Hopefully soon enough.

"Crawl toward Boone," Mason told her. "I'll be right behind you."

Abbie had been about to argue, until he'd added that last part. She didn't want Mason to stay put and take a bullet. But Boone was farther away from the shots.

For now.

With the shooter moving, it was hard to know where it would be safer.

Abbie scooted to the side, toward Boone, and when she was within reach, he pulled her closer until she was tucked up against him. The shots continued—slower now but seemingly getting louder with each one fired.

Mason was just a few inches from her when a bullet cut through the front tire. The air rushed out, causing the truck to sink down right on Mason. It wasn't enough to crush him, but Abbie didn't want to take the risk. She latched on to his arm and yanked him to her.

The sound of the sirens got closer, and then Abbie heard the screech of brakes into the parking lot. She couldn't see who'd arrived to help, but she did get a glimpse of Gage.

"Stay down!" Gage yelled to them, and he barreled out of the hospital doorway.

Abbie wanted to scream for him to stay put, to keep out of the way of those shots, but just like that, they stopped.

"The shooter's on the run," Mason said, and he glanced at Boone. "Stay here with Abbie."

Before she could ask Mason where he was going or remind him that he was out of ammo, he scrambled out from beneath the truck and ran in the direction where she'd last seen Gage.

"Be careful," she called out, but it was too late for him to hear her.

Boone heard, though.

Abbie met his weathered gaze, and she saw the realization in his eyes. She had fallen hard for Mason, and it was breaking her heart to see him in danger.

"Does he know?" Boone asked her.

"What do you think?" she whispered.

Boone blew out a weary breath. Nodded. Mason didn't miss much when it came to people. Especially her. So, yeah, he knew how she felt. That didn't mean he would do anything about it or even return her feelings.

The sound of the footsteps snapped her attention back where it belonged—on the shooter and the safety of anyone who might cross his path. She prayed it was Mason returning, but she soon saw Dade.

"Get Abbie inside the hospital now," Dade told Boone. And as Gage and Mason had done, he hurried away.

Boone didn't waste any time getting her to her feet, and with his gun still drawn, he hooked his left arm around her, and they hurried up the steps to the hospital. He pushed her inside, away from the windows and doors, and stood guard in front of her. They were alone. There were others in the waiting-reception area, and they'd all taken cover behind the chairs and furniture.

Abbie came up on her toes so she could peer over Boone's shoulder. Her heart sank when she couldn't see Mason, but she knew he was trying to run down the shooter.

"Mason's out of bullets," she mumbled, causing the panic to soar.

"He knows how to take care of himself," Boone reminded her, but there was concern and fear in his voice. And there was a reason for that. Three of his sons were out there with a killer.

Another police cruiser screamed to a stop in the parking lot, and Mel made a quick exit. She, too, was armed and went in pursuit.

"They'll catch him," Boone assured her.

Abbie hung on to that, but her hopes vanished when she saw Mason making his way back through the park and toward them. Judging from his expression, the shooter was still at large.

Abbie wanted to run to Mason, to make sure he was okay, but Boone anchored her in place. She didn't fight him, not until Mason stepped inside, and then she threw off Boone's grip and ran to Mason. He caught her in his arms and pulled her to him.

"You okay?" he asked.

She nodded and checked him for any signs of injury. None, thank God. Just that look of pure frustration on his face.

"He got away?" Abbie wasn't sure she wanted to hear the answer.

The muscles in Mason's jaw flickered. "The others will keep looking."

She wanted to be strong, needed to be because Mason already had enough on his shoulders, but Abbie couldn't help it. Tears burned her eyes.

Mason mumbled something. Not his usual profanity. She couldn't make out what he said, but it soothed her more than anything else could have. So did the way he kept her cradled in his arms.

But it didn't last.

Abbie had only a few seconds of that comfort before she heard the footsteps racing toward them. Mason obviously heard them, too, because he maneuvered her behind him again. However, this wasn't a threat in the same way gunman was. It was Dr. Mickelson, and he was hurrying up the hall toward them.

"Something wrong?" Mason immediately asked the doctor.

Dr. Mickelson nodded. "I need you to come with me. *Now.*"

Chapter Fifteen

Dead.

Mason figured that wasn't the worst news he could hear today, but it wasn't good. Ace Chapman was dead. Now, not only wouldn't he get the answers about who'd hired the man, but he also had another problem. A big one.

Because Ace hadn't died of natural causes.

"Looks as if someone smothered him," Dr. Mickelson explained. His voice was shaky. Heck, he was shaky. The doc had no doubt seen death before, but murder was a whole different story.

Mason had seen death, and yeah, Ace had been smothered.

"What's going on?" Mason heard Abbie ask from the doorway of the recovery room. He'd told her to stay put, but obviously she'd followed him.

Mason couldn't blame her. This was their lives here, and they had a dead hit man and another live one loose somewhere in town. He scrubbed his hand over his face and looked back at her. Mason didn't say a word, but she must have picked up on his body language.

"Who killed him?" she wanted to know.

And Mason wanted to know the same darn thing.

He glanced around the room. No surveillance cameras here, but there was one in the hall. Not outside the door exactly, but it might have enough range to show them who'd waltzed into Recovery and put a quick end to Ace's miserable life.

"I need the surveillance disks for the last hour," Mason told the doctor.

The doctor nodded. "You can use my office, and I'll have the disk delivered there." His attention drifted to Abbie. "Might do her some good to get off her feet for a while—and get away from this."

Mason couldn't agree more, and because he couldn't take her outside with the gunman still on the loose, the hospital was the safest place to be. Hopefully.

"What should I do with the body?" Dr. Mickelson asked.

"Don't touch it. I'll call the Rangers and have them send down a CSI team. Lock this door and don't let anyone enter."

Not that he thought there was any evidence to tamper with, but they might get lucky. Still, this was likely a case of premeditated murder, so the killer had probably covered his or her tracks.

"I'll go ahead and take Abbie to your office," Mason let the doctor know.

Where he could hopefully prevent anyone else from taking shots at her. While there, he intended to arrange for someone to question their suspects—all of them—and find out if they had alibis for these latest incidents—the shooting and Ace's murder.

Mason went to Abbie, slipping his arm around her waist to get her moving. She seemed frozen, unable to take her attention off the dead assassin.

Boone was there, too, just a few feet away from her. Standing guard. Mason considered thanking him for protecting Abbie, but he wasn't feeling that generous. Besides, it was possible that Abbie was in danger because of Boone.

And if so, there went any chance of ever feeling anything but the hatred he already felt.

"Should I go to the doctor's office with you?" Boone asked.

"No need. I'll take care of her." It sounded a little like marking his territory, but Mason was too riled and weary to tone it down.

But Abbie didn't budge. "You won't go outside?" she clarified to Boone.

Boone managed to muster up a reassuring smile. "I'll stay put. Go with Mason."

She hesitated a moment, as if deciding if he was being truthful, but the adrenaline crash must have been the tipping point because she nodded and got her feet moving.

While he led her down the hall, Mason made the first call to the Rangers to request a CSI team. Grayson was still likely tied up with his sick baby, Dade and Gage were in pursuit of the gunman, so Mason went to the next on his call list. His sister-in-law Bree, a deputy sheriff and former FBI agent.

"Ferguson, Stone and Nicole will just lie and say they know nothing about this," Abbie concluded after Mason had requested that Bree reinterview all of them.

"Probably, but Bree's good at what she does. She might be able to get one of them to snap." But Mason wasn't holding his breath.

Abbie stopped cold, and her eyes widened. "Bree won't be at the sheriff's office alone with that trio of vipers?"

"Not a chance. Kade will be with her. Luis, the other deputy, too."

Relief went through her eyes. Not much, though. Probably because they didn't seem to be any closer to ending the danger.

Mason ushered her into Dr. Mickelson's office, shut

the door and tried to maneuver her to the leather sofa. But again Abbie stopped, looked up at him and then slipped into his arms. Yet another dangerous place for her to be, but judging from the small sigh she made, she didn't think so.

She was wrong.

Yeah, this felt good. Right, even. But Mason knew this holding could end with a boatload of hurt for both of them.

"I really have to figure out better coping skills for nearly getting killed," she whispered with her breath hitting against his neck.

Because he was thinking about the hurt, and the heat, it took him a moment to realize she was talking about the shooting and not this latest hugging session.

"No one has coping skills like that," he assured her.

"You do," she challenged.

"Not a chance." Especially not where Abbie was concerned. Yeah, he'd been in danger before, but this was as bad as it got. Because it involved her.

And Mason wasn't about to give that further thought.

He pushed the wisps of hair from her face and pressed a chaste kiss on her forehead. Well, it was meant to be chaste, but it turned out to be a green light for Abbie to move even closer. Until she was smashed right against him.

"I'm not a real virgin, you know," she mumbled.

Mason felt the sucker punch of surprise, and he leaned back a little so he could see her face. "Excuse me?"

"I mean I'm not naive or innocent. Over the years I've made out with guys. I just didn't get to the big finale with any of them."

"Really." And Mason was more than sure he didn't want to hear the details. Ditto on that part about not giving this any further thought either.

"Really," she insisted. "I know the timing sucks for this

conversation, but I can't seem to find a peaceful moment to have a heart-to-heart with you."

She had a point there. They hadn't had much time for sleep, much less conversation. Yet they'd managed to fire up this attraction to a very uncomfortable level.

"Marshal McKinney will have a new name and place for you soon," Mason reminded her. While he was at it, he reminded himself of that, too.

Abbie shook her head. "I'm not going."

That was a couple of rungs up from a sucker punch. "What?"

"I'm not going," she calmly repeated. She stepped back, hiked up her chin. "Because wherever I go, the danger will just follow. I'm tired of running, tired of being scared. I'm making my stand right here in Silver Creek."

But then her eyes widened. "Oh, God. I can't do that, can I? Because it'll put you and your family in more danger."

"We're already in *more* danger," Mason reminded her. "And if you leave, that won't stop."

There. That was his argument for her staying. And it was a good argument, too.

Mason didn't have time to dwell on things because his phone rang. He glanced down at the screen, hoping it was Dade or Gage calling to say they'd captured the shooter. No such luck.

"Ferguson," Mason answered. Because Abbie was already trying to listen, he put the call on Speaker and hoped this moron didn't say anything to add to her already-too-high stress and adrenaline levels.

"I just heard about the shooting," Ferguson greeted. "Are you all right?"

"Peachy. Did you hire this guy to kill us?" Mason demanded right off the bat.

"Of course not. I keep telling you that I wish none of you any harm. When are you going to believe me?"

"When hell freezes over." And even that wouldn't do it. Ferguson was at the top of his suspect list. "Why are you calling me?"

"Because your sister-in-law just phoned and said I was to report to the sheriff's office for an interrogation and I'm to produce the letter that Senator Herrington left me."

"Why are you calling me?" Mason repeated. "If Deputy Bree Ryland told you to do those things, then you should be busting your butt to get it done. Unless you got something to hide."

"Nothing," Ferguson calmly said. "But there's a problem with the letter." He made a sound of disappointment mixed with frustration. Both exaggerated. Both fake. "I seem to have misplaced it."

Abbie huffed. Mason didn't even bother. He'd expected it. "We'll get a search warrant to look for it." Although if there was anything incriminating in that letter, then it was ash by now or else tucked away from the reach of a search warrant.

"No need. You can search my house anytime you like. Bring Abbie. You can both look."

Oh, yeah. As if that would happen. "What did the letter say?"

"Ford just wanted to thank me for my unwavering friendship." It sounded rehearsed. Probably was.

"You're sure he didn't ask you to put hits on all of us?" Abbie asked.

"Positive." With just that one word, the smugness was crystal clear in Ferguson's voice. Maybe he was just happy that he was able to torture Abbie a little bit more. "And even if I had, I would have declined. I don't blame you for your mother's sins."

No smugness in that last comment. It sounded, well, genuine. Of course, this was Ferguson, and he was a lying expert.

"Go to the sheriff's office," Mason told the man. "Don't keep my sister-in-law waiting."

The moment that Mason hit the end-call button, the door flew open. Abbie and he automatically flew apart as if they'd been caught doing something wrong, but it wasn't one of his siblings or Boone to cast a disapproving eye. It was Dr. Mickelson, and he held up a shiny silver disk.

"Here it is," the doctor announced.

From the surveillance camera no doubt. Mason certainly hadn't forgotten about it, but he'd had another lapse of focus because he couldn't get his mind and body off Abbie.

The doctor went to his desk and put the disk into his laptop. It took only a few seconds for the images to appear on the screen, and Mason wasn't disappointed. There was a clear angle of the recovery room where Ace had been murdered.

"I talked with the security guard," the doctor said as they watched. "And he moved to the front of the building when the shots started. He doesn't remember seeing anyone specific in the area of the recovery room."

Yeah, and that made Mason suspicious. Had those shots been fired to distract the guard and them so someone could kill Ace? If so, it'd worked.

Well, maybe.

There was no audio on the surveillance footage, but Mason saw the exact moment the shots started. The people in the hall began to run and scramble for cover. The seconds ticked off slowly until someone finally came into view.

The person paused at the top of the hall, glanced around and then walked forward.

"Who is it?" Abbie asked. She moved closer to the screen until Mason and she were shoulder to shoulder.

He shook his head, not sure who they were seeing on the screen because the person was wearing a baseball cap slung low enough to cover the forehead and the eyes. Whoever it was, he or she had attempted a disguise, which meant this probably wasn't a social call.

Mason watched, waited and finally the person stepped into view.

"Hell," he mumbled. And Mason reached for his phone.

ABBIE STARED AT THE WOMAN on the other side of the two-way mirror. Nicole didn't exactly look pleased about being escorted into the sheriff's office to answer some questions. But then, Mason didn't look pleased either, as he showed her the surveillance footage from the hospital.

"Oh, God," Nicole said when she saw herself on the screen. "It's not what you think."

Mason gave her one of his best glares. "Then you tell me what's going on—other than the obvious. Why did you kill Ace Chapman?"

"I didn't kill him." And as if on cue, Nicole began to cry. "I was set up to make it look that way."

That didn't help Mason's glare. "Of course you were."

Abbie heard a sound of mock agreement that mimicked Mason's, and she looked in the doorway to see Gage standing there. Uh-oh. She wasn't up to another round with a Ryland out to bash Boone.

But Gage didn't bash. He strolled closer and watched his brother and Nicole. "She's a natural-born liar."

Abbie couldn't argue with that. Nor could she be sympathetic to Nicole's nonstop tears. The woman was crying so hard that she couldn't speak. Abbie was too tired to have anything delay this interrogation and possible arrest.

Gage seemed disgusted with the display. "Rusty Burke just called and asked to speak to Mason. I guess Mason has his phone off for this little chat with Nicole."

That got Abbie's attention off Nicole. Rusty was the ranch hand who assisted her with the cutting horses. "Is something wrong?"

"Not really. Rusty's just having trouble with the new paint mare and wants Mason's okay to get rid of her."

"No," Abbie blurted out. She huffed. "The mare just needs some extra time and training, that's all. And Rusty's too timid with her."

Abbie suddenly felt stupid and overly emotional, like Nicole. Considering everything else going on, it was small potatoes, but she wished she had some time to spend with the mare. With any of the horses. Actually, she just wanted to do something normal again.

Gage stared at her. "For the record, I don't blame you for anything Boone's done." He paused. "But it's hard."

"I know," she admitted and moved on to another thought that she was overly emotional about. "I wonder if Mason will ever move past it."

He made a sound that could have meant anything. "Mason's a complex man." Gage went closer, propped a shoulder on the glass. "Does he know how you feel about him?"

Abbie opened her mouth. Closed it. Decided she'd already overshared too much in the emotion department. "That's a trick question."

"Could be," Gage admitted. "And unlike Nicole, you're not a natural-born liar, so you can't look me in the eye and say you don't have feelings for him."

He was right, and it was clear he wasn't going to leave until she gave him an answer. Abbie shrugged. The answer was obvious anyway. "I do have feelings for him."

It was an ill-timed confession. She realized that when

she looked past Gage and saw Mason. Standing there in the doorway. Listening to them. She snapped toward the mirror again and saw Nicole alone in the interview room.

"I needed to get some tissues for Nicole," Mason said. But he didn't budge. He looked first at Abbie. Then at his brother.

"Opening cans of worms?" Mason asked Gage.

Gage grinned. "Nope. Doing you a favor. And I'll do you a second one. Let me take a stab at Weeping Willow in there. You stay here and keep Abbie company. It appears y'all have some things to discuss."

He didn't wait for Mason to agree. Gage waltzed out, but not before Mason called him a smart-ass.

Abbie frowned. "I do have feelings for you," she repeated. "And I don't think you should get rid of the paint mare despite what Rusty thinks."

Mason blinked. With reason. She'd just tossed both apples and oranges at him when his mind was clearly on Nicole's interrogation.

Or maybe not.

"I never said I didn't have feelings for you," he grumbled. He crammed his hands in his jeans pockets and watched as Gage strolled into the interview room. "It's just that I'm not the marrying kind."

Abbie looked at him as if he'd sprouted horns. "You marry all the women you sleep with?"

"No." He slid her one of his glares. "But you're different, and you know it."

No, she didn't. "Different how?" she pressed.

But Mason didn't have time to answer. That's because Gage dropped down across from Nicole and started the interrogation. "Who are you claiming set you up?" Gage demanded.

"I don't know." Nicole shook her head, cried some more.

"I got a phone message, and the person said he was Ace Chapman and that he had something important to tell me. He asked me to come to the hospital."

Suddenly the tears stopped, and Nicole's head whipped up. She riffled through her purse, grabbed her phone and handed it to Gage. "Here, listen for yourself. The message is still there."

Gage did listen, but he didn't seem convinced that Nicole was telling the truth. "When you got this call, Ace was recovering from surgery. You didn't think it was suspicious that he'd be calling you?"

"No. He was very convincing. And besides, I've never spoken to him, so I didn't know it wasn't his voice."

When Gage just gave her a flat look, more tears came, and Nicole buried her face in her hands.

"You're different," Mason mumbled, getting back to Abbie's earlier question, "because you get under my skin." His glare morphed to a frown. "And what about the paint mare?"

"Rusty called and wants to get rid of her. I vote no on that. I can work with her…" She stopped. "If people will quit trying to kill me."

Mason eased his gaze to hers. Stared. And then the corner of his mouth lifted. He leaned in and brushed a kiss on her forehead. "Yeah, you're different." And he turned his attention back to the interview.

Abbie didn't want to let the conversation drop, but she had no choice—because of Gage's next question.

"Did Ford leave orders for you to eliminate all the Rylands and Abbie Baker?" he asked.

"No, of course not," Nicole jumped to answer. But then she stopped, shook her head. "Ford wanted all of you dead, I won't deny that. He used to say that if anything happened to him, the Rylands would be behind it and he'd made sure that all of you would pay."

The admission chilled Abbie to the bone. Yes, Ferguson had said that Ford wanted them dead, but this was confirmation that it'd been more than just talk.

"Who would do the paying?" Gage pressed.

"I don't know. That's the truth," she added when Gage huffed. "I do know that Ford kept tabs on Boone all these years."

Gage held up his hand in a wait-a-second gesture. "Ford knew where he was?"

"Yes. Ford said it was the only way to make sure Boone didn't come back to Silver Creek. That was their deal, for Boone to stay away."

"And he had," Gage verified. "Until now. But he wasn't in Silver Creek for the first attack and the fire at the ranch."

True. Boone had been miles away. So his return hadn't been the trigger for that attempt to kill her.

"Ford knew about Abbie, too," Nicole continued. That grabbed Abbie's attention. "He always said if necessary he could use Abbie to keep Boone cooperating."

"Use her how?" Gage asked.

Nicole met his gaze. "How do you think? You knew Ford, and he wasn't a Boy Scout."

Oh, mercy. Ford would have hurt her to make Boone toe the line. It gave her the creeps to think that both Ford and Ferguson had been watching and waiting all these years.

Gage leaned forward, put his elbows on the table. "Tell me about the letter you got at the reading of Ford's will."

"That," Nicole spat out. No more hunched-over shoulders. She sat up soldier-straight. "I'm not going to let you use that letter to arrest me for these attacks. Ford might have tried to blackmail me, but that doesn't mean I've done anything wrong."

Abbie didn't know who was more surprised—Gage, Mason or her. It was the first time any of their suspects had admitted that Ford had left criminal instructions in those letters. Of course, Nicole might be lying, Abbie reminded herself, but she wanted to hear the rest of what the woman had to say.

Gage made a keep-going motion with his index finger.

"Ford was a pig," Nicole snarled. "After all those years of working my butt off for him, he writes those three stupid letters, and he puts conditions on what he'd always promised he would give me."

"What conditions?" Mason mumbled at the exact moment that Gage asked Nicole the same thing.

Her eyes widened, as if she'd said too much. But there was still a hefty dose of anger there, too. Again, maybe it was fake. Hard to tell with Nicole.

"Did you ask Ferguson and Stone about this?" she tossed back at Gage.

"We did. Both said the letters weren't important."

The sound she made was part huff, part laugh. "Right. And I invented the internet." She got to her feet. "You want to know what Ford asked us all to do? Well, this is your lucky day, Deputy Ryland. I'll call my lawyer now, and within an hour he'll make a trip to one of my safety deposit boxes, and you'll have the letter I got from Ford."

Gage stood, too. "You can tell me now what it says."

Nicole shook her head. "Best to read it for yourself, and then you'll know why Ferguson and Stone lied."

Chapter Sixteen

Mason tossed the copy of the letter onto the desk in his room. The one that Nicole's attorney had delivered to the sheriff's office earlier. He'd read it so many times that the words were burned into his memory, but it was the bottom line of that letter that turned his stomach.

And that bottom line was money.

Ford had set up a forty-million-dollar offshore account, and the money would be paid to the person who delivered eight death certificates to Ford's attorney in the Cayman Islands. Death certificates for Mason, his five brothers, Boone and Abbie. There was even an order for them to be killed.

Abbie first. Then Grayson and his brothers. And finally, Boone.

Forty million was a lot of reason to kill.

But Ferguson probably hadn't needed the money as an incentive. Maybe not Nicole either. Despite all those tears during the interview, Mason suspected she'd been in love with Ford. How far would she go to carry out his dying wishes? But then, Mason could say the same for Rodney Stone, who'd been one of Ford's confidants and friends for years.

Mason understood why the Rylands were on that hit list, but he could only speculate as to why Abbie had been included. Maybe Ford considered her Boone's daughter. Or maybe Ford had wanted Boone to have to endure losing everyone he'd loved and once loved.

That sure didn't help the uneasy feeling in his gut.

Mason got up from the desk and headed for the shower. It was much too early for bed, not even 7:30, and too late for a ride to try to burn off some of that uneasiness. He felt like a powder keg ready to go, and it was best if he avoided everyone and everything.

The ranch was locked up tight. Every part of the security system was armed. And the ranch hands were standing guard. In other words, he'd done everything except figure out who'd taken Ford up on that offer to kill. More important, he hadn't figured out how to stop that SOB from killing Abbie.

Mason got in the shower, the water way too hot to be soothing, but he needed the heat to unknot the muscles in his neck and back. He needed other things, too.

Specifically, Abbie in his bed.

But it would be stupid for him to go to her room just across the hall. He knew that. His body knew that. Heck, the state of Texas probably knew it, but the ache still settled hard and hot inside him.

Cursing the ache and himself, he finished the shower and dried himself. While still scrubbing the towel over his wet hair, he stepped into his bedroom.

And came to a quick stop.

At first he thought he was hallucinating, that maybe the ache in his body had caused him to see Abbie in his room. Not naked as in his fantasies, but close. This mirage, or whatever the heck she was, was wearing a thin white dress, and she had her back anchored against his closed door. Some hallucination.

But then he caught her scent.

Hallucinations didn't smell that good.

It was Abbie all right.

"It's a bad time for you to be here," he snarled.

She ran her gaze down the length of his body. "That depends." She stayed put, watching him. "Are you going to make me leave?"

He should do just that. *Should*. But he knew that wasn't going to happen. He was going to screw things up beyond belief, and he would probably enjoy every minute of it.

Mason huffed, tossed the towel on the floor and walked to her. He should act like a gentleman and give her another chance to come to her senses and change her mind. He didn't do that either. He made it to her, hooked his hand around the back of her neck and snapped her to him.

Abbie did her own snapping.

Her arms coiled around him, and their mouths met. Man, did they. It wasn't a kiss exactly. More like a battle, and for some reason he couldn't make his mouth and hands be gentle. Abbie needed gentle. But then, she needed a better man than him. Too bad he was what she was going to get.

Mason kissed her hard and deep until they were both starved for air. And for each other. Of course, the starving for each other had started days ago, so it didn't need much fueling. Still, they added fire to fire when he lowered his mouth to her neck. Then her breasts.

He cursed the dress. Yeah, it wasn't much of a barrier, but it had to go. Mason stripped it off over her head and found a nearly naked, warm and willing woman underneath. He pulled off her bra and panties and tried those breast kisses again and took her nipple into his mouth.

She froze, made a sound of pure pleasure.

"Breathe," he reminded her. Reminded himself, too.

"I don't want to breathe. I want you." Her voice was all silk and sex.

"Yeah, I want you to want me. But we have to slow things down."

She didn't listen. Abbie unfroze, breathed and lifted herself to hook her legs around his waist. Oh, man. Sex against sex, and he was already hard as stone. If she changed the angle just a little, then that technical virginity was gone.

Abbie moved, changed the angle.

Of course she did.

Mason heard himself curse before the fireworks exploded in his head, and that hard-as-stone part went right into her with far more force than he'd intended. Yeah, fireworks all right and blinding, knee-weakening pleasure.

Abbie gasped, the back of her head hitting against the door.

That cleared his mind. Mason continued to curse, tried to apologize, but her gasp of pain, surprise or whatever the heck it'd been, turned to another sound. This one he had no trouble identifying.

It was a low moan of pleasure.

And more. That sound seemed to vibrate through her. Through him. Then she started to move.

The fireworks rifled off again, and he knew he was working on a thread of willpower. He couldn't take her against the back of a door, so Mason caught onto her hips to stop the blinding thrusts of her lower body, and he carried her to the bed. The moment he dropped her on the mattress, she tried to pull him back on top of her.

"Hold that thought a second," he insisted, and he reached for the nightstand drawer for a condom.

She didn't hold anything. Abbie was bound and determined to finish this in record time. Mason wanted to finish it, too, but he was already screwing up enough tonight without adding unprotected sex to the mix.

"I want you," she repeated at the end of one of those purrs.

"Yeah," Mason settled for saying.

It was another battle to get the condom on, and while he fumbled—something he hadn't done since he was sixteen—Abbie drove him crazy with some touches and kisses.

"Make the ache go away," she whispered.

For a moment he considered that might be a real ache, not one fanned by the need. But nope, it was need. Because the moment he had the condom in place, she drew him right back between her legs, lifted her hips and took him into her.

She looked at him, met his gaze. "It's better than I thought it'd be."

Unfortunately, Mason felt the same, and that was saying something because his expectation had been a mile high.

He was in big trouble here.

Trouble that got worse because he didn't just have sex with her. He kissed her. Tasted her. Gathered her into his arms. He forced himself to slow down. To savor every moment of this. Because in the back of his mind he had to admit he'd never felt this way and might never feel this way again.

Abbie did some savoring of her own. She slid her legs around him, using the strength of her toned muscles to thrust him deeper inside her. The purr became a throaty moan. Her hands pressed harder. Her embrace, tighter.

Mason knew she was close and wanted to ease back to make it last, but this wasn't something that could go on very long. Not with the ache burning them both. So he gave her what she needed. He slid his hand between their bodies.

And he touched her.

Abbie gasped again. Not from pain. The climax rippled through her. Through Mason. She fought, twisted, dug her nails into his back and did the only thing her body could do when past the point of no return.

She let go.

Mason didn't even try to fight it. But in that second when he was so near the snap in his head and in his body, he made the mistake of looking at her. At her sweat-dampened face. At her wide, surprised eyes fixed on him. At her mouth that he'd kissed too hard and fast.

At *her*.

And it was Abbie's face so clear in his mind that sent him falling. He was too far gone to speak, to do anything but fall. However, that didn't stop him from hearing Abbie.

"I love you," she whispered.

Chapter Seventeen

Abbie immediately felt the change in Mason. His grip loosened, and his lax muscles went stiff. She hadn't even allowed him a second to enjoy the climax of great sex before she'd no doubt ruined everything.

"I'll be back," she managed to mumble.

Mason didn't stop her. In fact, he rolled to the side, and Abbie scooted off the bed. She grabbed her clothes, slipped on the dress and got the heck out of there.

I love you?

Abbie might as well have taken a hammer and hit Mason in the head. Talk about the worst possible thing she could say. And the really bad part?

It was true.

She did love him, but that didn't mean he had to hear it. How she felt about him was her problem, not his, and she should have just kept her big mouth shut.

Abbie hurried back into the guest room, but she didn't stop. She had to keep moving. Had to do something to ease the smothering pain in her chest.

Oh, yes. Here was that broken heart that she'd been dreading.

She washed up, dressed in the borrowed clothes—jeans, dark red shirt and boots—and stormed out of the room. Down the stairs. And she would have raced right out the door if one of the ranch hands hadn't been standing in front of it. She didn't know his name, but he had a rifle clutched in his hands. Abbie hadn't forgotten the danger, but that was a clear reminder of it.

"I need to check on one of the horses," she insisted.

He hesitated but then nodded. "I'll call Rusty and let him know you're on the way out."

Better Rusty than one of Mason's brothers. Especially Gage. He already knew about her feelings for Mason, and he would have probably seen the panic on her face.

Abbie waited impatiently for the ranch hand to disengage the security system. The moment he did that, she was out of there, on the porch and then in the yard.

It wasn't late and with the nearly full moon and security lights, she didn't have any trouble following the path. Or seeing yet another armed ranch hand. Once she was past him, Abbie broke into a run and was practically out of breath by the time she reached the stables. And a waiting Rusty.

"Does Mason know you're out here?" Rusty immediately asked.

"I'm just checking on the mare you told Gage about," she said, dodging his question.

And thankfully the mare was inside and not out in the corral or pasture. Yes, she needed some air, some space, but she didn't want to risk being gunned by whoever had taken Ford up on his beyond-the-grave wish to have them all killed.

Abbie grabbed a carrot from the treat bin, something she wouldn't have normally done. Rewarding a horse who hadn't performed well was never a good idea. But then, she was apparently in a rule-breaking mood right now.

I love you.

Those three little words had sealed her fate and meant

she'd lost Mason forever. He'd made it so clear that he wasn't the commitment type. Heck, neither was Abbie. That's one of the big reasons why she'd stayed a virgin. Until tonight. Tonight had changed everything and not for the good.

She walked the length of the stable to the last stall, where she spotted the mare. All in all, it was a good place to do some thinking. The back stable doors were partially open to allow the crisp night breeze to flow inside. Abbie could look out at the moonlit pasture while staying hidden. And under guard. Rusty kept his distance, but he didn't budge, and like the other ranch hands, he was armed with a rifle.

"Rusty said you're causing trouble." Abbie offered the mare the carrot, which the horse immediately gobbled up. "Well, knock it off."

The mare snorted, but it didn't sound like much of an agreement. Abbie sighed, leaned against the wooden stable door and tried not to fall apart. She was failing big-time and on the verge of tears when she heard the footsteps and the too-familiar gait.

Mason.

He was walking slowly, deliberately, but he was coming toward her. Maybe to give her the boot. After all, he was her boss. Abbie preferred that to the alternative—a discussion about the *I love you*.

Mason, however, didn't say a word. He just kept walking until he reached the mare's stall, and he stopped right next to her. Abbie waited. And waited. But Mason just stuck his hand through the gate to stroke the mare.

"I figured you'd be running for cover," she finally mumbled when she couldn't take the silence any longer.

Mason took his time answering. "It appears I wasn't the one doing the running."

That snapped her gaze to his. "You can't be saying you're happy about what happened." Specifically about what she'd said.

"No." He drew out the word. "But I didn't figure running would help. I can admit when I've screwed up."

So there it was. His confirmation that it'd all been a big mistake. And although it was exactly what Abbie had expected, it still stung.

"I went to your bedroom," she reminded him. "I seduced you."

His eyebrow lifted, and he gave her the look that only he and the world's greatest skeptic could have managed. "If I hadn't wanted to get you in that bed, it wouldn't have happened." Another pause. His mouth tightened. "I didn't want to hurt you, though."

"You didn't," she lied. Except it wasn't even a lie. She'd hurt herself. Mason had spelled out the rules right from the beginning, and she'd still jumped in headfirst.

"I hadn't expected it to be, well, *wow*," she mumbled.

He flinched. "I'm not sure if that's an insult or not," he mumbled. "Because I always aim for wow."

She fought a smile, mainly because this wasn't a smiling moment. Abbie gave her feelings some more thought and came to a frustrating decision. If she had to do it again, she wouldn't change a thing.

"I love you," she repeated.

He stared at her, cursed and stared some more.

"And I don't expect you to do anything about it," she snapped. "Got that?"

It was a good exit line, and one of Mason's favorite shut-up-and-quit-arguing sayings, but it would have been better if she could have exited. But when she tried to storm off, Mason caught her by the arm. He did more of the staring. More cursing, too, and then he let go of her.

"I can never give you what you want," he said.

It took a moment for the words to sink in. Well, this wasn't the big surprise she was hoping for. The change of heart that she knew was a total long shot anyway. This was Mason being Mason, and if a woman played with fire, she should expect to get burned.

Because she was mad at herself, and at him, and because she was feeling ornery, Abbie came up on her toes and kissed him. "Never is a long time, Mason."

There. Now, that was an exit line. But once again, it didn't happen. That's because Mason's phone rang. And even though she'd already started to walk away, Mason's question stopped her in her tracks.

"Who is this?" he demanded.

Abbie turned and saw his expression go from the question to the concern. No, make that fear.

"What happened?" Mason asked, his voice louder now.

Abbie could only stand there and wait. It seemed to take forever, but Mason finally pressed the end call button and then jabbed another on the keypad.

"What's wrong?" Abbie asked.

Mason just shook his head. "The killer has Grayson's wife and baby."

"HOW THE HELL DID THIS happen?" Gage demanded the moment he stepped foot inside the ranch house.

Mason didn't fill his brother in as he'd done the others when they'd arrived in the family room. He let Kade give Gage the details so that he and Grayson could work out what needed to be done.

The ranch house was chaotic with all the brothers and their spouses present and everyone talking at once. Everyone trying to figure out how to rescue Eve and baby Chet. There was just one big problem—they didn't know where the kidnapper was holding them. And that problem was what had put the haunting look in Grayson's eyes. Thank God the other children and their nannies had all gone upstairs, because this wasn't something Mason wanted his nephews and nieces to witness.

"I shouldn't have left them in that hospital room," Grayson repeated.

"Hindsight's twenty-twenty," Mason reminded him. "You had no idea this was going to happen."

Especially because Grayson's mind had been on his sick baby. Dr. Mickelson had wanted to keep baby Chet overnight for observation, and both Eve and Grayson had stayed by his side. Until a nurse had come running into the room to tell Grayson that Mel had phoned the hospital to tell them that Gage had been shot.

"No cell reception in the hospital," Grayson repeated.

And that's why he'd run outside to call and verify what'd happened. When he realized it was a ruse, a fake call, it'd been too late. Eve and Chet had been taken. No one had seen anybody or anything.

"The killer will make some kind of ransom demand," Mason reminded his brother. "He or she doesn't get paid to hurt Eve or the baby. This is just to draw us out."

"Draw *me* out," Abbie corrected. She was standing in the doorway, her hand gripping the jamb. Probably because she wasn't too steady on her feet. "I'm the first name on Ford's death list. I'm the one the killer wants."

"You don't know that," Mason fired back. But no one agreed with him. They couldn't. Because Abbie's name was first.

She let go of the jamb, walked closer, her gaze nailed to Mason's. "When he or she calls, I'll be the ransom demand."

"To hell you will." Mason went to her, grabbed her by

the arm and pulled her out into the foyer. Of course, the nearly dozen Rylands and Bessie quit talking and focused on Mason and her.

"If you go to meet this SOB, he or she will kill you," Mason clarified, in case she hadn't understood his objection.

"And if I don't go, he might hurt Eve and the baby." She glanced over Mason's shoulder to address Grayson.

"The killer might do that anyway," Grayson admitted.

And Mason hated that he couldn't control that, that he couldn't stop it from happening. But what he could do was prevent Abbie from making herself a sacrificial lamb.

She tipped her head to the equipment bag that Nate had brought with him. A bulletproof vest was lying on top of it. "I could wear that and go in armed. You and the others could be at a safe distance. Then, when Eve and the baby are away from there, you could get me out, too."

"Yeah, with lots of bullets flying. That's not going to happen."

His cell phone rang, the sound shooting through the otherwise-silent room. *Unknown Caller* flashed across the screen, and he knew before he answered that this was the killer.

"I'm sending you a picture," the person immediately said. It was a man, but Mason didn't recognize the voice. But it could be the person who'd fired the shots at the hospital.

Mason put the call on Speaker so he could watch the image load. The others huddled around him to do the same. When the picture was ready, Mason's heart dropped to his knees. He'd hoped and prayed that all of this could be explained away.

But no.

The picture was of Eve cradling her sleeping son in her arms while a man had a gun pointed at her head.

Grayson cursed. "If you harm either of them—"

"I have no intention of hurting them," the man interrupted, "unless you give me a reason to do that."

"Where are you and what do you want?" Mason demanded. Beside him, Kade used his own phone to snap a picture of the image of Eve with her captor. No doubt to put it through the FBI's facial recognition software, because he went running toward his laptop.

Mason studied what he could see of the photo. Eve looked unharmed and was wearing a bulky down jacket that she'd used to tuck the baby inside. Good thing. Because Chet had a fever, the chilly night air wouldn't help.

"My demands are simple," the man on the phone continued. "I want each of you to come to me. I'll give you the location later, but the first person I want to see is Abbie Baker."

All eyes went to Abbie, and other than a slight intake of breath, she had no reaction. She'd already resigned herself to the demand, and that meant Mason had to change her mind. And the snake who was holding his sister-in-law and nephew.

"Having Abbie won't get you Ford's money," Mason pointed out. "Start with me and work your way down the list."

"Tempting," the man said, with sarcasm dripping from his voice. "But Ford's instructions were specific. Abbie first. The sheriff. Then you."

So it was about the money. Mason hadn't thought otherwise, but it sickened him to hear it spelled out. "We can pay you whatever Ford arranged in his will."

"Perhaps, but I have to decline. My boss says it's imperative that Ford's wishes be carried out. And here's how.

Abbie will leave *alone* and walk to the end of the ranch road where someone will pick her up. If she's followed or has anyone with her, Eve and the baby will be the ones who pay the price for you not following orders."

The color drained from Grayson's face. Mason was sure he wasn't faring much better. It sickened him to think of an innocent baby caught in the middle of all of this.

"Why does Abbie have to go alone?" Grayson pressed. "The goal is to kill all of us."

"My boss wants you to arrive one at a time. I'm not sure why exactly, and with what I'm getting paid, I'm not going to ask. All will be revealed when you need to know."

And with that, he ended the call.

Mason expected a flurry of questions and discussion, but everyone remained silent. And everyone continued to look at Abbie. She was no doubt about to remind them that she had volunteered to go, but Kade spoke before she could.

"I'm running the picture now," he explained, and that sent Gage and Nate heading in the direction of the computer. Grayson turned to go there as well, but his cell buzzed.

"Is it the kidnapper?" Mason questioned.

Grayson shook his head, answered the call on speaker. "Boone, this isn't a good time."

"I know." Boone's voice was barely a whisper. "An armed man has Eve and the baby."

Hell. What was going on now? And how the devil had Boone gotten involved?

"How do you know that?" Grayson asked, and yeah, he was suddenly suspicious.

"Because I'm looking at them now."

Mason snapped his gaze toward the phone and listened.

"Are they okay?" Grayson asked. "Have they been

hurt?" He was on the verge of panicking, and Mason doubted he could do anything to calm him down.

"They look fine. The baby's asleep, and Eve's just sitting there. The gunman is right behind her."

"Why are you there?" Mason wanted to know.

"It's not by accident. About a half hour ago, I got a call from a man who told me that if I'd come to the Ryland family cemetery, he'd let Eve and the baby go," Boone continued. "I parked my truck up the road and walked here, so I could see what was going on."

"Where are they?" Grayson demanded.

"By your mother's grave. But don't come," Boone insisted. "Not just yet. The place has been booby-trapped. I can see wires on the ground, and I'm pretty sure those wires lead to some explosives."

Not good. That made a sneak attack a whole lot harder. Not impossible, though. Somehow, they had to figure out how to do this.

Grayson had such a tight grip on the phone that Mason was surprised it didn't shatter in his hand. "Is there just one gunman?"

"Hard to tell. There could be others hiding behind the trees."

Yeah, and they had to anticipate that. But at least now they had a location, and that meant they could come up with a plan.

"The gunman's expecting me to show in fifteen minutes," Boone added. "What should I do?"

"Wait until you hear from me," Grayson ordered. He slapped the phone shut and looked at each of them. "Arm yourselves. We'll move on foot to the cemetery, but you'll stay back. I'll go in and try to negotiate their release."

The cemetery was a good mile and a half away. Still on Ryland land but outside the security fence that rimmed the ranch. And therefore not part of the surveillance system. No way to visually check what was going on. Plus, there was a problem with just driving in there—someone was no doubt watching the road.

"I got an ID on the gunman," Kade called out. "Sylvester Greer. He's a pro."

Mason hadn't expected anything less. "Any idea who hired him?"

"None," Kade answered. He hurried away from his computer and went to the weapons cabinet in the corner of the room. "But I'm betting we'll find out before the night's over."

Yeah, they would. But hopefully learning that wouldn't come at a sky-high price.

Like losing Eve.

"The gunman told you not to come," Mason reminded his brother.

Grayson spared him a glance as he, too, went to the weapons cabinet and took out magazines of ammo that he shoved into his pockets. "Would you stay back if they had Abbie?"

Mason hadn't seen that question coming, but he knew the answer was no. He wouldn't stay back. And he turned to let her know just that.

But Abbie wasn't there.

He tore out of the room and into the foyer. "Abbie?" Mason shouted.

No answer. And then he cursed when he looked at the equipment bag. The bulletproof vest was missing, and the front door was wide-open.

Chapter Eighteen

Abbie knew she didn't have much time. Probably less than a minute. She'd left the moment Mason ended the call with Boone and then had sneaked past Rusty, who was standing guard on the side of the ranch house. But it wouldn't be long before Mason or someone else realized she was missing, and they would try and stop her.

The night air was chilly, and the wind whipped at her, but she ran through the pasture. Toward the cemetery. And she tried not to think about how Mason was going to react to her leaving.

He wouldn't like it, that's for sure.

But there's no way she was going to put Grayson's wife and son at further risk, and the Rylands were too heroic to toss her in the line of fire. That heroism could endanger Eve and the baby far more than necessary.

All the danger and attacks had been leading up to this, and Abbie didn't intend to let anyone else face down a killer who was aiming for her. Well, for starters. If Ford Herrington got his death wish, then all the Ryland males would soon be in the line of fire.

Unless she could stop it.

This wasn't a suicide mission. That's why she'd put on the bulletproof vest and had brought a gun with her. She didn't have the aim of a professional hit man, but she had something that a hired gun didn't—the will to end this before Mason or any other member of his family got hurt.

That included Boone.

Yes, it was a long shot, but if Boone or she could take out the gunman, then this would finally end tonight. And she did have a little time on that front. Ford wanted her to die in front of Boone, and that meant the gunman would wait for Boone to arrive before he started firing. The gunman didn't know that Boone was already there, and unlike her, Boone had a deadly aim. If she could draw out the assassin, then maybe Boone could do the rest.

Abbie ran faster but kept glancing over her shoulder. No sign of Mason yet. She didn't have a clear view of the ranch road, but she couldn't see headlights either. Maybe the car that was supposed to whisk her away hadn't arrived yet.

When she made it to the back of the pasture, she ducked behind one of the white wooden fence posts. It wasn't wide enough to cover her, but it would have to do. She already had the gun drawn, but she got ready in case she had to take aim quickly. That would be a worst-case scenario, and it wouldn't get Eve and the baby out of danger.

She tried to pick through the darkness and the dense clump of trees so she could see the cemetery. Again, the angle was wrong. She couldn't see Eve, the baby, Boone or any gunman. She spotted one lone marble headstone. An eerie sight in the milky moonlight, especially with the wind fanning the veiny tree branches above it. Ford was one sick man to want his death wish carried out here.

Abbie levered herself up and heard the sound of footsteps. Not from the cemetery but from behind her. Before she could even look over her shoulder, someone grabbed her, hard, and shoved her to the ground.

She turned, ready for a fight, but thanks to the moonlight she had no trouble seeing her attacker's face.

Mason.

"What the hell do you think you're doing?" he snarled.

He was whispering, but Abbie could feel the anger in every muscle in his body. And there was a lot of him to feel because he literally had her pinned to the ground.

"I'm trying to save Eve and the baby," she fired back.

"This is *not* the way to do it." Mason didn't look at her. His gaze slashed all around them. With good reason. At least one gunman was out there, and he might see or hear the commotion.

"Don't move," he ordered, and he looked behind him.

Abbie did, too, and spotted several armed men making their way across the pasture. His brothers, no doubt. They were keeping low, but she could make out the silhouettes of their weapons.

She put her mouth right next to Mason's ear. "If the gunman sees all of you, he could hurt Eve. Let me go in there and try to defuse this."

"You can't defuse it. This is a death trap, and Greer, the hired gun, doesn't care a thimble of spit whether Eve and the baby get hurt in the cross fire."

Abbie wanted to argue. She definitely didn't want to think of a baby in this kind of danger. But Mason was right. Ford had set up these rules, and he wouldn't care who else died.

Oh, God.

What now?

"You're staying put," Mason insisted as if he'd heard her unspoken question. "Kade and Gage will figure out how to disarm the booby traps."

That sounded like a good start, but Abbie had to shake her head. "When the car arrives to pick me up, the driver will tell the gunman I'm not there. He'll be suspicious. And he'll know we're onto him."

"Then we have to work fast." Mason didn't hesitate, which meant he'd no doubt thought of this. "Any idea where Boone is?"

She shook her head. "I can't see Eve or the baby either."

"The picture of her and the baby was taken by my mother's grave. It's behind those." He pointed toward the thick clump of trees that were only about twenty yards from the fence.

Abbie groaned. If they were still there, it would be nearly impossible to sneak up on them. And that was no doubt the killer's intention.

"Wait here," Mason told her. "And that's an order. Move, and there'll be hell to pay."

Abbie didn't doubt that. But she wouldn't stay hidden if there was some way she could help. Of course, the trick would be to figure out how to do that without putting anyone else in even more danger.

Mason levered himself off her but then dropped right back down. Abbie followed his gaze and saw the movement to the far right of that clump of trees. It was a man. And for a moment she thought it was Boone. But it wasn't.

It was Ferguson.

Of course. So, he'd been the one to take Ford up on the offer to kill them. The money alone would have been enticing enough, but this was his chance to kill her and Boone, the man who'd protected her all these years.

Mason lifted his gun and took aim at Ferguson. He didn't fire, probably because he was waiting for the man to move a little. After all, Eve and the baby were likely just on the other side of those trees, and if Mason missed, one of them could be hit.

Abbie waited, her breath frozen in her throat. Her heart slamming against her chest.

But Ferguson didn't budge.

"What's he doing?" she mumbled. He wasn't looking out toward the ranch. Nor toward the road. He seemed to be focused on the cemetery itself.

That's when it hit Abbie. It was probably where Boone was hiding out.

She watched in horror as Ferguson took aim. She wanted to shout out a warning. But couldn't. She could only watch, wait and pray that Boone, Eve and the baby were out of the line of fire.

The seconds crawled by, making the wait unbearable.

Without warning, Ferguson suddenly dropped to the ground. Abbie shook her head, wondering why the heck he'd done that. But she didn't have time to wonder long.

A bullet slammed through the air.

Not toward Ferguson.

But at Mason and her.

MASON HELD HIS BREATH. Waited for another shot to come zinging their way. Especially because the last one had torn into the fence. This was exactly what Mason had hoped and prayed they could avoid.

Gunfire.

He tried to crawl over Abbie to keep her down, but she maneuvered to the side and took aim. Good grief, the woman was stubborn, but if their situations had been reversed, he sure wouldn't have stayed put either. Too bad Abbie was going to have to choke down her instincts and pride because he didn't want her in any more danger.

"Get down!" Mason insisted.

Abbie did lower herself, slightly, and like him, she looked around to pinpoint the origin of that single shot. It had come from the general direction of where he'd spotted Ferguson. However, Abbie's nemesis was nowhere in sight now. Probably because he'd fired that shot and then gotten down.

Mason glanced around to make sure everyone was okay. He could see just the outlines of his brothers who were scattered around the pasture. Six guns, plus Abbie. Mason had wanted more, but he couldn't leave the wives and kids unprotected at the house. That's why he'd asked every available ranch hand to stand guard outside the ranch house.

"Listen," Abbie whispered, her voice trembling now.

And Mason knew why. He heard the same sounds she had. The baby. Crying. Grayson no doubt heard it, too, and there was no way he would continue to lie in wait in the pasture with his son's cries filling the night air. No. This could get even more dangerous, fast.

Abbie apparently thought so, too, because she shouted out before Mason could stop her. "You said you'd let Eve and the baby go if I came. Well, here I am. Now let them go."

Mason braced himself for a shot to come their way. But it didn't.

"Come out where I can see you," the person shouted back. Mason recognized the man's voice from the earlier phone call. It was almost certainly Greer.

"You're not going to do this," Mason told her, and he latched on to her arm just in case she tried. He should have clamped a hand over her mouth.

"I'll come out there when Eve and the baby are safely away from all this," Abbie answered.

Silence. But Mason kept watch while he waited for Greer to respond.

Where the devil was Ferguson? Was he trying to sneak up on them? Maybe. But it could be worse than that. Mason had no idea how many other gunmen were working with

Greer and Ferguson, and here Abbie was willing to walk right into the middle of that viper's nest.

"I'm coming out," someone else shouted. Not Greer this time but Boone. "You can release Eve and baby and hold me at gunpoint instead. Abbie will do whatever you tell her if you're holding me. Isn't that right, Abbie?"

"Stay back, Boone!" she yelled. And she no doubt meant it. She was terrified for his life.

But Mason saw this from a different point of the view. From Ferguson's. If he had Boone, he did indeed control Abbie, and it'd be easier to kill them both.

"All right," Greer answered. "Boone, you have a deal. Come out so I can see you, and keep your hands in the air."

"No!" Abbie shouted. But it was too late.

Mason saw Boone step from the clump of trees. Not too far from where he'd spotted Ferguson earlier. Mason couldn't see Greer, but he had no doubt that the assassin had his weapon trained on Boone.

"They're coming out," Greer announced.

"What about the booby traps?" Grayson yelled.

Greer took his time answering. "Eve knows where she has to run."

Oh, mercy. It was dark, and Eve was scared. Not the best of conditions for navigating what could be a minefield.

Mason held his breath. Waited. Prayed. Hoped that if his prayer failed, his aim wouldn't.

Boone moved to his right and eventually out of sight. On Greer's orders probably. Finally, Mason saw something he actually wanted to see.

Eve and the baby.

His sister-in-law had a crying Chet clutched to her chest, and she ran out from the trees. Grayson got up and raced over the fence toward them.

Mason and his brothers responded, too. They all ap-

proached, ready to fire if anyone took a shot at Grayson.
Thank God that didn't happen. Grayson helped them over
the fence and pulled them down to the ground so he could
shield them. The next step would be to get them completely
away from there.

Abbie, too.

But that thought had no sooner crossed his mind, when
there was movement in the trees again. Mason could see
Boone, and he appeared to be arguing, but he couldn't
make out what he was saying.

"Eve and the baby should go now," Greer ordered.

Grayson lifted his head, looked around. No doubt wondering if it was a trap.

"Just the two of them," Greer clarified. "Not her husband. Not Abbie. Not anyone else. And hey, if I'd wanted
them dead, they wouldn't be out there with you."

True, but Mason didn't trust Greer or the snake who'd
hired him.

"Go now, Eve!" Greer insisted. "Last chance to get that
baby away from here before all hell breaks loose."

Grayson gave her a nod, and she started moving. She
stayed low. Kept the baby close to her. She made her way
back to the house.

"Oh, God," Abbie mumbled.

Just as Boone dived to the side.

There was no time to figure out why he did that because
the shots started, and one of them slammed into the fence
right next to Abbie and Mason. As close as that shot was,
Mason still took a moment to glance back, to make sure
Eve and the baby were out of harm's way.

They were.

That was something, at least. Now he had to do the same
for Abbie by taking out the shooter.

Shooters, Mason corrected.

There were two sets of shots, and both were coming right at them. Greer and Ferguson probably. But where was Boone, and was he in a position to help?

"What happened to your plan of taking me?" Abbie shouted over the shots.

"Stay quiet," Mason warned her so the shooters couldn't pinpoint their position, but he wanted to know the same darn thing.

"This is the plan," Greer calmly answered.

None of them responded. They just waited. But Mason suddenly got a very bad feeling in the pit of his stomach.

"You'll stand up, climb over the fence and come stand by your grandfather's grave. That's where Ford requested that you all die."

Yeah, Ford was a sick SOB all right. "Any reason we'd just walk to our slaughter?" Mason asked, figured the answer he was about to hear was obvious.

Ferguson and Greer were going to use Boone to lure them out.

Not the wisest of plans, especially because all but Abbie hated him. Well, maybe not hate. But there was no love lost there. Maybe their attackers were counting on the fact that six lawmen weren't just going to stand by while Boone was gunned down.

"You've got no leverage," Boone called out to the gunmen. "I won't have any of my sons or Abbie dying because of me."

"Oh, it's not you they'll try to save." And Greer let that hang in the air for several bad moments.

"What do you mean?" Grayson finally asked.

"I mean your wife is wearing a jacket with an explosive device. She's probably inside the house now with all the others. The wives, the kids, the ranch hands. And even if she's taken off the jacket, the device is still there."

Oh, hell. And Mason just kept repeating it. Across from him, he heard Grayson utter something much worse.

"All of you, stand up now," Greer ordered. "Drop your weapons, put your hands in the air so I can see them. And start walking toward me. One wrong move, and I detonate the explosive, and everybody in that house dies.

"Oh," Greer said, his tone mocking, "you've got thirty seconds."

Chapter Nineteen

"Stay behind me," Mason warned Abbie.

She would for now, but they both knew that wouldn't last long. Soon, Greer would want her since she was first on the list.

"Put down your guns," Greer reminded them.

Abbie dropped hers, lifted her hands into the air. Mason dropped his, too, but Abbie saw the pistol he had tucked in the back waist of his jeans. He didn't remove that one, but he did lift his hands and started over the fence.

"Behind me," Mason emphasized to her.

Abbie did that, as well. She climbed over the fence, along with the others, and they started trudging toward the cemetery.

"Those thirty seconds are almost up," Greer taunted.

That got them hurrying, even though Abbie hated that Greer was playing with them like puppets. Still, they couldn't risk an explosion. They all came to a stop in the clearing, just a few feet away from the first grave.

Boone was already there, waiting for them to join him.

It took a moment for her to spot Greer because he was partly hidden behind a tree. And armed, of course.

"You sent a text to your wife," Greer accused, looking directly at Grayson. "Don't bother to deny it," he continued when Grayson didn't answer. "It's all right if you told her about the device. I'm getting paid to finish things with all of you, not them."

Despite the circumstances, Abbie believed him, and she was glad that Grayson had managed to warn Eve. Maybe now the Ryland wives and children would be safe. That was something, at least.

Greer pointed to one of the trees on Abbie's left, and when she followed his pointing finger, she spotted the rifleman perched on one of the branches. That explained the two sets of shots.

Well, maybe.

"Where's Ferguson?" Abbie just came right out and asked. "Or does he plan to stay in hiding when he shoots me?"

"He's not going to shoot you," Boone growled. And like Mason, he also stepped in front of her.

However, the shift in position didn't block her from seeing Greer's reaction. He certainly wasn't jumping to answer, and he seemed annoyed. She hoped that meant Greer and Ferguson weren't seeing eye to eye on how this should all play out. Dissension could work in her favor.

Greer pointed to two other trees. "Cameras," he explained. "Senator Herrington left the money for this job in the hands of an attorney in the Cayman Islands, and the lawyer requires proof."

Mason glared at the cameras, at the gunman in the tree and at Greer. "I hope your boss is paying you enough to have this much blood on your hands."

"Who says I have a boss, other than the late senator, that is?" Greer fired back.

Mason shrugged. "You're not smart enough to set this up on your own."

Abbie gave Mason a warning groan, which he ignored.

Maybe he figured he could goad Greer into doing something that would violate the rules of this nightmare.

"Besides, Ford left only three letters," Mason continued, "and you didn't get one of them." He put his hands on his hips, close to his gun. "But it does make me wonder—will your boss keep you alive? Because I gotta say, you are a major loose end that could tie you to multiple murders and a boatload of other felonies."

"Yeah," Gage chimed in. "And because your boss isn't showing his face, then I'm thinking he wants you to do all the dirty work. Then he takes out you and your wingman in the tree, sends the video to the lawyer, and he doesn't have to pay you a penny."

Even in the darkness, Abbie saw the anger flash over Greer's face. "That's not going to happen." He turned that anger on Mason. "And time's up. Step to the side."

So that Greer could kill her.

Mason would try and stop that from happening. So would Boone. Abbie, too. But she doubted all of them would make it out of this alive, and she darn sure didn't want someone else dying in her place.

Abbie glanced at Mason, making eye contact, even though she could see him inching his hand toward his gun. He didn't have to tell her what he wanted her to do. He wanted her to get down while he had a shootout with Greer and the rifleman.

In other words, suicide.

Abbie snapped toward Greer. She figured she had seconds, or less, to try to stop that from happening. "I don't want to die in front of the Rylands," she told Greer. Not a lie but the next part was. "I have no connection with any of them other than through Boone, and they haven't exactly given me a warm and fuzzy welcome to Silver Creek."

Mason shot her a glare, which she ignored.

"Ford's instructions were that I was to die in front of Boone," she continued. "*Just* Boone."

That wasn't an amused look Greer gave her. More like a suspicious one. He paused for several seconds. Then, he shook his head. "No deal. All of you stay together. And you die together. One at a time."

Abbie had expected that response, but she wasn't giving up.

Greer aimed his gun directly at her. She got ready to dive to the side. Away from Mason and Boone. And she hoped they did the same.

Everything happened fast but in slow motion, too. She saw Greer's hand tense, ready to pull the trigger. But before he could do that, Mason rammed his body into hers, sending her crashing to the ground.

A shot cracked through the air.

But Abbie couldn't tell who had shot or where the bullet had landed. That's because Mason dropped right on top of her, and the fall and the impact knocked the breath out of her.

There was another shot. Then another. But Abbie couldn't move because she was gasping for air. Mason, however, moved her. He dragged her behind one of the trees, and he came up to return fire.

Abbie heard the sound then. Not just a bullet. But the deadly thud of a bullet slamming into something. Into *someone,* she mentally corrected. There was a groan of pain.

And then nothing.

With her heart racing out of control, she looked at Mason. He had ducked behind the tree but was also still firing. He wasn't hurt, thank God. Well, not yet anyway.

She frantically looked around for Boone. No sign of

him. And she hated to have to consider that he might have been the one who was shot. If not him, then one of his sons.

"I have to take out the rifleman," Mason mumbled. "Don't move," he ordered her again.

Abbie couldn't anyway. She was still fighting for breath. Plus, going out there now would only get Mason and her killed.

Mason scrambled to the next tree over, then another, and Abbie got her first glimpse of the war zone playing out in front of her. Grayson was behind one of the trees, and he, too, had taken aim at the rifleman. She was thankful that Grayson had a gun as well, but that wasn't stopping the rifleman. He was firing nonstop, and he definitely had a better vantage point.

She shifted a little, still keeping cover behind the tree but also searching for Boone. No sign of him or Mason's other brothers. Definitely no sign of the person who'd been shot. It was too much to hope that it'd been Greer or Ferguson.

Abbie thought of the Ryland wives back at the house and prayed that none of them would try to come into this. Of course, that was a strong possibility. She imagined herself in their place, with the men they loved in danger, and Abbie knew there was no way she could stay put.

With her breath level again, she searched around the tree for something, anything, she could use as a weapon. She latched on to a small limb and was dragging it closer when she saw the movement from the corner of her eye.

There was no time for her to react. No time to get out of the way. Something bashed right into her head. The pain was instant. Searing. And before Abbie could even call out to Mason, the darkness came.

MASON CURSED. THE RIFLEMAN was out of range of Mason's Colt. Probably the reason the would-be killer had chosen that particular spot in the first place. Not good. Because as long as he stayed in that tree, none of them were safe.

He glanced around, trying to work out everyone's position, but the only one he could see was Grayson. When the shots had started, everyone had scattered, and Mason only hoped that one of them was in a better position than he was to eliminate the rifleman.

"Abbie?" he heard someone shout. Boone.

Mason swung his gaze in her direction. And his heart went to his knees. He saw her all right, but she was being dragged into the bushes. Oh, mercy. Had she been shot? Or worse?

But Mason refused to believe that.

"Abbie!" he shouted. Mason ignored the rifleman and ran toward the spot where she'd disappeared into the thick underbrush.

She didn't answer, and that revved up his heartbeat even more. He wanted to call out her name again, but that wasn't a wise choice. Her captor could use the sound of Mason's voice to aim and take Mason out. That couldn't happen. If Mason got shot, he couldn't save, and it was clear that Abbie needed saving.

Staying low, Mason shoved some of the underbrush aside. No Abbie. It was too dark to follow the drag marks, and the gunfight was drowning out sounds that he needed to hear.

What the devil was going on? Had Greer managed to take her? If so, it wasn't hard to figure out why. According to Ford's rule, Abbie had to die in front of Boone. Greer wouldn't just give up on the kind of money he was earning for this. No. He and maybe even his boss were still trying to set up the kill.

And Mason had to stop it.

He tore his way through the underbrush and came to

some trees that rimmed the west part of the cemetery. Where his mother's grave was located.

Where Greer would try to kill Abbie.

But there were no signs of either of them here.

However, Mason did hear something. He tried to pick through the din of gunfire to pinpoint the low sound he'd heard. A moan. But not just an ordinary moan.

This was one of pain.

He tried not to panic. Hard to do when it could be Abbie who'd made that sound. Abbie, in pain. Mason scrambled to the side and nearly tripped over something.

Except it wasn't a something.

It was a *someone*.

The moonlight helped him, and Mason looked down at the twisted face of Vernon Ferguson. The front of the man's shirt looked shiny black, but Mason knew it was blood.

He'd been shot.

Ferguson clutched Mason's arm. "I didn't do this," he got out.

Mason made a yeah-right sound, and he picked up the gun by Ferguson's side, but something wasn't right. After all, Ferguson had been shot. He was dying.

And someone had done this to him.

"If you didn't put this plan together, then why are you here?" Mason demanded.

"Greer called and said if I wanted to watch Abbie die, I should come."

"Hard to believe that's the only reason. Did Greer decide to kill you—his boss—and collect the money for himself?" Mason asked. He didn't look at Ferguson. He kept watch around him in case this was some kind of ambush.

"I'm not his boss." Ferguson's mouth stretched into a creepy smile. "I wanted to keep Abbie alive. It's more fun when she's alive."

Mason shook his head. In some sick twisted way, that made sense. Ferguson couldn't torment a dead woman. Did that mean Greer was working alone? Maybe. But it didn't matter. Greer and the rifleman were just as dangerous.

He had to get to Abbie.

"Where is she?" Mason demanded, and he threw off Ferguson's grip.

Ferguson shook his head, and Mason knew he couldn't waste any more time. With his gun in one hand and Ferguson's in the other, Mason ran toward the clearing. Toward his mother's grave.

And that's when he saw Abbie.

She was alive, thank God, but there was blood trickling down the side of her face. In the pale moonlight, she looked like a ghost.

Mason started to run to her. But he came to a dead stop. Because Abbie wasn't alone. Someone was standing behind her.

And that someone had a gun pointed directly at her head.

EVERYTHING WAS SWIMMING in and out of focus, but Abbie blinked, trying to fight her way out of the arm that was vised around her neck. Hard to do with the blow to the head. It had not only made her temporarily lose consciousness, she was now woozy and weak.

Who was behind her? Who had the gun to her head?

Greer probably. And she was betting he didn't intend to keep her alive much longer.

"Let her go," she heard Mason say. His voice was low, a dangerous growl, and despite the gunfire on the other side of the cemetery, she had no trouble hearing him.

Or seeing him.

Every muscle in his face and body was rock hard.

Primed for a fight. But it didn't take a clear head for her to know that he didn't have a shot. Not with her captor using her as a human shield.

"Stay put, Mason," her captor called out. "Boone, get out here now!"

For a moment Abbie thought her injury had caused her mind to play tricks on her ears. She'd expected Greer's voice, but it wasn't.

It was Rodney Stone's.

"You don't have to do this," Mason said. "There are other ways to get money."

"Not Ford's money," Stone fired back. "He was my friend, and he would expect me to do this for him."

Abbie groaned. So it wasn't just about the money. It might have been easier to talk him out of it if it had been.

"Boone?" Stone shouted again. "The camera's waiting for you."

Abbie glanced up and saw the camera mounted in the tree. It was pointed directly at her.

"Get out here now or I shoot Mason," Stone warned.

"You're planning to shoot me anyway," Mason countered, and he inched forward, his gun aimed and ready in case he got a clear shot.

"True," Stone verified. "But I can make it quick and painless. Or I can make you suffer. Make Abbie suffer, too."

The threat went through her. And Mason. She could see the fear on his face. The raw frustration, as well. He couldn't stop this, and it was killing him.

Abbie wasn't ready to say goodbye to Mason just yet, but she had to accept that it was exactly what she might have to do. And it broke her heart. It had taken her more than three decades to fall in love, and here she'd had only minutes to savor it.

"Boone!" Stone yelled again. He moved the gun to Abbie's belly. "How long will it take her to bleed out? Get out here now or you'll learn the answer to that the hard way."

Mason took a step closer. "You set the fire at the ranch?" he asked.

The question threw her, and judging from the way Stone's arm tense, it threw him, too. "Why the hell would that matter now?"

"Because I want to know why I'm about to die." Mason kept his eyes trained on Stone. "I figure the fire was to draw Boone out. It was the fastest way to get him to Silver Creek."

"You want a gold star, Deputy?" Stone mocked. "Because I'm fresh out of them. And Boone's fresh out of time."

Stone was ready to pull the trigger. Abbie had no doubt about that, and while the shot probably wouldn't kill her, she braced herself for the pain that she would feel. And the pain she would see on Mason's face.

There was movement to her right. It happened so fast that Abbie only got a glimpse of Boone before he dived right at them. He crashed into them, sending all three of them to the ground.

Stone fired, the sound of the bullet so close that it was deafening.

Abbie rolled to the side, trying to move away from Stone's gun. She also tried to move Mason and Boone out of the way.

She failed.

Mason was there, right in the tangle of bodies. Fists were flying. Blood splattered across her face, but she had no idea whose it was.

Abbie reached out and held Stone's hand so he couldn't fire again.

But it was too late.

He fired.

The blast went through her, and it took her a moment to realize she hadn't been hit.

Boone had.

Stone's shot went straight into Boone's chest.

Abbie heard herself scream, and she tried to get to him. She failed at that, too. Stone lifted the gun again, ready to kill Mason.

But the other shot came first.

The moment seemed to freeze. She glanced at Mason. Then at the gun in Boone's hand. The one he'd just used to shoot Stone.

Stone fell back, his eyes wide-open and lifeless.

Because the world was starting to spin around, Abbie would have fallen, too, but Mason was right there to catch her in his arms.

Chapter Twenty

Mason handed Abbie the small carton of orange juice that he'd gotten from the vending machine. "You should drink something," he insisted.

She looked up at him from the seat in the surgical waiting room. Her eyes were glazed with fatigue. Her shoulders, slumped. It had been a long night, and the end wasn't in sight yet because Boone was in surgery, and the initial report was that he was in critical condition from Stone's gunshot wound.

A wound that could ultimately kill him.

"You should drink something, too," she insisted right back.

Mason held up his cup of black coffee for her to see. It was his third.

She managed a frown. "Something healthier."

He would do that. Later. Maybe they could have a big family breakfast, especially because all his brothers, their wives, the kids, their nannies and even Bessie were scattered around the room. All waiting for Boone to get out of surgery.

His father, Mason mentally corrected.

Because he had certainly come through for them tonight. He'd saved Abbie, and Mason would be eternally grateful to him for that. It didn't erase the past. Or the hurt. But it was a start.

"Mel just finished questioning Nicole," Dade told everyone after finishing yet another call. His brother had taken over tying up the loose ends of the investigation. Good thing, too, because Mason just wasn't up to it.

It would take a while for him to get over how close Abbie had come to dying tonight. Grayson clearly felt the same about Eve and his baby because he had both of them in his lap and was holding on for dear life. Gage was doing pretty much the same to Lynette.

"It doesn't look as if Nicole had anything to do with this," Dade added. "Nor Ferguson."

Mason agreed. Ferguson was dead but had used his dying breath to say he hadn't been involved. Even though Ferguson was a slimy snake, there had been no reason for him to lie at that point. Plus, even if he had, it didn't matter. He'd died on the way to the hospital. The man was no longer a threat to Abbie or anyone else.

Abbie opened the orange juice, took a sip and handed it to him. Mason surrendered and put his coffee on the floor so he could drink. It tasted like acid, probably because his stomach was still churning.

She took his hand and drew him down into the seat next to her. Mason went one step further and slipped her arm around him so he could pull her closer. His brothers would notice.

But he didn't care.

He brushed a kiss on her forehead. Then her cheek. And what the heck. He kissed her. In hindsight, he wished he'd done it sooner because the heat from the kiss melted some of that ice in his blood.

When he finally pulled back, Abbie made a small sound

of approval and eased right back into his arms. "Don't sell the paint mare."

Now, that was not something Mason expected to hear her say. He cocked his head so he could meet her gaze. And her second frown of the past five minutes.

"It settles my mind to think of the horses and the ranch," she mumbled as if he would understand.

And he did. Because it was exactly how he felt. The ranch was what centered him. Always had. Well, until now. It disturbed him a little to think that the kiss with Abbie had done the same thing. Maybe better.

"The only person who can handle the mare is you," Mason pointed out. He hadn't intended that to sound like an invitation with strings attached.

But it was.

She stared at him. "Does that mean I have my job back?"

He stared back at her. "As a minimum."

A really low minimum.

Mason realized he had things to say to her, but he needed to lay some groundwork first. "We'll need to get official approval from Marshal McKinney, but with Ferguson and Stone out of the picture, there's no reason for you to go back into witness protection."

"So I could work with the mare." Abbie nodded. Paused. Her mouth quivered a little. "Would I get to sleep with the boss?"

Okay. The groundwork was going pretty darn fast. "As often as you want."

Now she smiled. "Good, because I'd like that *often*." She slipped her hand around the back of his neck, drew him closer and kissed him.

She tasted like sunshine, and Mason didn't think the juice was responsible for that.

He kissed her until his breath was thin. Until his mind was jumbled from the heat. And until he heard someone clear their throat.

Gage.

He was grinning at them, but Mason realized that they'd become the center of everyone's attention. None of the adults were sleeping now. All eyes were fixed on them.

Oh, man.

He was not the sort of person to make public announcements about his feelings, but every single one of them probably knew or suspected that he'd taken Abbie to his bed. And not just to his bed. Heck, he'd taken her virginity.

But even that didn't seem to play into this.

Strange. Mason had thought that being Abbie's first would somehow make him feel as if he'd been trapped in a foxhole. However, what he was feeling wasn't of the trapped variety.

Mason looked at his family. Then at Abbie. And he thought about the future. Not about the mare she'd train. Not about sleeping with the boss.

Even though he really liked that idea.

However, what he liked most was that she loved him. She'd said it—more than once—and Mason believed her. She loved him. He didn't know why. He damn sure didn't deserve it.

But she loved him anyway.

And there was something else.

"I'm in love with Abbie," he let everyone know. Best to get it out there in the open.

Then he looked at Abbie to see what her reaction was. She smiled. Just smiled. Before she kissed him again.

"About time you figured it out," Grayson mumbled.

"He's always been slow," Gage piped in, causing Nate, Kade and Dade to bob their heads in agreement.

"I'm sitting right here," Mason reminded them when he broke the kiss. "I can hear you."

They were clearly all aware of that, and they were also enjoying this a little too much. Later, he'd sneak Abbie off for some private kisses and some other stuff—if he got lucky.

"You love me," she whispered against his mouth.

"Yeah, I do. You okay with that?"

"Better than okay." The next kiss was a little too long and hot, considering they still had an audience. "And it means I get to work with the mare." She winked at him.

Mason laughed before he could stop himself. "You're right. I think you got a pretty good shot at job security."

The smiles and the light mood vanished when the waiting room door opened, and Dr. Mickelson walked in. Mason had known the doc his entire life and had never been able to read his face. This time was no different.

"Boone made it through surgery," he finally said.

That set off a flurry of long breaths and sighs of relief, but none of them said a word. A few stood. All stared and waited.

"The bullet damaged his lung and one of his kidneys, but we managed to repair everything. He's still listed in serious condition and in the recovery room next door, which normally means he wouldn't be seeing anyone right now, but he's asking for all of you.

"There are some rules," the doctor said when they all started to move in the direction of recovery. "This visit will last a minute, maybe less, and none of you will say anything to upset him."

"He saved Abbie," Mason said. "I just want to thank him." He paused. "And welcome him back to the ranch."

Mason stared at the others, waiting for an objection.

He got a few raised eyebrows. A shrug or two. But no one objected.

"All right." The doctor nodded. "This way. But for the record, I'm getting a little tired of stitching up Rylands. The next time I see any of you back in here, it'd better be for baby deliveries, and nothing more serious than sniffles."

Dr. Mickelson looked first at Lynette and then at Darcy, who were both in the early stages of pregnancy.

"Kayla, too," Dade proudly announced, and he gave his wife's belly a fatherly pat. "We just found out this morning."

Normally, this was the point where Mason would have groaned and made a comment about not changing diapers or babysitting, but those things were starting to grow on him, too.

A little.

"Boone better get well fast," the doctor remarked. "That'll make, what, six grandkids and three more on the way? Y'all got your own baseball team there."

While the doctor herded them into Recovery, he also scooped Chet from Eve's arms and gave the baby a quick examination. The baby was fine, Mason knew, because both Eve and Chet had been examined after they'd brought Boone in for surgery.

Somehow Mason and Abbie ended up at the head of the clan, but they all managed to stuff themselves into the room. Abbie made a small sound in her throat. Definitely not a happy sound. Probably because Boone looked weak and pale. His eyes were barely open. Barely focused. But his gaze swept over them and he smiled.

"The doc says you can come home in a day or two," Bessie volunteered.

His smile was weak but it widened. "I'd like that, but I don't want to cause any trouble."

No one uttered anything. You could have heard a blasted pin drop.

"It won't be trouble," Mason finally said. And it was the truth.

Boone's eyes watered and he nodded. Truth was, Mason's eyes watered, too, and when he looked at Abbie he saw the tears rolling down her face.

"The minute's up," the doctor announced. "Boone needs his rest."

"We'll be back in the morning," Mason let his father know. And when Boone reached out for him, Mason gave his hand a squeeze. "Thank you for saving Abbie and for everything else you did tonight."

The others came forward, echoing what Mason had said, and then they each filed out.

"That was kind of you," Abbie whispered when they were in the hall.

Mason wiped the tears off her cheek. "Saying I love you must have put me in a good mood." He shrugged. "That, and the fact that we're all alive and mostly in one piece."

"Yes, there is that." She slipped her arm around his waist, pulled him closer.

It not only felt good. It felt right.

"Get a room," Kade joked, nudging Mason with his elbow. It was a little funnier than it should have been because Kade was practically wrapped around his wife, Bree.

But a room wasn't a bad idea. Maybe when Boone was out of the hospital, Mason could whisk Abbie off on a much-needed vacation.

That felt right, too.

In fact, despite the ordeal they'd been through, the whole moment seemed as right as it could get.

Mason stopped, and as his family streamed past them, he looked down at Abbie. "I don't want to be just your first lover. I want to be your last."

Except that didn't sound the way he'd meant it to.

"What I mean," he tried again, "is that I don't want you to be with anyone other than me."

She smiled. "Well, considering I'm in love with you, that won't be much of a hardship." Abbie got them moving again.

But again, Mason stopped. "No, it won't. But I want more than a lack of hardship." Which sounded stupid, but he was tongue-tied here.

Heck, he just went for it. "I want to marry you," Mason blurted out.

The sea of streaming Rylands froze, and once again, all eyes were on them. Abbie just stared, too. And she was holding her breath. She had a frozen look on her face.

"Say yes so we can go home," Dade complained.

Grayson leaned in. "Say yes only if it's what you want to say," he said using his big-brother tone.

"Make him suffer a little bit first," Gage joked.

Mason gave them all dirty looks. "Can we have some privacy here?"

"No," they answered in unison. "Say yes, Abbie."

She released the breath she'd been holding. Probably because she didn't have a choice. She was starting to turn a little blue.

"Yes," she whispered, but it was loud enough for everyone to hear. The whoops and cheers came, followed by a yell from Dr. Mickelson for them to hush and leave.

They started to trickle out again, but Mason wasn't going to wait until they got outside to clear this up.

"You don't have to say yes because my brothers pressured you," he let Abbie know.

She came up on her toes. Smiled. "No pressure," she assured him. "Mason Ryland, I want to spend tonight and the rest of my life with you. Got that?"

Yeah, he got that. Mason pulled Abbie closer and sealed the deal with a kiss.

* * * * *

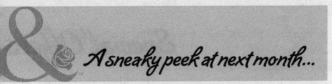

A sneaky peek at next month...

INTRIGUE...

BREATHTAKING ROMANTIC SUSPENSE

My wish list for next month's titles...

In stores from 15th March 2013:

❏ Soldier Under Siege — Elle Kennedy

& Hostage Midwife — Cassie Miles

❏ Deadly Sight — Cindy Dees

& The Awakening — Jana DeLeon

❏ A Widow's Guilty Secret — Marie Ferrarella

& Colton Showdown — Marie Ferrarella

❏ Beyond Valour — Lindsay McKenna

Available at WHSmith, Tesco, Asda, Eason, Amazon and Apple

Just can't wait?

0313/46

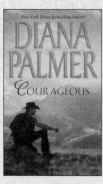

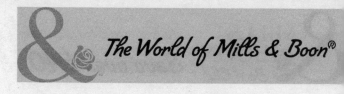
The World of Mills & Boon®

There's a Mills & Boon® series that's perfect for you. We publish ten series and, with new titles every month, you never have to wait long for your favourite to come along.

Blaze®
Scorching hot, sexy reads
4 new stories every month

By Request
Relive the romance with the best of the best
9 new stories every month

Cherish™
Romance to melt the heart every time
12 new stories every month

Desire™
Passionate and dramatic love stories
8 new stories every month